W9-BCQ-192

JUPITER'S
BONES

JUPITER'S BONES

FAYE KELLERMAN

G.K. Hall & Co. • Chivers Press
Thorndike, Maine USA   Bath, England

This Large Print edition is published by Thorndike Press, USA and by Chivers Press, England.

Published in 1999 in the U.S. by arrangement with William Morrow & Co., Inc.

Published in 1999 in the U. K. by arrangement with Headline Book Publishing.

U.S.   Hardcover   0-7838-8782-5 (Core Series Edition)
U.S.   Softcover   0-7838-8783-3 (Core Series Edition)
U.K.   Hardcover   0-7540-1386-3 (Windsor Large Print)
U.K.   Softcover   0-7540-2290-0 (Paragon Large Print)

The text of this Large Print edition is unabridged.
Other apsects of the book may vary from the original edition.

Set in 16 pt. Plantin by Juanita Macdonald.

Printed in the United States on permanent paper.

British Library Cataloguing in Publication Data available

Library of Congress Cataloging-in-Publication Data

Kellerman, Faye.
  Jupiter's bones : a novel / Faye Kellerman.
    p. cm.
  ISBN 0-7838-8782-5 (lg. print : hc : alk. paper)
  ISBN 0-7838-8783-3 (lg. print : sc : alk. paper)
  1. Large type books. I. Title.
  PS3561.E3864 J86   1999b
  813′.54— dc21   99-046903

For those who have made it worthwhile to get up in the morning.

To Jesse for the projects and excitement.
To Rachel for the elegance and style.
To Ilana for the fun and games.
To Aliza for the snuggles and the warmth.
To Anne, my mother, for the unconditional support.
To Barney, the suffering agent, for the twenty-four-hour ear.

And to Jonathan — my partner in crime as well as love.

Special thanks to Special Agent Gayle Jacobs
for giving me a clue.
Any mistakes are mine, not hers.

Prologue

Because her recent days had been filled with scientific data and research, Europa had paused only for the most basic of human necessities — food, water, bathroom breaks. Her nights had been equally jammed as she tried desperately to play catch-up — exercising on the stationary cycle, calling friends and attempting a life. Time had taken on a pace as unstoppable as the biblical flood. The rushing tempo had given her sporadic anxiety attacks as well as migratory bouts of heart palpitation — unusual since she was in peak condition and excellent health. She'd probably live a long time, judging by her parents' genetics. Her mother had been in her early sixties when she had died, but she had been a broken woman.

Unlike her father.

Her father. He'd be in his seventies. And like most narcissists, he'd probably be in wonderful health.

Or so she thought.

But no time for any musings. Her professional calendar had been too demanding.

Except there had been that recurring daydream, a fragment from her past, a sneaky little devil that kept insinuating itself into Europa's brain when she least expected it.

A remembrance of things past, thank you, Proust.

Sitting by the lake, watching the water gently lap up on the shoreline. For her tenth birthday, her father had decided to take her camping — just the two of them, leaving her squalling younger brothers at home with Mom. Dad had taken her somewhere up in the San Bernardino Mountains. To this day, Europa wasn't sure of the precise location, and after she had become estranged from her father, she hadn't bothered to ask.

The moment to remember had been at night. Back then, the stars weren't subjects of scientific scrutiny nor were they inanimate objects of cosmological theory. They were millions of diamonds set into a velvet sky. The moon had been out — a waning moon, Europa recalled that. Its beams had bounced and rolled along the caressing waves. They had just finished a trout dinner cooked on the campfire . . . roasted marshmallows for dessert. Snuggling under her sleeping blanket with her father by her side.

Just the two of them.

When her father had been the most important person in her life.

To help her fall asleep, he had told her stories, something he rarely did. Tales of evil empires in faraway places called black holes. There were also the heroic, fleet-footed knights of Quasar. And when demons of black holes tried to capture

8

the knights of Quasar with their secret destructive weapon called *gravity*, the knights would turn themselves invisible, weightless rays, and escape faster than the speed of light.

A fantastic story because her science teacher had told them that nothing traveled faster than the speed of light. And when she had mentioned that fact to her father, he had laughed, then kissed her cheek. The only time in her life when Europa remembered being the recipient of her father's affection. Not that Dad had been overtly cruel, just inconsiderate. But mostly absent.

She thought of that night when she received the news — that her father was not only dead, but had died under suspicious circumstances.

1

"The thing is, they moved the body, Lieutenant."

"What?" Decker strained to hear Oliver's voice over the unmarked's radio static. "Who's they?"

"Whoever's acting as the head honcho of the Order, I guess. Marge did manage to seal off the bedroom. That's where Jupiter was found —"

"Could you talk up, Scott?"

"— point being that the crime scene is screwed up, and the body has been messed with because of the shrine."

"Shrine?"

"Yeah. When we got here, the members were in the process of dressing him and constructing this shrine —"

"Where's the body now?"

"In a small anteroom off some kind of church —"

Temple, Decker heard a male voice enunciate from the background. "Someone with you, Detective?"

"Hold on, lemme . . ."

Decker tapped the steering wheel until Scott came back on the line. It took a while.

Oliver held his voice low. "I told them to stop messing with the corpse until you got here. Not being a trusting soul, I've been guarding the body with some self-appointed guru who calls himself Brother Pluto. I sent an officer in there to keep him company so we could talk more privately."

The electronic noise cracked through Decker's ear. He said, "You need to talk louder."

Oliver spoke up. "This Pluto person doesn't want the police here. He keeps insisting that the death was natural, waving this bogus death certificate to prove it, disregarding the empty fifth of Stoli underneath the bed. Which *he* claims wasn't Jupiter's because Jupiter didn't drink."

"*Death* certificate?" Decker said. "Has the coroner been there?"

"Nope. It was signed by a gent named Brother Nova."

"Who's he?"

"Got me, sir."

"Did you explain to them what we're doing is standard procedure in sudden deaths?"

"I've tried to explain it, but Pluto's *not* listening." A laugh. "I've been biting my tongue, refraining from asking him where Goofy was."

Decker smiled. Oliver was showing unusual discretion. "Did you tell him that we have to transport the body to the morgue for autopsy?"

"Been saving the good news for you. Because right now, Pluto and his toons are not happy campers, though I suspect they've never been a cheerful lot. Who called the death in?"

"Jupiter's daughter. Her name is Europa

Ganz. She's on the faculty at Southwest University of Technology. Jupiter used to be a hotshot professor there years ago. His real name is Emil Euler Ganz. Apparently, the daughter's not associated with the Order."

"So how'd she find out about the death?"

A good question. "I don't know, Scott. The details are sketchy." He hesitated. "Find out about Ganz's death certificate. This Nova must be a member of the Order, right?"

"I'd assume so. Probably some kind of in-house doctor. But that doesn't qualify him to sign off on Jupiter."

True enough. Decker's finely tuned psycho-BS-detector was on max. He said, "The static is really bad. I'm having trouble hearing you. Just keep status quo until I get there."

"We're trying. But the parishioners are getting feisty. Is 'parishioners' the right word?"

It was fine with Decker although cult followers seemed more apropos. "Just try to keep everyone quiet."

"How far are you from the holy spot?"

"Four, five miles. Traffic's a little thick. I'll be there in about fifteen minutes."

"See you." Oliver clicked off.

The initial call had come through while Decker was still home, eating breakfast with his younger daughter, who was as skinny as the stick figures she drew. Hannah thought it was great fun to pick the raisins from her oatmeal, leaving behind the grainy mush. Decker was trying to spoon-feed her, attempting to get some nutrition down her gullet until Rina aptly pointed out that the child was five, and capable of feeding herself.

He lived about twenty minutes by freeway from the station house, about thirty-five minutes from the crime scene. That was on good days, and today wasn't one of them. Decker ran his left hand through strands of ginger hair now streaked with white, and settled into the seat of the unmarked Buick. He guzzled strong coffee from a thermos. Across the passenger's seat was the front page of the *Los Angeles Times*.

Eight-oh-five and nothing was moving.

Inching his way up to the next off-ramp, he decided to exit and take Devonshire. The boulevard was one of the main east-west arteries through the San Fernando Valley, six lanes lined with strip malls, wholesalers and industrial warehouses. Going farther west, the street's industry gave way to residences — stucco ranch houses sitting on flat land that once held agricultural orchards — oranges, lemons, apricots. He and Rina had recently purchased a house in the area, intending to move in after a few minor renovations.

Which had turned (predictably) into a major overhaul.

He could have done the job himself *if* he hadn't been gainfully employed. So they bit the bullet, hiring subs while Rina acted as the contractor. One day, Decker had come to the property to find his wife precariously balanced on a ladder, pointing out to the roofer a defect near the chimney. Her skirt blew in the wind as she spoke animatedly, though Decker couldn't hear a word of the conversation. Apparently the roofer had run the hose over the top of the house for twenty minutes, proudly pronouncing the place water-tight. But Rina had been skeptical. She had run the hose for three hours, discovering a leak after two hours and twenty minutes.

(The first rain would have ruined the hardwood floors, Peter.)

Decker smiled, thinking about her image — that of his Orthodox Jewish wife perched on the highest rung of a tall ladder, one hand pointing out flaws while the other held down that hat she wore to cover her hair.

The scene helped to buoy his spirits. The day was gray and dirty, typical overcast May weather in Los Angeles. At least the cars were moving. He proceeded west into open terrain, the foothills on the right greened by the recent rains. They had become rolling waves of wild grass and flowers, spewing their pollens, making it a miserable allergy season. What Decker wouldn't have given to have the Allegra concession this year.

He thought about Europa Ganz's call to headquarters — reported as a suspicious death. In this case meaning suicide as opposed to death by natural causes. How could she know anything if she wasn't there?

Someone tipped her. Who? And why?

Decker found suicides annoying because ev-

14

erything was left pending until the coroner made a definitive ruling. In the meantime, Homicide was saddled with the unpleasant job of keeping everything and everyone on hold, plus preserving the integrity of the "crime" scene — *just in case.* If Ganz had been someone less noteworthy, Decker wouldn't have been called down. But since the corpse had once been a luminary prizewinner in astrophysics — a visionary for his generation eons ago — as well as the current leader of a two-hundred-plus-person enclave, Strapp thought it a good idea for someone with a title to make an appearance. The captain would have come in person, except he'd had a morning meeting downtown.

From what Scott Oliver had said over the radio, the members of the Order of the Rings of God were griping about the police. Of course, they'd gripe about anything establishment. Decker had been inside the compound once. It was not the stark and sterile place he had imagined. The interior had high ceilings with lots of skylights — blueness and sunshine visible from all angles. A complete view of the heavens, as if Ganz hadn't quite given up cosmology.

Lots of skylights, several gable vents, but very few windows.

Decker had been called out to investigate a kidnapping charge, which turned out to be another case of a wayward kid exchanging the complexities of freedom for straightforward rules and regulations. He hadn't talked to Ganz. Instead, he had been given some underling with a celestial name. (Had it been Pluto?) The sect member had insisted that no one was ever held against his or her will.

He seemed to speak the truth. He had allowed Decker inside the entry hall to interview the kid. Clearly, the boy had wanted to be there. Although Decker's heart went out to the parents, he was hog-tied. Their son was over eighteen and legally — if not emotionally — an adult.

Looking into his rearview mirror, Decker saw the meat wagon about thirty feet behind him. He led the way to the compound. Together, they pulled up curbside, parked and got out.

The Order of the Rings of God had placed itself on five acres of flat land blending into mountainside. The structure was a series of square, gray stucco bunkers linked together chock-a-block. From this view, Decker could see the tops of the skylights peeking out from the roofs. And his memory had served him correctly. There were very few windows — small, square panes more suitable for an attic. The domain was enclosed by a six-foot chain-link fence. A pack of Doberman pinschers had materialized, greeting them with vicious snarls.

The driver of the van wore blue scrubs. His name tag called him Postham. With him was the deputy coroner, Dr. Judy Little, a misnomer because she stood about five-ten and weighed around 175. She reminded Decker of Marge, both of them being large-boned, attractive and in their mid-thirties. But Marge's eyes were softer, brown and doelike. They were one of her best features.

Postham squinted into the glare of the steely sky. Judy Little growled back at the dogs, which made them bark louder. "I don't envy the mailman. Where's the gate? Surely they don't expect us to drive around the entire perimeter."

Decker picked up his mobile phone and called Oliver. "How do we get in?"

"Where are you?"

"In front, being sized up by a trio of maniacal Dobies. Have someone come out here and direct us." Decker punched the end button, regarded the stucco cubes. From his perspective, he could see seven.

"A real architectural masterpiece." Little had to shout to be heard over the dogs. "What's the style? Neo-Cult military?"

"Squares are the way to get the most space for the least money."

"May be practical, but no aesthetics."

"Agreed."

Little asked, "Got any background for me?"

Decker tried to stare down the dogs. No success. "Call came into headquarters as a suspicious death. Detective Oliver found an empty fifth of vodka under the victim's bed. I'm thinking like a Heaven's Gate suicide — a combination of drugs and liquor. The victim was Dr. Emil Euler Ganz. He was once a big wheel in academic physics. Then he suddenly disappeared for ten years. When he finally showed up, he had reinvented himself as Father Jupiter. He's been running the Order for fifteen years."

Little screamed at the dogs to shut up. They didn't listen. "Oh. *Him.* So you think he left this galaxy to ascend to a better universe? Well, good luck to him. I wonder if he took anyone with him?"

The thought made Decker shudder. "We've only found the one body." He waited a beat. "It's a good point."

"What is?"

"Ganz's taking his disciples with him. Maybe he left some instructions for them to join him. Even if he didn't, there're bound to be a few unbalanced individuals in there who could play follow the leader."

"A *few* unbalanced individuals?"

Decker raised his eyebrows. "Look, if adults inside want to kill themselves, I'd try to stop them, but you can't save the world. In this case, though, there're kids involved. That concerns me."

Little made a face. "Now that's a *very* good point."

Decker rubbed his forehead, wondering how he could possibly ensure the kids' collective safety. As always, responsibility weighed him down, much more than his two-hundred-plus poundage.

A silver van was approaching from the other side of the fence. When it stopped, a girl of around twenty stuck her head out. No makeup or jewelry. She had a heart-shaped face and a smooth complexion. Her murky pond-colored eyes were swollen, her nose was red and drippy. Her hair was tied up in a bun and covered by a white, crocheted net. She wiped her nostrils with a tissue and said, "How many more of you are coming down?"

"Pardon?" Decker asked.

"Police," she sneered. "How much longer must we put up with this invasion of our cherished privacy? What we do is no one's business but our own."

Decker didn't speak for a moment, letting the silence hang in the air. Pausing always helped him to deflect anger and control his tongue. Finally, he said, "Ma'am, are you supposed to direct us to the compound's entrance?"

"I am not *Ma'am!* I am Terra!"

"Okay," Decker answered. "*Terra!* Are you supposed to direct us to the compound's entrance?"

She nodded. "Yes, I am."

Decker opened his car door. "So why don't you do just that?"

2

Ignoring hostility was part of the profession. Decker was used to stony glares and the occasional hurled epithet. But there was something disconcerting about the group. So many disciples, all of them displaying a curious mixture of fury and fragility. Or maybe it was the white cotton robes they wore, making them look like zombies housed in shrouds.

He thought a moment.

That wasn't fair. Jews also wore white robes — *kittles*. Men wore them when they married, during the High Holy Days, and at the *seder* — the festive Passover meal. The garment was also used in burial. A morbid association, but Decker couldn't help thinking about it.

Most of the sect members simply stared as Decker, along with Oliver, draped the yellow crime tape across the temple door.

Brother Pluto, on the other hand, expressed himself verbally. "Is that yellow ribbon *really* necessary, or are you two just looking for something to do until that doctor is done?"

He was thin and short and balding. He also wore a robe, but his was blue and appeared to be fashioned from silk. He had a belt on it, but it was partially open. Underneath, Pluto wore a white T-shirt and jeans. The acting head guru was irritated. He spoke in a reedy voice. If Decker were to personify him as a planet, Pluto would have been the logical choice.

Decker finished pinning the tape and straightened his back, towering over the little man. "Sorry about spreading the investigation all over the place. Since the body was moved, we can't confine ourselves to just the one room —"

"A clear violation of our civil rights!"

Decker smoothed his mustache, then said, "Tell me whose civil rights are being violated and I'll put a stop to it!"

Pluto spoke bombastically. "You know what I mean! Your *people* questioning our grieving family."

Oliver ran his hands through his black hair, wondering if the guy really was an alien. He sure as hell looked like one. "We're trying to find out what happened to your leader, sir. Don't you want to know?"

"But we *do* know, Detective! Our Father Jupiter has gone to a better place."

So why all the grieving? Decker glanced upward at a peaked skylight of stained glass — swirls of blue, yellow and orange. It looked like something Van Gogh would have designed. Huge mother. It was supported by beams of steel and wire mesh.

He returned his eyes to Pluto and said, "Spiritually, I'm sure you're right, sir. Unfortunately, we need to know what happened physically —"

"Spiritual and physical are one and the same.

21

Of course, the violators will never understand that. Society's thinking has been fractured irreparably, constantly separating the soul and body. Just as you've done now, Lieutenant. It's not your fault, though. You've just never been schooled."

Decker said, "Perhaps, at another time, you can enlighten me."

"You're being sarcastic. Your attitude is typical for a violator. Even more in sync with your work as a policing agent."

Pluto's vitriolic words had drawn a little crowd. It was growing by the moment.

Now what was the friggin' purpose of all that? But of course, Decker knew the purpose. To embarrass him, to make the outsider — the *violator* — look like the ignorant fool. Still, he held his tongue. He wasn't about to start a riot for what appeared to be an open-and-shut case of suicide.

"I'm not trying to be contentious. Just curious. If I were an outsider interested in joining the Order, how would you explain to me the true nature of the universe?"

Pluto sneered. "Our philosophy is not a parlor game, Lieutenant!"

"I didn't say it was. Tell me your philosophy. And if we have time, I'll spout off a few theories of my own."

Pluto seemed amused. Folding his arms across his chest, he leaned against the temple door, breaking the crime ribbon. "Very well. We'll trade philosophies. But you two go first —"

Oliver's brown eyes darted across the masses. He held his hands up. "Hey, leave me out of this one."

"As you wish." Pluto turned to Decker. "Lieutenant."

Spitting out the title as if it were a swear word.

Decker picked up the yellow tape and tacked it back onto the door, aware that the gathering was waiting for him to begin. "Interesting that you should mention the universe. Because I remember reading one of Ganz's —"

"Father Jupiter," Pluto interrupted.

"Excuse me." Decker was deferential. "I was reading Father Jupiter's lay articles on the universe . . . back when he was a cosmologist."

Like Pluto, Decker knew he was playing to an audience. He divided his glances between the cotton-robed followers and the silk-robed Pluto.

"As an observant Jew, I was struck by one of Jupiter's statements — that the universe has neither a past nor a future. It was something that just was . . . or is. Sort of flies in the face of the Big Bang theory —"

"The Big Bang?" Oliver smiled. "I like the sound of this theory."

Decker held back laughter. "It stated that the universe came from one massive explosion."

"Explosion of what?"

"An explosion of . . . stuff."

"How'd the stuff get there?"

"That's an open question," Decker answered.

Pluto broke in. "It's not the universe that al-

23

ways was. It's *matter* in the universe that was, is and always will be. The physical component of course explains nothing about the spiritual."

"Agreed. Which is why we Jews have kind of combined the two aspects. We believe that God — whom we call Hashem, which means *the name* in Hebrew — is the source of all matter and is neither a creation nor susceptible to destruction. Hashem just *is*. God is material and God is spiritual. And He described His heavens as limitless way before science got into the act."

Pluto continued to slouch with his arms across his chest. "Precisely why Father Jupiter left science and returned to the spiritual." He waved a dismissive hand. "I don't think you've said anything too profound about God's existence. In fact it's rather simplistic."

Decker was winging it now. "Well, I was just thinking . . . now correct me if I'm wrong — if the universe or at least *matter* was, is and always will be, and if matter has existed forever . . . and all matter is conserved, then Jupiter's still a part of the universe —"

"More simplicity —"

"So if your leader isn't dead, just . . . transformed, then why grieve for him? Why the shrine? Why all this hoopla for someone who — as you stated — is in a better place? You shouldn't be grieving. You should be having a party."

Oliver added, "Yeah, like a wake or something. BYOB. Judging from the fifth under Jupiter's bed, maybe your leader was doing just that."

The crowd's eyes went back to Pluto. The short man's cheeks had taken on a deep blush. "Your cavalier attitude to our Father Jupiter the Beloved is obscene!"

Pluto turned on his heel and stomped off.

Oliver and Decker exchanged glances. Decker shrugged. No one spoke for a moment as the crowd stood shell-shocked in the absence of a leader. Decker cleared his throat. "I'm sure you'd like us out as soon as possible. And we'd like to give you back your privacy. So could you all please keep the aisles clear so we can conduct our business?"

No one moved.

Decker said, "Come on. Let's break it up. Debate club is over."

As if programmed, the people began to disperse. After the crowd had thinned, Oliver whispered, "Think the lobotomies are done before or after they join up?"

Decker smoothed his pumpkin mustache. "Some people just have a rough time coping."

Oliver shook his head. "You did pretty good . . . being put on the spot like that."

"I plagiarized from Rina. Actually, she made the connection between the universe and how Jews view God. We were watching some science yawner on PBS or the Discovery Channel . . . 'Nova' or 'Omni' or something with a short name."

"You mean there are human beings who actually *watch* those shows?"

"Rina does. She likes that stuff. I don't remember much. I fell asleep." Decker looked up at the skylight. The gray overcast was beginning to burn off. "We pissed Brother Pluto off. That wasn't smart. It's going to make our job harder."

"Loo, what exactly is our job?"

"To bring the body to the morgue for a complete autopsy. Once Dr. Little formally declares this a suicide, we can button this case up."

"So let's load the body into the meat wagon."

Decker shook his head. "Not yet. Let me talk to the Doc. If she sees no overt sign of homicide, I'm inclined to let these guys have their shrine and their last good-byes."

"*Why?* Let's just get the hell out of here."

"Patience. I'd like to give you and Marge more time to check out the bedroom. It would also give the people here some closure. Maybe make them feel a *little* less hostile toward us. And maybe that would mean fewer problems if we need to come back."

"Body temperature hasn't dropped much. I'd guestimate that he's been dead for less than six hours. No rigor, but it was cool last night. If the room wasn't heated, the lower temperature could have delayed its onset. Lividity was shot to hell because the body was moved." Little consulted her notes. "No stab wound, no gunshot wounds, no overt bruises, contusions or ligature marks. Nothing to suggest foul play by brute

26

force." She leaned over the body. "But there are subtler ways of doing a guy in."

Decker's interest perked up. "Meaning?"

"He had a few puncture marks in his arm — the left bicep. A neat job. No evidence of hitting a vessel or a subdural hematoma. Just a tiny prick. See this little dot right here?"

"Sure do. Is it self-inflicted?"

"Possibly," Little said. "He also had some punctures in his buttocks. Could be harmless, but I won't know anything definitive until I get the bloods and gases back. I'm about done here . . . ready to take Professor Ganz to the chophouse —"

"Uh yeah, that might be a problem —"

"They don't want to autopsy the body."

"Exactly."

"It's the law."

"Exactly." Decker smoothed his mustache. "How much time before the body chemistry starts changing?"

"The sooner I get him in a meat locker, the better."

"The folks here want to have some kind of processional, walk by the body to say good-bye to their leader."

"How long?"

"There's two hundred and thirty-five of them —"

"Two hundred and thirty-five?"

"Including children, yes. Still, I think we could wrap it up in a half hour . . . forty-five minutes."

27

Little made a face. "Can we put him on ice?"

"Will it mess up your tests?" Decker asked.

"It's certainly not ideal." She smiled, showing big, yellow incisors. "You want to do this for them, Pete?"

"It would give me a chance to look around and allow my homicide team to finish up with the bedroom. Once we're kicked out of here, we may have a hard time getting back in."

"Someone going to stand guard here to make sure they don't screw up the body?"

Decker winced. "They'd like to dress him . . . throw on his royal robe."

"*Royal* robe? What the hell is a royal robe?"

"Some purple silk job with gold embroidery. Wouldn't mind having it for a smoking jacket."

"You smoke?"

"If stressed enough, I even burn. They also want him to hold his royal scepter. Can they squeeze his fingers around the staff without screwing you up?"

"This is all very odd."

"Can they do it? Yes or no?"

Little smiled. "Sure, dress him in a robe. Put the scepter in his hand. And while you're at it, add a crown on his head and a ruby in his naval. Let them pay homage to their Grand Imperial Poobah!"

3

The processional gave Decker the opportunity to skulk around. Assigning two uniforms to watch over the body, he slipped away just as Pluto took center stage. As he left, he caught a glimpse of the guru, who still wore his blue silk robe, but had overlaid it with a long, purple vest, which was no doubt meaningful of something.

Carefully, he tiptoed down a hallway which held one door after another, like a hotel corridor. He jiggled a couple of knobs — closed but not locked. Glancing over his shoulder, he saw nary a soul.

Just a quick peek.

He opened a door.

The space was spare and tiny. Bare walls except for a postage-stamp, square window opened to let in a wisp of cool air. On the floor was a cot with a brown blanket. A shelf above the bed held a pot, a mug, a ceramic bowl and several black-spined books. More of a prison cell than a bedroom.

Again, he looked around.

The foyer was empty.

He went inside, managing to squeeze his giant frame into a cavity's worth of square footage. Then, he shut the door.

Time's a tickin'. If you're gonna do it, get to it.

He took the pot from the shelf. It had been used, but was scrubbed clean. The mug was also clean, and contained one tablespoon and one teaspoon. The pottery bowl held ashes of burnt incense. Decker sniffed. Sandalwood maybe? No evidence of pot. He put the accoutrements back. The books turned out to be videotape cases. No labels. He hesitated, then took a tape at random and tucked it under the strap of his shoulder harness. He buttoned his jacket.

Just borrowing, he told himself. No harm in that.

No sign of a closet. With care, he crouched down and peered under the bed. A suitcase. He pulled it out. Inside were two neatly folded white cotton robes, and two pairs of denim jeans along with two white T-shirts. Several pairs of woman's white cotton briefs — the only indication that the room's occupant was female. Gingerly, he restored everything back to pristine condition, and stowed the valise under the bed.

No connecting doors to any room. Ergo, no connecting bathroom.

And that was that. Opening the door a crack, he scanned the foyer. Still empty. In a swift move, he glided out to safety, then came through another corridor, opening several doors and peeking inside. Replicas of the bedroom he had just seen. Spartan surroundings, even for those without material attachments. Were they also without *emotional* attachments? Maybe, but maybe not. There had been a lot of weeping following Father Jupiter's death.

Eventually, the pathway led Decker to a set of double doors. He pushed on one, revealing the Order's kitchen. It was cavernous and industrial with metal cabinets, stainless-steel counters, massive sinks and a built-in refrigeration system. It was also flooded with light from the ceiling's giant glass dome.

The cooking area was devoid of people but not of smells. A wave of something savory tickled Decker's nose, causing his stomach to do a little tap dance. He checked his watch — ten forty-two. Twenty-three minutes had passed since the procession had begun.

Go for it, he told himself. Worse came to worst, he could say he was just looking for a drink of water.

He walked into the area, running his index finger along the countertop. Spotless and dust-less. Lots of heavy cauldrons hanging from an oval-shaped central rack secured by chains from the ceiling. Four mammoth-sized kettles sat on the cooktops. Using the cloth of his jacket as a pot holder, Decker lifted a lid and got a faceful of steam. Blinking back the heat, he was looking at some kind of soup or stew. He replaced the lid, then pulled forward on one of the oven doors. Warm, but not hot air. A pan with loaves of bread still in the rising stage. He returned the door to its original position, hoping he didn't screw something up.

31

Lots of light coming down from on top, but still, not much in the window department. There were long but narrow fenestrations running along the top of the walls. Hands on his hips, he looked around.

Alone.

He opened one of the cabinets above the counter — sacks of flour, a dozen packets of dried yeast and jars of dried spices. Another had the same contents. A third held a dozen canisters of different types of teas. The cupboards seemed to hold provisions only. The bottom storage area was filled with water bottles — at least a hundred five-gallon jugs. He closed the doors and leaned against the counter.

No plates, no bowls, no cups, no eating utensils and no other cookware except the hanging kettles. Soup or stew in the cauldrons, and a small pot and a mug in each room. Probably stew or soup was the sect's usual fare, and each person was allotted an individual pot and spoon for his or her portion. Maybe a personal cup for the tea. And that was that for tableware. It would sure save on the kitchen labor if each person took care of his or her own vessels.

Pulling the handle of one of the built-in refrigerator doors, Decker saw rows of jars, each labeled with a specific fruit or vegetable. Some of the produce was pickled, others had been made into purees or sauces. Some of the citrus fruits had been candied. He had to hand it to the Order. The members were earthquake-ready, better prepared than he was. In the case of absolute shut-down, the sect could go on for months.

He took out his pad and made a quick sketch of the physical layout. As his eyes panned over the room, Decker noticed another door along the back wall. It opened to an immense garden with rows of produce, sided by orchards of fruit trees. The plot seemed big enough to qualify as commercial agriculture.

Tucking his notepad into his jacket, he climbed down the three steps, then ambled along a dirt path lined with trellises woven with plant material — vines of tomatoes and cucumbers dotted with their small, yellow flowers. The twisted suckers of pole bean plants climbed along a steel vegetable cage. There were also raised beds made out of brick. They housed squash plants abloom with mustard-colored flowers, two-foot-high eggplant with purple blooms and a panoply of pepper plants. Also included were remnants of the winter vegetables — lettuce and spinach heads on the verge of bolting. Sprinkled among the edibles were beds of flowers — newly planted marigolds and petunias. Aesthetically pleasing as well as practical because marigolds were insecticidal. Strike another notch for the Order's self-reliance. The patch was damn impressive.

The area looked to be about a couple of acres with two fruit orchards sandwiching a vegetable garden. Beyond the arable portion was scrubland overrun with wild fauna and airborne spores: dandelions, orange nasturtiums, purple statice, wild daisies, sage plants and chaparral. Copses of silver eucalyptus gave the land some texture and height. Gnarled California oaks sat dormant in ground water, grumbling because El Niño had overwatered the turf.

Decker stopped walking, his ears hearing more than ambient sounds. Dogs barking — the Dobies. He hoped they were locked up somewhere, but suspected they were close at hand. Stupid to explore with them on the prowl. Yet he kept going.

He came upon a good-sized tool and potting shed — around two hundred square feet. The usual stuff — trowels, claws, rakes, hoes, weeders. Shelves with terra-cotta pots, and dozens of plant starts sitting in egg cartons. There were also shelves containing bags of fertilizers, boxes of nutrients, plant food sprays and aerosol cans of weed killer. There were also jars of rat killer, all clearly marked with the skull-and-crossbones logo, some pest traps and animal cages as well. Apparently the Order of the Rings of God had decided that bugs and pests took a backseat to human needs.

Not that Decker found that philosophy objectionable. He embraced the Jewish philosophy that had animals serving people, and not the other way around. God had given the human race the gift of reason, although in Decker's line of work he rarely saw it utilized. That being said, people — with their theoretical gift of reason —

had obligations to their animals. Cruelty was strictly forbidden. As a matter of fact, pets and livestock had to be fed before sitting down to one's own meal, the rationale being that though people don't forget to eat, they are occasionally remiss about that bowl of dog chow. *Tsar Ba'alei Chayim* — kindness to animals.

The shed was neat, the garden implements hanging on the walls or stowed in one of the built-in slots. There were several plastic trash cans for dirt and leaves. The floor had been swept clean.

Cleanliness and godliness — hand in hand.

Decker mulled over the adage.

The sect must believe in some type of a god. Why else name yourself the Order of the Rings of God? Why not just . . . Order of the Rings. Or just plain Rings. Much thought often goes into naming. Decker remembered how he and Rina had endlessly debated baby names even *after* they decided to name Hannah Rosie after Rina's grandmothers. Then how much *more* important would the name be if it denoted a personally tailored philosophy? Or a new *religion?* Each word would be important.

Decker heard a throat clear, and turned around. The man wasn't as tall as Decker, but must have cleared six feet. He appeared to be in his late thirties with a thin face and brown eyes. He sported a goatee, and had a black ponytail, which fell between his shoulder blades. Like Pluto, the man wore a blue silk robe overlaid with a purple silk vest. Decker wondered about his name. Mars? Maybe Uranus. That would be fitting. Because the whole investigation was a big pain in the ass.

The man walked over to Decker and held out his hand. "Bob," he announced.

Involuntarily, Decker let out a chuckle. He shook the proffered hand. "Lieutenant Decker."

"You find me funny?"

"Just the name."

"Why's that? Bob's a common name."

Again, Decker smiled. "Yes, sir, it is indeed. I hope I'm not trespassing —"

"You are. You're lucky I locked the dogs up. With the police coming and going, I had no choice. They don't like strangers."

"Good guard dogs never do."

"You'd better believe it." Bob smiled. "Their names are Donner, Dancer and Rudolph. Santa has his reindeer, I have my friends."

"They're your dogs?"

"No." Bob wiped sweat from his brow. "They belong to the Order. But I'm outdoors a lot so we enjoy a personal relationship."

Decker sensed an underlying message — a veiled warning that said, "Don't mess with me."

Bob said, "When I first arrived, Father Jupiter asked if I wanted to change my name to something more . . . far-reaching — celestial or heavenly, if you will. That was the trend. To follow our great leader's lead. But, being an individualist and a bit of an oppositionalist, I declined.

36

Unlike most of the people here, I wasn't running away from *myself* per se. Just running *to* something better, my spirit being my compass."

Decker nodded, waiting for more.

Bob mulled over his words. "I've found peace that had previously eluded me. I found my personal god."

Decker kept his face flat. "Father Jupiter is your personal god?"

"Perhaps that's an overstatement." Bob smiled, showing tea-stained teeth. "He's not a god, but a leader. Showing me the way. My own personal . . . Tao. I feel that we were birthed from the same matter."

"Is he related to you by blood?"

Bob chucked. "How I wish." His eyes swept over the vista. "Look around, sir. This is a type of modern-day Eden. Rephrasing it into scientific parlance, I'd say here we have ideal Newtonian physics — a perfect world of action and reaction, and absolute time. Out there . . ." He cocked a thumb over his shoulder. "It's strictly Einstein where everything's relative. Or Max Planck and quantum mechanics where things are random and unpredictable."

Decker waited a beat. "You tend the garden by yourself?"

"I have help. But I've been here longer, so *I* get to wear the blue robe and purple vest."

"Which means?"

"I'm an official privileged attendant to our Father Jupiter. Like Socrates, we get to sit at his feet

37

and listen his words. We hold the title of guru. So I'm officially Guru Bob. But you may call me brother. After all, we're one big family."

The guru's face remained neutral, but Decker suspected that Bob was speaking tongue-in-cheek.

Bob explained, "There are four of us who hold the rank."

"Ah. I see. I've only met —"

"Pluto. He's quite the organizer."

Decker said, "I had assumed he was the acting head of the Order now that Father Jupiter is gone."

Bob continued to be unreadable. "I suppose you could call him the *partial* acting head. He certainly is a talking head."

"He has opinions."

"That is true," Bob answered. "Let's get back to Newtonian physics. Because basically that's the same concept we're dealing with. For our everyday reactions, Newton's laws hold. You know his laws, right?"

"Refresh my memory."

"A body at rest stays at rest . . . a body in motion stays in motion. The orbits of the planets. What comes up, must come down. Any of this sound familiar?"

"The up and down part."

"The specifics are not important. What is consequential is that his laws hold in ordinary life, but they break down when objects start approaching the speed of light. Then time no longer is absolute, but is relative and lumped into this category called space time. Not to mention the effects of the space warp — the curved topology of our universe. And the effect of huge gravitation bodies we can't see called black holes. In other words, you get massive distortions, you understand what I'm saying?"

"The analogy is eluding me, sir —"

"Bob."

"Bob, then." Decker paused. "Were you a scientist in your past life?"

"A graduate student in astrophysics at Southwest University of Technology. I worshiped Dr. Ganz as a scientist, as a physicist, as a cosmologist and as a brilliant philosopher and thinker. I devoured his texts, could quote his writings word for word. He became the idealized father I never had. Mine was a washed-out old coot. Even after he made money, he wasn't happy."

"But you hadn't met Ganz before he disappeared."

"Of course not. My hero was pure fantasy because I, like others, had thought him dead. When I found out that Ganz was still alive, I rejoiced. My hero had leaped from the dry pages of publication and into real life. When others ridiculed his abrupt transformation, I had to find out for myself what brought about his startling change. So I came here. I heard him speak, I talked to the man, thought about his ideas. Once I entered his world, I never left. To me, Father Jupiter is still king of the universe."

Melach Haolam, Decker thought. A hefty title for a mere mortal. "So you've been with Father Jupiter how long?"

"Fourteen years. But getting back to Newton's absolute time versus Einstein's relative time, the analogy is this: I have no objection to Guru Pluto stepping in as acting head of the Order under *most* circumstances — i.e., Newtonian physics. Just as long as he doesn't try to impose absolute time under Einsteinian conditions. Because if he does, I'm going to clean his relative clock, so to speak."

Decker opened his mouth and closed it. "Are you saying he can act as the Order's head just as long as he doesn't overstep his bounds?"

"Precisely," Bob stated. "You're quick for a cop."

Decker stared at him.

Again, Bob grinned. He swept his arm over the vista. "Father Jupiter loved the garden. Next to the heavens, he loved this world the most. Can't say that I blame him."

"It's beautiful."

"You know, to get here from the front of the compound is quite a trek. Certainly *not* within arm's reach from the procession . . . which is where you're supposed to be. Been doing a little space travel, sir?"

"I got lost."

"I'll bet." Bob scratched his head. "I don't care, but the dogs wouldn't like it. Certainly, Pluto wouldn't approve."

"And that matters to you, Bob?"

The guru thought about that. "Let's put it this way. At the moment, Pluto's nerves are frayed. It's best that you don't taunt him. He's handy with an ax."

Decker was surprised by the implicit threat. "I beg your pardon?"

"Woodcutting." Bob smirked. "I'll show you a shortcut back."

"Actually, if you could show me to Father Jupiter's bedroom, I'd be much obliged."

Bob tapped his foot. "Ordinarily, that's off-limits. But since a birdie has told me that you've parked a couple of your lackeys there, guess I might as well show you the proverbial light. Or at least the way." Bob started walking, but Decker didn't follow. Bob stopped. "Yes?"

"You all going to be all right here? Maintain status quo, so to speak?"

Bob said, "*You all? Much obliged?* Originally from the South, sir?"

"I guess that's true if you consider that Florida was part of the Confederacy." Decker turned grave. "I have *concerns,* Bob. I don't want any unbalanced members trying to join Father Jupiter. An individual adult suicide is one thing. But mass suicide that includes *children,* well, that qualifies as murder."

"And you're wondering who would you arrest as the culprit if we were all dead?"

"Bob, I'm not *screwing* around anymore. I'm *very* concerned for the kids."

Bob said, "Here we believe in free will. Father Jupiter said that nothing is sincere if it's done under coercion. As far as I know, there are no plans for us to jump to the next level. Not that I can predict anyone's individual behavior any more than I could predict the position of a photon at any given moment. But I do understand what you're saying."

Decker wasn't too sure about that. "And if you hear anything about mass suicide, you'll let me know immediately, correct?"

Bob said, "I don't recall you being assigned to our welfare and safety." A tap of the foot. "I suppose I could take your concern as a compliment. You care."

"Especially when it comes to protecting kids."

"Lieutenant, I live here, but I don't live in a vacuum. I have a son. I want to see him grow to be a man."

"So we have an understanding."

"Up to a certain point."

"Meaning?"

"As long as Newtonian physics hold, we're fine. But when we get to Einsteinian travel in space time . . . what can I say? Things get pretty warped out there. I'll show you the way to Father Jupiter's bedroom now. Once you're there, Lieutenant, you're on your own."

4

Guru Bob walked Decker back to the Order's entryway before deserting him for the young girl van driver known as Terra. He whisked her away, leaving Decker to flounder among the white-robed mourners. Standing solo, Decker felt as welcome as a leper. He hunted around the hallways until he saw yellow crime tape strung across a doorway. He stepped over it and went inside the room. The scene wasn't much to speak about. In general, overdose suicides weren't messy or bloody. It was just a matter of finding out which specific agent stopped either the breathing or the beating of the heart. More a matter for a doctor than a detective.

Ganz's bedroom was significantly larger than his parishioners' cells, but not grandiose by any means. He had a queen-sized bed instead of a cot, a dresser for his clothing instead of a trunk under the bed and a wall of bookshelves. Most important, he had an attached bathroom. The techs had just finished dusting; black powder covered Ganz's nightstand, bookshelves and bedposts. At the moment, Scott Oliver was rifling through Ganz's clothes. Marge Dunn was scribbling in her notepad. She wore beige slacks, a white blouse and a black jacket. On her feet were basic black loafers with rubber soles. There were gold studs in her ears — no other jewelry. The simplest necklace could become a noose when dealing with a violent felon. She wore no perfume either, because alien scents can screw up evidence.

She looked up. "Lieutenant."

"Detective." A smile. "What do you have?"

"A headache." Marge pushed blond bangs from her brown eyes. "You have any Advil on you, Pete?"

"Always." Years ago, Decker had been shot in the shoulder and arm. The wound had healed without motor nerve damage, but pain lingered like an unwanted relative. He tossed her his bottle. She took off her gloves and plunked out two pills, swallowing them dry. Then she hurled the bottle back. Decker caught it with one hand.

"According to Pluto . . ." Marge dropped her voice. "Have you met Pluto?"

Decker smiled. "I have met Pluto."

Marge rolled her eyes. "A piece of work."

"Wouldn't want him for a houseguest."

She smiled. "Anyway, Pluto's story is that Ganz was found roughly in this kind of position." She flung her hand back, opened her mouth and flopped her arms out at her side. "Rag doll style. Head and left arm hanging off the side of the bed. He was lying on the diagonal, the body skewed to the left. You can still see part of the outline on the sheets."

Decker examined the depression in the rumpled coverings. It ran from the left top of the bed to the right bottom corner. "Who found him?"

"Venus — Jupiter's significant other — did." She paused and thought. "You know, there're only nine planets. Wonder what the rest of the group call themselves?"

"There're always the asteroids," Oliver said as he rooted through the pockets of Jupiter's purple robes. "Isn't a mile-long asteroid gonna hit earth in something like twenty years?"

"Yeah, I heard something like that on the news." Marge scratched her head. "Wonder if I should take an early retirement?"

"Where's Venus?" Decker asked. "And please nobody say second rock from the sun."

"At the processional, washing Jupiter's feet as the people pass by," Oliver answered. "It's a full-time job because his followers keep kissing Jupiter's big toe. And no, I don't know what that means."

Decker said, "Mennonites wash their feet before praying."

"Why's that?" Marge asked.

"I think Jesus used to wash the feet of his followers before praying out of humility. So did Abraham — he did it out of kindness. Of course, way back when, washing feet was a standard Middle Eastern custom. You live in the desert and wear sandals, you're going to have dirty feet."

Marge said, "Most of the people here wear tennis shoes."

Decker thought a moment. "You know, Jews wash the dead bodies before corpses are buried. In addition to their own philosophy, maybe the Order co-opted bits and pieces from different, established religions. A little of this, a little of that."

Oliver asked, "What is the group's philosophy?"

"I'm not sure." Decker pulled out the videotape. "Maybe this'll help us find out." He dropped it into a plastic bag.

"Where'd you get *that,* Loo?" Oliver asked.

"I'll return it. Don't worry." Quickly, Decker changed the subject. "What time did Venus find the body?"

Marge said, "Pluto said around five in the morning."

"*Pluto* said," Decker stated. "Has anyone talked to Venus?"

"I've tried but she's been in seclusion," Oliver said. "*Incommunicado* until she took her place at the processional."

"She's going to have to be interviewed." Decker rubbed his eyes. "So all the information about Jupiter's death is via Pluto?"

Oliver nodded. "He's the official spokesperson."

"I don't know about that." Decker explained the cult's pecking order, mentioning that there were three other privileged attendants. He told them about Bob.

Oliver asked, "So who are the other two?"

Decker said, "Count the purple vests."

"Venus was wearing a purple vest," Oliver stated. "That leaves one more. Want me to go out to the processional and take a look, Loo?"

"Are you done here?"

Oliver shut the dresser drawer. "I'm done. I don't know about Detective Dunn."

Decker turned to Marge. "Find anything to suggest that this was anything other than a suicide?"

"Nothing at first glance, at least." She consulted her notes. "Empty fifth of vodka under the bed, empty vial of . . . let me get the exact name . . ." She paged through her notes. "Nembutal sodium capsules . . . twenty milligrams per capsule. Vial was empty, prescribed originally for ten capsules, no refills. I also bagged a vial of diazepam —"

"Valium," Decker said. "Diazepam is the generic name."

Marge looked up. "Whatever you say. I don't use that stuff. I found an empty vial prescribed for twenty tablets, also twenty milligrams per tablet."

"Ganz's name on the labels?"

"Not Ganz, Father Jupiter."

Decker asked, "The label read 'Father Jupiter'?"

"Yes."

Decker asked, "Where'd you find the empty vials?"

"On his bed stand," Marge said. "All the vials were dusted and bagged. To me, it plays out like a typical case of mixing drugs and alcohol."

"What about anything injectable?" Decker asked.

No one spoke for a moment. Then Marge asked why.

"Because the ME found recent IM needle marks in his arm and butt."

Oliver smiled sheepishly. "Uh . . . there's a slew of shit in his medicine cabinet. I wrote it all down, but I didn't bother to dust or bag it. Not with the two empty vials at his bedside."

"I'll bag it," Decker said.

"It's not that I screwed up —"

"Who said you screwed up?"

"You've got that look on your face, Deck."

Oliver had screwed up, but Decker let it go. "Go out and find the remaining guru —"

"Yeah, yeah," Oliver muttered, stepping over the crime tape. Deck wasn't a bad guy. He never lorded his position over those in his command, and he didn't buddy up to the brass. Begrudgingly, Oliver was forced to admit that Deck *probably* made it to the position on merit.

"Come back here when you're done, Scott," Decker called out.

"Fine, fine," Oliver answered.

When he had left, Marge asked, "Needle marks?"

"Yep."

"Self-inflicted?"

"In the arm, maybe. But in his butt?"

Marge regarded his face. "The empty fifth of

vodka . . . the pills. Everything's too neat. You have doubts, don't you? So do I."

"I just don't like it when the crime scene has been altered. It would have been one thing if someone had tried to revive the body — moved it just enough to do CPR. But to *move* a corpse in order to place it in a shrine before contacting authorities? I find that odd. People are usually nervous around dead bodies."

"The group's strange. Maybe they have odd ideas about death and bodies."

"Even so, Marge, *someone* should have known better. Then you have the fact that the death wasn't called in by *anyone* in the group. It was called in by Ganz's daughter. So how did she find out about it? And if no one in the Order of the Rings called the police, what exactly *were* they planning to do with the corpse?"

"Bury it on the grounds?" she suggested. "They seem antiestablishment enough to do something like that."

"That's certainly true." Decker slipped on a pair of latex gloves. "We have two immediate tasks."

"We have to talk to Venus," Marge said.

"Exactly. Do you want to do it? Might be better woman to woman."

"Sure. I'm just about done here, so I can do it now. Unless you want me to bag the vials in the bathroom."

"No, I'll bag 'em. The second thing we need to know is —"

"Who from the group called Jupiter's daughter?" Marge interrupted. "Which means someone should talk to her. You'll do that, right?" She smiled. "Anything to get out of here."

"Why waste my breath if you know what I'm going to say?"

Marge laughed. "No need to get peevish, Loo. All it means is that you trained me well."

The bathroom was a closet crammed with a toilet, a washstand and a shower without a stall — a curtain cutting across one of the corners, and a mounted handheld water spray. White tile walls, white tile floors, all of it slippery when wet. A drain had been cut into the floor. Above the washstand was the medicine cabinet. Decker opened the cupboard, plastering his body against the opposite wall to avoid getting hit by the swing-out door. There appeared to be around thirty different white plastic bottles, each with its own label. At first glance, nothing was in duplicate form. Which meant everything would have to be bagged separately. Decker draped a clean cloth over the toilet seat — which was surprisingly in the down position (had a woman been in there?) — and laid the plastic evidence bags down on the clean surface. He also placed a cloth over the washstand. Then he took out his pad and pen.

He started at the left upper corner:

Echinacea Purpura — For supporting the im-

50

mune system. One hundred capsules at 400 mg each.

Decker wrote down the name of the drug, the number of tablets per bottle and the dosage of each pill. Then he spilled out the remaining capsules on the cloth draped over the washstand and counted them. Twenty-six still in the container. Carefully, he picked them up and put them back into the bottle, counting each kerplunk as they dropped to the bottom. Twenty-six tablets on the first count, twenty-six tablets on the second count. It's a wrap. He bagged and labeled the bottle.

One down, around twenty-nine more to go. He glared at the vials, knowing the same routine awaited him. Aah, the glamour of police work. Perhaps a little gray matter helped solve a few cases. But the true tricks of the trade were patience and an eye for detail. Of course, a confession never hurt. With any luck, he'd finish the bagging before the procession ended. And if he didn't, he hoped that the gurus would leave him alone to do his thing.

He took another bottle from the shelf: *Zinc tablets* (as citrate). One hundred tablets at 10 mg each. Forty-two tablets remaining.

Bottle three: *Calcium* (as calcium citrate). One hundred tablets at 200 mg each. Eighty-six tablets left.

Bottle four: *Manganese*. One hundred tablets at 100 mg each. Seventy-seven left.

Bottle five: *Vitamin C* (as ascorbic acid). One

hundred tablets at 100 mg each. Forty-two left.

Bottle six: *Sublingual B_{12} with folic acid and biotin*.

Decker read the instructions.

This unique formula is in sublingual (under tongue) form, the most effective form known for the absorption of vitamin B_{12} and folic acid (other than injection).

He thought a moment.

Other than injection.

Maybe that explained the IM needle marks in Jupiter's arms and butt. He was shooting up B_{12}. Maybe this was going to turn out to be simple.

One can hope. Decker turned the bottle in his gloved hand. It held one hundred tablets, each containing 800 mcg of vitamin B_{12}, folic acid and biotin. Seventy-one left.

Bottle seven: *Super-Antioxidants*. One hundred and twenty tablets, each containing 100,000 IU of vitamin A (one hundred percent as beta-carotene), 500 mg of vitamin C, 200 IU of vitamin E and 25 mg of selenium.

Decker emptied the bottle onto the cloth. They looked like horse pills. Fifty-seven left.

Bottle eight: *Healthy bones supplement*: For a healthy skeletal system. This one contained calcium, zinc, manganese, magnesium, copper (as gluconate), boron, horsetail herb extract, yucca juice and vitamins C, D, B and K.

Decker perused his notes, then looked back at the shelves. Lots of concoctions containing the same supplements — vitamins C, D and K. And the minerals zinc, magnesium and chromium. There were five bottles holding megadoses of vitamin C. If Ganz had taken all of the pills, all at once, he would have been overdosing on many of the vitamins and minerals, some as much as ten thousand milligrams more than the recommended daily dose.

Is it possible to OD on vitamins? Decker didn't see why not. Vitamins were drugs. Judy Little would know.

Moving from the first shelf to the second, Decker found more of the same — vitamins, minerals, extracts and supplements. Interestingly enough, as he waded through the bottles, he found no prescription drugs, nor did he locate any over-the-counter medication. Not even a lowly bottle of Tylenol. Yet on Ganz's nightstand were recent prescription vials of Valium and Nembutal. And according to Marge, his name was typed on both of the labels.

Speculate later, Deck. For now just finish up.

Fifteen minutes later, the cupboard was empty. As he gathered the numerous evidence bags, Decker felt hostility over his shoulder.

"Just *what* do you think you're doing?"

Pluto's voice. Decker turned around, knocking into the little man with his shoulder. "Are you all right?"

"No, I'm not all right." Pluto rubbed his shoulder. "You clobbered me."

"It was an accident. There's not enough room

in here for two people."

"Agreed. *You* shouldn't *be* here." Pluto's face was bright red. He continued to massage his shoulder.

Decker felt the hairs on his neck rise in protest. But he managed to check his temper. "Sir, this is a crime scene. And you, being here, are in violation of the law. Now I know you want me out of your hair. So make it easy for me and leave —"

"You're taking personal property —"

"I am taking evidence from a crime scene. Now if you don't get *out* of my way, and *out* of this room, I'm going to handcuff and arrest you in front of all your people."

"Which will only serve to stoke their simmering anger —"

"I'm willing to chance it if you're willing to spend a night in jail. Now move it!"

Pluto rocked on his feet, faltered, then stepped aside. Decker stomped out of the bathroom, bags in arms, then placed them on the floor. He searched around for shopping bags for easier transport. "Is the processional done?"

Pluto sighed. "Yes." Another sigh. "Yes, it's done."

Decker regarded the man's face. He seemed genuinely saddened. But as soon as he realized Decker's eyes were on him, he hardened his expression. "I suppose you ghouls are going to take Father Jupiter's body now. When will it be released for our private burial?"

"We won't keep it any longer than necessary." Decker spoke softly. "I'm very sorry for your loss, sir. Father Jupiter was a great man."

Pluto held the stare, then looked away. "Yes, he was. Thank you for your words."

Decker paused. "Perhaps you can explain something to me. The death was called in by Ganz's —"

"Father Jupiter."

"Yes, of course. The call to us came by way of Father Jupiter's daughter. Now, as far as I know, no one in the Order of the Rings of God called it in."

Pluto was silent.

Decker asked, "Were you planning on reporting the death, Guru Pluto?"

Pluto whispered, "It makes no difference now."

"So you weren't planning on reporting it —"

"I didn't say that."

"Sir, in the future, please be advised that you *must* report any death. It's the law."

"It's irrelevant now," the guru stated.

Again, Decker hesitated. "Out of curiosity, were you planning to bury the body on the grounds?"

"What might have been is *no* longer a concern."

"Fair enough," Decker answered. "No point in speculation. Just one more question, Pluto. Who called Father Jupiter's daughter and told her the news?"

"I wish I knew. Whoever did it needs to be addressed."

"Addressed?"

"For breaking the vows and overstepping the chains," Pluto orated. "You have your laws, we have ours."

5

It took some time and a little internal maneuvering, but eventually Marge was given the go-ahead to interview Venus. She had expected her bedroom to adjoin Ganz's, but it was located on the other side of the compound. She was led to the chamber, flanked by two gendarmes in white robes, each one looking very grave. One had facial hair, the other was clean-shaven, but both had close-cropped haircuts. The bearded man knocked on the door. It was answered by a smoky, female voice asking who was there. After Marge identified herself, the voice told her to come in. Beard opened the door, but didn't dare cross the threshold — as if restrained by an invisible net.

Marge went inside, then took a moment to look around. Spare but bright, the room held a double bed, a Shaker-like chair and a bookshelf. Venus was propped up by pillows, her legs stretched out atop the bedcover.

Talking to her guard, she said, "You may go now, Brother Ansel."

The man hesitated, then spoke in a nasal voice. "Are you sure you want to be left alone with a violator, Mother Venus?"

"Yes, I can manage. Thank you for your consideration. You may go."

"As you wish." He left, throwing Marge a hostile look as he shut the door. The two women made eye contact.

Marge said, "Thank you for seeing me, Ms . . ."

"Just call me Mother Venus. Or just Venus." She'd been reading a paperback. She put it down in the spine-up position, and pointed to the chair. "Have a seat."

"Thank you." Good-looking, Marge thought. Even with red eyes and no makeup, her features were striking. Appearing to be around thirty, Venus had shoulder-length, chestnut hair that framed an oval face. Translucent green eyes were shaded by enormous lashes. Her silken complexion was wan — to be expected — but Marge detected a hint of pink at the cheekbones. She wore a bright blue robe that plunged at the neckline and fell open mid-thigh, exposing graceful legs. She wasn't wearing a bra, but even without the support, she had cleavage. Her feet were bare and her left ankle was adorned with a gold bracelet. She lowered her gaze, then flung the bottom of the robe over her uncovered legs. Crossed and recrossed her ankles.

Marge felt funny addressing her as Venus, although if one needed a model for the goddess of love and beauty, this one could fit the bill. She craned her neck and managed to read the paperback's title — *Faith and Beyond*. She couldn't make out the author. Extracting a notepad from her jacket, she asked, "Would you mind if I took some notes?"

"Why would I mind? I have nothing to hide."

Marge digested her words, translating them. *She has something to hide.* "I'm sorry if I have to probe into sensitive areas —"

"You're just doing your job." Again, Venus recrossed her ankles.

"What are you reading?"

The question seemed to momentarily stump her. She glanced at her side and picked up the paperback. "This?" A shrug. "Something in Jupiter's library. The metaphysical part is interesting, but the science is complex." She tightened the robe around her neck. "That was Jupiter's forte — science . . . physics . . . cosmology. The very origins of existence. But you know that already, don't you."

"Yes, we know who Jupiter was."

"He was a great, great man." Venus's voice tightened. "I can't believe . . ." A sigh.

Marge asked, "How long have you lived here, ma'am?"

"Venus, please. Ma'am is for your world, not ours."

"Venus, then. How long have you been here with Jupiter?"

"Around ten years. When Jupiter took me in, I was really messed up — drugs, alcohol, two abortions. I had no faith, no beliefs, no . . . nothing. Just a self-destructive idiot. Jupiter saw right through me."

She looked at the ceiling.

"Anyway, this isn't relevant to your investigation. I'm telling you this because . . ." Tears fell from her eyes. "You don't know what a savior he was. I truly mean that. That's what Jupiter did. He dropped a brilliant career as well as fame and fortune to save souls. More than that, he taught others to save souls — me, Bob . . . Pluto. You wouldn't know it, but Pluto has rescued many homeless under Jupiter's guidance."

More tears. She wiped her face with the corner of her robe. "I suppose you want to know about this morning."

"Please. Had he passed away when you found him?"

"Yes . . ."

"How did you know?"

Venus wiped more tears. "He wasn't moving! He wasn't breathing! His heart . . . it had stopped."

"You felt for a pulse?"

She licked her lips. "Actually, no. I . . ." She closed her eyes and opened them. "I thought he was sleeping. It was time to get up for morning ablutions and prayers. I went into the room and called out his name. When he didn't answer, I went over to the bed and . . . and shook him a little. He . . ." She stopped to catch her breath. "He fell over when I touched him. His head . . . falling over the mattress . . ."

She swallowed.

"I screamed. Pluto . . . Pluto came in. After

that, I really . . . don't . . . one of my attendants ushered me out . . . brought me back to my room . . . waited with me. Later, Pluto came to me with the news."

Marge engaged her with sympathy. "Do you remember what time it was when you came into Jupiter's room?"

She spoke with effort. "The usual time. Around five."

"You say he . . ." Marge tried to be as gentle as possible. "You say he fell over when you shook him. Was he lying down or propped up —"

"Propped up. Jupiter often slept semiupright. He had a sinus condition. Being completely prone stuffed him up."

"And when you found him, he seemed to be asleep."

Venus nodded.

"Eyes closed?"

Again, Venus nodded.

"Anything odd about his position?"

"Meaning?" Venus asked.

"Did he appear to be comfortable? Were his limbs contorted, or was anything awry in the room?"

Venus shook her head no. "Everything seemed . . . fine."

"Did you see bottles of medicine at his bedside? Things like painkillers or sleeping pills —"

"Jupiter didn't take painkillers or sleeping pills. He didn't ascribe to any sort of Western medicine."

"Did you see any needles —"

"No," Venus answered. "No needles. Although Jupiter sometimes injected himself with vitamins."

Marge took in her words. "We didn't find any syringe."

"I keep them in my bathroom. Take a look. I have a case of disposables. We use them for hygienic purposes."

How convenient. Marge asked, "Did you inject him with vitamins?"

Venus raised her eyes. "I injected him a couple of times in the butt."

"Recently?"

"Three, four days ago."

"Ah," Marge said. That explained the needle marks. At least, that was *her* explanation. She said, "What can you tell me about the bottle of vodka —"

"Ordinarily, Jupiter did not drink. So if he drank himself . . . himself comatose . . . or . . . or dead . . ." She gulped air. "It could have only been for the purpose of transporting himself to a higher level of faith."

Transporting himself. Marge would have to get back to that one. "Did you see the bottle in view when you went to wake him up?"

Venus shook her head.

Marge said, "Let me review for a moment. Just see if I have it right. You went into Jupiter's bedroom around five in the morning to wake him for prayers. He was sitting upright —"

"Semiupright."

"Semiupright," Marge corrected herself. "You called out to him and he didn't answer. You went to shake him awake, and he slumped over, head over the edge of the mattress. At that point, you screamed, and Pluto came in. Is that accurate so far?"

"Yes."

"Did Pluto come in alone?"

"I believe so. But within seconds, there was a crowd. It was horrible." Her eyes welled up with tears. "Just . . . dreadful."

"Then someone brought you back here, to your bedroom, correct?"

"One of my attendants — Alpha-two, if I'm not mistaken."

"Alpha-two is your attendant's name?"

"All my attendants are Alphas."

"Do they wear vests and robes like Jupiter's attendants?"

A slight smile. It gave light to her face. Venus said, "Someone explained the color-coding to you. No. My attendants wear white robes with pink collars. They are privileged among the women, but none of them are as privileged as Jupiter's attendants. This is a male-dominated society. You are told that upfront. Besides, it doesn't affect me. As Jupiter's chosen mother, I'm second in command . . . well, I guess at the moment, I'm officially *in* command although temporarily Pluto is handling things. Until I can *compose* myself. But that's only *temporary*. I have no intention of letting *Pluto* step into Jupiter's shoes. I don't believe that even Pluto wants that onerous responsibility."

Marge nodded, scribbling down the cult's pecking order. "Who will succeed Jupiter?"

"I don't know who could possibly succeed him. As far as I know, Father Jupiter did not leave any line of succession. And with his sudden death . . ." Venus's eyes darted from side to side. "It will have to be worked out. But I assure you the Order of the Rings of God will remain intact. We owe it to Father Jupiter to further his ideals of love, charity and spirituality."

"Lofty goals."

"From a lofty man."

"One more thing," Marge said. "Pluto came back to your room to tell you the news."

"Correct."

"Do you recall the time?"

"Around a half hour later. So maybe it was five-thirty. But I wasn't clocking him."

"Of course. So as best as you can remember, Pluto came to your room and told you the news about five-thirty?"

"I suppose." She buried her face in her hands, then looked up. "It all happened very quickly . . . very surreal. I still can't believe . . . I knew he hadn't been himself, but . . ."

"Hadn't been himself in what way?" Marge asked.

"He wasn't exactly ill, but he seemed . . . *drained*. He hadn't been in his ordinarily high spirits for least six months. And he often held his head — like he had a bad headache. I was concerned. But when I asked him about it, he shrugged me off and assured me it all very normal. That it was part of the process."

"What process?"

Venus eyed Marge. "If I told you, you'd scoff. All the violators scoff."

"Try me."

Again, Venus hesitated. "Part of the communication process with the beyond. Father Jupiter knew that his body was being tapped of its life energies because he had begun to make serious contact with the forces."

Again, the room fell silent.

Venus said, "You wouldn't understand. You couldn't understand."

Marge tried to keep skepticism out of her voice. "What kind of forces?"

Venus waved her off.

"Please. I *want* to understand, Venus. Who had Jupiter contacted?" *Maybe someone was threatening him.* "Tell me." *Keep the voice even, Dunn.* "Were they humans? Were they aliens?"

To Marge, it appeared that Venus was appraising her sincerity. Finally, the alluring woman said, "Not aliens as you perceive them — little beeping things with five eyes and antennas."

Her voice became intense.

"For about six months, Jupiter had been receiving signals . . . electromagnetic waves that he felt were coming from an alternative universe. He was particularly excited because these signals were not classic Big Bang background radiation. You know . . . stuff given off when the universe was created. They seemed to be organized signals. How he could tell, I don't know. But that's why Jupiter was Jupiter. Only a man of his scope could interpret such things."

Marge tapped her pad. "He was a brilliant man."

Venus's expression took on a slight sneer — the upward curve of her lips, the roll of her eyes. "An understatement, Detective."

Marge ignored the condescension. "Tell me about these signals, Venus."

The young woman's smile was patient. All in all, Venus appeared cooperative.

"Jupiter said these were far-away stellar signals — many, many light-years away. So distant that they may have come from the original creation of matter. When the universe was still in ten dimensions instead of four. You know about the four dimensions, don't you — length, width, depth and time as a function of space. Space time. Einsteinian time. Do you know about Einstein's special theory of relativity? E equals MC squared?"

"I wasn't great in science," Marge said. "Maybe you could skip the equations and just tell me in layman's terms about the signals?"

The female guru seemed relieved and went on. "According to Jupiter, there are other universes that parallel our own. You get to them through the black holes. Unfortunately, once you enter the event horizon, you can't come back. Even if Jupiter's space travel theories are eventually accepted, and time is proven to be multidirectional, travel through black holes is strictly one way. So no one can ever come back to tell us about the experience."

No one spoke. Marge glanced at her notes — *black holes, ten dimensions, time multidirectional.* She was lost, but so what? She was investigating a suicide, not exploring the Order's whacked-out philosophy. Still, it was not something to be completely overlooked. The Order's "isms" may be the reason why Jupiter killed himself.

Venus's eyes clouded over. "I think I may have mixed up a few points. All I know is that it made perfect sense when Jupiter explained it. He was preparing us for the eventuality of it all. Especially because of the millennia. The timing just seemed to work out perfectly."

Marge's ears perked up. "Eventuality of what?"

"*Space travel* to a different physical as well as metaphysical plane. He claimed that time was closing in. From the Big Bang to the Big Crunch. Of course, Jupiter's concept of time is different from ours. A short time to him could have been a million light-years. Which is a very long time." She looked down. "Anyway, this is all tangential. I guess I'm just trying to figure out *why*." She exhaled. "Life as we know it is so . . . short . . . so *temporary*."

"Jupiter's space travel . . ." Marge leaned forward. "Did part of the process include suicide?"

"In theory, I suppose that suicide could be made part of it. Not that Jupiter ever mentioned suicide as a mode of transport. He spoke in more theoretical terms. Let me assure you, Detective, that the Order of the Rings of God is no Heaven's Gate. Jupiter was no crackpot. He certainly didn't believe in castration. We have children here. Mass suicide isn't part of our philosophy."

Marge said, "Still, it appears that Jupiter did take his own life."

"If he made that choice, he had a very good reason."

Marge asked, "Did you happen to notice any suicide note?"

"No. But I was taken away so quickly . . . there could have been." Seconds ticked by. "Did you find something?"

"Did Jupiter ever talk about suicide?"

"Mostly he spoke of the temporal issues of life. Was there a note, Detective?"

"That's what I'm trying to figure out. If Pluto removed something from Jupiter's bedroom —"

"I'll find out. Whatever is in Jupiter's bedroom now belongs to me." A beat. "Once you're done with the questioning, how long is your involvement going to last?"

"Not too long —"

"What's the process? You determine the cause

of death, then release the body?"

"Basic —"

"And if the death was natural, there's no problem?"

"None —"

"But if the death was caused by suicide, then what?"

"The coroner issues the death certificate based on his findings —"

"And then you release the body for burial?"

"Yes."

Venus rubbed her eyes. "So why are the police involved? Why do you care if he killed himself or not?"

Marge hesitated. "Jupiter's demise may be ruled a suspicious death, Venus."

She raised her hand to her mouth. "You think . . . that someone could . . . that's impossible!"

Marge said, "We have to rule out murder. Once we've done that, we're out of here."

"No one here would have killed Father Jupiter. Everyone loved him."

Marge nodded. "You know, his daughter called in the death —"

"His *daughter? Europa?*" Venus raised her eyebrows. "Well, maybe not *everyone* loved him."

Marge wrote frantically. "What can you tell me about her?"

Venus hesitated before she spoke. "I don't think I should talk about her."

"Why not?"

"Because if you are investigating a murder, I

don't want to be the one who . . . never mind. I've said enough."

"I take it Europa's not your best friend?"

"She rejected her father. That hurt him very much. Of course, I have feelings about her. But I don't see how she could have had anything to do with his death. She hadn't seen her father in fifteen years."

"Yet she called the death in."

Venus was quiet. Then she got up. "I must get dressed. I need to be a public figure for my people now. I certainly don't want to give them the misguided impression that Pluto is in charge. So if you'll excuse me."

"Of course." Marge stood. "Venus, don't you find it strange that Jupiter's daughter called in the death?"

"I find it very strange."

"How'd she know that her father had died?"

"Detective, that's a very good question."

6

The thermos of coffee had run dry. Reluctantly, Decker traded the one vice for another. Reaching in the glove compartment of his unmarked, he pulled out a loose cigarette. This one happened to be a Marlboro, but it really didn't matter. It had nicotine; it would do. He cranked the windows down, sat back in the driver's seat and lit up, staring out the windshield as smoke exited from his nose and mouth. Chiding himself for the weakness although not too harshly.

He had quit the noxious habit for almost six years. But then came a bloodbath, and the horrific images just wouldn't quit. The dreaded flashbacks — over a year old — popped up at inconvenient times. It was at those moments when Decker went for the rush. He didn't fully understand why he'd been thinking about that grisly scene at Estelle's restaurant. If he had to rationalize it, he'd most likely chalk it up to a hinky feeling about the safety of the children still residing within the compounds of the Order of the Rings of God.

He smoked slowly . . . leisurely, washing his nerves with a chemical calm. Since becoming a detective lieutenant, he rarely visited crime scenes — only in the extraordinary cases. Like

Estelle's . . . like this one. The death of famous people always made news, although Ganz hadn't been an important figure in science for a long time.

The meat wagon had left ten minutes ago, Ganz's body safely aboard and heading for the morgue. Decker's job was basically over. Now it was up to the pathologist. If all went well, he'd close shop here within fifteen minutes. He was hungry — it was past two in the afternoon — but wolfing down a sandwich in the car was bound to create a storm of stomach acid. Better to wait and grab a late lunch at home if possible. If not, even his desk was a better place to dine than behind the wheel of a car. He had just finished his smoke when Marge and Scott Oliver came through the gate of the compound. He got out of the car and waved them over.

"What did you learn from Venus?" he asked Marge.

She took out her notes. "The story goes like this. She went into Jupiter's room around five in the morning. He had been sitting semiupright in his bed and appeared to have been sleeping."

"Eyes closed?"

"Yes, eyes closed. At least that's what she said. Venus called out to him. When he didn't answer, she tried to shake him awake. At that point, he fell over lifeless, and she screamed. Her yells brought Pluto to the room. Immediately, she was ushered out, and taken back to her room. Half hour later, Pluto came to her and told her that

Jupiter was dead."

Oliver said, "So she was in her room for a half hour, just waiting to hear something?"

"Yep."

"Alone?" Decker asked.

"With one of her attendants." Marge hesitated. "Alpha-two."

"That's the name?"

"Apparently."

Oliver asked, "So what was happening with Jupiter between the time she discovered his *supposedly* dead body and the time Pluto brought her the news?"

"I don't know. We should speak to Pluto —"

"Wait, wait, wait," Decker interrupted. "Scott, why did you say his '*supposedly* dead body'? Any reason to think that Jupiter *wasn't* dead at that point?"

"Loo, if someone would have done the normal thing — call in the paramedics or 911 as soon as the body was discovered — I would feel a lot better about this being a suicide. The way it stands now, with no official around to verify Ganz's death until we arrived, which was around . . . what, Margie? Around seven?"

"Closer to seven-fifteen."

"When'd you get here?" Oliver asked Decker.

"Quarter to eight."

"So between the time that Venus went into Jupiter's room and someone from the outside actually *saw* the body — that's two hours. What do we think happened during that time? We've assumed that someone moved the body from the crime scene to the temple. Because we were told that Jupiter died in his bed. But we're not even sure if that's true. We also know that some dude named Nova signed a death certificate."

"Anyone talk to him?" Decker asked.

Oliver said, "They couldn't seem to locate him — which also makes me suspicious. Pluto said I could come back after dinner — around six. Being as it's after two, I figured why push it for four hours. Now I know they're going to prep Nova — tell him what to say and what not to say. But if he's not a pathological liar, I'll be able to see through that crap."

Decker agreed. Oliver turned to Marge. "You want to come back with me?"

"Yeah, I'll come back with you."

"So what are you doing for dinner? Want to do Chinese?"

"I'll do Chinese."

Oliver turned to Decker, "I don't suppose you'll be joining us."

"Thanks anyway, but I'd like to see my wife."

Oliver said, "I used to have one of those."

Decker smiled. "Yeah, well . . . tell you what. You two come over to the house after Nova's interview."

Marge chuckled. "Rina would love that."

"She won't be thrilled, but besides being a good sport, she genuinely likes you two."

"Aw shucks, I'm a-blushin'." Oliver grinned. "Exactly how much does she like me?"

Decker wagged his finger, then turned serious. "So you think something nasty went down, Scott?"

"Yep. Moving the body is a cardinal sin, and they should have known better."

Decker organized his thoughts. "Let's back it up . . . to your statement about the body being *supposedly* dead. For the moment, let's assume that Venus was telling the truth: that she found Jupiter either dead or near death. If Jupiter was *near* death instead of *actually* dead, are you saying that someone, during those unaccounted for hours, knocked him off?"

"Why not? It's possible."

"But why would someone bother to commit murder if Ganz was already dying?"

"Because maybe Jupiter had a chance of surviving if *someone* called the paramedics. Could be that Venus was about to call 911, and Pluto stopped her. He sent her back to her room, so he could do dirty work."

"Why would Pluto wanted Jupiter dead?" Decker asked.

"Because Pluto wanted control of the Order."

Marge said, "Venus claims the Order is now under *her* control."

"There you go," Oliver said. "Jupiter isn't even dead for twenty-four hours and already they're at each other's throats. Who knows? Maybe they're in it together."

"Who? Venus and *Pluto?*" Marge shook her head. "I don't think so." She flipped through her scribblings. "Point of fact. Venus *claims* not to have noticed any medication on Jupiter's nightstand. She said she was taken away and didn't have time to absorb her surroundings . . ."

"And that would jibe perfectly with my theory," Oliver said. "Pluto pushes her away before she can call the paramedics. Then he places the empty Valium vial in the room to make it look like a suicide."

Decker said, "If someone wanted to fake a suicide, don't you think the vial would have been placed in the room *before* Venus arrived?"

"Maybe Pluto was about to do it, but was interrupted by Venus's sudden appearance." Oliver rocked on his feet. "Loo, what makes the whole thing suspicious is that the body was fresh. Coronor places the time of death within two hours of the discovery. Rigor mortis hadn't set in."

"Most common time of death is in the early morning," Marge said.

"But we're not thinking death by natural causes, Margie."

Decker said, "Maybe it took Jupiter all night to summon up the nerve to do himself in. First, he drank the vodka to lower his inhibitions. Next he finished himself off with the pills." He ran his hand through thick tufts of hair. "Or maybe Jupiter was a lush and a pill popper, and this was a simple accidental overdose."

Oliver looked dubious. "He downed a fifth of vodka."

"We've all known alkies who drink that much for breakfast."

"Venus said he didn't drink or take pills," Marge stated.

"According to her." Decker stuffed his hands in his pocket. "We've got a suspicious death — three options. Accidental OD, suicide or homicide. We may never be able to distinguish between accidental OD or a suicide. But that's not *that* important for us. The only thing that gets us involved is a homicide. So the question is this: Can you force someone to chugalug a fifth of vodka and/or down a bottle's worth of Valium?"

Oliver said, "If the guy was a secret drinker, someone could have dissolved the pills in the booze."

"Valium's insoluble in water," Decker said.

"Then maybe someone ground the pills up in his food."

"Valium has a bitter taste —"

"So Pluto *injected* it into Ganz's veins," Oliver tried again. "In case you've forgotton, the body had fresh needle marks."

"Venus said Jupiter often injected himself with vitamins," Marge commented.

"Inject himself?" Decker asked. "He had IM needle marks on his butt."

"Sometimes *she'd* do it," Marge said.

"How *convenient*," Oliver mocked. "The logical assumption is that someone stabbed him with an IV needle, telling Jupiter that it was his vitamins. Meanwhile guy's being shot up with a lethal dose of Valium." "The drug burns like hell when you inject it," Decker said. "Jupiter was a scientist. He would have known immediately that he wasn't being shot up with vitamins."

"But by that time, it would have been too late —"

Decker said, "I don't like it. Too many 'ifs.'"

"So maybe Jupiter was dead drunk when he was dosed up with Valium," Oliver retorted. "Maybe he had already been knocked out with the vodka."

"You're saying Ganz drank himself comatose, then someone finished him off with the Valium?"

"Why not?" Oliver asked.

"For one thing, it's messy." Decker paused. "You're saying that someone went to all this trouble just to take over as leader of the Order."

"Loo, you met that twerp, Pluto. He *lusts* for control."

Decker said, "So you not only have a theory, you have a prime suspect."

"Pluto had the means, the motive and the opportunity. He was Jupiter's privileged attendant."

"He was one of four privileged attendants," Decker said.

"But the *first* one on the scene after Venus, *and* he's the only one who's come forward as the leader. He needs to *dominate*. I'm telling you, there's something off with that guy."

"Scott, Pluto has been with Jupiter for years. Why *now?*"

"Because Jupiter was out cold from the vodka.

78

The perfect opportunity presented itself."

Decker conceded Oliver some points. He said, "Even if the path report comes back with drugs and booze in Jupiter's system, we'll still have no way of knowing if Jupiter's death was suicide or homicide. Not without other overriding evidence. If you have something up your sleeve, Scott, I'm all ears."

"No direct evidence," Oliver answered. "Just twenty years experience."

"I don't discount that," Decker said. "But we can't open a murder case based on your experience."

"Can I put in my two cents for suicide?" Marge asked.

Decker said, "Let's hear it."

"Venus said that Jupiter hadn't been himself lately. That he hadn't been exactly ill, but . . . how'd she phrase it?" Marge consulted her notes. "He hadn't been his usual spirited self. He'd been drained of his energy, he held his head a lot . . . like he had headaches. But when she asked him about it, he assured her that this was all part of the process."

"What process?" Decker asked.

Marge let out a small chuckle. "Well, here goes nothing." As Marge recounted the leader's supernatural ideas, they sounded even stranger than the first time she had heard them.

"So he was receiving radiation from all these parallel universes." Oliver gave her a sneering smile. "Well, *why* didn't you just say so. That explains everything."

"I'm not giving credence to her hypotheses, Scott. I'm just saying maybe he was ill with something serious and he decided to mask it in quasi-scientific theory."

"Why would he do that?" Oliver asked.

"So as not to upset his followers," Marge said. "Maybe he decided to go out with dignity rather than suffer an agonizing death."

"What makes you think he was suffering from a physical illness?" Decker asked. "To me, it sounds more like psychosis . . . voices telling you to do strange things."

"Or like a drunk after imbibing a fifth of vodka," Oliver put in. "I've heard those kinds of voices before. They sound a lot like my buddies egging me on."

"I'm serious," Decker said.

"So am I," Oliver retorted. "If Ganz drank a lot, I'll bet he heard voices."

Marge said, "To hear Venus describe Jupiter . . . he sounded like a man with something on his mind." She tapped her foot. "There's more to Jupiter's illness than what Venus told me. I feel it in my gut."

"I'm sure you're right," Decker said. "But I can't base a case for suicide on your gut feelings any more than I can base a homicide on Oliver's experience."

"So what do you suggest?" Oliver asked. "We keep poking around until we find something that throws us to one side or the other?"

"Exactly. And you can start with Nova. Find out what on earth possessed him to sign a death certificate. Even if he is a doctor and it's not strictly illegal, it's a gross irregularity." Decker looked up at the sky. "Let's keep the files on the Jupiter/Ganz case *open* for a while, if for no other reason than to look after the Order's kids. I don't want this death paving the way for another Heaven's Gate or Jonestown."

"Absolutely," Marge said. "With Jupiter gone, who knows what they're thinking."

Decker said, "Meanwhile, there are loose ends that we can clear up, the first being who told Ganz's daughter about her father's death. When I asked Pluto about it, he claimed he didn't know. Seemed pissed about the leak, grumbling something about the chain of command being broken. The guy does walk around like he has a ramrod up his ass."

"You don't like him either," Oliver said.

"I don't like lots of people," Decker said. "But not all of them are criminals." A pause. "Just a high percentage."

Marge smiled. "Venus doesn't know who called Europa either," she said. "She claims that Europa hadn't seen her father in over fifteen years." She turned to Decker. "Weren't you planning on interviewing her?"

"Planning to do it sooner or later." Decker looked at his sack lunch, sitting on the passenger's seat of his unmarked. Guess he was going to eat in the car after all.

7

Over the phone there were no signs of tears, no long sighs, nor any mawkish sentiment. Europa was polite but all business. Of course for her, the loss of her father happened years ago, so Decker supposed her grief had happened then. She was still in her office when Decker had called, and would be there for at least another hour. She told him to come down although she wasn't sure why he wanted to talk to her.

"Just a few questions," Decker said. "Tie up a couple of things."

"For a few questions, a telephone is very expedient," Europa answered.

"I'm a face-to-face kinda guy," Decker answered. "I hope you don't mind. It shouldn't take too long."

"Well, I'm an e-mail-to-e-mail kinda gal. But I suppose it wouldn't hurt me to make human contact. Sure, come down."

Decker got into his unmarked, apologized to God for not ritually washing his hands, then bit into his turkey sandwich. The fresh meat was thinly sliced with lots of mayo and Dijon mustard, just the way he liked it. No, the food wasn't the problem. It was the lack of company. He picked up the cell phone and dialed home.

Rina answered after three rings. "Something tells me you're not on your way here."

"How'd you know?"

"You're talking with your mouth full. You're also on the cellular. Which means you're probably driving. Driving and eating mean you're in the field working."

"You should be in my profession."

"You're not only driving and eating at the same time, you're also talking. If a cop sees you, he's going to pull you over."

"I'll fix the ticket. I know people."

"It's not the citation I worry about. Just be careful, Peter. Traffic is getting worse and worse each year."

"That's true. Is the baby home yet?" *The baby being five years old.* "Or is today her long day?"

"Today is her long day at school."

"So we could have had some real time together?"

"Yes."

"Ouch!"

"Your choice. What are you working on?"

"The Ganz thing."

"The news is saying it was a suicide."

"Maybe."

Rina said, "Maybe as in *probably* a suicide? Or maybe as in *maybe yes* but *maybe no?*"

"Maybe as in I have to investigate every angle before I close up the file."

"And the department requires a second-grade lieutenant to do the investigation?"

83

"Ganz was once a famous man."

"I see. Am I wrong or do I smell politics?"

"What can I say? Strapp said he'd have someone cover for me in the division. When he says that, it means the guy is on the hot seat. Man, you make a mean turkey sandwich!"

"Thanks. You're my best customer."

Decker placed the borrowed videotape in the glove compartment of his car. "I've got a tape for us to watch when we get home."

"What kind of tape?"

"Don't know."

"Sounds exciting," Rina said. "Should I breathe hard?"

"Don't bother. It's probably more spiritual than physical."

"Now I'm curious."

"Good, it'll keep you up in case I'm home late."

"Before I forget, Cindy called."

Decker's heart took off. "What happened?"

"Nothing," Rina said. "She's taking four-day, twelve-hour shifts, that's all."

"But she's okay?"

"Great! Never sounded happier."

Thrilling, Decker thought.

"She wants to go with you to the range," Rina said. "Call her when you get a free moment."

Shooting forty-fives and Berettas at the head and chest regions of paper felons — a real father/daughter bonding experience. Decker said, "I'll call her tonight. Maybe we can go next week if it's okay with you."

"It's fine with me." She hesitated. "And if you go to a public range, maybe you can take Sammy?"

Decker was taken aback. "Why in the world would I do *that?*"

"Because Sammy has made up his mind where he wants to study in Israel next year. He wants to go to a yeshiva in Alon Shvut — Gush Etzion. It's behind the green line and —"

"Hold on! What do you mean *behind the green line?*"

"It's in the territories, so they do *Shmerah* there — guard duty. It wouldn't hurt him to have a jump-start on how to handle a weapon —"

"*What?!*" Decker suddenly realized he'd missed his turn-off. He also realized his heart was still hammering inside his chest. He pulled onto the shoulder of the freeway, and killed the engine. "Hold on a friggin' minute! When was this decided?"

"He was going to say something to you this morning but you rushed off —"

"Excuse me, I was *called* off!" He was shouting, but he didn't care. "Rina, how could you agree without at least talking it over with me! How could you agree to it *period!* You're his mother, for goodness sakes! Don't you care about his safety?"

"Peter, I used to live in Gush —"

"And cavemen used to grunt instead of talk." He took a deep breath, resisting the urge to reach for a cigarette. "Allowing Sammy to go to Israel was a big concession for me. I love that boy!"

"So do I —"

"I'll be damned if I'm going to put him in danger! Going anywhere within the disputed territories is out of the question! End of discussion."

The line went dead for a moment.

Decker said, "Are you still there?"

"Yes, I'm still here."

"Rina, I'm expecting a united front on this one!"

"Peter, as his mother, I agree with you one hundred percent. Except we're not just two parents, we're three. He told me that if Gush was good enough for his father, then it's good enough for him. Now *what* do I say to that?"

Decker felt his head throb.

His *father.* Of course that meant Rina's late husband, Yitzchak. Decker had been Sammy's father for over seven years, almost two years longer than Yitzchak had been with the boy. Still, the word *father* was reserved for this ghost.

Rina said, "Are *you* still there?"

"Yeah, yeah." Decker smoothed his mustache. "All right. At least I see what the problem is. Not that I'm agreeing to anything. But I understand . . . we'll talk about this later."

Rina said, "It was wrong of me to bring it up."

"No, it wasn't," Decker answered. "I know it's easier dealing with me on the phone than it is in person. I'll try to behave civilly about this. But no promises."

"Fair enough."

"I love you," Decker said.

"Love you, too."

Decker said, "No, I really mean that. I love you."

"And I really mean I love you, too. We'll talk later. Finish your sandwich in peace . . . and hopefully without indigestion."

Fat chance of that! Decker said good-bye, then cut the line and leaned back in the driver's seat. As always, after these types of issues, he debated his efficacy as a husband and father. Would his children — unlike Ganz's — mourn for him when he was dead? Would it make a difference if they did? To him, life wasn't about memories, it was rooted in the here and now. Yet there was his stepson, Sammy, desperately trying to communicate with the departed. What was the point of telling him it couldn't be done? It would only build resentment.

But better resentment than to risk his son's welfare. Youth had no concept of danger. Decker knew that because once he had been young. He waited a few moments, then started the engine. When the lane was clear, he pulled out into the void and joined up with the smooth flow of oncoming cars.

Southwest University of Technology had set its roots in Pasadena, a quiet, staid town northeast of Los Angeles. A small place compared to its overcrowded sister, it harked back to gentler times — less traffic, street parking and even some small cafés without a franchise logo. Once a year,

Pasadena still grabbed the spotlight with its annual Rose Parade. But the day after January 1, the city seemed to fade like the flowers on the floats.

The Tech's campus hosted an amalgamation of low-profile structures nestled among ancient pines and majestic oaks. Some Ivy League architecture had crept into a few of the buildings — the administration house and the student union — but most of it was postmodern and utilitarian. The air was cool, and Decker enjoyed walking around. The backpack-toting students were a diverse lot of ethnicities, and seemed younger every year. Since the weather was inviting, many of the kids studied outdoors, sprawled out on the lawns or sitting at a café table drinking lattes, poring over texts of particle physics or nonlinear topology. Jeans and T-shirts appeared to be the corporate dress, and no one gave Decker or his typical cop-suit a second glance. Judgments here were made on the basis of what was inside the package rather than the wrapping.

Dr. Europa Ganz was stationed in a triangular-shaped corner office on the fourth floor of the astrophysics building. She had the requisite institutional desk, metal chairs and file cabinets and bracket bookshelves. It was fluorescently lit, but it did have a window that showed a patch of steel sky and the quad area below. Hanging on the walls were two black-and-white photographs of some planetary surface, excellent in their clarity and resolution. Decker took a moment to study them, both chalky white, pockmarked and completely barren.

"The moon?"

"This one's the Mohave Desert at night," Ganz answered. "The other one's the moon. Hard to tell the forest from the trees, eh?"

"You fooled me."

"We were all one once — the moon, Earth and planets, the sun, the entire universe. And when you're young — like babies — you all look alike. Later on comes the process of differentiation. Look at me. Forty years old and still trying to pull away from my father's ghost."

Decker nodded while studying the scientist. Her hair was light brown and had been clipped short across the back. Feathered bangs softened her wide forehead. Her face was square-shaped with a strong jawline. Pale, white skin and intense blue eyes. Her gentlest features were her lips — lush and red. No makeup, but there were gold studs in her ears. She wore jeans, a white T-shirt and a black jacket, the sleeves rolled up to the elbows. She pointed to a chair.

"Have a seat. Is it *Lieutenant* Decker?"

"Yes."

"My father must rate."

Decker smiled. "Only you can answer that."

Europa's lip gave a half-smile. "Snappy retort. I hope you're not intending to delve into my family's psychodrama. I don't have time."

Decker sat down. "Why would I do that?"

"Now you're really sounding like a shrink."

He took out his notepad. "Actually, Doctor, I came here to find out who told you about your father's death. No one at the Order of the Rings of God seems to know who called you."

"Can't answer that because I don't know who called." Europa sat down at her desk. "I hope you didn't drag yourself all the way out here just to ask me that."

"No idea?"

"No idea."

"Male or female?"

"That I can answer. Female. She was probably making the call on the sly."

"Why do you say that?"

"Because she spoke quickly and in hushed tones." Europa stood. "Coffee?"

"Sure."

"How do you take it?"

"Black."

"Caffeinated?"

"The more drug-laden, the better," Decker answered.

Europa laughed. "You'd do well here." She brought out a bottle of water and poured it into the coffeemaker. "She also told me to alert the police."

"The police?" Decker wrote as he talked. "Did that make you suspicious?"

"Of course it did."

"You made the call around seven?"

"I suppose. You'd know better than I would. Don't you tape incoming phone calls?"

"Just trying to get your recollection."

She paused, heaved her shoulders as if they held granite epaulettes. "It's been a long day."

"I'm sure it has. Thanks for seeing me." Decker smoothed his mustache. "Recall as best as you can the exact words this female caller used."

"Something like . . . 'I thought you should know. Your father just died. I'm not sure how it happened. It's suspicious. Call the police.'" Europa measured out coffee. "Then the woman hung up. I knew it was useless to call the Order back. They wouldn't tell me anything. So I found out the number of the closest police station and reported it as a suspicious death. The news is saying it's an apparent suicide. Is that your conclusion?"

"One of them."

"Cagey fellow. What are the others?"

"Too early to speculate," Decker answered. "People at the Order have said you haven't spoken to your father in years."

"Not true. Maybe it's wishful thinking on their part. If he *completely* denies his real children, then they've co-opted the right to be substitute children."

"So you've seen your father recently?"

"No, not recently. The last time I saw him was maybe fourteen . . . fifteen years ago. But I have talked to him. He would call me every so often, usually *around* my birthday. I'm surprised he remembered it. Not that he'd ever wish me a happy birthday. Instead, he'd say something like he'd been thinking about me. He'd ask me about what I was doing. I told him my latest research. If I asked him about an idea, he'd offer an opinion. If I didn't, he wouldn't. We'd talk for about twenty minutes. Then nothing until the next year."

"Why do you think he called you?"

She shrugged. "Maybe he missed me. More likely, he missed his science — real science. Not the pseudoscientific garbage he's been professing for the past fifteen years."

"You don't approve."

"No, but that doesn't matter."

"Have you ever been down to the Order?"

"Way back when."

"And?"

"And nothing. I came and I went. Jupiter wasn't the father I remember. Nor did I want him to be. I found the entire experience disconcerting. Also, back then, I was mad at him. Your dad deserts you at a crucial moment in your life . . . disappears for ten years, well, you don't suddenly welcome him back into your arms."

"Do you remember any of the people there?"

"No, not really. Well, this one guy named Pluto. Short, obnoxious fellow. Hated me from the get-go simply because I was Jupiter's daughter."

"He's still there."

"It doesn't surprise me. My dad likes people he can push around."

Decker paused for just a fraction. "He was pushing Pluto around?"

92

"He was pushing everyone around. Dad always liked his underlings subservient."

"Your father was a notable man," Decker said. "I'm sure he had underlings in academics."

"Yes, he had underlings, but he also had *colleagues*. Sometimes it's hard to be challenged."

"Your father felt that way?"

"I'm second-guessing, but yes, I think he didn't like to be questioned. I think that's one of the reasons he dropped out. As his ideas drifted farther and farther from the mainstream, he became a target for intense criticism. I don't think that set well with him. But this is all very beside the point. I don't know who called me. I certainly don't know why she did. But I'm glad she did. It's good to have the police involved."

"Did anyone from the Order other than your father ever call you before this?"

"No."

"So this woman who called you . . . it was the first time you had heard her voice?"

"Are you asking me if her voice sounded familiar?"

"Did it?"

"No. It wasn't Venus, if that's what you're getting at."

"I'm not getting at anything. How do you know it wasn't Venus?"

She took down two mugs from the bookshelf. "Because I know what Venus sounds like. You see, Venus, née Jilliam Laham, *was* my girlhood best friend."

8

Sipping coffee, her feet propped on the desk, Europa said, "Once upon a time, I had friends just like any other little girl. Jilliam was one of them. We formed an alliance out of mutual loneliness. Both of us had absentee fathers and narcissistic mothers, but her situation was more extreme. At least my father and I had occasional talks because I was scientifically inclined. Jilliam and her father had nothing in common. He was a high-powered attorney who hated children but loved sex with teenage girls. Looking back, I suppose her relationship with Dad was a natural sequela of her own father's misbehavior."

She paused.

"Our mothers had points in common as well. Mine was self-absorbed, but hers was selfish and egotistical. We met when we were eleven. I took pity on her. She seemed needy." She rolled her eyes. "Little did I know."

Decker put down his mug. "When did she actually become involved with your father?"

"Hard to say." She took another drink from her cup. "My father vanished when I was fifteen. When he was resurrected as Jupiter some ten years later, I knew I had to see him. Jilliam came with me for moral support. It was a reunion from hell."

"In what way?"

Europa's eyes glazed over. "I wanted a father." A pause. "I didn't get one. I felt betrayed, but not surprised."

"How did you find out about his return?"

Europa's eyes took in Decker's face. "A phone call."

The room fell quiet, the only sounds coming from the wall clock's ticking and ambient noise from down below.

"It wasn't that he was cruel. He just couldn't help being who he was. And that was good enough for Jilliam. She lapped up every word of his bizarre pseudoscientific ramblings. I don't think she understood a word of it. But she did react to the force of his personality. Then I realized that the rapture was a two-way street. The way he *looked* at her — such naked hunger. Though in denial at the time, deep down I knew something was going to happen."

"Do you think they had a prior relationship before that reunion meeting?"

"You mean *before* he disappeared? I doubt it." A grimace. "She was only fifteen."

"Was your father inclined to seduce women?"

Europa stared at him. "Why are you asking about Dad's sexual proclivities?"

"Your father's death is under investigation." Decker tapped his pencil. "I was just wondering if your father could have angered someone — like an irate husband or jealous boyfriend."

Europa immediately broke into laughter. It was so abrupt it took Decker by surprise.

She said, "Lieutenant, the more *appropriate* question is who in this world *hasn't* my father angered. Before he disappeared, he must have burned every bridge in existence. Often my brothers and I would muse that he had disappeared because he had done something even more nefarious than ruin careers — which, by the way, was a favorite hobby of his."

Quickly, Decker turned a page on his notepad. "Your father ruined careers?"

Europa started to speak, then stopped herself. She peered at him with intense blue eyes. "Somehow you suckered me into talking about our family's sordid saga. Although *what* it has to do with Dad's death, I don't know. No, Lieutenant, I really don't think he murdered anyone. Back then, my brothers and I were engaging in childish fantasy, giving my father an exotic alibi to excuse his devastating and inexplicable behavior."

But Decker was persistent. "How did your father ruin careers? Did he sabotage experiments? Did he steal someone else's research?"

Europa stared out of the window. "No, nothing illegal. If he had done that, he wouldn't have been so feared. Instead, he decimated within the proper channels." She hugged herself. "To understand my father's potency, you'd have to know the academic world."

Decker said, "I've heard its moral accountability falls somewhere between politics and Hollywood."

"You've got it." Europa gave him a beleaguered smile. "In academia, to be associated with the right people is all-important. And Dad was *the* right person to know. His stamp of approval added prestige to anything it touched. He was on the board of many scientific organizations and peer-review journals. A good word from him could immediately advance a career just as a well-placed barb could set it back ten years. During his scientific years, Dad doled out much more criticism than praise. He had brought down many a promising career with a single, snide comment. Presenting a paper to Emil Euler Ganz was an ordeal akin to being placed on the rack. A few of Dad's remaining colleagues have enlightened me as to how truly sadistic he was, taking pleasure in smashing someone's life's work."

Decker formulated his question. "Of all the people your father . . . offended —"

"Ruined."

"Is there any specific person that sticks in your mind?"

"No. My older colleagues might be able to help you."

"I'll ask around," Decker said.

"Approaching my father's colleagues might be akin to entering the enemy camp." She smiled. "Maybe not now that he's dead. I'm sure they got their revenge witnessing my father's downfall in cosmology. Since Emil Euler Ganz had become an object of derision, Dad's enemies could discredit his previous criticism of their past work."

She seemed bitter. Decker asked, "When you entered the field, did they hold your father's behavior against you?"

She thought for a moment. "I'm sure a few did. Mostly, people felt sorry for me. As a girl, I had been abandoned by him. As a scientist, I was now saddled with this embarrassing nutcase called Father Jupiter. In reality, even before Jupiter, my father had lost his scientific luster."

"Why was that?"

"He was espousing some way-out theories even before he took his famous hike. Now, the few times *I've* spoken to him, his mind was as scientifically sharp as ever. But we kept our conversation on neutral ground, never talking about his postulations." She got up and poured herself another cup of coffee. "Which are not as crackpot *now* as they were then."

Decker asked, "What kind of crackpot theories did he hold?"

Europa returned to her desk. "It's a long story as well as a complicated one."

"I've got time. Try me."

"How's your working knowledge of physics?"

"I know Newton had three laws of motion."

"That's a start."

"Actually someone at the Order clued me into that one."

"Who?"

"Someone named Bob."

"Ah . . ." Recognition. "Tall, thin . . . I think now he sports a beard."

"Goatee." Decker tried to hide his surprise. "Does he have a last name?"

"Changes with the wind. When I knew him, it was Robert Ross."

Decker wrote it down in his notes. "Where do you know him from?"

"From Southwest. We were fellow students — actually dated for a couple of months. He was a fanatic admirer of Emil Ganz the scientist. With my father gone, I was his sole link to the great man. But when Dad was resurrected as Jupiter, Bob went directly to the source. At one time, he had a working brain. By now I'm sure it's mush."

"He impressed me as being sharp. But what do I know?"

Europa shrugged. "Maybe."

Decker regarded her with a swift glance. She wasn't as separate from the Order as Decker had thought. She had kept in contact with her father via phone, she had dated one of the members, and had been best friends with her father's woman. Also, she remembered Pluto, albeit not fondly. And this was what she *admitted* to. Who knew what she wasn't telling him. He said, "Explain your dad's whacked-out theories."

She sighed heavily. "Dad had developed some far-out theories about teleportation and time machines into alternative universes — a combination of H. G. Wells and *Beam me up, Scotty.*"

Again, a sigh. "Not that this bears any relevancy to your investigation."

"Actually, it may be very relevant," Decker answered. "Maybe he chose to end his life because he believed that he was transporting himself to a better place with a time machine."

"Even so, why would that be relevant to the police?"

"Because we have to make sure no one tries to follow in your father's footsteps. I don't want another Heaven's Gate — not anywhere and certainly not in my district."

"How can you guarantee that?"

"With adults, we can't. Kids are another story."

"I see your point." She held up a finger. "So you *are* viewing this as a suicide."

"Everything's open," Decker said without emotion. "Especially since your father had enemies."

"That he did."

"Getting back to your dad's theories . . . did any of them have any scientific bases?"

"Of course. Before my father vanished, he'd been working on superluminal loopholes — things that could scientifically account for instantaneous time travel, backward-in-time travel and faster-than-light travel."

Decker raised his brow. "Okay."

"Not a science fiction reader, Lieutenant?"

Decker smiled. "I liked it when Han Solo did that warp speed thing on the *Millennium Falcon*."

He leaned forward. "What travels faster than light?"

"Undiscovered subatomic particles called tachyons —"

"Undiscovered?"

"They're out there. We just haven't found them yet. Also photons coming from the same electromagnetic wave. Subatomic particles called kaons travel *backward* in time. With them, we see the result of the event before the actual event takes place."

"I don't follow you," Decker said. "I was taught that nothing travels as fast as light. Are you saying that's not true?"

"I believe you mean that you were taught that nothing travels as fast as electromagnetic radiation. Visible light is only one small part of the spectrum. You've got UV waves, microwaves, radiowaves, infrared waves . . . any of this ring a bell?"

"No."

She tapped a pencil on the surface of her desk. "All right. I'll try to sum up twentieth-century physics in a couple of paragraphs."

"I'm taking notes."

"Stop me if I lose you." She finished the dregs of her coffee. "For years, physics was based on Newton's three laws of motion. The second law deals with the orbits of heavenly bodies. The fact that some of the orbits didn't comply with Newton's mathematics bothered no one. They just added a fudge factor, an arbitrary number that makes the math fit the physics."

"You can do that?"

She chuckled. "It's not ideal — something akin to smashing a square peg in a round hole — but physicists do it with theories that *almost* work until someone comes along with a theory that works better. Newton's theories worked for most cases so why quibble with the few exceptions? Something wasn't right, but no one knew how to fix it."

"I've known a few cases of that."

"I'll bet." Europa leaned over her desk. "Then along came Einstein, who ushered us into the modern world. His theories on the curvature of space explained the inconsistency in Newton's planetary laws. But he is best known to the layman for his remarkable theory of relativity. It changed our concept of time from something absolute and immutable to something relative from party to party."

"Which means?"

She stopped, took in a breath and let it out. It appeared as if she was used to confusing people. "Words don't do it justice. The mathematics is beautiful, but that won't help you either. Please interrupt me if I'm going too fast."

"Oh, I will. Go on."

"All right. This is the standard model used to explain it. Picture a train pulling away from a platform. To the person on the platform, it appears as if he is standing still and the train is moving, right?"

"Right."

"But to the person on the train, it seems as if the train is standing still and the platform is moving —"

"But we know the train's moving."

"Only because you've been taught that it's the train that moves."

"But the train *is* moving. It's going from place to place. The platform isn't budging."

"In space, Lieutenant, you have no way of knowing who or what is actually moving. You always have the option of assuming that you're moving and other guy is standing still."

Decker said, "But if you're moving, you're moving."

"Sorry. Motion is relative. So is time, distance and mass. And the faster you go, the more relative it is. Now, at slow speeds, the relativity factor isn't going to make much difference. Suppose you're cruising at sixty miles an hour on the freeway and I'm stalled on the shoulder with a flat tire because I didn't have the time to take my bald retreads into the garage. If you zoom past me at one o'clock in the afternoon, what time will my car clock read?"

Decker said, "It's not going to read anything because your motor's turned off."

She laughed, showing teeth. She had a nice smile when she chose to use it. "It wasn't a trick question, sir."

Decker smiled boyishly. "One o'clock."

"Brilliant."

"Thank you." Decker noticed that talking

about science loosened her up. That was good. Loose people had loose lips.

She continued. "But as your speed approaches that of light, everything changes. For instance, say you're in a spaceship going ninety percent the speed of light. Now, inside your ship, everything looks normal to you. The clocks run on time, your spaceship has the same dimensions and your clothes still fit you. Are you with me?"

"I'm here."

"But to another ship out in space, *your* rocket will look shorter by a factor of two, your clock will appear to run half as fast and your weight will be twice as heavy."

"So you're saying fast speeds distort things. I can buy that."

"But here's the entire point of relativity. To your eye, everything inside *your* spaceship is normal. To your eye, it's the *other* guy who's distorted. His clock is slow, his rocket is shorter and his mass is twice as heavy. To *your* eye, he's distorted. But to *his* eye, you're distorted."

"So who's right?"

"You both are."

"A Solomonic approach to physics," Decker stated.

Again, she smiled. "It's all perspective."

Decker said, "Getting back to your father, you're saying he based his theories of teleportation on Einstein's relativity. Something like he could transport himself from one place to another because everything's relative?"

"Actually, Einstein wasn't a major factor in my father's theories."

"So there's more." Decker held up his pencil. "Shoot, Doc. I'm ready for you."

She chuckled. "Einstein's theories kicked off a revolution, but he wasn't the final word on cosmology. That belongs to quantum physics."

"Is this going to make me feel really stupid?"

"I'll keep it simple," Europa said. "There are two distinctly different aspects to how we view light or any electromagnetic radiation. Now, Newton stated that light acts like a wave, that it's continuous and uninterrupted, that it has rises and falls, peaks and troughs. Okay so far?"

"I'm with you."

"Quantum theory says light is *not* a wave, but discreet packets or bundles made up of particles called photons. Two contradictory theories — light as wave, light as particles."

"Dare I ask? Which one is right?"

"They both are. Sometimes light behaves as a wave, sometimes it behaves like photons. If you thought relativity was bad at pinning things down, you don't even want to know about Heisenberg's Uncertainty Principle. It says that although you can make predictions on how these photons will behave over the long run, you can never say exactly how they will behave over the short run. At any given moment, you have no way of knowing which energy state any given photon will occupy. Are you with me?"

"No. Can I ask what photons have to do with teleportation?"

"You're a single-minded man, Lieutenant."

"A bad physicist, but a decent cop."

"Photons, sir, have been one of the links implicated in instantaneous travel. Before Dad dropped out, he was one of the few men who was trying to prove that photons originating from the same packet of light had this instantaneous link between them. Whatever was happening to photon one was also happening with photon two no matter what the distance between them was. All because once they had shared the same light bundle. Are you with me?"

"Instant communication."

"*Instantaneous* communication," Europa corrected. "Now, since mass can convert to energy at the speed of light — E equals MC squared — then atoms — like the kind that make up your body — can be converted to electromagnetic energy or light in the form of photons. And since there is an eternal, instantaneous link between photons from the same packet, you can transport *your* atoms — now in photon form — instantaneously from one position in space to another using this superluminal link. Which is considered a scientific lost cause. Although things can move faster than light, they can't seem to transport meaningful information . . . things like *organized* atoms. Which is what my father spent his scientific life trying to prove. He hit walls, but that didn't stop him. When he couldn't do it as

Emil Euler Ganz, he went metaphysical and tried to prove it as Jupiter."

She frowned. "But you know how things get messed up going from theory to actuality. Sometimes we physicists predict it right on — like with the atom bomb. We knew the math *way* before we had the technology. But most of the time, we sit there and wallow in our own mistakes. Like a baby with a dirty diaper, just crying and squirming while waiting for someone who knows better to clean it up."

9

Oliver said, "I can buy the thing about time slowing down. Ever been to an opera?"

Decker laughed, but Marge said, "I like opera."

"That's 'cause you're a woman." Oliver bit into an egg roll. "Sure you don't want one, Deck? They're vegetarian."

"No thanks." He added sugar to his tea. "So when are you two meeting with the death certificate guy . . . what's his name? Omni?"

"Nova," Marge said. "We found out he's a podiatrist."

Decker made a face. "A podiatrist signed Ganz's death certificate?"

"Maybe Jupiter's feet were cold." Oliver polished off a wonton.

"I'm sure they were if he was dead," Marge said. "For your information, Scott, there are plenty of men who enjoy opera."

"None of them heterosexual."

"That's ridiculous!"

Oliver thought it over. "Okay. Maybe there are a few effete Englishmen who like opera. But I dare you to find *one* straight guy who likes ballet."

Decker tried again. "What time are you meeting Nova the podiatrist?"

"Six-thirty," Oliver said.

Decker looked at his watch. "That's in a half hour."

Oliver pointed to Marge's entree. "Put a dent in your cashew chicken or we'll never make it."

"I'll take the rest to go. The soup filled me up."

Oliver said, "That's another gay thing — soup. Straight guys would never get filled up by soup. Straight guys don't even eat soup. Soup is a broad thing."

Marge said, "Were you always this concrete or am I just noticing it more?"

Oliver rolled his eyes. To Decker, he said, "So Ganz was a schmuck. Doesn't surprise me. All these cult leaders are megalomaniacs." He attacked the remnants of his Mongolian chicken. "I mean look what he was into — time machines, alternative universes . . . instant travel through space. Playing God basically. Good sci-fi, but for a man of Ganz's stature . . . he was freaking out." He turned to Marge. "You know, the whacked-out ideas combined with the headaches that Venus told you about . . . maybe he had a brain tumor."

Decker said, "When Europa spoke to him, she said he was still scientifically sharp."

"That's her opinion," Oliver said.

"I found it interesting that Ganz had made enemies."

"It's irrelevant, Deck. Unless one of them sneaked into the Order and laced his vodka with cyanide."

Decker said, "You never know when the past can come back to haunt. Besides, Ganz wasn't completely divorced from his former life. He kept in contact with Europa, his significant other was Europa's girlhood friend —"

"What?" Marge broke in. "You said that Europa's around forty."

"She is."

"Venus looks about thirty."

"So she looks young," Decker answered. "Europa said she was a pretty girl." He told them Jilliam's background.

Marge said, "So Ganz was the father Jilliam never had. Where have I heard *that* one before?"

"And she was also a young piece of ass," Oliver said. "Yes, it's the same-old, same-old. But so what? Why the fascination with the past, Deck? Do you have a former associate of Ganz who you think was out to get him?"

Decker admitted he didn't. "This Bob — the one who dated Europa — she said he was obsessed with Emil Ganz the scientist."

"But Bob met Ganz *after* he had become Jupiter, right?"

"Right."

"So Bob couldn't have been a past enemy. He would have been too young to be one of Ganz's colleagues."

Decker conceded the point. "In fact, he was Europa's former schoolmate."

"Look, Loo. Even if every single one of Ganz's former acquaintances hated his guts, *I* don't see what that would have to do with his death. Ganz stopped being Ganz twenty-five years ago."

Marge said, "*If* someone murdered him, it has to be a current member of the Order. Someone who wouldn't arouse suspicion by being there, don't you think?"

"Maybe."

Oliver wiped his mouth. "You like this *past coming back to get him* theory, don't you?"

Decker said, "I'm trying to get a complete story. So *if* it turns out to be something other than suicide, I've got avenues to explore."

"Then start with Pluto," Oliver said. "He's my nominee for asshole of the month."

"Actually, I like *Europa*," Decker said. "She phoned the police about her dad's death, *and* she knows the key players in the Order —"

"Including Pluto?" Oliver interrupted.

'She claims she didn't *know* Pluto, only that she met him and didn't like him."

"Something in her favor," Oliver said. "Why would she want to hurt her father now?"

"He was a lousy father," Marge said.

"He was *always* a lousy father," Oliver retorted. "I repeat. Why now? You think she's been harboring a murderous grudge for twenty-five years?"

"I like simple reasons," Decker said. "Like money —"

"Ganz had been a professor in his former life," Oliver broke in. "How much money could he have saved up?"

Marge said, "If he had won a major scientific award, maybe lots. What's the Nobel Prize worth these days?"

"He didn't win the Nobel Prize," Oliver grumped.

"There are plenty of other organizations that give money to genuises just for being genuises," Marge answered.

"Or Ganz could have worked for NASA or some other scientific government agency," Decker said. "Maybe he moonlighted in industry as a consultant — in aviation or aeronautics or even a think tank. Point is, we don't know what Ganz was worth. We don't even know who holds the deed for the Order."

"The building?"

"The building, the land, its bank accounts. Does it *have* its own bank accounts? Since this is a suspicious death, maybe we should find out."

No one spoke for a moment. Then Marge said, "Looking into Ganz's finances . . . do you think it's a good use of our time, Pete?"

The implication was right on. Decker blew out air. "Probably makes more sense to wait for the pathology reports to come in. Could be I'm obsessing." He sipped tea and gave his words some consideration. "How busy is tomorrow, Margie? Could you give it a couple of hours?"

Marge said, "Not a problem."

"Okay, do the basics. Bank accounts, brokerage accounts, insurance policies —" He stopped himself. "That's going to take longer than a couple of hours. Margie, you do the bank and brokerage accounts. Scott, you call the assessor's office and find out who holds the deed to the land, then poke around for insurance policies."

Marge said, "Pete, insurance isn't applicable in cases of suicide."

"They'll pay death benefits if it's accidental death. And if he took out whole life insurance, there'd probably be a nice little nest egg cash policy *as well as* death benefits."

Oliver was dubious. "You want me to cold call insurance companies? That seems kinda . . . screwy."

He was right. Score another for his crew. Decker said, "How about this? Ganz was a full professor at Southwest University of Technology. Faculty usually gets all sorts of perks — health insurance, car insurance, life insurance. Start there with the insurance angle. If you reach a dead end, call it quits and we'll reevaluate."

"Simple enough." Oliver looked at Marge. "Are you gonna take that last egg roll?"

"It's all yours." She turned to Decker. "If Ganz had secret money, don't you think Venus would make a better suspect than Europa?"

Decker said, "Venus wasn't officially married to Ganz. Kids would be first in line to inherit."

"Unless he made other provisions in a will," Marge said.

Oliver said, "Jupiter didn't seem like the 'will' type."

"I'm not so sure about that," Decker said. "For a guy who was into spirituality, he had his feet firmly planted in earthly trappings — a pretty, younger girlfriend, attendants who waited on him, people who worshiped him. We found an empty fifth of vodka under his bed." He shrugged. "Doesn't sound like any capuchin I've ever known."

Marge smiled. "Exactly how many capuchins have you known, Pete?"

Oliver said, "What does cappuccino have to do with this? Speaking of which. How about some dessert? Ever try litchi nuts, Loo?"

"Have to pass." Decker finished his tea. "I've already missed breakfast and lunch with the family. Don't want to press my luck by missing dinner."

Each time Decker pulled into the driveway, he grew wistful. Because each passing day brought him *that* much closer to the end; good-bye to the acreage, the horses, the ranch land, the orchards, the *freedom* of his carefree divorced days.

Well, carefree wasn't exactly the right word.

Truth be told he was miserable in that interim period — lonely and disagreeable. Ah hell, who was he kidding? He hadn't been the Marlboro Man in over seven years. Only thing he and Marlboro had in common was sucking nicotine.

After killing the motor, he got out of the car. The front door opened and a little stick figure with orange ringlets and open arms came running to him.

"Daaaaddeeee!"

"Hannah Roseeee!" He bent down, scooped her up and threw her over his shoulder — a small, chortling sack. He opened the front door with his foot and threw his briefcase onto one of the buckskin living room chairs. He tossed Hannah onto the couch as she squealed with delight. Within moments, Rina materialized, drying a dish. She wore a maroon sweater over a denim skirt. Her thick, black hair was secured by a barrette. She had recently trimmed her long locks. Now they fell just past her shoulders. A becoming style for her beautiful face. Except that most of the time, as required by her religious beliefs, she kept her hair covered with a scarf or a hat, or, at the very least, tied up in a braid or a bun.

"You're home." She glanced at the wall clock. "And at a reasonable hour."

Hannah started jumping on the couch. Again, Decker picked her up, threw her up in the air and set her down.

"Something smells very good."

"Chicken with garlic."

"Do I have enough time for a quick shower?"

"It's not a problem for *me*." Rina looked at Hannah, who was tugging on Decker's sleeve.

"Let's play, Daddy," the little girl shouted.

"In a minute, honey," Decker answered.

"Hannah, let Daddy take off his jacket."

"You can take off your jacket in *my* room!"

Hannah's room was an outpouching off their master bedroom. Decker had built the house with only two bedrooms. In retrospect, poor planning. But after his divorce, he never assumed that he'd be hosting anyone other than Cindy.

Hannah pulled at her father's hand. "Let's go, Daddy!"

"Hannah, hold on!" Rina chided.

The little girl looked disappointed, but remained quiet. Rina immediately felt guilty. "Oh, go ahead! We'll talk later."

The five-year-old brightened. "Goody! Let's go!"

"A minute, sweetie." Decker held back impatience. "Boys okay?"

"They should be home any minute."

"Do you need me for anything?"

"It's all right. Go with your daughter. We'll have the evening to catch up." She looked at him with piercing eyes. "You are *done* with work, right?"

Decker winced. "Scott and Margie are coming over around eight. But just for an hour or so."

Rina didn't speak. She had heard that one before.

"No, really," Decker reassured her. "We'll wrap it up quickly. It's the Ganz thing. Which seems pretty straightforward . . . at the moment."

She had heard that one before as well. "It's

fine, Peter. I put Hannah to bed at that time anyway."

Again, Decker grimaced. "Didn't I say that I was going to put her to bed tonight?"

"You can do it tomorrow night."

"I said that last night, didn't I?"

"*C'mon*, Daddy! Let's go do puppets!"

"Go, Peter," Rina told him. "I'll call you when dinner's on the table."

Hannah said, "You can sit on the floor while I get the show ready."

"Can I change my clothes first, Hannah?"

"*Sure* you can change your clothes!" she shouted with generosity.

"Maybe I can look at the paper while you set up?"

Hannah's face darkened.

Rina said, "Now you're pushing it."

"Silly me," Decker said. "I meant *after* dinner."

Hannah recovered her cheer. "Sure you can look at the paper after dinner, Daddy. *After* we play squiggles."

"She's made plans," Decker said.

"Yes, she has." Rina smiled sadly. "Lucky her. She has yet to learn how futile plans can be."

Pluto led the detective duo into an alcove off the main sanctuary. It had enough room for a trestle table and four chairs. The walls were covered by bookshelves. As she sat, Marge caught some of the titles, all of them having to do with the metaphysical. No surprises there. Nova, the podiatrist, paused before choosing the seat opposite Marge. Immediately, Oliver took up the chair next to the Doc, closing in on the man's personal space.

Chunky and balding, Nova appeared to be in his middle thirties. He wore the costume of a privileged attendant — the blue robe and purple vest — but the vest sported an embroidered caduceus. His round face held an almost hairless complexion as well as dark, saucer eyes. Probably his hair was once dark brown, but because of its thinness and streaks of gray, it had taken on the sandier tones. His fingers were stumpy, his nails cut short. His hands were shaking — nervous. Marge felt he should be. He had no business signing a death certificate.

Pluto remained at the entryway, his arms folded across his chest. His position made it clear to all that he had no intention of leaving. Marge looked up at him and said, "Thank you, sir, you can go now."

"I'd prefer to stay," he answered.

"I realize that," Marge said. "I'm trying to be polite."

Pluto remained rooted to his spot.

Oliver shrugged. "If our presence here is problematic, sir, we can take Nova down to the station house —"

"On what grounds?!" Pluto blurted out.

Nova's voice held a tremolo. "Brother Pluto, I appreciate your show of solidarity. But if they want to talk with me in private, I have no objection."

Pluto's eyes narrowed.

Quickly, Nova added, "Brother Pluto, you know how much I respect your wisdom. If I require your help, I shall ask for it immediately."

Marge said, "Make it easy on all of us."

Pluto glared at the detectives. "We all have work to do. Be quick." Then without another word, he turned and left.

Oliver stood up and peeked around the opening. Pluto had remained nearby. Oliver gave him a wave. The short man turned an angry red, but finally left the temple.

Oliver returned to his place. "I think Brother Pluto has a trust problem."

Nova said, "He's protective."

"I think it goes deeper." Oliver took out the tape recorder and handed it to Marge. "I think he doesn't want you saying the wrong thing."

Nova bristled. "I can speak for myself."

Marge made the necessary identifications for the tape, then placed the recorder in front of Nova. "So you take full responsibility for your own actions?"

"Of course!" Nova was indignant. "We're all adults."

Marge said, "So tell me why you signed Jupiter's death certificate when you're only a podiatrist."

Nova raised his voice. "Detective, I am a trained medical practitioner. I was the most qualified here to make such a determination."

"And if you were on a desert island, I'd say fine and dandy," Marge said. "But here in L.A. there are *better* people to make that determination. As a medical practitioner, you must know that suspicious deaths require investigations —"

"I had no way of knowing that the death was suspicious —"

"Exactly," Marge interrupted. "That's why you should have called the police and let them handle it."

"I resent this line of inquiry!"

"You can resent it just so long as you answer me," Marge said. "Why didn't you call the police?"

"I saw no need —"

Marge interrupted. "Sir, as a podiatrist, how many autopsies have you conducted?"

Oliver broke in, "Sir, we're not challenging your abilities. We're just wondering why you went out on a limb."

Marge asked, "Were you pressured to wrap the thing up?"

"Certainly not!"

"So why'd you do it?"

"Because Father Jupiter was dead!" Nova was flushed, droplets falling down his forehead. "Someone had to make it clear to the followers that *he* wasn't returning to earthly life. I felt that I was the chosen one for the mission."

Oliver asked, "Doctor, when did you first check him out?"

"When?"

"What *time?*" Marge asked.

Nova took in a breath and let it out. He wiped his face with a tissue. "Around five in the morning. Perhaps a little later."

"And you examined him thoroughly?"

"Of course —"

"Took his pulse?"

"This is insulting —"

"Checked the heart?"

Nova leaped to his feet. "I will not stand here and be abused like this!"

"A standard death certificate asks for time of the demise," Marge said. "What time did you put down?"

The brother faltered. "I don't remember the exact time to the minute. As I stated, I was called in a little after five."

"But that really wasn't the time of his death, sir," Marge said.

"What do you mean?"

"I mean Jupiter didn't actually *die* at five in the morning." She glared at Nova. "Or did he?"

"Detective . . ." Oliver warned. Time to play off her aggression. He turned to Nova. "I know this sounds like we're . . . doubting your competency —"

"It certainly does!" Nova looked pointedly at Marge. "I was just doing my duty — to the Order and to my profession —"

"Meaning you checked Jupiter's feet for corns?"

"Detective . . ." This time Oliver was chiding

her in earnest. To Nova, he said, "Why don't you sit back down?"

With reluctance, Nova returned to his chair, refusing to look at Marge. She stood up. "I gotta use the bathroom. Don't bother with the directions, I'll find it myself."

As soon as she left, Nova wiped his brow with a blue silk handkerchief. "She is a detriment to your department!"

"She's a good cop," Oliver said flatly.

"She's got a rotten disposition." Nova imitated her. " 'Meaning you checked his feet for corns?' She hasn't the foggiest notion of what a podiatrist is or what he does. We're extremely well trained."

"I'm sure you are," Oliver said. "But we are bothered by your not calling the police right away."

"What difference does it make?" Nova said. "The police were obviously called in."

Oliver asked, "So you called them?"

Nova fidgeted. "No, *I* didn't."

"But someone did. Any idea who?"

"I was told it was Ganz's daughter — Europa."

"Any idea who called her?"

"None."

But he squirmed as he uttered the word. Oliver didn't press him on it . . . not yet. "Who called you into the room?"

"Brother Pluto. He asked me to make some kind of assessment as to why he died . . . to tell the people something. I had to make a split-second decision as to the cause of death. Remember I was stunned myself. Shocked! Although Father Jupiter wasn't feeble, he was in his seventies. A coronary didn't seem out of line. I knew that if there was more, it would come out later on."

Oliver scratched his nose. "Sir, what do you mean by *more?*"

Nova stuttered. "Well, if the death was something other than a heart attack."

"The empty liquor bottle didn't make you a bit curious?"

Again, Nova faltered. "Alcohol can bring on a heart attack, especially in an older man."

"Did Father Jupiter drink?"

"An occasional sacramental glass of wine."

"But not usually an entire bottle of vodka."

"Of course not . . . at least, not that I'm aware of."

"Meaning he might have, but you didn't know about it?"

The podiatrist grew flustered. "I've never known Father Jupiter to be immoderate. Besides, *you* have no way of knowing how much alcohol he imbibed. That bottle could have been drunk over a year's time."

"The pathology report will tell us his blood alcohol level," Oliver said.

"Then I suggest you save your questions until then."

Oliver said, "We like to ask our questions right away. Memories are fresher."

"There's nothing to tell. I signed a certificate because he was dead."

Oliver stared at him. "How'd you get hold of an official death certificate? They are the property of the coroner's office. Why would you even *have* them here?"

"I have no idea why we have them. But we do."

Oliver noticed Nova was looking over his shoulder, not making eye contact.

The podiatrist said, "Perhaps I shouldn't have put down natural causes. But if it's something more, I simply made an honest mistake."

Marge returned. "An honest mistake as opposed to a dishonest mistake?"

Nova said nothing, a sour expression stamped on his face.

Marge said, "By the way, you signed the time of death as five thirty-two A.M. You said you were called in around five. What were you doing for a half hour?"

Nova's face held a triumphant look. "A good examination takes *time*, Detective." He looked at Oliver. "Anything else? I really do have other obligations."

Marge tossed out, "Any idea who called Europa about Jupiter's death?"

"The detective and I have already crossed that territory."

"Please answer the question."

"No, I *don't* know who called Europa."

But Marge noticed that Brother Nova had blushed.

10

Timing was everything. As Decker debated the wisdom of bringing up a hot issue around the dinner table, Sammy jumped the gun by saying, "Did Eema tell you my decision about Israel?"

Decker's fork stopped midair. "Yep."

"So what do you think?"

Laying it on the line. Decker emptied the fork and chewed slowly, his elbows resting on the cherrywood tabletop — one of his carpentry projects from his bachelor days. He had finished the set right before he met Rina, and it gleamed thanks to her assiduous polishing. Not all of his woodworking got such attention. She just had a thing for this set. His eyes drifted around the table — first to his daughter, then his stepsons. Nearly sixteen, Jacob would be taking his driver's license test in a couple of months. Fun and games that was going to be. The boy caught his gaze and smiled at him with twinkling baby blues inherited from his mother. Decker managed to smile back.

Then there was Sam — sullen and serious. At seventeen, he had recently topped six feet. Lanky kid. Still, Decker could spot an underlayer of muscle. Dark eyes and thick, sandy-colored hair — a good-looking boy and brilliant. In one sense, he was almost an adult. The key word was *almost*.

Decker laid down the fork and wiped his mouth. He chose his words carefully. "Are you open for other opinions or is it a closed matter?"

"Well, I'd like to know what you think."

"Know what Sarah did today, Daddy?" Hannah interrupted.

"Believe it or not, I am interested in your opinion," Sammy went on.

Hannah spoke louder. "She ate up all my snack. Isn't that silly!"

"Great, Hannah," Sammy muttered. "So what do you think?"

"Isn't that silly, Daddy?"

Decker answered. "I'm concerned about you being in the disputed territory —"

Hannah shouted, "Isn't that *silly*, Daddy?"

"Hannah, quiet!" Sammy said.

The little girl's face fell.

"Yes, it's very silly," Decker answered. "Sam, maybe this isn't the right time —"

"Why do her needs always come before mine!" Sammy argued. "This is important to me! Don't you think she can learn to wait a minute before interrupting?"

"It's not a matter of her needs before yours." Decker held his sulking daughter's hand. "But she is only five —"

"Fine!" Sammy dismissed him. "Forget it. I'll write you a postcard from Gush —"

"Shmuel —" Rina tried.

"I said *forget* it!"

"Don't yell at your mom," Decker said. "For one thing, she's on your side."

"I'm not on any side," Rina stated.

Jacob got up from the table. "Hey, Hannah. Wanna go play draw-a-face on the computer?"

The child still had tears in her eyes. She looked at Jacob, then looked at her mother expectantly. Rina said, "For a few minutes only, Hannah. Your brother needs to eat."

Jacob extended his hand to his little sister. "C'mon, peanut. You want to draw the girl with a mustache again?"

Hannah giggled and leaped up, knocking down her chair.

"Thank you, Yonkeleh," Rina said, righting the seat.

"Yeah, Jake's the *good* son," Sammy muttered.

"He's trying to help you out, Shmuel," Rina said.

"I know, I know . . ." He looked at Decker. "I'm nervous. I'm afraid you're going to say no without even listening to me. And even if you do listen — which I don't think you'll do — you'll still say no."

Decker tried to stifle his frustration. "So basically, you've got me programmed before I've said a word."

"I just know you."

"Then what's the point in talking?"

"I'm still interested in your opinion."

"As worthless as it is —"

"I didn't *say* that —" Sammy interrupted.

"All right," Decker answered. "Just calm down —"

"I'm very calm," Sammy snapped back. "You're the one who isn't calm."

Cool it, Deck, you can't win. Take a breather. Decker took a long drink of water. "Sam, I wasn't wild about you going to Israel period. But going to a yeshiva that's beyond the green line makes me very nervous. I have legitimate concerns about your safety."

Sammy said, "Dad, I've talked to tons of people who have been there. They say it's very safe. Much safer than Jerusalem. You know, the biggest problem in Israel is the crazy drivers — a much bigger problem than terrorism. And Gush is out in the country so it's real quiet —"

"When they're not sniping at you —"

"Dad, the Arab villages are down below. Gush is up on a hill."

"So you're going to stay in this very small vicinity for an entire year and never travel in or out of Israel proper?"

"No, of course not." Sam played with his food. "It's twenty minutes from Jerusalem on this new *kfeesh* which bypasses —"

"What's a *kfeesh*?" Decker asked.

"Roadway," Rina said. "Around three years ago they built the tunnel road, which bypasses some of the Arabs —"

"The *tunnel* road?" Decker asked.

Rina nodded. "They dug a couple of tunnels

underneath the mountainside."

"Why a *tunnel?*"

"I guess it was easier to dig under the mountain than to build on top of it. The road bypasses Bethlehem —"

"That's the main trouble spot, Dad," Sammy said.

"Sam, the entire *area* is one big trouble spot." All Decker could think about was how easy it was to blow up a tunnel. "You're sitting in the middle of Arab territory —"

"Gush isn't in the *middle* of anything," Sammy retorted. "It's its own place. It's been around for . . . how many years, Eema?"

"Around thirty," Rina said.

"Dad, it's not this camp settlement with tents and sleeping bags that the papers make it out to be. It has markets and schools and houses —"

"How many Jews are out there versus how many Arabs?"

"Dad —"

"Sammy, I'm not debating politics. I'm talking *bodies.* There are many, many *more* of them than of us. And every time some president has trouble here at home, he starts poking around for foreign countries to dominate. Which usually brings him to the Mideast and a peace plan. And every time America starts hawking a peace plan, *someone* over there gets riled. And *I* don't feel good about planting you — *my* son whom I love very much — in the middle of danger."

"It's not dangerous!" Sammy insisted.

"Why? Just because a couple of immortal, teenage boys say so?" Decker said. "Look, *maybe* I'm just being a stupid American, believing all this press about the area being a hot zone. Maybe the Arabs really do love us and want peace and if you're stuck out there on the road at three A.M., they'll be happy to help you —"

"It's not safe to be stuck on the road at three A.M. here either," Sammy shouted.

"Difference is you've got a car phone and you can call me. Who are you going to call over there, Sammy?"

Sammy put down his fork and slumped. No one spoke for a minute. Finally, the boy said, "Abba went there."

Another period of protracted silence. Then Decker said, "I know he did. Do you think he'd want you to put your life in danger —"

"My life wouldn't be in danger! You're overreacting. As always!"

Decker started to speak, then stopped. He pushed his plate away. "Fine, Sammy. You asked for my opinion. You know how I feel. If it would be up to me, you'd go to Yeshiva University directly —"

"I told you, I'll get credit for my year in Israel."

Decker bit his lip. "I'm staying out of this one. It's your decision."

"Fine, so I'll go to Gush."

Decker shrugged. "Can I ask you one thing?"

"What?"

"If Gush wasn't an option, where else could you go?"

"Kerem b'Yavneh," Rina said. "Shalavim."

Decker looked at Rina. "Are those bad places?"

"Bad?"

"In dangerous areas?"

"They're inside the green line."

"Are they good yeshivas?"

"They're excellent."

"As good as Gush?"

"Definitely," Rina said.

Decker turned to Sammy, the obvious unspoken. The teen threw up his hands. "If you're going to *forbid* me to go to Gush, I suppose I could go to Shalavim."

"Isn't David going to Shalavim?" Rina asked.

"I don't have to do everything David does, Eema. We're not joined at the hip."

"I was just saying —"

"Look, it's up to you," Sammy burst in. "You're paying for it." He stood. "I'm going to take over for Yonkie. Let the *good* son eat his dinner." He walked away.

Silence hung in the air. Then Decker whispered, "Where'd he get this good son, bad son bit?"

"He probably feels like a bad son — both to you and to Yitzchak," Rina whispered back. "He wants you to make the decision for him."

"I'm not going to do it." Decker nibbled on a floret of broccoli. "I've had my say. Rest is up to him . . . or you." A beat. "Do you have any feelings about it?"

"I'd like him behind the green line."

131

"So why didn't you *say* something?"

"I figure one of us is enough. Why overwhelm him?"

"Wouldn't have anything to do with being loyal to your husband's memory, would it?"

Rina was taken aback. "Peter, *you're* my husband. Your opinion is *paramount* over anything else. I thought we were over this."

Decker rubbed his forehead. "I'm sorry."

She leaned over and kissed the top of his head. "It's been a long day, hasn't it."

"Yes."

"And you still have Marge and Scott to deal with. You work too hard."

"Probably."

"Want to take a drive in the Porsche after you're finally done with work? The boys can baby-sit."

"Only if you promise not to call it a Nazi car."

Rina smiled. "I promise."

Decker grumped. "A ride to where? To the new house?"

"I have some samples of wallpaper hanging in the kitchen."

"And this is your idea of a good time? Choosing wallpaper for the kitchen?"

"If you behave yourself — and I know that's a big stretch — I'll point out the new mattress in the bedroom."

Decker broke into subdued laughter. "Well, that has possibilities."

"Indeed."

He smiled. "You come up with great ideas, you know that."

Rina patted his hand. "I have the knack."

Decker set up shop in the living room because it held a TV. Marge sat on the couch, Oliver took up one of the chairs. Rina was standing by the wayside, curious but silent.

He slipped the "borrowed" videotape into the feed.

The monitor filled with the image of Jupiter. He appeared younger than seventy, but Decker figured that the video was old. The film did have that grainy appearance found in time-worn cameras.

Everyone watched in silence. Five minutes passed, then ten. Still, no one spoke.

Ganz's hair was silver-white but there was plenty of it. His skin held a few creases, but no prominent sags. Its tone was somewhere between red and orange and seemed to glow, but that was no doubt due to the TV's faulty hues. His eyes were of indeterminate color — blue-green-gray-black — and flashed as he spoke. Although the guru was looking directly into the lens of the camera, he was hard to understand. The volume of his voice seemed rise and fall at will, having little to do with the points he was making.

Truth be told, even after fifteen minutes, Decker wasn't sure what the points were. Something to do with charity and duty, love and honor. Most of the language was florid and arcane. Yet there was something magnetic about his manner. A force of personality. He said, "The man is definitely possessed by a spirit."

Oliver asked, "Anyone understand what he's saying?"

"Not important," Marge said. "I'm sure even he doesn't understand what he's saying. But he sure has a fever to him."

"Hallelujah!" Oliver said. "There's a sucker born every minute."

Marge looked at Decker. "How much longer?"

"Don't know."

"That man can talk a spell — and nonstop."

"Maybe the tape was edited," Decker suggested.

"I don't think so," Rina said. "It looks continuous to me." She smiled. "It's because he's standing in front of a pulpit. It could magically transform a deaf-mute into a motor-mouth."

"Man, ain't that the case," Marge said. "In church, it seemed like the pastor would never shut up."

"Really?" Rina smiled. "I thought it applied only to rabbis on Yom Kippur. Thrilled to be talking to a full house."

Decker smiled. "I see neither of you have ever been to a Baptist revival meeting. We're not talking hours, we're talking days."

As Rina watched the TV, she furrowed her brow, concentrating on the words shot back in poorly reproduced audio. "That's sounds familiar." She repeated the words. " 'Surely as I have thought, so shall it come to pass —' . . . can you replay that, Peter?"

"Not a prob." Decker stopped the tape, back-tracked, then pressed the play button. Rina listened assiduously as Ganz preached.

The great Jupiter spoke in stentorian tones. His Day-Glo red face filled the screen. "That I will break them in my land . . . this is the purpose that *I* purposed upon the whole earth. The whole earth, my brothers and sisters. Who shall void my purpose? Who shall void my word? Who shall void it? Who shall turn back?"

"Peter, can you pause it for a sec?"

"Yes, ma'am," Decker answered.

Rina went to her Jewish library and pulled out a book. "It sounds like the words from one of the prophets. Let's try Isaiah. It sounds like his voice." She riffled through the pages of the tome. "What a memory! Here were go!" She read the passage to herself. "He's paraphrasing a bit."

"What *purpose* is Jupiter talking about?" Marge asked.

Rina shrugged. "I don't know what purpose *he's* referring to. Isaiah was talking about the Babylonians. That Hashem — er, God, rather — was going to punish them for destroying the land of Israel."

"So far the only people Jupiter destroyed was himself," Marge said.

Oliver said, "Or maybe someone destroyed Jupiter before he could destroy him . . . or her."

"You really like homicide, don't you, Scott," Decker said.

"I really do."

" 'That I will break them in my land . . .' " Decker clicked the stop button. "Now that is open to all sorts of interpretation. The Order calls us outsiders 'the violators.' Maybe he thinks we have violated this land, meaning earth, like the Babylonians did to Israel."

"Do you think Jupiter was planning to do something?" Marge asked.

"It sounds to me like he's just spouting," Rina answered. "Cribbing actually. Quoting from previously written material without citing references. I bet most of his speeches are cribbed."

Oliver frowned. "This Isaiah fellow doesn't sound very cheerful."

"All the prophets were morose," Rina said. "Maybe that's what happens when you have visions." A pause. "Sounds like Jupiter was having visions of his own. And not exactly the divine kind."

Decker said, "Not to be contentious, Rina, but if you read the prophets . . . the straight text . . . they sound a little weird."

Rina said, "Could be the reason why no one listened to them. It's hard to be the purveyor of doom and gloom. Telling people what they don't want to hear. But the chief difference here is Jupiter is plagiarizing. At least the biblical prophets were original." She checked her watch. "I've got to put Hannah to bed."

Decker ejected the video. "I think we've seen enough."

Rina said, "Even as an older man, Jupiter was handsome."

Marge said, "Powerful features."

Decker asked, "Or is that only because you *know* who he is?"

"No, there's something . . . charismatic about him."

"What?" Oliver asked with disdain.

"The way he looks into the camera," Rina said. "Straight at you. As if you were the only person who mattered." She smiled. "Something to be said for that."

"I don't talk to you like that?" Decker asked his wife.

"Of *course,* you do," Rina countered. "You're very charismatic, Peter."

Decker gave her a look. "Why do I detect sarcasm?"

"She complimented you, Loo." Marge nudged him in his bicep. "Say thank you."

"Thank you."

Rina smiled. "Why is it that only we women know these things?"

Oliver said, "Better question is why do women like opera and soup?"

"Pardon?" Rina asked.

Marge waved at her. "Old conversation, Rina."

"So you think Ganz was charismatic?" Decker asked.

"Yes, I do. And I couldn't be *all* that off-base.

How many members does the Order have?"

"Someone told me two thirty-five," Decker said. "But I think there're babies, too."

"So how many kids in all?"

"Too many," Decker answered.

Marge waited until Rina left. Then she said, "The thing is that Nova blushed when I asked if he knew who called Europa."

"I asked him the same question while you were in the john," Oliver said. "He denied it to me, also. Guy's a pisspoor liar. Which is good. Means he's probably not a total psycho."

"Why do you think he's a psycho?" Decker asked.

"*Anyone* involved in that cult is psycho."

Decker pondered the words, wondering how ultra-religious people fit into the definition of a cult. He thought about that aspect of his own faith every time he entered a yeshiva. After eight years, Orthodox Judaism was still foreign to him. Alien, but not oppressive. Certainly the yeshiva *he* knew wasn't a cult — not with Rabbi Schulman at the helm. Everyone came and went as they pleased. Look at Rina. After having lived there for four years — two with her husband and two on her own — she walked away with the rabbi's blessing.

He glanced at his watch. It was almost nine. They'd been watching the tape for the last half hour. A waste of time. The case merited one more day of probing. Something to work on until the path report came in.

He picked up the thermal coffeepot sitting on an end table. "Anyone for seconds?"

Marge pushed her mug to him. "To the brim."

Decker refilled her mug then his. "Scott?"

"Pass," Oliver answered. "By the way, that was smooth operating, Dunn." He turned to Decker. "You should have been there in person. She got him riled, but not so over the top that he didn't want to talk."

Decker said, "Good job."

"All in a day's work," Marge said. "Point is, we *know* that Nova had something to do with the phone call."

"Europa said the caller was female," Decker said.

Oliver said, "So he got someone else to do the deed. It all makes sense now, Loo. Pluto put the screws on Nova to assign a cause of death and to ink the death certificate. Now Nova may be loyal to the Order, but he wasn't stupid. He knew he wasn't a qualified pathologist. So he had someone call the death in to the police, knowing that would cover his ass."

"Except that the caller phoned Europa, not the police," Decker said.

"Whatever," Oliver said. "I'm just saying that Nova was smart enough to pass the buck. He didn't want to take final responsibility for diagnosing Jupiter's death." He chuckled. "I can't believe these names — Nova, Jupiter, Venus . . . it's like kids playing outer space. They might as well put foil on a box and call it a rocket ship."

"Except Jupiter's dead," Decker said.

Marge brushed hair from her eyes and said, "What are you thinking, Pete? That if Europa had been out to get her father, she would have needed inside help. The call could have been the inside help telling her that the job was done."

"You got it."

Oliver asked, "If Europa whacked her dad, why would she want to be associated with the death by phoning it in?"

"Someone had to tell the police," Decker said. "If they'd waited much longer, the death would have looked *really* suspicious, and we would have been obliged to launch an all-out investigation. Also, since Europa did the calling, the police don't have a voice tape of her accomplice. So we have no way of knowing who from the Order helped her." He thought about his words. "Actually, we have no way of knowing who really called her. We don't even know if it's male or female. We're taking Europa's word for it."

"You have something against the girl, Deck?" Oliver asked.

"Not a thing," Decker said. "I'm creating a 'just in case' script."

"Why?"

"For a variety of reasons," Decker said. "Ganz was a famous man whose death was far from straightforward. His demise is bound to be scrutinized, and I want to make sure we're prepared. Also, we know that the body was moved . . . some of the evidence was bound to get messed up — or maybe even cleaned up. I'm not saying it *was* a homicide. But *if* the Order is intentionally covering up Ganz's suicide, I'd like to know *why*."

11

With the phone at his ear, Decker looked up from his desk, saw Oliver leaning against the door frame. Decker beckoned him in, then held up splayed fingers, indicating five minutes. "The court case is at three, Captain. It's going to be tight for him to get downtown and then back here again . . . no, that's what I'm telling you, sir. It came out of CAPS, not Homicide . . . right, an assault with a deadly which, for some reason, was moved to downtown . . . No, I don't know why the change of venue. More than that, I don't know why the judge agreed to it."

He whispered to Oliver to pull up a chair. The detective closed the door and sat. Decker's office was small, but it was enclosed, affording a semblance of privacy even though the walls were panes of frosted glass — a step up from the usual cubicle.

Into the receiver Decker said, "If I recall correctly, the DA originally filed it as an aggravated assault, which he later filed as a homicide . . . about two months ago . . . I think this is the third continuance. The time lag is ludicrous. The incident happened a year ago, and the DA hasn't even settled on charges of man one or two. But this isn't our problem. It's all internal politicking over there. Meanwhile, they want me to give up one of my valuable men, so they can look good. I don't see the purpose . . .''

Again, Decker glanced toward the door. Jane Heard, the squad room secretary, had come in. She handed him a fresh batch of phone messages, leaving without a word. Decker's watch read eleven-thirty. He'd been making calls since seven. If his right ear got any hotter, it could double as a griddle. As he listened to Strapp make his points, he flipped through the notes — routine business, routine business, routine, routine, routine, routine, a call from Rina reminding him that she wouldn't be home until three, more routine business —

"Yes, I think it would be better if someone filed a continuance for tomorrow morning. First and foremost, it'll give them time to get their act together. At the moment, Wiggins's out in the field, handling a hot domestic. Why should I pull him off when they haven't even finalized the charges . . . all right . . . all right. That sounds good. I'll call you as soon as he's done.''

Decker hung up the phone and mugged a madman's grimace, shaking his hands at the world. He picked up a pen and made a note for the trial tomorrow morning on his crammed-to-the-margins desk calendar. "What brings you to the bowels of bureaucracy, Detective?''

Oliver stated, "He had insurance.''

"What? Who?'' *Attention shift, Deck.* He sat up. "Ganz had insurance? How much?''

"A mil for death benefits, *and* a cash policy roughly equal to another mil."

"Whoa!" Decker rolled his tongue in his cheek. "Who's the beneficiary?"

"Europa Dawn Ganz."

"Sole beneficiary?"

"She was in the policy he had held with Mutual Guard via Southwest University of Technology. For all we know, he could have had dozens more. You want me to keep probing? I'll have to start from scratch. It's going to take time. Your call."

Decker picked up a mug sitting on his desk. It held tepid coffee, but he drank it anyway. "How crowded is your day?"

"My time's free at the moment. But Webster and Martinez were just called to the field. Marge and I are in line to catch the next case."

"If you get called, you go. In the meantime, see if you can do some follow-up."

"Not a prob. I'll phone while I eat lunch at my desk."

Mentioning lunch brought a rumble to Decker's stomach. He took out his own brown bag. "A very big policy for a professor. Especially when you consider that Ganz took out the policy twenty-plus years ago."

"Twenty-five. Nineteen seventy-two."

"I wonder if Europa had filed a claim after Ganz's initial disappearance?"

"Funny you should ask. Mrs. Ganz, Europa's mother, made a claim around five years after her husband vanished on behalf of her daughter. But Mutual Guard denied it. No proof of death."

"So someone was aware of the policy way back when."

"The mother was. I don't know about Europa."

"But she still would have been twenty — an adult."

"Absolutely," Oliver said.

"And this policy has remained in effect all these years?"

"More than that, Loo. It was paid off a year ago. Europa is not only the beneficiary of a million in death benefits if we come back with an 'accidental death,' she can also lay claim to the policy itself." Oliver let go with a knowing grin. "All of a sudden, it seems that she has center stage."

Decker absorbed the words. "I wonder if Ganz had planned to cash in the policy and live off the money when he did his disappearing act. Then again, he couldn't have had much into it. Maybe two or three years' worth of payments. Hardly enough to sustain himself."

Oliver scrunched up his eyes. "Just where did Ganz go for ten years?"

"No one seems to know . . ."

"Weird . . . just to take off like that." Oliver shook his head. " 'Course, I couldn't imagine what it would be like to be that smart. Contemplate the beginnings of the universe. It's gotta do strange things to your psyche."

This brought to Decker's mind the Talmudic story about the four rabbis going into the forest to discuss the meaning of life. One of them died, one went insane, and the third became an apostate. Only Rabbi Akiva came out with his faith intact. The sudden relevancy became so apparent as to be transparent.

Decker said, "Scotty, back then, when Ganz took out the policy, premiums must have been very stiff on a million dollars. Why would he insure himself for that much? Take on that much debt when he was only a professor?"

Oliver said, "You know, I bet Ganz had been planning his Houdini for a long time. Could be he did it to take care of his family."

"Ah," Decker said. "So the money was guilt money to his family for deserting them. Or at least, guilt money to his daughter."

"Sounds good to me."

"But you said Mutual Guard didn't pay off."

"Obviously they had suspicions. And they were right because Ganz returned fifteen years ago."

Decker said, "At that time, Ganz knew his daughter wasn't a millionaire. Somewhere along the line, he must have figured out that the claim wasn't paid. So he couldn't have felt *that* guilty." He took out a sandwich from his brown bag. Roast beef and it looked good. But if he was going to eat bread, he'd have to ritually wash his hands. So instead, he liberated a piece of roast and downed it in one gulp. "To keep the policy active all these years, someone was paying the premiums. Was it Ganz?"

Oliver shrugged. "I'll make a couple of calls. See if I can find who was keeping it alive, though the logical choice is Europa. She's the only one who had something to gain."

"How would she get the money to pay the premiums?" Decker stared at his sandwich, suddenly realizing that his head was pounding. He needed sustenance. "I'm hungry. I've got to go wash."

"Go ahead. I'll get my lunch."

"If Marge is out there, bring her in." Decker got up, went to the bathroom and washed his hands, saying the blessing *outside* the facilities. Rule number one. No blessing God in the john. By the time he came back to his office, Marge and Oliver were at his desk, lunches in tow. While Scott brought her up to date, Decker ate his sandwich, polishing off a couple of bottles of Snapple. When Oliver had finished, Decker wiped his mouth with a napkin and said, "Suppose Jupiter suddenly discovered that the policy was still alive."

Marge said, "You're thinking that suppose Jupiter decided to cash it in. Maybe even change the beneficiary to Venus. Europa took exception and bumped him off, and made it look like an OD accident."

Decker scratched his nose. "Can you at least let me get the thought out?"

"Am I right?"

"That's *not* the point," Decker said. "*If* Europa's

guilty, she had to have had inside help."

"What about Guru Bob?" Oliver suggested. "She dated him."

"Why not Venus?" Marge asked. "They were girlhood friends."

Oliver said, "Don't you think that if Jupiter was going to change the policy, Marge, he would have changed it in favor of *Venus* as the beneficiary?"

"Not necessarily," Decker said. "If he pictured himself as Father Jupiter of the Order of the Rings of God, could be he intended to leave the money to the Order for the mutual benefit of all its members. Or maybe he backtracked and decided to leave it to science. I like Marge's idea. Just maybe the women got together out of mutual interest in money." He turned to Marge. "Did he have any other money stashed away elsewhere?"

"Nothing like the insurance policy, but he had savings upward of fifty thou between three or four bank accounts."

"Maybe that money was used to run the day-to-day operations of the Order."

"Could be," Marge answered, "although the accounts are in *Ganz's* name. Ganz — not Jupiter."

"The guy was rich," Oliver said.

"True," Decker said. "However, he was still worth more dead than alive."

The preliminary path report hadn't come

through, and probably wouldn't be available until tomorrow afternoon. No sense in poking around the Order, upsetting the mourners, until there was something concrete. Again, Decker flipped through his phone messages. He picked up the receiver, then realized he could make the calls as easily from his home as from his desk. Besides, he was still hungry and the station house only had nonkosher vending machines. He telephoned his house, but no one picked up.

Then he remembered that Rina had accompanied Hannah on a class trip to the zoo. They'd be gone until three.

Which meant his house was empty. If he left now, he could grab two hours of quiet, uninterrupted work time. He loaded his briefcase with files from his most pressing cases, slipping in Wiggins's folder for tomorrow's court case. Lastly, he added his file from the Ganz case, and his message slips. He checked himself out, leaving his pager on for emergencies.

The idea of solitude made him salivate, a part of him understanding the Ganzes, Gauguins, and all those disappearing *artistes;* that overwhelming desire to chuck it all and search for something more meaningful. But then he thought back to his divorced days, to the oppressive loneliness that dragged him down like an undertow. He had yet to find a meaningful relationship devoid of responsibility. A small case in point being the dog. There had been times when Ginger had been underfoot. But he had been depressed for days after the setter had been put down.

He thought about his dog as he opened the front door, stepping quietly into his living room. He still missed Ginger's maniacal greetings. He and Rina had discussed getting another puppy, but with the impending move, it wasn't the right time —

Decker's ears suddenly perked up.

He realized that he was hearing things . . . noises.

Listening with trained precision.

It sounded like panting, and it was coming from the kitchen, which didn't make sense at all. Instinctively, his hand went to his gun. He tip-toed through the living room, stopped at the bedrooms. The boys' bedroom door was open, but *his* bedroom door was closed.

His mind flashing to Jan . . . to that day and what he had walked into . . . to feelings of deep humiliation and betrayal.

But this was *Rina!* She couldn't . . . It was impossible! She'd never . . . he'd stake his life on it!

Still, as unexplained anger welled up in his chest, he unstrapped his shoulder harness.

One sweaty hand grasped the knob as his heart pounded. The other hand wrapped around the butt of his gun.

He threw open the door.

One glance to take it all in. Two half-naked bodies on his bed. He was on top; she had her legs wrapped around his waist. His hand was on her bare chest. He bolted up into a sitting position, then threw a shirt over his friend's face as she let out a high-pitched scream. All of it taking just seconds.

"Jesus!" Decker muttered aloud as he slammed the door shut. From the outside, he pounded once on the portal and yelled, "You got five minutes to get dressed and get your butt over here."

Feeling his heart jump through his throat. *Half-naked, Decker. They were half-naked.* Jake had his pants on — more or less.

Securing his gun back into his harness, Decker stormed into the kitchen and poured himself a glass of water — something to grasp to prevent his hands from shaking. He was angry at the situation, but even more so, he was pissed that his dream of solitude was abruptly rent asunder, leaving him with yet another crisis with which to deal.

Suddenly, he heard the girl cry. She was weeping hysterically — big, deep sobs that ripped through Decker's heart. What he couldn't understand was why he could hear her so clearly. She was panicked.

"Oh, God, I'm dead! I'm really, really dead! I'm in big, big trouble —"

"Sha—"

"Oh, God, I'm *dead*. Like really dead! Like I'm in such bad trouble, I'm gonna kill myself! I'm — Don't *touch* me!"

Silence.

Again, the girl started crying, but softer this time. Through tears, she said, "I'm sorry, Yonkie, I didn't mean it. I really didn't mean it. I'm just so scared! I am so dead —"

"Listen —"

"You don't know my father, Yonkie. I mean, you don't *know* him like I *know* him. He's going to *kill* me." She began to imitate him. "We've got to take a *meeting* on this! A meeting! Let's take a meeting! A family meeting! It's time for a family *meeting* to discuss our feelings! He's gonna *level* me. I'm dead! This time, he's going to *kill* me!"

"My stepfather won't tell him," Jacob said quietly.

"He's going to kill —"

"Did you *hear* what I said?" Jacob repeated in a louder voice. He seemed more irked than scared. "My stepfather won't tell him."

Abruptly, the girl quieted.

Decker looked around the room. The voices had been coming from the baby's intercom. Often, Rina left it on to hear Hannah when she was in the room by herself. Obviously, she had forgotten to turn it off. Generally, he was a big one on respecting privacy. But he felt justified because (a) his son had cut school, (b) had sneaked into the house and (c) decided to play doctor with some anonymous girl on *his* friggin' bed.

The girl asked, "How do you know he won't tell?"

Yeah, Decker thought, *how the fuck do you know I won't tell?*

Jacob said, "I just know."

"What does *that* mean —"

"It means I just *know, all right!*" Jacob's voice had turned harsh. "I'm not saying it's going to be gravy. But I'll handle it. Shayna, my stepdad grew up in a goyish family in southern Florida. He got in fistfights. He played football. He was in Vietnam. He's a cop. I'm sure he had more than his fair share of backseat humping —"

"Don't talk like that!"

Again, no one spoke.

Then Jacob said, "My dad goes postal on religious issues because he doesn't understand them. But stuff like this . . . he understands." Silence. "Just like . . . like climb out the window. I'll . . . I'll handle it."

"What are you going to do?"

"I'm going to go out there and keep my mouth shut. Let him do all the talking until he talks himself out." A beat. "Something my brother hasn't learned to do. Because Sammy's the *honest* one. *Contentious* you'd better believe it, but deep down, he's that way because he's so *sensitive.* He just needs extra attention because he's the *only* person in the world who ever suffered. Not like me. I'm the *easy* one in the family. So easy that it's like I'm not even there . . . just a grinning, village idiot."

More silence.

Then the girl said, "What are you talking

153

about? You're the smartest person I know. I'm sure they don't think that way at all."

"On some cosmic level, I'm sure you're right." His voice sounded bitter. "Look, Shayna, call your sister and tell her to pick you up. I'll deal with my dad. No reason for both of us to get detention."

Another stretched silence.

Then Decker heard the slide of a window being opened, and being slammed shut. At this point, he turned off the intercom, waiting for Jacob in the kitchen. When the teen did enter, he broke Decker's heart. Toting an oversized backpack like a donkey with a load. Jake was clearly upset, but attempting to hide it with apathy. His smooth face was flushed — wet and red — his black hair askew and falling over his eyes. His white shirt was untucked, resting over blue slacks, the fringes of his *tallit katan* hanging from under his shirt like four, thin tails. He dropped his backpack in the corner, ran his fingers through his locks, then secured his yarmulke on the crown of his hair with a bobby pin. His blue eyes were focused on some imaginary spot on the floor.

Jake still had some room to grow, but he was on his way to manhood. Around five-ten with a lean body and the kind of matinee-idol looks that made girls swoon. Not hard to understand where his beauty came from; he looked just like Rina. Likening him and his wife to Joseph and Rachel. Another beautiful man whose astonishing face caused him problems.

But Decker had never perceived his son as a heartthrob because to him, Jacob was simply Jacob — a social, *frum* kid with lots of friends, an easygoing personality, a winning smile. Not a grinning idiot — Jacob was very bright — but someone whom Decker didn't think about because he *was* so easy. Now with that myth destroyed, Decker regarded his stepson through newly opened eyes. Definitely, Jake was a girl-magnet. If they didn't talk soon, there'd be real trouble.

Wearily, Decker pointed to a kitchen chair and Jacob sat. Decker turned the other seat around so his stomach was resting against the chair's back. "Next time you do this, you might want to turn off Hannah's intercom."

The boy reddened, eyes darting around the kitchen. When he spied the contraption, he let his eyes rest on it for just a moment, then looked down. "So you heard everything. Then I don't have to repeat myself."

Decker asked, "Anything you want to add?"

Jacob didn't say anything.

"Nothing?" Decker asked.

The teen cleared his throat. "I guess I would really appreciate . . . if you didn't . . . if you kept this between us. I'll take whatever punishment you give me. But I'd like to keep it between us."

"Noble of you."

"Why should both of us go down?"

"She was there, same as you. One might even say I have a parental obligation to let her folks know."

Jacob was silent.

"Is her father that bad?"

The boy glanced up, sensing a reprieve. "He's a pompous jerk. Some real rich entertainment lawyer who has an opinion on everything. And it's usually wrong. He's a *ba'al tshuva*."

"And that's why he's a jerk? Because he's a born again?"

"No, of course not. It's . . . admirable to be a *ba'al tshuva*. But he's like . . . forcing it on the family. Shayna . . . the girl I was with . . . she came to the school about a year ago. Her father made her change her name from Shane to Shayna because it sounded more Jewish. She's trying hard, but it's . . . you know, new to her. She can barely read Hebrew. She misses her old friends from public school." A pause. "You should understand."

Decker did understand, but damn if he was going to give Yonkie any points. He asked, "Anything else?"

He tried to look at Decker, but his eyes didn't quite make it to the face. He was trying to get a grip on himself, but his legs were shaking. "Well . . . if you wouldn't tell Eema, I'd appreciate that also."

"No go, Jacob. You're her son. She has a right to know."

The boy shrugged. "Okay."

"Can I ask you a question?"

"Sure."

"Why *my* bedroom?"

The teen's eyes stared about an inch over Decker's shoulder. "The bed's bigger."

Decker forced the boy to make eye contact. "You violated *my* privacy, you violated your *mother's* privacy. That was a rotten thing to do."

"I'm sorry." Water welled up in Jacob's eyes. "It won't happen again. I promise."

Decker stood and pulled the kid toward him. The kid melted in the embrace. "Jacob, I don't know where you've come up with this grinning idiot thing. Your mother and I have untold love and respect for you. But obviously, after today, we need to do some talking."

He broke away, almost pushing Decker aside. "We weren't doing anything."

"Well, you were doing *something* —"

"It's nothing compared to other kids I know." He sank into his seat. Staring at the ceiling, he was quiet. Decker had no choice but to wait him out.

Finally, Jacob whispered, "There's something wrong with me. I'm . . . I'm just . . . like . . . wired *all* the time."

"Wired?"

"You know what I mean."

"Aroused?"

He nodded, his eyes still upward. "I think about it constantly. I'm obsessed with it."

"Sex?"

Jacob didn't answer.

"It's called being fifteen and male."

"I don't know . . ." Jacob shook his head. "Sammy's not like that."

"You're not Sammy."

The teen spoke haltingly, his eyes staring off in space. "One of the guys in my class got hold of some porno films about six months ago. We've been watching them every *motzo Shabbos* . . . after his parents go out."

The room fell silent.

Jacob went on, "I feel real sleazy doing it — some of them are really . . . disgusting — but I can't stop."

"You can't? Or you don't want to?"

He shrugged. "The thing is . . . all of the guys at school who are into girls . . . are also into booze and dope. They're *real* jerks." A beat. "They're . . . idiots."

"Who? Like Dovid? Steve?"

"Dovid, Steve, Ronnie, Joey . . . all of 'em."

Decker waited.

Jacob again spoke slowly. "But the guys who are good students are . . . are like *shomer negiyah* — that means they don't touch girls. Not that that's *bad*. Sammy's *shomer negiyah*." A sigh. "It's just in my class the religious guys are dorky . . . and real self-righteous. I can't talk to them without feeling . . . dirty. So I hang around the jerks. I know it's dumb. Because how long can you hang around jerks without turning into one?"

158

"They drink and take drugs?"

The boy nodded.

"What about you, Yonkie? Do you drink and take drugs?"

The boy looked away. "A few times. No big deal." But as soon as he said it, he cringed.

Decker kept his face flat. He wasn't all that surprised. It was always the quiet ones . . . "What did you do?"

"Nothing much. They pass it around while we watch . . . you know . . ."

"No, I *don't* know.

"I've taken a couple of hits —" He stopped himself. "Maybe more than a couple. But just pot. No big deal."

Decker was quiet.

"I mean I've never even gotten like *really* buzzed. I mean maybe a little buzzed, but . . . just . . . you know —"

"No, I don't know."

Again, the boy looked up — anywhere but at Decker. "Funny thing is, if I pass it up, nobody cares. I don't have to use to be accepted. But I just feel like I should."

"Why?"

"To belong. Except I don't fit in anywhere. I'm too . . . too academic to be a head, and too . . . wired to be one of the little rabbis. I can pass through both groups without a problem. I've got lots of friends. I don't know *why* I do stupid things. But I do them and . . . and later, I *hate* myself."

He rubbed his face, made a swipe at his eyes.

"I keep thinking, like what if Eema saw me. It would hurt her so much." He looked at Decker with plaintive eyes. "I know you have to tell her about this. But I really wish you wouldn't." His eyes widened as anxiety gripped his heart. "You're not going to tell her about the pot. I told you that in *confidence*."

Decker asked, "What do you think I should do?"

"Oh, God!" He tilted his chair back and regarded the ceiling, a defeated look stamped across his face. "What if I promise that I won't do it again? Smoke dope, I mean."

"Should I believe you?"

No one spoke. The kid seemed to be thinking about it, or at least, faking it out.

"I think you can," Jacob answered. "I *hope* you can. Anyway, feel free to check up on me — go through my things . . . listen to my phone conversations. I know I'll have to earn back my privacy."

He was on the right track. Decker asked, "What about drinking, Yonkie? Do you drink, too?"

The boy became more animated. "Seriously, I don't drink. I got drunk once when I slept over Steve's house. I got so sick, I swore never again. I *don't* drink. I mean I'll drink wine on Shabbos. But I never drink just to drink."

"That's good."

"So are you going to tell her? About the dope?"

Again, Decker forced the boy to make eye contact. "Well, Jacob, that's up to you. If you prove yourself to be trustworthy, why should I distress your mother? But if I see an *inkling* of erratic behavior . . . son, I'm a cop. If you mess up, you'll see just *what* a cop I can be."

The boy nodded gravely. "Fair enough. That's one of the good things about Shayna. If I'm around her, I'm not around them."

"Are you two an item?"

"We're . . . good for each other. Something to hold on to — literally."

"Have you two had sex?"

Jacob shook his head no.

Decker peered into his eyes. "Are you lying to me, Yonkie?"

"No." He sighed. "She made me promise to keep our underpants on. Actually, that's okay with me. I couldn't handle it . . . not yet. Not that I haven't had opportunities. It's a really . . . *different* world outside of the yeshiva. I guess I don't have to tell you that."

"Go on."

"Just that there're *tons* of girls out there who are really *aggressive*. You wouldn't believe what they've said to me. Well, I guess *you* know. But Eema would be shocked out of her mind. In the last two months alone, I've had like five or six invitations to go over to houses when the parents aren't home."

"Girls from your high school?"

"No. Secular private or public school girls."

"Shayna's old friends?"

"Yeah, some of them are."

"Are they Jewish?"

"Some yes, some no. Some are older than me. They're real messed up. Divorces and affairs and all sorts of stuff. It's sad. All I'm saying is compared to them, I'm a monk."

"So you haven't had sex, Yonkie? What about oral sex?"

"No . . . just . . ." He fidgeted. "How much detail are you going to ask me?"

"Enough to make sure you're not going to contract something that could kill you."

Jacob looked away. "You can't get AIDS if you're a virgin."

"That's not true. If you don't believe me, I'll let you talk to a thirteen-year-old girl that Juvey pulled in last night. She's wasting away from consumption and AIDS, and she swore up and down that she only did it to guys orally."

Jacob was stunned. "Thirteen?"

"Yep."

"Is she like . . . from a poor family or something?"

"Middle class. To quote from her mother, 'She fell in with the wrong crowd.' "

Jacob was silent. "Is the girl HIV positive or does she have AIDS?"

"She has AIDS. But that really doesn't matter. Her lungs are going to crash before her immune system." Decker leaned over and put his hand on Jacob's shoulder. The boy bristled, but didn't pull away. "*Don't* have sex. You're *way* too young emotionally and physically. First times are often disasters. But if you're older, you can handle it better."

Jacob was quiet.

"Do you hear me, Yonkie?"

"Yes, I hear you."

"But if you mess up, don't be *stupid*. *Wear* a condom."

"It's against Jewish law."

"Yonkie, I don't know that law, but I do know it's against Jewish law to endanger your health, let alone kill yourself. Don't have sex. But if you do something impulsive, I don't want you to die, or knock up some girl. You understand?"

Jacob nodded.

Decker said, "If you're too embarrassed to buy condoms, I'll do it for you. This does not mean I approve of the behavior. I don't approve. All it means is I don't want you to die."

"I'm not going to need them."

"But you'll come to me if you do?"

The teen nodded. Then he appeared to really give Decker's words some thought. "If something does . . . I'll let you know. I promise." For the first time, the boy initiated eye contact. "I'm really sorry."

Decker stroked the boy's cheek, then withdrew his hand. "Jacob, I want you to *stop* watching porno films. They only increase your arousal, and you have no outlet to bleed off your libido except masturbation. Now, I know that's also against Jewish law. But I have no problem with it. It's clean, it's easy and it'll keep you from going off the deep end. Even so, there's no sense in *feeding* your sexual appetite. When your friends put on the flicks, *walk* out. Also, if you stop watching films, it'll get you away from that crowd and force you to do healthier things."

"Like hanging out at Nate's Pizza Shop," Jacob said drolly. "There's a real riot."

"After sex and drugs, I'm sure it seems mundane. But it's what you should be doing. Or take Shayna out to the movies. Or go bowling —"

The kid rolled his eyes.

"Bowling's fun," Decker insisted.

"If you're fat and forty and like to guzzle beer." He rolled his eyes. "Anyway, if you saw *what* hung out at bowling alleys, you wouldn't recommend it as an alternative behavior. You know, I used to do regular stuff. You used to take me riding every Sunday. Then you got rid of the horses —"

"We can't keep the horses in the new house."

"That's not the point. We just don't . . . do anything. We used to go ATVing in the mountains. You used to take me go-carting. You never even take me for a drive in the Porsche anymore. Since you got promoted, all you ever do is work or go fix up the new house." A sigh. "Not that I'm blaming you for my stupid behavior. But I do miss —"

Decker's beeper went off. Instinctively, he looked at the pager. The station house was calling him. His head was reeling, his stomach lurching. Responsibility was a leech that just wouldn't quit. He said, "Go on."

"No, go answer it," the teen said with resignation.

"You're more important. Go on."

"I can't talk if I know some kid out there is being raped. We can pick this up another time."

But Decker knew they wouldn't. Feeling crushed, he stood and went to the phone. "It shouldn't take long."

"Whatever."

Decker punched in numbers on the phone. While he waited to be connected, he stole some juice and cold meatloaf from the fridge. A half minute later, Marge came on the line.

"Got a call from the Order. There's been an incident."

Decker almost choked on his food. "Another body?"

"A missing body. One of its members — a young woman around nineteen or twenty. Her given name is Lauren Bolt, but she was renamed Andromeda by the Order. Her room is undisturbed, but she's nowhere to be found. Pluto's claiming she was kidnapped by one of our officers —"

"*What?* —"

"Who was paid off by the girl's parents —"

"You've *got* to be kidding —"

"And the whole thing was coordinated by Reuben Asnikov —"

"The deprogrammer?"

"That's the one. Pluto stated that he wouldn't be surprised if Asnikov was behind Jupiter's death. As far as he's concerned, Asnikov planned the whole thing just to get the girl out. You know, ends justify the means. He claims that Asnikov is a ruthless, murdering bastard."

Decker pulled out a notepad from his jacket. "When did all this happen?"

"We caught the call about ten minutes ago. Scott and I are on our way."

"Secure the area with crime ribbon tape. No one goes in or out. Get a couple of uniforms to help you keep the area sealed off. And check the ID on everyone including the officers. Just on the rare off-chance that someone was actually impersonating one of us yesterday."

Marge paused. "It's happened before."

"I know. Let's hope Pluto's being hysterical. If he isn't, we've got a problem. Do you have the parents' phone number and address?"

"We called. No one's answering."

"Anyone in the squad room from Homicide?"

"Bert and Tom came back around five minutes ago."

"Do this for me. Send Bert Martinez over to the girl's parents, and send Tom Webster over to talk to Asnikov."

"Why? At the moment, Pluto's accusations have no basis."

"The girl's parents need to be told about their daughter. She *is* missing. If they had a hand in it

166

and it was against her will, then it's kidnapping. If not, maybe they know something to help out the police. To Asnikov, go under the pretext of warning him that the Order is angry at him —"

"They *are* angry at him."

"Then Webster's job is legit. In the meantime, he can feel Asnikov out. See if he squirms. Although in his line of work, I doubt he sweats much."

"When will you make it down to the Order?"

"Give me fifteen, twenty minutes. I've got to drive my son back to school."

"Your son?"

"I'm at my house."

"What's your son doing there? Shouldn't he be in school?"

"Don't ask."

Marge said, "See you in fifteen."

Decker hung up and looked at Jacob, "Something came up. I've got to go."

"The Ganz case?"

Decker stared at him.

Jacob said, "It's all over the news." The teen walked over to the corner and picked up his backpack, swinging it over his shoulder. Again, he ran his fingers through the front of his thick black hair. James Dean with a *kepah*. "Believe it or not, I'm interested in what you do."

"I know." Decker felt the pit of his stomach drop. "I realize I've been busy . . . too busy. The Daytona's coming next month. How about if I get us some tickets — just you, me and Sammy?"

Jacob smiled. "Sounds great, but don't make promises you can't keep."

Cutting to the quick. Decker was silent. Together they quickly left the house. Decker locked the front door while Jacob threw his backback into the unmarked. After they had both buckled up, the teen said, "Are you going to write me an excuse?"

"For cutting class?" Decker revved the motor and pulled out of the driveway. "Do you think I should?"

"No. But they're going to want to know where I was."

"Tell them you were at the house. I'll vouch for that. But I'll also tell them that you didn't have my permission to cut school."

He said, "I'll probably get detention."

"You'll live."

"No, I mean I'll probably get detention instead of being suspended. You're supposed to be suspended for cutting. But kids cut all the time. Half the time they don't even get detention. Nobody even knows they're gone."

"Really organized school I send you to."

"Don't blame me." Jacob fidgeted. "So . . . like am I grounded or what?"

Dying to get punished. It cleanses the soul. Or maybe it was a wish for some kind of attention. Decker said, "I want you to start coming to the new house with me. I'm putting dry wall up in the new bedroom. I can use another pair of hands."

The boy grimaced. "Dad, I can't screw in a

lightbulb. I'll be more harm than help."

"So you'll learn. Not just you, Jacob, Sammy, also. I'ven't wanted to burden you two with your parents' project. But I think that was a mistake."

"I have lots of schoolwork over the weekend."

"So budget your time. As far as Saturday night goes, you stay home and baby-sit Hannah for a month. After that, you're on your own just as long as you stay away from pot, booze and porno. I think I'm being more than fair."

"Yeah, actually it sounds pretty liberal."

The remainder of the ride was silent. As Decker pulled up at the school's curb, Jacob said, "You really like your job, don't you."

His first instinct was to downplay it. But after all this, Jacob was entitled to some honesty. "I like it very much. It's stressful, but at least it's not routine. I'm probably a little like you. I get bored easily."

"Ain't that the truth. Two and half hours of *gemara*. It's . . . stultifying." Jacob opened the door. "I wish I was like Sammy, and believed all the junk they throw at us. I'd be a lot happier. Trouble is, I just don't buy most of it." He slid out of the car. "We'll pick this up later." He smiled. "Over drywall."

Jacob shut the door and walked away. Decker watched him go, feeling inadequate and unsatisfied. A moment later, the teen was joined by four other boys who were obviously glad to see him. Decker wasn't sure but he thought he detected a sudden swagger in his son's walk. Jacob was a real charmer.

Jails were full of them.

12

They had amassed for the confrontation in the main hall. As the sun stood upright in its pathway, its rays poured through the ceiling's windows, bleaching the faces of the spotlighted. The combination of the afternoon heat, the compressed bodies and the greenhouse factor had turned the area steamy, and it smelled as ripe as a gym. In the harsh glare, Pluto's face appeared neon orange as sweat dripped down his face and onto his shoulders. Perspiration had also darkened the armpits of his blue robe. The two detectives and four officers were managing to keep the crowd from turning unruly, but they were badly outnumbered. Who knew how long order would last?

Seeing this as he stepped inside, Decker radioed for all units to be on alert in case backup was needed. The situation was tense, but not as grueling as dealing with his family. Hell, he didn't have to see these yahoos every night for dinner.

When Pluto spotted Decker, the guru turned his wrath on the higher authority. He pointed an angry index finger at the lieutenant, shaking it as if sprinkling baptismal waters. "I hold *you* responsible for the *kidnapping!*"

Over one hundred angry adult faces turned toward him, each adding a hostile grunt or remark of his or her own.

Pluto orated, "We expect the police to conduct an all-out manhunt until our Sister Andromeda is returned to us. We demand this. We will not put up with anything less."

Again, the crowd shot back some righteous amens.

Decker said nothing, waiting for the noise to die down. A moment passed, then two, then a full minute, Pluto waiting for him to say something. Lacking sagacious words, Decker smoothed his mustache. "Where's the bathroom?"

Oliver almost broke up, but Marge elbowed him just in time.

Pluto had turned pumpkin from outrage. *"What?"*

"I have to use the facilities," Decker said. "Happens to the best of us. Afterward, I'm here to listen —"

"To *listen!*" Pluto sneered. "We don't want your *therapy!* We want action!"

A chorus of support from the parishioners.

"One of our members was *stolen* from us!" he yelled. "Find her!"

Again, the masses erupted.

"We're here to serve," Decker yelled over the noise. "But first things first. Someone direct me to the john, please?"

Silence. Then a male voice answered, "Third door on the left."

Decker scanned the room in the direction of the voice. Bearded and thin — Guru Bob with a cryptic smile. Decker nodded. Then he told Pluto to meet him in the temple.

Once inside, Decker locked the door. The place was closet-sized and barely accommodated his size. He turned the water on full blast and washed his hands and face while trying to formulate a plan. He didn't want a one-on-one with Pluto, either in front of an audience or alone. He needed input from other less volatile members. He decided to request a meeting of *all* the privileged attendants. He had wanted to meet Nova, and now seemed as good a time as any.

Coming out of the bathroom, he saw that people were dispersing slowly. Apparently, a breakup announcement had been made. He couldn't find Marge, but Oliver was deep in conversation with some members, taking notes and acting official.

Decker searched the room for other blue robes, hoping to find Nova, but he could only make out Bob in the crowd. He elbowed his way through the swarm until he was within talking distance of the goateed man.

The attendant acknowledged him with a curt nod. He said, "Pluto's waiting for you." Bob glanced at Oliver, in conversation with a blond, stocky man. "Just you, not him. He was firm about that."

Decker said, "Why don't you come join us? You and Venus and Nova." He hesitated.

"Where is Nova?"

His sentence was interrupted by a white-robed, thirty-something man who had turned his bullish face toward Decker. Standing nose to nose, the man shouted, "This is outrageous! Are you cops going to do anything? Or are you going to sit on your ass and fart onions!"

Decker backed away, trying to regain personal space. "You got some bedside manner, guy!"

Immediately, Bob stepped in. "Something will be done, Brother Ansel. One way or another—"

"I hope so!" Brother Ansel broke in. "We cannot let this crime pass unchallenged —"

"Of course not —"

"An invasion of our privacy! *Satan* took advantage of our tragedy! Struck in our moment of sorrow!"

"Everything will be dealt with. Now go back to your room. Meditation is in five minutes —"

"This is hardly the time —"

"On the contrary, Brother Ansel, it's the perfect time," Bob answered. "Spiritual growth happens during life's challenges. Please return to your room now." A chastising look. "You don't want to risk a fine, do you?"

The pugnacious Ansel growled, but eventually left. Not before throwing Decker a sneer. When he was gone, Decker asked, "Who's the Satan?"

Bob said, "Pluto's expecting you at any moment. If he gets angry again, who knows what he'll say to the crowd."

"Come with me."

"That wouldn't be wise."

Decker paused. "I thought you said that you and Pluto are of equal rank."

Bob reddened in anger. "We are. But I have other business to take care of. We all have jobs to do."

Meaning he didn't want to cross Pluto? Decker said, "Of course. Come if you can."

Bob was clearly in a quandary. "I'll be there, but it'll take time. Start without me."

"Great. Bring Nova along if you find him."

"Uh huh." Bob became distracted, his eyes resting on a girl of about twenty. Her eyes were mildly green, and her brown hair was tied back in a bun. He nodded and she nodded back, passing an unwritten note of sexuality. She looked familiar.

Then Decker remembered. It was Terra. The girl in the van who had led them through the gate — and past the dogs — yesterday morning.

Bob said, "I'll see you later."

Decker asked, "By the way, where *is* Nova?"

Bob tensed. "You're getting downright pesky."

Decker shrugged. "Sorry about the persistence. It's my job. Still, I don't want to alienate you. You've been helpful."

"Yeah, well, that can change quickly."

"I saw Europa yesterday. She offered me some interesting insights. Maybe we can talk about her some time."

"Then again, maybe not." Bob's face was flat. "Good-bye."

Decker said, "I'll see you in a bit." He walked toward the temple. After taking a dozen steps, he stopped, then turned and looked over his shoulder. Bob had disappeared, no doubt going off to chase a much more tangible celestial body.

The rooms were clones of one another, and Sister Andromeda's was no exception. Hers was just as Decker had described the others. A cot, a coarse wool blanket and a makeshift shelf on which sat a cup, a spoon and several books on spirituality and lay physics.

As a matter of fact, the bookshelf dared to have a novel. Nothing big . . . a romance title from a couple of years back. Still . . .

Marge tapped her pencil on her pad.

There was something eerie about the cubicle. All of the girl's earthly possessions remained — from the books to the suitcase underneath the cot. It certainly didn't *seem* as if she was planning on going somewhere. Everything was in place. Only thing missing was the occupant.

Hearing scuffled footsteps, Marge turned around. A young woman barely out of her teens stood at the doorway. Her complexion was smooth and pale, her hair medium brown and tied up. Pretty in a waifish way. Full lips and pronounced cheekbones. Her hands and fingers were long and smooth as if sculpted from marble. She wore a white robe. On her feet were white slippers.

"She was taken, you know," the woman stated

in a soft voice.

Marge said, "Tell me about it."

"It was him. The one we call *Satan!*"

"Does he have a more . . . conventional name?"

Her delicate fingers gathered in a fold of her snowy gown. "Reuben Asnikov. Her parents hired him. They paid him lots of money. Andromeda was terrified of being snatched by him. He has a sordid reputation."

"In what way?"

"In his methods of brainwashing."

Or deprogramming, depending on your perspective, Marge thought. "Tell me about it."

"Just that he will stop at nothing."

"Can you be more specific?"

"Is there a way to categorize the evilness of the devil?" A tear fell down her cheek. "None of us are incarcerated here. We can leave if we want. Yet we stay because here we can live under the glow and guidance of Father Jupiter."

She started to cry. Marge waited her out. It took about a minute. When the young woman finally calmed down, Marge said, "I didn't catch your name."

"Terra." She wiped her eyes with the back of her silky hand. "It's Terra."

"And you were friends with Andromeda?"

"We are both teachers of the children. The sweet, sweet children. The future of the Order." A new batch of tears escaped. "It is intolerable to think that they will not grow up with the holy hand of our venerated Father Jupiter."

"Where are the children now?" Marge asked Terra.

"Come." Terra straightened her spine and took Marge's hand. "I'll take you."

Leading her down a hallway, Terra tiptoed until they reached a kind of cul-de-sac of three doors. Small, muffled cries bled from one of the rooms. Terra smiled. "The nursery."

"Mind if I take a look?"

Terra opened the door just a crack, enough for Marge to see but not wide enough to be noticed.

Three women in white gowns were tending to a dozen small children — babies and toddlers. Each was doing a job. One was rocking a two-year-old, singing lullabies to a Botticellian face. Two infants were sleeping in cribs. One woman was on the floor building with Legos with a group of toddlers. Another was setting up food on a picnic table for what appeared to be an afternoon snack.

"Would you like to go in?" Terra told Marge.

"No, that's fine." Marge faced her. "Don't want to disturb anyone."

Terra closed the door and opened another. "This is one of our two primary classrooms for grade school." She walked inside the room. Immediately, a group of children stood at attention, all of them dressed in white cotton pants, a white long-sleeved T-shirt and white socks and sneakers.

The clothes were *bright* white — dead white. Either these kids didn't do much dirty work or the compound owned shares in Chlorox.

In *white* and standing *erect* — like little angels. Around thirty of them of varying ages, but they all seemed to be under twelve. A quick ethnic breakdown put around sixty percent of them as Caucasian, about thirty percent Asian, while the remaining ten percent were of mixed race.

Tender, small faces with bright eyes too big for their faces, smooth cheeks unravaged by hormones and red but unchapped lips that, when parted, produced the crooked smiles of half-erupted teeth. They stood in a state-of-the-art classroom replete with writing desks each holding a PC computer, a monitor and a printer. A marker board sat on the front wall, various equations scrawled across the white surface in red ink. The remaining three walls were made up of bookshelves. All the texts seemed to deal with the physical sciences or the spiritual. Not a novel in sight. Like the other rooms in the compound, there were no windows — only skylights.

No windows.

Making access into the compound — except through the exterior doors — just about impossible. With all the goings-on yesterday — the police, the techs, the people from the coroner's office — Asnikov would have had a rare opportunity to strike.

Terra stood at the front of the classroom. Her manner was grave. "Good morning, our future generation."

In unison, they answered, "Good morning,

our Sister Terra."

"You may sit."

They sat.

"I will be with you in a moment. You are to use this interlude to say your prayers, asking once again for the safe journey for our Father Jupiter into the next universe. We all hope to join him soon."

The last sentence drew hackles from Marge's neck.

Terra asked, "Our dear son Gamma, will you lead the chant?"

A ten-year-old Asian boy stood. Within moments, the class broke into a mantra — hushed drone as whispery as the wind. Terra took Marge out of the classroom. As soon as they were alone, Marge asked Terra about the meaning of *joining* Father Jupiter.

The young woman gave Marge a startled look. "It's a formality, Detective. They need to feel part of the grief process. Yet we insist that they know there is a better future." She paused. "Surely, you don't think we have something more . . . more *permanent* in mind."

"There have been precedents."

"Father Jupiter was never one to force anything upon anyone. I assure you that those in charge feel the same way."

After interacting with Pluto, Marge wasn't sure at all. "I noticed those kids were preteens."

Another tear slipped down Terra's cheek. "The older ones were Andromeda's charges."

Again, the young woman took Marge's hand. She shook it with urgency. "You must find her soon. For the children's sake. She relates so *well* to them . . . to the *teenagers*."

Slowly, Marge extracted her hand from Terra's. "How many kids were in her charge?"

"Eight. They're simply *lost* without her."

"Who's taking her place in the meantime?"

"I am," answered a deep, male voice. He was tall, thin and bearded. He extended his hand to Marge. "Guru Bob. And you are . . . ?"

"Detective Dunn."

"Ah. That's right. You were here yesterday."

"Yes, I was. I didn't expect to be called back so soon."

"We didn't expect it either. What are you doing here? I mean here specifically . . . in front of the classrooms."

"Sister Terra was just showing me around."

"I'll bet she was." He took in Terra with fiery eyes. Marge came to her rescue. "I was looking over Andromeda's room and Terra was kind enough to take an interest in her welfare. She said that Andromeda was a teacher. One thing led to another."

But Bob's eyes never left Terra's. He said, "I'll finish up. You have children to take care of."

"Yes, Brother Bob." Terra was petrified. "Right away."

The older man softened his tone. "Don't worry. The transgression will not go beyond me. I know you meant well. How about if we meet in an hour . . . to discuss the children's lessons?"

Terra licked her full lips, her big eyes growing even wider. "Of course." She managed a slight smile. "Of course."

Marge waited for more, but no one spoke. Something more than lessons was going on between them.

"That's all," Bob said in a casual tone. "You may go."

Again, Terra gave him a smile — a bigger one. She pivoted and returned to the safety of her classroom.

Bob had a gleam in his eye. "You have nothing better to do than to harass a young woman?"

Talk about harassment. Marge said, "What transgression did Terra do? Show some independent thinking?"

"Independent thinking is not a transgression. *Any* opinion is welcome as long as it's between family members. But showing you around without proper clearance is not acceptable. It's how we keep order."

"Sort of like the army."

"Paramilitary. If you don't like it, you can leave." His eyes honed in on hers. "Pluto's not spouting hyperbole. Andromeda *was* kidnapped. She's over eighteen. Her parents have no right to keep her against her will."

"The law agrees with you."

"Yeah, well, that's not enough right now. The sooner you resolve this crisis, the better. If you don't do it with quasar speed, the trust between my people and yours is going to deteriorate exponentially."

"Any suggestions?" Marge said.

"Yeah. Lean on Asnikov. Haul his ass into jail. Torture him until he confesses."

"We've got a thing called due process in this country."

Bob sneered, "Asnikov doesn't care about due process. Why should I?"

13

"What do you know about cults?"

Webster thought about the question. "I'm no expert —"

"Then it's good you're with me," Asnikov broke in. "You might as well learn from the best."

The intercom beeped, a disembodied female voice saying, "Jay on line two."

"I'll take it in the inner office." Asnikov regarded Webster from across his desk. The cops had sent him Surfer Dude — blond and well built. He stood about six even . . . boyish face though he was probably about thirty-five. Mr. Southern Boy, sitting in his blue serge suit with a *well, shut-my-mouth* grin. Sneaky demeanor. He bore watching.

"The call's important." Asnikov stood. "Help yourself to another cup of coffee, Detective, I'll be right back." He paused. "You poke around, you're asking for a lawsuit. I've got cameras everywhere."

Webster pointed to an overhead, geometric stained-glass ceiling fixture, and then to an air-conditioning grate.

Asnikov said, "Try to find all of them. It'll keep you busy until I'm done."

As soon as the deprogrammer left, Webster sat back in his chair, and tried to maintain a relaxed pose because the cameras were recording him. He was sweating internally if not through his shirt. Reuben Asnikov was a steel vault without a millimeter of give.

Webster liked how the office had been done up — arts and crafts style. The ceiling was low and made from cherrywood planks set in a running board pattern. The illumination came from recessed, ceiling canisters. The overhead fixture, which was rectangular and ran the length of the ceiling, was assembled from small, opaque squares of yellow, red and blue glass; it probably held a half-dozen cameras. Webster looked upward and waved.

All the furniture was constructed from slats of pure, polished teak: stark in design and hard on the butt. Even the couch Webster was sitting on had no fixed cushions on the back. Sitting was made tolerable by the use of yellow silk pillows. Asnikov's desk was an enormous chunk of rosewood grained with deep swirls of brown and black. The desk chair was a modular piece of blue leather. The walls, like the ceiling, were built with cherrywood planking. No artwork was hung on them because the picture windows provided the color — palettes of leafy green elms and sycamores. Through the windows, Webster caught sight of a rock waterfall.

An attempt at serenity was marred by the six-foot-high gun safe in the corner, the locked shelving unit holding the newest of surveillance equipment and the fully loaded computer ticking out reams of paper. Asnikov's phone system had more lights than an airplane's cockpit.

A few moments later, Asnikov returned, hanging up his jacket on a brass coatrack. The man was built as solidly as a welder. His face was hard, his green eyes were intense and his square jaw had a mandible that worked overtime. His clothes were more Hollywood exec than PI. He wore a loose-structured tan Armani-type suit over a blue-and-brown striped shirt. For his sartorial accessories, he had chosen a yellow tie and matching pocket handkerchief.

He said, "Get out your writing pad and take notes."

Webster held his tablet up. "Ready when you are."

"Cults." Asnikov started ticking off fingers. "You need a charismatic leader — someone with *it*. Because it's the leader who attracts the followers. Which is the second thing you need."

"Followers," Webster said.

Asnikov smiled with closed lips. "You got it. Cults require adherents — *ites*. They're the ones who guarantee survival, the drones who work the jobs and spread the *word* — which is the third thing you need."

Up went three fingers.

"The *word!*" Asnikov said with emphasis. "The philosophy, the *ism*. Cults are always ritualistic and more than likely have an *unorthodox* philosophy specifically designed to develop an us/them attitude. The *ism* is the key to a successful cult. It must isolate and alienate its members from the outside world. Ergo, a successful cult is one that erases its members' pasts. If the cult eradicates its adherents' history, it's free to create its own, substituting one that glorifies and extols the cult's values *and* the values of the charismatic leader who, in fact, determines those said values. Are you with me?"

"I'm with you," Webster replied.

"To recap, three things. The *it,* the *ites* and the *isms,*" Asnikov continued. "There are open cults and closed cults. Most of your religious variants started as open cults, founded on *isms* by a charismatic leader who held a vision. Some examples: Christian Science developed by Mary Baker Eddy, the Shakers forwarded in this country by Ann Lee, Mormonism with Brigham Young's sighting of the angel, Maroni, Jewish Chasidism with the Ba'al Shem Tov. Today, many of these cults have been integrated into standard American religious practices. But way back when, these leaders were ridiculed and ostracized."

"Just like Ganz," Webster stated.

"Ah, but there's a big difference," Asnikov answered. "In these open cults, the adherents stick to a strict set of *isms, but —* a big *but —* they are free to come and go. No one is *forcing* them to stay. The leaders are generally nonobstructionist, and access to its participants is easier."

"And that makes your job easier," Webster said.

"Absolutely. If I can talk to a person alone, and on *my* turf, I may be successful in returning that adherent to the former life *or* I may *not* be successful. If I am sure that there is no coercion, I let well enough alone. The parents may be very unhappy, but if the kid's over eighteen, them's the breaks.

"It's the closed cults that are my stock-in-trade — the ones that keep their followers under lock and key."

"And you feel that the Order of the Rings of God falls under that category?"

"Without a doubt. When was the last time you ever saw one of its adherents in the supermarket?"

"I've never looked."

"Well, Detective, I *have* looked. And let me tell you something. No one ever went in or out without Emil Ganz's — i.e., Jupiter's — say-so. You ever wonder how a cult that big survives when no one residing there has a conventional job?"

"How?"

"Two things. First, the group pools its followers' collective money. You join the Order of the Rings of God, you give up all your worldly assets for the good of the group. Guess who determines how that money is spent?"

"Jupiter."

"Two points, Detective." Asnikov took out a

bottle of water, and drank it empty. "Over the years, Jupiter must have conned hundreds of thousands from his adherents. How much Jupiter had pocketed for himself is anyone's guess. I do know he bought a chicken ranch about a hundred miles north. It produces eggs and chicken for the Order with enough leftover eggs and feathers to sell for pocket change."

"So Jupiter has used the money for the good of his followers."

"Except that the ranch is under *his* name as the sole owner." Asnikov glanced at his watch — a Steel Oyster Rolex. "Now this is a prime example of a closed cult. To get the chickens and eggs, someone from the Order has had to go up there on a regular basis. It's a time-consuming and menial job — collecting eggs and chickens and feathers. You assign a chore like that to an underling. Yet the only people who *I've* ever seen leave the confines and drive up there were Jupiter and his attendants — Pluto, Bob, Nova and the lady Venus. No one else. Ever. You've got to ask why."

"Jupiter doesn't want to give his followers freedom."

"Exactly. He keeps his adherents *away* — away from freedom, away from their pasts and from parents or old friends or, God forbid, me. If Jupiter loses his followers, he loses his power base. Personally, I'm always suspicious of people who love power."

Asnikov's jaw muscles started working.

"People say I'm a kidnapper. Uh uh, not a chance. I'm a *redeemer.* It's people like Ganz who are the kidnappers."

"But if the member is a willing participant —"

"No such animal. As long as the person is not permitted access to the outside world, he or she is a captive. Maybe one who is treated nicely — fed and clothed and fucked — but as dependent as a pet. You have children, Detective?"

"Indeed, I do."

It came out as "In*deed,* ah dew."

Asnikov asked, "How'd you like if some goat treated your son or daughter like a circus animal — blindly obeying orders like some freak?"

"I could understand the heartbreak." Webster looked at the deprogrammer. "But taking someone who is over eighteen and whisking them away — even for his or her own good — is against the law. Then again, I think you know that. I've doubts whether something like a law would stop you."

"If those idiots at the Order say that I've been within ten feet of their compound within the last month, they're lying. Even worse, Detective, they may be hiding something truly nefarious."

"Like what?"

"A girl's missing, sir. *You* figure it out."

"You think they've murdered her?"

"I don't think anything is beyond them."

"You wouldn't be trying . . . for instance . . . to deflect the attention away from yourself, now would you?"

Asnikov was straight-faced. "I don't need to deflect attention away from myself. Watch me all you want. If I break the law, arrest me. I'm not worried."

Webster asked, "So you're not involved in Lauren Bolt's kidnapping?"

"No, I'm not involved. And who says she was kidnapped? With all the confusion yesterday, the girl could have taken the opportunity to slip."

"And if I looked into your books, I wouldn't find Millard and Patricia Bolt listed as your clients?"

"Now that is truly a theoretical question." Asnikov gave him a hint of a smile. "If you could break into my books, which are written in code, I'd hire you in a snap at a starting salary of six figures." He paused. "If you don't believe me, Detective, ask Lauren Bolt's parents."

"We've been trying to get hold of them," Webster answered. "Mr. Bolt's secretary says they're on vacation."

"It's America. They have a right."

Webster slouched, trying to get comfortable on the rock-hard sofa. "Why don't I believe you?"

"I don't know why," Asnikov answered. "We're basically on the same side."

"It's the basically part that bothers me," Webster said. "Y'see, my tactics always fall within the law."

"Hence the high failure rate among the police." Asnikov grinned, showing white-capped teeth. "I reiterate. You think I break the law, arrest me. You do your job, I'll do mine."

Webster licked his lips, deciding to redirect the interview. "In your opinion, what's going to happen with the Order now that Jupiter's gone?"

"An interesting question." Again, Asnikov checked his watch. But he didn't appear to be in a hurry. "There are four under him with a supposedly equal power base. But anyone who knows anything about the Order knows that Pluto is the number-two man."

"So Pluto takes over?"

"Notice I said the number-two *man*. Problem is there's also a number-one *woman*. And she holds just as much sway as Pluto. Right now, I'd say Pluto is probably in charge. No doubt, he's trying to stonewall Venus. But once she gets her bearings that could all change."

"Who do you think will win out?"

"Can't tell. But there's bound to be some sort of power play by Pluto, then a counter by Venus . . . a jockeying back and forth until someone will eventually come out the victor."

"How long do you think that'll take?"

"Who knows?" Asnikov's eyebrows bunched in concentration. "A week, a month, a year. The longer it takes, the better it is for everyone. If the power play is made too hastily — without thought to consequences — things could get ugly. If I were the police, I'd keep a close watch on the compound. The Order's a fecund bunch. You don't want a pile of dead kids on your conscience."

14

Pluto appeared to be praying, giving Decker a few extra moments to take in the temple *sans* the processional hubbub. The sanctuary was retangular in shape except for the northern wall, which was rounded and arched with a domed ceiling. The north side also held a spectacular mural of the nighttime heavens painted in deep jeweled blues and brilliant silvers and whites. In the middle of the heavens hung an idealized screen-sized, midtorso portrait of Emil Euler Ganz. Father Jupiter looked down sternly on his worshipers, his exaggerated, too-sharp jawline jutting outward from his face, stern, steely eyes that could cut through granite. He wore royal purple vestments, embellished with gold thread, and ruffed with a monk's cowl fashioned from fur. Either a halo or spiral galaxy rested over his silver hair. His right hand held a scepter made from iridescent cosmic dust while his left hand twirled his namesake planet. It might have been comical had Jupiter not looked so godlike, as if he could inflict harsh punishments through plagues.

The three remaining walls of the temple were adorned with stained-glass windows of the other eight planets, each sphere held aloft by its respective mythological Greek god or goddess. Ten rows of twenty north-facing pews filled up the center floor space. Pluto was kneeling in the first row, his head bowed, his clasped hands resting against his forehead. His lips were moving but no sound came out. Decker cleared his throat. Pluto looked up and over his shoulder.

"Do you always sneak up on people?" His voice echoed across the room although he wasn't speaking loud.

Decker said, "You learn a light touch when you do surveillance work."

The attendant stood and faced him. "And is that what you're doing now? Surveillance work?"

Decker approached him with measured footsteps. "You reported a missing girl, I'm here to investigate. We're on the same side."

"I certainly hope you mean that. We need action!" The small man's face had become red. "Starting with that maniac!"

"Asnikov —"

"Of course Asnikov!" The little man began to pace — up and down the aisle . . . up and down, up and down. "That monster has been out to get us for years! Unsuccessfully, I'm proud to say. All his cajoling and bribing and heavy-handedness has failed miserably. So he has resorted to unscrupulous methods like this."

"You think he's kidnapped her."

"No, I don't think he did it. I *know* he kidnapped her!"

"Okay." Decker paused. "Assuming you're right. Any idea where he might have taken her?"

Abruptly, Pluto stopped pacing. "No. You're going to have to do a thorough investigation of him. All-out manpower hunt. He needs to be tailed . . . talk about surveillance work. If you're willing, I can help you work out a plan."

Evidence of a crime would help. Decker ran his tongue in his cheek and looked upward. The ceiling had been painted with stars and celestial bodies. Funny he hadn't noticed it before. "I've asked Bob and Nova to join us. Working together, maybe we can come up with a better solution —"

"Totally unnecessary! Too many people make for too many problems."

Decker tapped his foot. "Aren't they your equals?"

"How we utilize our manpower isn't of your concern. Do what is your concern. Go find Andromeda!"

"Who decides when others are needed?"

"A *very* good question," answered a husky female voice.

Both Decker and Pluto turned toward the entrance. Venus paused so they could take her in, then approached them with slow, purposeful steps, her red and gold robe sweeping across the floor as she walked. Her posture displayed a position of royalty, and not an unrehearsed one. "Why was I *not* informed about this latest development?"

Pluto made fists, then slowly relaxed his fingers. "I had every intention of telling you —"

"When?"

"As soon as I found the time! While you were meditating and praying in your room, I was quelling a near riot in the community hall!"

Venus said, "From what I heard, your words seemed more incendiary than calming."

"Then you *misheard!*"

The two faced off in stony silence. Decker felt like a child caught between divorcing parents. Moments ticked by.

Venus spoke. "I am not a hothouse flower, Pluto. I will not be kept in the dark about things concerning my family! This is especially important to me because Andromeda was one of my favorites. I love her dearly."

Pluto decided to give ground. "If it is your desire to dirty your hands, so be it. After all you've gone through, I was trying to save you the misery."

"I appreciate the concern, albeit misguided." Venus focused her attention on Decker. "I'm counting on you to return Andromeda to her home. Here! It's where she belongs!" Hard eyes landing on his face. "If you can't bring her back, I know others who can and will."

Meaning illegally. Empty threats or does she have sources? Decker asked, "Do you know where she might be?"

"No. Asnikov is hiding her at some undisclosed location. You have your work cut out for you."

Decker said, "To mobilize the kind of manpower you're requesting . . . it would help if we had evidence that a crime was committed."

Pluto broke in, "The girl is missing —"

"She's over eighteen, sir, she's entitled to come and go as she pleases —"

"She would never leave here!" Venus said.

"How do you know?"

"She loved it here. She was happy here. And she'd never leave the children. She loved the children!"

Decker asked, "Does she have children of her own?"

A male voice joined in. "No, she didn't have children. She *taught* children."

The trio turned toward the newcomer. Guru Bob.

He said, "She taught the teenagers. She related well to them. Probably because she wasn't much older herself."

Pluto was perturbed. "Didn't you say you were going to take over her class?"

"He wanted me here." Bob cocked a thumb toward Decker. "For today, I combined the teens with Terra's class. There's only seven of them."

"Seven?" Venus said. "I thought we had eight teens. I'm sure we have eight."

Bob's eyes grew restless. "No, seven —"

"No, I'm sure there's eight." Venus tapped her toe. "Vega, Rigel, Gamma's two girls . . . Asa and . . ."

"Myna," Bob said. "She was there."

Venus continued, "Orion, Leo, Ursa . . ."

"They were all there, Venus."

"No. We're missing someone!" Venus insisted. "God, don't tell me that monster got hold of one of our children!"

"Hold on, hold on!" Bob said with irritation. "Vega, Rigel, Asa, Myna, Orion, Leo, Ursa . . . I think that's all —"

"No, it's not all!" Venus grew nervous. "Lyra!" She said triumphantly. "Moriah's kid. She's thirteen now . . ."

"I didn't see her today," Bob answered. "Maybe she wasn't feeling well."

"What does that mean?" Venus scolded. "She was under your care."

Abruptly, Bob's demeanor darkened. "Out of the goodness of my heart, I agreed to teach them, not to baby-sit! Look, Pluto, I don't mind you stepping in temporarily for Jupiter to give the family stability just so long as you realize that you're not Jupiter —"

"I'm not trying to *be* Jupiter!" Pluto insisted. "But someone has to keep the Order running until things have calmed down. Certainly the *others* weren't up to it —"

"And just what does *that* mean?" Venus interrupted.

"I was referring to Nova!" Pluto muttered. "Not you!"

Decker broke in. "Why don't we look for the girl. We can start with her room."

Venus explained, "Lyra's housed with the teens."

"Take me to the quarters." To the men, Decker said, "You two go round up the roommates. I'll want to talk to them."

"Oh, God!" Pluto muttered. "And just what are we supposed to tell Moriah?"

"She won't care." Bob brushed him off.

"What do you mean, she won't *care!*" Once again, Pluto was outraged. "Of course, she'll care!"

"Pluto, she's incapable of caring. She's whacked out —"

"This is how you refer to one of our most spiritual —"

"Pluto, she isn't spiritual, she's *psychotic!*"

"She's mentally ill?" Decker asked.

"Without a doubt," Bob answered.

Decker was appalled. "You house a psychotic woman here?"

Without warning, Bob turned into something wild and furious. "Before you start passing judgment, let me tell you something. Moriah had been in and out of treatment centers and hospitals for nearly fifteen years of her thirty-year-old life. When Brother Pluto found her, she and her daughter — who was about five at the time — were living in a cardboard box dirtied by their own excrement. Pluto, out of charity, took them in. For eight years, we've been caring for Lyra as one of our own *and* have kept Moriah clean, neat and well fed, which is more than her own parents have ever done. When we found her, they had disowned her. Except now that Lyra is growing into a young lady, they're making noise, sending threatening letters to the Order —"

"Oh my God and Jupiter!" Venus broke in.

"Oh, no!" Bob slapped his forehead. "Andromeda wasn't the target! It was *Lyra!*" Again, he hit his brow. "Those bastards! With all the confusion, they finally managed to snatch her." He began to pace. "This is even worse than I thought. Andromeda was probably protecting Lyra when Asnikov struck. I hope to God and Jupiter that he didn't hurt Andromeda while trying to get Lyra!"

Pluto turned his wrath on Decker. "*Now* do you believe us?"

The unfortunate scenerio had the ring of truth. Because this time, the victim was a child.

Bob was muttering. "This is just terrible!" He turned a furious face on Decker. "You gotta mow that monster down!"

"Priorities." Decker was talking as much to himself as he was to Bob. "First, let's see if Lyra's under your roof."

15

Trying to narrow down a time frame for the missing woman and teenaged girl, Marge sat in a makeshift headquarters set up in a spare bedroom cell. Barely enough room for two chairs and a card table, but it would serve the purpose. Guru Bob had offered it as a workstation, a sign that official intervention was welcome although it wasn't apparent from Pluto's attitude. The little man continued to spout accusations.

Vega, one of Lyra's roommates, was sent in to Marge before evening meditations, around 4 P.M. The fourteen-year-old seemed small for her age. But Marge knew she was judging not only by American standards but by her own taller-than-average height. Or perhaps it was the girl's posture: the stooped shoulders and the hunched back, thin arms hugging her books when she walked in the room.

Garbed in white — like the dress of the other children Marge had seen — Vega was of mixed race. She had a bronze complexion, poker-straight black hair and blue, almond-shaped eyes that slanted upward. Marge pointed to the chair and the teen sat down in a ramrod-stiff position. Clearly, she had been instructed to sit that way. She was still embracing her tomes, so Marge took them from her and placed them on the floor. The girl clasped her hands and laid them in her lap. Marge smiled, but Vega did not smile back.

Marge pressed the record button on her machine and placed it close to Vega. She asked, "Do you know why you're here?"

Vega nodded.

"An affirmative nod," Marge said into the machine. "Tell me why you're here."

"Because Andromeda and Lyra are missing. You are asking us for help."

Her voice sounded flat . . . robotic. Marge asked, "You're roommates with Lyra, aren't you?"

Vega nodded.

"Again, an affirmative nod," Marge stated. "Vega, could you please answer yes or no? The recorder can pick up your response that way. Did Lyra sleep in her bed last night?"

"Correct."

"Do you remember seeing her when you woke up?"

"Correct."

"Do you remember seeing her dressed and ready for school?"

"I believe you mean ready for morning meditation and breakfast."

"Okay. Do you remember seeing her ready for meditation and breakfast?"

"Correct."

"Around what time did you leave for . . . what

comes first? Meditation or breakfast?"

"Meditation."

"And what time is that?"

"Seven in the morning."

"So you remember seeing her at seven this morning?"

"Correct."

"Then you ate at what time?"

"Seven-thirty."

"Did she eat breakfast with you?"

"Correct."

"And then what do you do after breakfast?"

"More meditation."

"Okay. What time was the second meditation?"

"Eight o'clock."

"And was Lyra with you at eight?"

"Correct."

"Then what did you do after the second meditation?"

"We went to the classroom."

"Did Lyra go with you to the classroom?"

Vega pressed her lips together. "I . . . think . . . so. But I am not positive. Our teacher Andromeda was not there. So things were confusing."

"What time was this?"

"Class instructions start at eight-thirty. So it must have been eight-thirty. We are always punctual."

"And Andromeda wasn't there in your classroom at eight-thirty."

"No, she was not. This confused all of us."

"Was Lyra with you at this . . . confusing time?"

"I think so. But as I said, it was confusing."

"Was any adult waiting for you in the class-room?"

"No one. This is what was so confusing. Eventually, our teacher Terra came in. She was surprised to find that our teacher Andromeda was not in. She was confused as well."

"Around what time was that?"

"Around nine. I believe one of the boys went to get her. Because we were so confused."

"So from eight-thirty to nine, there was no teacher in your class."

"Correct."

"What did you do?"

"What did we do? I do not understand the question."

Marge said, "You didn't have any teacher for a half hour. What did you do while you waited for someone to show up?"

"We sat in our seats."

Marge waited for more. When it didn't come, she asked, "You sat in your seats?"

"Correct."

"Did you talk?"

"No, we did not talk. We waited quietly. Perhaps a few of us meditated. But that is allowable as long as it is silent."

"Just sat there meditating . . . or waiting?"

"Correct."

"No talking?"

"No. No talking."

Marge put down her pencil. "Do you like it here, Vega?"

The girl's eyes registered confusion. "It is my home. Of course, I like my home."

"What do you like about it?"

"Like?"

"Yes, like. What do *you* enjoy doing?"

"I enjoy everything."

Marge paused. "You enjoy *everything?*"

"Correct." She still maintained her rigid posture.

"Do you like any one thing . . . something special?"

The girl gave the question some thought. "Our Father Jupiter was an expert at science. I suppose I like science the best."

"Science is a big category. What part of science do you like the best?"

"Perhaps particle physics — the different colors of the electromagnetic spectrum that are elicited when atoms are excited then fall back to their resting states. This week, Guru Bob is to teach us about the different family of mesons, bosons and tau mesons. I think that should be very interesting."

Marge tried not to stare with an open mouth. "Very interesting."

For the first time, the girl gave a half-smile. "So you must also like quantum physics. I see we have much in common. You would like it here, too. Perhaps you can become one of our beloved teachers."

Marge felt a sharp ping inside her chest — this little, stilted and stifled girl, trying to relate to her. It was hard to fathom that she was fourteen. When Marge had worked juvey, the teens she had pulled in were cynical and world-weary. This one was so naive, it hurt. Just a kid, begging to be liked. "I would like that, Vega, except I'm not trained as a teacher. I'm trained as a police-woman. You do know what that is, don't you?"

"Of course." She remained grave as she spoke. "You protect and maintain the outside disorder from falling into absolute chaos. But you only make temporary, remedial solutions. The out-side society is far too entropic for any permanent state of rest."

Obviously spitting back lines she had learned from her fearless leaders. But the assessment wasn't all that far off. "If we could get back to Lyra and Andromeda now?"

The girl nodded in sincerity. "Certainly. Whatever is your wish."

Marge tried not to sigh. "You said that Terra came into your classroom at around nine in the morning."

"Correct."

"And then what happened?"

"She asked where our teacher Andromeda was. Of course, no one knew. We were all con-fused."

"And then what happened?"

"She told us to go meditate with her class — with the younger children — while she sorted

206

out the confusion. We waited with our teacher Terra's class of younger children."

"Now this is very important, Vega. Do you remember if *Lyra* came with you into Terra's class?"

"No, I do not remember if Lyra came. The last time I distinctly remember seeing Lyra was at breakfast."

"Vega, did Lyra seem happy here at the Order?"

"Of course."

"So she never complained to you about the Order?"

"No, never."

"Did she ever talk to you about her grandparents?"

"I did not even know that she had living grandparents."

"Do you have living grandparents, Vega?"

"I do not know. My true family is in the Order of the Rings of God."

Marge forced herself not to pass judgment. It wouldn't help the case, and it could cause her stress. She said, "So Lyra never spoke to you about her grandparents."

"Correct."

"And you don't remember if she went with you over to Terra's class?"

"Correct. I do not remember."

"The last time you remember seeing her was at breakfast."

"At breakfast. That is correct."

"Do you have any idea where either Lyra or Andromeda might be?"

"No."

Marge looked deep in the teen's flat eyes, projecting her own emotions back through the vacant mirrors. "Vega, are you worried about Lyra? Or about Andromeda?"

The teen bit her lip. "It would be nice to locate them. I like Lyra. And I like our teacher Andromeda very much."

"Why did you like her?"

The girl's bottom lip quivered. The first hint of honest emotion. "She was very kind. And she has a very nice and wide smile. If you do not find her, I will miss her."

Slowly, a real tear rolled down her cheek. She made no attempt to wipe it away.

"She read us a book about a little prince boy once. He flew all over the galaxies and had many adventures."

"*The Little Prince*?" Marge asked. "By Saint-Exupéry?"

"Correct. That is the book."

Marge smiled. "You know, Vega, we do have much in common. I loved those stories, too. I had to read them when I was around your age in French class."

"We read them in English, but Andromeda said that maybe one day we would learn them in French."

"So she read you *The Little Prince*, huh?"

"Correct." A sigh. "They were very silly stories

and eventually Guru Pluto took the book away, saying it was too fanciful — which it was. Still . . ." Another deep sigh followed by another tear. "They were beautiful stories."

When it became clear that Lyra wasn't anywhere in the compound, Pluto called a meeting in the temple. Decker showed early, with Oliver and Marge following a few minutes later.

Oliver said, "I don't see what good a meeting's going to do."

"Agreed," Decker said. "What about talking to Lyra's mother?"

Marge said, "She doesn't talk, Loo. She rocks on her butt and babbles. I don't think she's faking either."

Oliver added, "Looks like the real labonza."

"Well then, we've exhausted our use here," Decker said. "If we think Lyra was genuinely kidnapped by her grandparents, interviewing them is the next step."

"Do we think that Lyra was kidnapped?" Marge asked.

"I don't know," Decker said.

Oliver said, "You know, it's like someone's trying to dismantle the place — first Jupiter, then a missing woman and child."

"What do the missing persons have to do with Jupiter's suicide?" Marge asked.

"I don't know if it has anything to do with it," Oliver answered. "It could be like Pluto claimed — that someone took advantage during all the confusion to kidnap the kid or the woman or both."

Decker asked, "Does anyone have the names of the grandparents?"

Marge shook her head. "Too busy interviewing adolescent girls." She sighed. "God, I feel for them. They're trapped here, living in a lifeless world of particle physics and Einsteinian relativity. Whatever happened to proms, dances and Friday night football games?"

Decker nodded, often having similar thoughts when he scrutinized his own sons' school. The boys attended classes from seven to five-thirty, and two nights a week were filled with evening lessons. The school was mixed, but the classes were single-sexed. No big surprise that a "wired" kid like Jacob would cut school to steal a quick feel. But Decker would never voice his opinion to Rina. Certain things were immutable and had to remain so if the marriage was going to survive. Rina's religious lifestyle was as programmed in her as her genes for black hair.

Oliver said, "None of the kids I talked to remember Lyra going into Terra's class. Which means she'd been missing since . . . what . . . around nine in the morning?" He turned to Decker. "When did you get the call, Loo?"

"Around twelve-thirty."

Marge asked, "About four hours and no one notices she's gone?"

Decker said, "They were focused on Andromeda, not on the kids."

"Still . . ."

"I agree," Decker said. "Something's funny."

A moment later, Guru Bob arrived with a deferential Terra in tow.

Marge said, "Hi, Terra, we meet again." She introduced the girlish woman to the others.

Guru Bob said, "Terra worked with Andromeda. I thought she could give you nice people here some insight." He urged her with a pat on the back. "Tell them if Andromeda would just pack up and leave the Order on her own."

"No, she would not!" Terra's voice was ethereal. "Never would she leave us."

Bob circled Terra, sizing her up as if she were on the witness stand. "What about Lyra? Would she leave on her own?"

"Lyra would never leave. She was a child, and unlike Andromeda, she had no resources. She was clearly taken — kidnapped."

Bob looked at Decker as if to say, "There you go."

Well, that solves everything, Bob. Decker asked, "Do you have any ideas *where* she might have been taken?"

Bob started, "She was taken by her grandparents —"

"So you've said," Decker interrupted. "You've mentioned threatening letters that the grandparents sent the Order. I'll need to see them —"

Pluto burst into the temple, charging down the aisle. "What is *she* doing here?" He pointed to Terra, stabbing her with his cold eyes. "Who did you leave in charge of the children?"

In the same ethereal voice, she said, "They are at dinner, Guru Pluto."

"And *who* is supervising dinner?"

"Brother Ansel and Brother Bear," Bob said. "With those two in charge, things will be under control."

Pluto seemed barely mollified. But he didn't add anything.

Bob said, "Terra, tell them what you told me . . . about Andromeda."

Terra talked as if programmed. "Andromeda had grave concerns about being abducted by Reuben Asnikov —"

"That monster!" Pluto spat out. "When is he going to be held accountable for his crimes?"

"We're getting to that," Bob answered. "Go on, Terra."

The young woman said, "But Andromeda was equally worried about Lyra. Her grandparents — Moriah's parents — had been writing her letters. The letters stated that they had hired Asnikov to return her to them —"

"Wait a minute, wait a minute!" Decker interrupted. "The grandparents had written letters to their grandchild?" He turned to Bob. "I thought you said they'd written threatening letters to the Order."

Bob said, "Maybe they were writing letters to everyone."

"Can someone please show me these letters?" Decker asked.

Terra said, "Lyra showed the letters to

Andromeda. Later on, Andromeda confided in me and said —"

"*Who* has the letters?" Decker interrupted.

No one spoke.

Decker asked, "I take this to mean that *no one* has them?"

"I don't have them," Bob said. "But I remember reading them. That's how I know the contents. Maybe Venus has them."

Decker tried to keep his face neutral. "How'd you get hold of these letters in the first place, Bob?"

"Jupiter showed them to me," Bob answered.

"Jupiter?" Pluto bellowed. "He *showed* you letters written to the Order?"

"Yes, he did, Pluto. Anything else I can answer easily?"

"Did Jupiter routinely go through the mail here?" Decker asked. "I take it you censor mail on a regular basis?"

"I don't *censor* anything," Pluto said.

"Well someone must *censor* it," Decker said. "This isn't a public institution. It's a private place and you have strict rules. Something's not adding up. You would never allow Lyra to read a letter from her grandparents that spells out plans for her abduction."

"It could have been hand-delivered without our knowledge," Bob said.

"Who could sneak inside and hand-deliver letters to a thirteen-year-old girl?" Decker asked. "This is crazy. For all I know, this entire kidnapping is a ruse —"

"Then why is Lyra missing?" Venus appeared in her full glory. She paused, posed then promenaded to the front of the temple wearing her festive robe. This one was more elaborate than the other — all sparkles, beads and embroidery. Like a haute couture evening gown. She stopped in front of Decker. "I've been talking to Moriah —"

"You're kidding me," Bob said.

"No, I'm not kidding," Venus said. "The woman talks —"

"She babbles. She's incoherent —"

"Coherent enough to cry for her daughter —"

"You *told* her?" Bob was aghast. "I thought we agreed —"

"I thought she may have some insight as to where the child was taken."

"And did she?"

Venus sat down in the front row of pews and smoothed out her dress. Her gaze fell on the portrait — a stern Jupiter casting his disapproving eyes over his constituents. "Unfortunately, no. We let the poor woman down."

"You shouldn't have told her," Bob stated. "By the way, has anyone seen Nova? I can't seem to find him."

Absent looks all around.

"You know, I'm getting a really weird feeling about this." Bob looked at Decker. "You show up and suddenly people start disappearing."

Pluto smiled meanly. "Well stated, Guru Bob."

Bob turned to Terra. "Go find Brother Nova."

She looked scared. "Me?"

"Yes, you," Bob insisted. "Last I checked, you have eyes and legs. Go find him now!"

The young woman ran off, the hem of her white robe dragging on the ground.

To Decker, Bob said, "You have two missing persons, both associated with Asnikov —"

"I beg your pardon," Decker said. "We have *nothing* to tie Asnikov to the missing persons. For all I know, Andromeda and Lyra could have run off together. If you expect *me* to go after Asnikov, get me something concrete."

"Why can't you question him?! What's the holdup?"

Decker gave Bob a slow burn. "Let's get something clear, sir. I am running this investigation. And just like the Order, I have an established procedure. You want to help your own cause, find me those letters."

"What letters?" Venus asked.

"The ones that Lyra's grandparents wrote to the Order, threatening to file suit against us," Pluto said. "Do you have them?"

"I don't have them," Venus said. "I don't even remember *seeing* them."

Decker asked, "Where would Jupiter have kept his important files?"

Venus said, "I don't recall any files — his or otherwise."

Decker asked, "Hey, what about that chicken ranch? Could he have kept files there?"

Pluto and Bob exchanged quick looks, but said nothing.

Decker asked, "Mind if we look around out there?"

Bob asked, "How'd you know about the chicken ranch?"

Because Webster told me about it, that's how. Decker ignored the question. "Any objection to us poking around? For all you know, Andromeda may be hiding out there with Lyra."

Pluto said, "Absurd! She doesn't even know of its existence."

"I know it exists," Decker said. "Maybe you don't keep secrets as well as you think. Can I go out there and look around? Yes or no?"

"For what purpose?" Pluto asked.

"To find these letters," Decker said. "How about this, Pluto. Take Detectives Oliver and Dunn out there with you. If we find the letters, we'll have something concrete —"

"I don't see why Jupiter would keep files out there," Pluto said. "I'm against it . . . strangers poking around our business." He looked at Bob.

The lanky man said, "Don't matter to me."

Venus said, "The kitchen is getting low on supplies. One of us needs to go out there anyway —"

"I'll do it." Pluto threw a distasteful look toward Marge and Oliver. "Get the inevitable over with."

Bob smirked. "Yeah, you do have a way with Benton."

"Who's Benton?" Decker asked.

"A good man," Pluto answered. "Let's get this fiasco over with."

Decker said, "I've done everything I can do here. It's time to hit the pavement. I'll need the names of the grandparents. And I'll need a good photograph of both Andromeda and Lyra."

Venus took out a snapshot from her dress. "Funny you should ask. Moriah just gave me this."

It was a black-and-white snapshot of a girl with that preteen crooked smile — big upper and lower incisors followed by spaces and gaps where adult teeth should be. The girl in the picture must have been around ten or eleven. She had big, dark eyes, a broad nose, pronounced cheekbones and thickish lips. Her hair was pulled back into a ponytail. She had a wide forehead and arched eyebrows. Adorable.

"Is she black?" Decker asked.

"Half-black," Pluto answered. "Her father was black."

"So these grandparents . . . Moriah's folks . . . they're white?"

"Moriah's white," Venus said. "Stands to reason her parents are."

"So if Lyra's in the neighborhood, she's going to be noticed. What are their names and address?"

"Their names are Herbert and Cecile Farrander," Bob said. "I've got the address written down in my cell. As far as a photograph of Andromeda, Terra can probably dig one up . . ."

Decker hit the photograph with the back of his hand. "This is a start." He turned to Pluto. "When can you take them out to the ranch?"

Pluto said, "I usually lead the fold in evening meditation." He checked his watch. "We're going to get a very late start."

Giving someone a jump-start and a chance to rifle the files. Not a chance. "Can't Bob lead the prayers?" Decker asked.

"It's not my job," Bob answered.

"So let someone else fill in," Decker said. "The ranch is what — about an hour . . . hour and a half away? If you start out now, you can probably make it back before ten. When's your prayer session?"

"Ten-thirty."

"Then let's hustle," Marge said.

Pluto growled, "You're not leaving me any choice."

Decker said, "You're catching on."

Marge swung her purse over her shoulder. "Call you when we get back?" she asked Decker.

"Absolutely," Decker said.

Venus asked, "And we'll be hearing from you if there's good news?"

Decker said, "Madam, you'll be hearing from me no matter what."

16

Beyond Pasadena and the Rose Parade, beyond Southwest University of Technology lay the dowager city of Santa Martina — an old-moneyed town of towering magnolias, canopied sycamores, manicured emerald lawns and two-storied manses. Wide, shaded streets quiet enough to host a stickball game *if* the neighborhood had had any children. Instead, it served golf-playing grandparents who took lunch at the club, garbed in brightly colored polo shirts and pressed white trousers. The home of the Republican Party, Episcopal churches, martinis before dinner and cardigan sweaters. The enclave might have been considered exclusive except that bad topology had condemned it to a smog-laden basin choked with ozones during the summer months. But that was okay with the residents. Hot weather meant donning cruise wear and sailing for cleaner pastures.

Farrander's address put Decker in front of a putty-colored hacienda set back on a rolling hill of kelly green. Two forty-foot weeping willows framed the house, and the front plantings included coral, red and white azaleas so resplendent with blooms as to be gaudy. He parked curbside, walked down a flagstone pathway up to an arched and recessed doorway. He rang the bell; deep chimes emanated from inside the house. A bubble-coiffed blond woman in her late sixties or early seventies answered the door without asking who it was. She had a wide face with ironed skin that had been stretched over pronounced cheekbones, and ultra-thin lips painted rose-colored. Her brown eyes were rimmed with lifted bags. Her neck was the dead giveaway of her age; it held wattles set into cracks and creases. She wore knitted beige pants and a white cable-knit sweater. Her sockless feet were housed in brown leather loafers.

"Yes?"

"Cecile Farrander?" Decker asked.

"Yes. That's me."

Decker took out his identification billfold. "Lieutenant Peter Decker from the Los Angeles Police Department. May I talk to you for a minute?"

She checked her watch, although she didn't act as if she were in a hurry.

"Are you in the middle of something?" Decker asked. "I could come back."

"What is this about?"

"It concerns your granddaughter."

Her mouth made an O shape. "Which one?"

"Lyra."

A blank stare.

"Lyra . . . Moriah's daughter . . ."

Another vacant look.

"Moriah?" Decker repeated.

"Mori . . ." The lightbulb went off. "Oh, you mean Maureen." She blushed from embarrassment. "Is she all right?"

"She's fine," Decker said. "Actually, I'd like to talk to you about your granddaughter. May I come in?"

But the woman was tentative. "My husband isn't home right now . . . maybe I shouldn't be saying that. You could be anyone. He always says I'm very naive."

"I could come back," Decker said. "When would be convenient?"

"How about Wednesday?"

"Today is Wednesday."

"I meant Wednesday of next week."

Putting off her grandchild's welfare for seven days. She certainly didn't appear like the obsessive, letter-writing, suit-threatening relative that the Order had made her out to be. Decker tapped his foot, trying to figure out his next step. From inside, he could make out the slow ticks of a grandfather clock. "It would be better if we talked sooner."

Again, the O-shaped mouth. "Well, all right. Come in." She hesitated. "Maybe I should look at that billfold again?"

Decker handed it to her. She studied it at extended–arm's distance. "Well, you certainly look like the man in the picture." She nodded. "A bit grayer."

Decker smiled. "That's true."

"When was this picture taken?"

If she had anxiety about Lyra, she was hiding it very well. "About two years ago."

She looked at the picture, then scrutinized Decker. "A hard two years, Lieutenant?"

"I've paid my dues," Decker said. "May I come in?"

Finally, she stepped aside.

Decker walked into a two-story entry hall, which housed the audible grandfather clock, then entered a living room filled with light and accumulated dust. Tall multipaned windows, clouded with particles, had been cut into the textured stuccoed walls, providing Decker with a view from wherever he looked. Through the grime, he could make out the backyard — a parklike area of green bleeding into a copse of thickly planted specimen trees. The floors of the room had been constructed from thick oak planks stained coffee brown. The furniture must have been decades old — overstuffed couches and chairs upholstered in a faded pattern of green-leafed red roses weaving through a white trellis. The coffee and end tables — made from glass set into walnut frames — held year-old magazines and out-of-print art books.

"You can sit anywhere," the woman said.

Decker chose one side of the couch, Cecile chose the other. He said, "Thank you for seeing me on such short notice, Mrs. Farrander. I wouldn't impose except I do think this is important —"

"You can call me Ceese."

Decker paused. "Okay." He took out his notebook. "This concerns Lyra . . . your granddaughter."

The woman clasped her hands and remained silent, waiting for him to continue.

"She's missing," Decker said.

No response.

Decker asked, "Does that concern you?"

"Well, I don't know if it does," Ceese said. "I've never met Lyra. I haven't talked to Maureen in years."

"Do you know where your daughter and granddaughter have been living?"

"Oh, yes," Ceese responded. "In some hippie community in the West San Fernando Valley." A sigh. "She has been there for a while, hasn't she?"

"Around nine years."

"I'm glad she's found some stability." A pause. "Has she had any more children?"

"Uh, no, I don't think so."

"So the little black girl . . . that's the only one?"

"Lyra, yes. I believe so —"

"And it's this little black girl who's missing?"

"Yes. Her name is Lyra. Any idea where she might be?"

"Me?" She shook her head. Her sprayed-stiff hair didn't move with the motion. "Why would I have any idea?"

Decker cleared his throat. "You haven't written to the commune asking for Lyra's custody?"

Ceese looked shocked. "Now *why* would I do that?"

Why indeed. Decker said, "For starters, she is your granddaughter."

Ceese stared at him. "Lieutenant, do you have children?"

"Yes."

"More than one child?"

"Yes."

"Then you know how children can vary."

"Of course."

"I've raised three daughters, Lieutenant. Mo was the youngest. From the day she was born, I couldn't control her. She was collicky, irritable, a raw bundle of random energy. As she grew older, she just grew worse — obstinate and sassy. She smoked, drank, she engaged in promiscuous behavior with black boys. She took drugs which ruined her brain. She turned very strange. Even so, I didn't abandon her, Lieutenant. I tried! I really *tried!*"

Her face became animated with determination.

"I enrolled her in drug rehab, not once but *twice!*" Holding up two fingers. "Twice! How did she react to my acts of kindness? By escaping responsibility, by calling up her father and me and screaming obscenities. *Then,* after all that, she had the nerve to show up here — at the house — asking for money, holding this little black baby in an obvious play for sympathy. Well, she got nothing. She was filthy . . . smelled like garbage. I

224

wouldn't let her in the house!"

Ceese made a face.

"When that hippie commune took her in, I was grateful even though my husband and I knew it was nothing but a scam to get her money —"

"Maureen has money?"

"She *had* money. I'm sure the hippie commune's got it all now. Thank God my father's dead. It would have killed him if he knew what had happened to the trust fund he gave her."

"Maureen had a trust fund?"

"Yes, she did."

"Can I ask how much?"

"A lot. At one time it was over a hundred thousand dollars. I'm sure she spent most of it on drugs. But I bet there was a *little* left over for that hippie commune. Why else would they take her in? Those cults only want money so their leaders can buy Rolls-Royces."

Decker rubbed his eyes. "So you haven't been in contact with Maureen, Mrs. Farrander?"

"Ceese, please! And no, I haven't been in contact with her. Neither with her nor with her child."

The door opened. A stocky, elderly man shuffled into the room. He had stooped shoulders and a bent spine — probably Herbert Farrander. He had a bald pate that was ringed with gray. He wore a white polo shirt and blue serge pants. He regarded Decker with watery, smog-soaked eyes.

Ceese stood up. "Herbert, this is Lieutenant Decker from LAPD —"

"LAPD?" Herbert's voice was shaky. "What's LAPD doing out here?"

"It's in regard to your daughter, Mo—"

"Her?" Herbert made a face and waved Decker off. "I don't even want to know." He turned to his wife. "You want to go out with the Harringtons for dinner?"

"Where?" Ceese asked. "At the club?"

"They were thinking about the Grillway."

"The Grillway sounds nice for a change."

Herbert regarded Decker. "Are you still here?"

"Herbert!" Ceese chastised. "Be polite."

"Not when it comes to Maureen." He plopped down into one of the armchairs. "What'd she do?"

Decker ran his tongue against his cheek. "She didn't do anything. Her daughter is missing. Your granddaughter —"

"That black baby isn't any relative of mine," Herbert pronounced. "Not that I wish her any harm. Just don't get me involved."

"Still, I'd like to ask you a few questions."

"I suppose you would," Herbert said. "Ceese, how 'bout a gin and tonic?" He faced Decker. "And for you, sir?"

"I'm fine —"

"How about a beer? You look like a beer drinker."

Decker resisted the temptation to size up his gut. It was flat . . . relatively. At least his pants were still the same size . . . although he had let his

226

belt out a notch or two.

"No, I really am fine. I'd just like to ask a few questions about your daughter —"

"Oh, go ahead!"

Herbert was annoyed. Probably, he was annoyed whenever he didn't have a drink in his hand.

Decker asked, "Have you written to her since she's taken up residence in the Order of the Rings of God?"

"I haven't. Ceese hasn't. The lawyer has. She kept asking for more money . . . from her trust fund. Ceese tell you about the trust fund?"

"The one set up by your father in-law —"

"He was trying to avoid inheritance tax for the grandchildren. Well-meaning idea, but it backfired. Left behind a lot of lazy grandchildren."

"Here you go," Ceese said, handing him his gin and tonic. "Are you speaking ill of the dead?"

"Just expounding on the evils of inherited money." He sipped his drink. "Me? I worked for every penny I ever owned. If Mo had done the same, she wouldn't have been in the straits she's in now. Not that I'm unsympathetic to the plight of the mentally ill. Didn't we attend that dinner for Orlando Hospital?"

"That we did —"

"Some people have problems . . . big problems. But you have to knuckle down and work. Maureen? She never knew the meaning of work."

Decker asked, "So you never tried to contact

her at the Order regarding her daughter, Lyra?"

"No," Herbert answered. "Never."

Decker was suddenly tired. "The Order said you've been writing threatening letters —"

"What?" Herbert took another sip, then a gulp. "That's an outrage! Untrue! That Jupiter fellow has it all mixed up."

"Herbert, didn't you read the papers a few days ago? That Jupiter fellow died —"

"No!"

"Honest to goodness —"

"I don't believe it! How old was he?"

"In his early seventies —"

"A young man —"

Decker broke in. "Sir, what did Jupiter have all mixed up in regards to threatening letters?"

Herbert thought a moment. "*We* never wrote any letters. The estate lawyer — what's his name, Ceese?"

"Anthony Ballard."

"That's right. Anthony Ballard. *He* wrote to the Order. They kept trying to get hold of Maureen's money, threatening the trustees. Which didn't hold water because my father-in-law was smart enough to put spendthrift clauses into his grandchildren's trusts. Ballard got mad and wrote them up a *cease and desist* letter. It shut 'em up. The cult couldn't touch the trust money, but it still managed to raid Maureen's bank account. Which wasn't insignificant."

"About how much in her account?"

"Twenty, thirty grand."

"So Maureen's flat broke now?"

"No, she still has her fund. She just can't get her hands on the money unless she proves herself to be competent mentally. Which so far hasn't been the case."

"If Maureen would suddenly die, who'd get the money?"

"It should revert back to her siblings." Herbert pointed a finger. "But now that she has this daughter, the girl could make a legal claim. Not that it's any concern of mine. Let the vultures fight over it. I'm content with what I have."

"How much is left in her fund?"

"I suppose around fifty, sixty grand." He turned to his wife and held out an empty glass. "How about one more?"

"You should be getting ready for dinner."

"One more."

"You're a terror!" But Ceese took the tumbler anyway.

Decker asked, "So you haven't been contacting the Order, threatening to take Lyra away from them?"

"How many times do you want me to answer the same question?" Herbert protested. "The answer is no." He took the refilled glass from his wife and turned to Decker. "Sure you don't want a beer?"

"Positive." Decker stood up, suppressing anger at the two of them that perhaps wasn't justified. Cold, smug and distant, the Farranders were a parental nightmare. Still, Maureen must have put them through hell. "Thanks for your help."

Ceese said, "I do hope you find Lydia."

"Lyra," Decker corrected.

"How old is she now?"

"Thirteen. Would you like to see a picture of her?"

Ceese knitted her brow. "Well, all right."

Decker showed her the black-and-white snapshot. Ceese glanced at it, tried to look away, but the expression held the old woman's gaze. She sighed. "Oh, dear. I'm getting a little misty." She averted her eyes. "Thirteen's a difficult age. Maybe she ran away. Have you considered that?"

"Yes, ma'am —"

"Ceese!" She wagged a finger at him. "I'm not that old."

Herbert began to chortle, his face turning deep purple. "Depends on who you're looking at."

"You're awful!" Ceese said. "I'm getting dressed." She turned to Decker, her eyes still watery. "You can see yourself out?"

"No problem."

Herbert hoisted himself from the chair. "Better start sprucing up." He stopped, coughed up something into a handkerchief. Then he faced Decker. "If you see Maureen, tell her . . . tell her, *if* she calls, I won't hang up."

Slowly he trudged toward the staircase, climbing each riser with the effort of an old man.

17

Beyond the edges of the Order's compound, beyond the last remnants of urban life, lay stretches of open Southern California land. The eastern landscape should have been scrub as far as the eye could see, but the recent rains had turned the area lush with brush and wildflowers. The gnarled trunks of the oak trees had greened with moss, and soaring eucalyptus trees were covered with white, papery blossoms. As the sun fell low in the sky, Marge's eyelids grew heavy. The ride was long and monotonous. With Pluto in the backseat, she and Oliver couldn't discuss the case, which would have galvanized her mind, keeping her alert. Rather than succumb to slumber, she opened the thermos of leaded coffee.

"I'll take some of that." Oliver spoke over the hum of the engine.

"Are you tired?" Marge handed him the thermos. "I can drive."

"No, thanks. I'm fine." Oliver swigged coffee and cocked his head toward his shoulder. "At least, he's out."

Marge regarded Pluto. The little man's eyes were closed, his mouth was open, and his chest was moving up and down in rhythmic pattern.

Oliver kept his voice low because people often heard things in their sleep. "I'm also hungry. Think we can grab a quick dinner after we're done?"

"If it doesn't take too long."

"When does Deck want to meet with us?"

"We're supposed to call him when we're done," Marge said. "I figure around ten or eleven. I'm not expecting to find much in the way of letters. But you never know." She tapped the steering wheel. "I've got some tickets to a concert Friday night — Mozart. Nothing too heavy. Want to come?"

"What about James?"

"The ER's shorthanded this week. He's picking up the slack."

Oliver said, "I've got a blind date."

"A *blind* date —"

"Shhhh!"

Marge dropped her voice. "Sorry."

"It's not *totally* blind!" Oliver qualified. "I saw a picture of her . . . good-looking girl."

"Don't tell me — blond, blue eyes, big tits —"

"Three for three —"

"Around fifteen years old, Scotty?"

"Twenty if she's a day —"

"Probably stunted in the cerebral cortex —"

"Don't doubt it. Why else would a cute girl date a guy old enough to be a patriarch —"

"You're not that old —"

"Frankly, I don't care if she's blank between her ears. You don't fuck a brain."

232

"Then you wonder why you can't sustain a relationship."

"Well, you're not winning any medals in that department."

"I beg your pardon! I've been with James for nearly six months."

"La-dee-dah. Tell me where to send the anniversary present."

Marge smiled while regarding her partner. Objectively, Oliver was a good-looking guy, with a head full of black hair, strong bone structure and intense dark eyes. He didn't hold a whit of attraction for her — she knew him too well — but she could definitely understand how he got women.

Oliver smirked. "Maybe she's premed."

"And I'm the next supermodel, Scotty."

Oliver glanced at her. "You know, Margie, you really sell yourself short."

Marge's first instinct was to buck. Instead, she held back. "Was that a compliment?"

"I think it was."

"Well then, thanks . . . I think." Marge was whispering. "What are we actually looking for? Letters? Secret files?"

Oliver shrugged ignorance. "I think Deck wants us to make sure that Andromeda and the kid aren't hiding up there."

"Why would they hide up there?"

"Beats me. But I know Deck just wants everything buttoned up and shut tight. Right now, the ranch is a question mark. He wants to rule it out."

Marge looked out the side window. Night had blanketed the hilly landscape. All that remained were shadows and inkspots. "How much longer?"

"Why? You have to use the potty?"

"Just answer the question?"

"Around a half hour."

"Thank you."

Silence.

Oliver turned on the radio. "You like country?"

"Probably all we can pick up around these parts."

"I like country." He adjusted the dial until he found Shania Twain belting out a torch song about long-lost love. "Ever see this girl? She's a real piece. She and the Dixie Chicks. Man, those gals are hot babes."

"The Dixie Chicks?"

"I'm not making it up."

"The Dixie Chicks," Marge repeated. "Used to be an insult to call a woman a chick. Whatever happened to feminism?"

"Look at it this way, Marge," Oliver said. "Dixie Chicks is a much better band name than the Hairy Armpits."

She glared at him. "Did I just invite you out?"

"You did."

"Momentary lapse of insanity."

"Or sanity. I'm what keeps you going. Let's face it, Dunn. Any guy you date looks better than me."

With no city lights to keep the sky aglow, the

place was as dark as pitch. Straining to find the turnoff, Oliver kept the car at low speed, kicking up clouds of dust from the unpaved pockmarked roadway.

He muttered, "Someone should've told me that I'd need a four-wheel drive."

Pluto said, "You should have thought of that before your boss dragged me out here. Exactly *what* is the purpose of this trip?"

"Lieutenant Decker wants to locate those threatening letters." Marge added under her breath, "*If* they ever existed."

"Why would we make them up?" Pluto asked.

"So you'd have someone to blame for Andromeda's absence."

Pluto tightened. "Andromeda wasn't a prisoner. If she wanted to leave, she could have done so. Need I remind you that *Lyra* is also missing. Why would a little girl leave on her own?"

Marge had no answer.

Pluto said, "I'm worried sick about the both of them . . . that Asnikov really crossed the line on this one. If Andromeda got in the way . . . well, let's just say that people like Asnikov get nasty when crossed." The little man's eyes studied the darkness. "You'll need to slow down. The driveway's hard to see. We're almost there. Over to the left just beyond that stunted oak tree. There!"

Oliver reduced his speed even further. The only thing he saw was a narrow pitted rut. He turned the wheel sharply, and the car plowed through a cover of loose feathers. "Jesus!"

"Keep going —"

"How much longer?"

"About twenty more feet. You can park there."

Oliver crawled forward to the designated spot, stopped, then killed the motor. The cackles of fowl could be heard even with the win-dows closed. He opened the door and stepped into piles of dirty plumage. It smelled like shit and dust. "Man, they're loud. Do they ever sleep?"

"The artificial lighting keeps them going. It promotes egg laying." Pluto wiped dust from his black T-shirt and jeans. For the dirty assign-ment, he had taken off his purple vest and the blue robe he normally wore. "We turn off the lights around twelve. Then they quiet down."

Marge came out of the car and made a face. "How can you sleep with that noise? Don't the neighbors complain?"

"What neighbors?" Pluto started fast walking toward a dark shadow. "Let's get this nonsense over with."

Oliver had to march to keep up with him. His newly polished black Oxfords were dusted with grime. They looked muddy brown. "How long has the Order owned this place?"

"Around eight years."

"Long time. Is it profitable?"

"Profit is immaterial. It provides the Order with a source of food, which means indepen-dence from the violators of the outside world."

"You have someone who maintains and guards it?" Marge asked. "To make sure that no one steals the chickens?"

"I've already answered that. A farmhand named Benton lives on the premises."

"Ah, yes," Oliver said. "Good old Benton. Is he a member of the Order?"

Abruptly, Pluto stopped walking. "A charity case. Not unlike Moriah. He's a decent watch-dog and he doesn't mind shoveling bird shit."

Oliver asked, "Is this guy crazy?"

Pluto broke into a slow grin. "He isn't Norman Bates, if that's what you're thinking."

"Oh, that's reassuring —"

"He's very dedicated to Father Jupiter. We haven't told him the news." Pluto picked up his pace. "Someone'll have to break it to him. It will be quite a shock to his psyche. But tonight's not the night. Not with you around."

Marge asked, "How often do you come out here?"

"Someone from the Order comes up once or twice a week — to collect the eggs and do a chicken count."

Marge used long strides to keep up with the little man. "Which of you come up here? You? Bob —"

"Both of us . . . Nova and Venus as well. And of course, Jupiter. He used to come up as often as he could. He said the long ride served as medita-tion time for spiritual enlightenment. Eased his tired mind —"

"And his headaches?"

Pluto stopped walking. "*What* headaches?"

Marge waited a few moments. "Venus said Jupiter used to have these headaches. He'd hear voices . . . voices that spoke to him. It made him weary."

Pluto clenched his fists, but said nothing.

Oliver asked, "First you've heard of it?"

No answer. "This way," Pluto said softly. He stopped in front of a broken-down, one-story structure and swung open a squeaky screen door. He tried the door. When he found it to be locked, he took out a ring of keys.

"Where's Benton?" Oliver asked.

"Probably out slaughtering some chickens. I told him I needed around three dozen." Pluto's eyes bore into Oliver's. "You can watch, Detective, if you'd like."

Scott took the bait. "I'll do even better. I'll shoot the suckers in the head for you."

Marge said, "Not a good use of your service revolver, Detective."

"You spoil all my fun," Oliver answered.

Pluto kept monkeying with the bolt. "For some reason my key is jamming."

Marge assessed the house as the guru played with the lock. Even in the dark, she could tell it was in disrepair. The clapboard siding was a mass of peeling paint like a giant reptile in various stages of molting. The wooden planks of the wraparound porch were splintered and, in a few places, had broken through. Finally, she heard the bolt click.

"Water must have rusted it. I'll have to tell

Benton to oil it." Pluto opened a creaky screen door. "Here you go." He pushed the door forward. "Help yourself. Watch out for spiders and scorpions. And don't pet the rats. They bite."

Marge kept her voice flat. "Is there a light switch somewhere?"

Pluto stuck his hand through the door frame and turned on the light. "I'm going to see about the chickens."

"I'll come with you," Oliver said.

Pluto said, "I don't know if Benton would like that."

Oliver turned hard. "It was a statement, sir, not a request."

Pluto shrugged. "Watch your suit jacket, Detective. Blood is notoriously hard to clean out."

The little man took off, but Oliver dogged his heels. Someone had to watch Pluto, so Scott had given *her* the job of searching around a rat-filled, insect-laden, broken-down hovel.

It was the preferable of the two assignments.

Thousands of stars salted the sky, but it did little to enhance the terrain. The topology was as flat as stale beer. In the distance, Oliver could make out a few stunted shadows casting ghoulish figures on the hard-packed ground — probably century-old, disfigured oaks. The air smelled like overripe produce. As he neared the bunkerlike coops, the squawking turned to shrieks of terror — panicked cries on a sinking ship. Oliver knew his imagination was working overtime, but the cackling was *loud*. It blotted out the sound of the gravel crunching beneath his feet.

The chickens were housed in thirty-five hundred feet of wood-planked bungalows. Jaundiced light gave the hay roof an eerie, postnuclear glow, and shot out beams from the knots in the wood. Amid the cackling, a high-pitched screech stabbed Oliver's ears. It made his heart jump involuntarily. He found his hand patting down the butt of his gun from under his jacket. Pluto seemed unfazed.

"Benton?" he yelled out.

No answered.

"This way."

He motioned Oliver around the structure, to the back of the coops. The odor was more pronounced: a stench — metallic and fecal. The outdoor area was dimly lit by two kerosene lamps. Scattered on the ground were wire cages of clattering hens protesting like inmates. Oliver had to sidestep around them. A metal stake had been driven into the surface like a tetherball pole. Tied to it was an industrial battery pack flashlight, which illuminated the scarred, flat surface of a three-foot-high tree stump. Across the top of the stump was the stretched neck of a bound hen, its dirty wings flapping spasmotically, its legs kicking helplessly. Desperately trying to break loose from a lost cause.

Beside the stump was a stump of a man — not exceptionally tall but built like a fireplug. His square, hairless head sat on a blocky neck. He had a wide, protruding forehead. Dark, dull eyes were inset in a sunken trough of skull. The orbs landed on Oliver's face for just a moment, before returning their focus to the ground. One beefy hand was squeezed around the neck of an upside-down, headless chicken, its legs frantically striking at air because the motor impulses hadn't died with the bird. The man's other hand held the bloodied ax.

He didn't look up. He spoke over the din of the clacking chickens. "Welcome, Brother Pluto."

"It's good to see you, Benton."

The plug's eyes remained on his feet. Gunboat-sized shoes. His sausage-shaped fingers loosened their grasp around the chicken's neck. Blood poured out of the newly opened aperture and splashed into a waiting bucket. Benton threw the corpse into a large, metal tub. "I'm not done yet."

"That's fine, Benton, we made good time." Pluto relieved him of the ax and walked over to the chopping block. Lifting the hatchet, he slammed down the metal edge across the wooden surface and severed the tethered chicken's neck. As blood spurted out, Oliver did a little two-step backward, his eyes still on the chopping block. Slowly, he looked up at Pluto.

Leaving the ax in the tree stump, the little man said, "Her squawking was giving me a headache."

Though shaken, Oliver kept his voice even.

"Yeah, it was pretty loud."

Pluto regarded Oliver. "Sorry. I should have warned you. Did you catch any spray?"

"No, I jumped back in time."

"Good." Pluto walked over to the tub and looked down. "How many birds do we have, Benton? Around twenty?"

"Eighteen. But I ain't even defeathered and gut 'em yet."

"That's all right. I'm not in a hurry. I'll take around three dozen back with me —"

"Not in my car, you won't," Oliver blurted out.

Benton's eyes lifted from the ground to Oliver's face. His eyes narrowed. Oliver met the stare dead on, but he was disconcerted. Again, he felt his hand patting his gun underneath his jacket.

"I'm not coming back with you, Detective," Pluto said. "You do what you have to do. I'm going to help Benton finish up with the chickens. I'll take the truck back if that's okay with you, Benton."

"You shouldn't dirty up your hands with the slaughterin', Brother Pluto," Benton said. "You're a clean man. Dirtyin's my job."

Pluto gave him a pat on his solid shoulders. "How about if I pack up the eggs? Would that make you feel better?"

"It's dirty in the coops, too." The square man untied the dead chicken from the block. He threw the disconnected head in a plastic bucket, then once again drained the body of its blood by holding it upside down. "I hate for a godly man like you to be walkin' in feathers and chickenshit. House ain't much better. I'da cleaned it more if I'da knew you was coming."

"Shit is good for the soul, Benton," Pluto philosophized. "It brings us back to the ground. Back to Mother Earth."

The farmhand looked confused. "If you say so, then it must be true." A pause. "When is Father Jupiter comin'?"

Pluto hesitated. "Father Jupiter hasn't been feeling well."

Benton's lower lip jutted out. "Did I make him mad?"

Pluto smiled kindly. "Oh no, Benton, not at all. He's just been tired. He needs rest."

Well, he's getting plenty of that, Oliver thought.

"You ain't lyin'?" Benton asked.

"No, I'm not lying."

"I thunk that mebbe I did somethin' wrong."

"Not at all —"

" 'Cause he ain't been out here in a couple of weeks."

"Father Jupiter has been very tired —"

"He likes comin' out here."

"Yes, he does —"

"He sits over there." Benton pointed out to some unknown place in the dark. "He does his lookin' there. You know, with that telerscope. Sometimes he lets me look through it. You see stuff up close . . . stuff you cain't see with just

243

your eyes in your head."

"I know. Interesting, isn't it?" With a single pull, Pluto liberated the ax from the tree stump and handed it back to the farmhand. "I won't keep you from your work."

Benton nodded, opened the cage and pulled out a clattering bird. The hen pecked at Benton's calloused skin. If he felt anything, he didn't show it. "This one's real fat. Get a lot of stew from her."

"That's good because we have lots of mouths to feed —"

"Yo, Oliver!" Marge was screaming to be heard over the chickens. "Scott, can you hear me?"

Oliver shouted back, "I hear you —"

"Where are you?"

"Behind the chicken coops —"

"Come over to the house!" Marge yelled at full voice. "I think we've got a problem."

18

Except now that Lyra is growing into a young lady, someone's been making noises . . .

It sure wasn't the Farranders.

By seven, Decker pulled into his driveway.

Either the missing letters were pure invention or someone else wanted Lyra. But who else did she have? An unknown father, no siblings to speak of, apathetic and dismissive grandparents . . . something wasn't adding up.

He shut the motor and got out of his unmarked.

It would have been nice to take a hot shower, eat, then crawl into bed. Instead, Decker had to be Dad. Not the Emil Euler Ganz kind of dad — unfettered, egotistical, bombastic and irresponsible. And not the Herbert Farrander type of dad, who wrote off his daughter as if she were a bad debt. No, he had to be a *good* dad, the TV dad — understanding, wise, stern, cheerful, childlike without being childish. And he had to act these roles even though his mind was on a stolen child, along with a missing girl not much older than his teenaged sons and a bit younger than his own daughter, and hundreds of men, women and children whose lives were determined by a few unbalanced individuals as solid as holograms.

At the door, Rina greeted him with Hannah and the newspaper. She kissed his cheek. "Glad you made it home. How are you?"

"Beat." He held the folded paper up. "What's with this?"

"Look on page fourteen."

"What's on page fourteen?" Somehow, Hannah had climbed onto his back and was hanging from his neck like a spider monkey.

"Editorial section," she said. "Yesterday there was an op-ed piece about Great Ganzby, the scientist. Today, it's clear he isn't being mourned by everyone if the letters to the editor are to be believed. Hannah, you're choking him."

Decker brought the little girl around into his arms. She wrapped her thin legs around his waist. "My daddeeeee. I love my daddeeeee!"

"I love my Hannah Roseeeee!" He flipped through the newsprint as best he could, trying to find page fourteen. Hannah hit the paper with a closed fist, ripping a page in two. "Hannah!" Decker barked with irritation.

Instantly, the girl reached out her hands to Rina who took her. "Let's let Daddy change his clothes first."

"Thank you." Decker picked up the broken paper and headed for the shower.

There were three letters, one mild in its condemnation, the second medium hot while the last one was scathing:

Epistle number one:

At one time, Emil Euler Ganz may have been a luminary of the scientific community of cosmology. But that time has long past, and it was a man called Jupiter who died. That man was nothing but a two-bit sideshow con who bilked suckers out of money, and spewed out watered-down pseudoscientific drivel. From an informal poll taken by my colleagues, I assure you that the Guru Ganz will not be missed.

Dr. Kevin Doss, Ph.D.
UCSD Department of Physics
San Diego, California

The second letter:

I don't know why society finds it necessary to praise men and women simply because they had talent, even remarkable talent. A case in point being the death of con man Jupiter aka Dr. Emil Euler Ganz. Yes, the man *might* have been brilliant, but so what? He was a scamster who kidnapped unsuspecting children and wrecked many lives. I should know. Our lovely but naive daughter was taken into his cult — the Order of the Rings of God — over two years ago. No matter how many times we have reached out to her, our overtures have gone unanswered, and our letters have been returned. This is the most painful point as I don't know if she's even getting our

247

communications. And every time I've tried to see her, a door has been shut in my face. A long time ago, Ganz may have done something for humanity, but the man who died was anything but human.

Emily White
Brentwood, California

Number three:

Emil Euler Ganz was the ultimate con man who had honed his skills years before becoming Father Jupiter. A mediocre physicist himself, Ganz was smart enough to surround himself with brilliance, and crafty enough to exploit the talent around him. He was a pirate, a plagiarizer, a thief, a kidnapper and an adulterer, and I can document every single one of those accusations. I'm not surprised that he disappeared for ten years. He wasn't seeking spirituality. He was probably on the run from some irate husband who just got tired of Ganz messing with his wife. My wish for Jupiter is to be sucked into a black hole and come out the other side as shredded cabbage. Good riddance to bad rubbish.

Dr. Robert Russo, Sr.
Russo Holistic Supplements
Lancaster, California

Decker folded the paper and put it in his brief-case. Europa hadn't being lying: her father had made enemies. The last note was especially ven-omous. But it was the second letter that in-trigued him. The woman spoke of unanswered and returned mail. If the Order had received let-ters concerning Lyra, why weren't they sent back unopened? Who determined which letters were opened and which were returned?

Stepping into the shower, Decker took a deep breath and tried to turn it off. He washed away grime and tension with hot, burning needles. By the time he came out, his skin was pink and his head was pounding from the heat. He did some arm circles and stretches to loosen his stiff back. The exercise helped the tightness but did little to mitigate the knot in his stomach.

Maybe he needed food.

By the time Decker made it to the dinner table, he felt battle-scarred. To his surprise, the boys were seated at their usual places. Jacob was staring at his hands — Mr. Lothario.

Ah, yes, there was *that* to deal with.

Decker asked, "Where's Hannah?"

Rina said, "I fed her an hour ago. She's drawing pictures in her room. Maybe we can have a nice quiet meal . . . for once."

Decker asked, "You waited for me to eat dinner?"

"The boys wanted to wait."

He regarded his sons. "Thank you."

"You're welcome," Sammy answered. "How was your day?"

"Fine . . . busy." Decker looked at Jacob. The boy had his eyes glued on his food. Rina had made turkey breast with stuffing. It smelled and looked delicious. But truthfully, Decker was so hungry, he would have wolfed down gruel. Still, he remembered his manners and his religion. After the ritual washing and breaking bread, he dug in and chomped on a slab of white meat. "It's wonderful. I'm starved."

"Great, Eema," Sammy said.

"Very good," Jacob agreed.

"Thanks." Rina smiled. "Isn't this nice?"

For as long as it lasted, Decker thought it was very nice.

No one spoke for a few minutes, the table occupied by chewing, drinking and swallowing.

Very quiet.

Rina took a stab at conversation. "The Israel Philharmonic is in town. I thought I might get some tickets."

"Sounds great," Decker said. "Do we take Hannah?"

"I don't think so, Peter. My parents can baby-sit."

"Even better," Decker said. "It's nice to relax at a concert."

"I agree." Rina turned to her sons. "You boys want to come?"

"When?" Jacob asked.

"Sometime next week. I figure maybe Wednesday evening."

The teen hesitated. "I can't."

"Why not?" Rina asked.

He laid down his fork. "I have detention all next week."

Decker felt his stomach tighten.

Rina looked confused. "You have *detention?*"

"Yes, Eema, I have detention."

Sammy asked, "All *week?*"

Jacob nodded.

"*Why?*" Rina cried out. "What did you *do*, Yaakov?"

Jacob looked at Decker, then at his lap. "I cut school today."

"You *what?*" Rina shrieked. "Why? Where'd you go?"

"Here."

"Here?" Rina exclaimed. "Meaning home?"

Jacob nodded.

"Guess who caught him?" Decker asked. "I came home to do some work and there he was."

"*You* caught him?" Rina exclaimed. "Why didn't you *tell* me about this, Peter?"

"Rina, I've been tied up all day. I just got home —"

But she wasn't listening; her attention was on her son. "You cut school to come home when you *knew* I wouldn't be here. You knew I was on Hannah's field trip. You did that on purpose!" Rina's face had taken on an irate blush. "You were with Shayna, weren't you. You both came here." She turned to Decker. "She was with him, wasn't she?"

"As a matter of fact, she was —"

"And were you going to tell me *that* as well?"

"If you'd give me a chance —"

Again, Rina cut him off, her indignation directed at Jacob. "You cut school to be with her. Well, that's just great! That girl is a *bad* influence on you —"

"That is *such* a prejudiced statement, Eema!" Sammy butted in. "You'd never say that if she was from a *frum* family."

"What are you *talking* about!" Rina snapped back.

Sammy said, "You know Shayna hasn't had it exactly easy. Matter of fact, the whole family is messed up. Her brother, Ben, is in my class. You know what his father did to him? He pulled Ben out of high school in his *senior* year and put him in a Jewish school because the old man suddenly decided to become religious. The poor guy doesn't speak a word of Hebrew and doesn't have a clue as to what's flying. So of course, he doesn't learn a damn thing —"

"Will you please not *swear!*" Rina said. "What happened to your mouth?"

Sammy was unperturbed. "The guy is totally lost. He just hangs around the druggies all day, getting stoned —"

"The druggies?" Rina asked. "What *druggies* —"

"All I'm saying is that if Yonkie brought Shayna here, he probably had a good reason. She was probably really depressed or something. And you know if he tried to talk to her at school, he'd have a thousand rabbis down his throat telling him the evils of speaking to the opposite sex —"

"That's nonsense!" Rina said.

"It's *not* nonsense, Eema, it's a fact," Sammy insisted. "I'm sure she was really needy. For sure, her brother is. So instead of being happy that Yonkie's trying to *mekarev* someone, you're putting him down."

"Mommeeeeee!" Hannah cried out from the other room.

Rina turned a furious face to Sammy. "You know I just *love* this." She pointed a shaky finger at Jacob. "He cuts school and somehow I'm to blame —"

"Mommeeeee!"

"I'm coming!" Rina screamed back. "I'm through with dinner. Clear your plates when you're done!" Then she stomped away.

Seething, Decker looked at his older stepson. "And *what* was that all about?"

Sammy said, "I just believe in tolerance."

"So how about showing some tolerance as well as *respect* to your mother?" Decker shot back. "Your behavior just now was deplorable. We'll deal with this later." He threw irate looks at both his stepsons and left the table.

Sammy waited until his stepfather had shut the door to the bedroom. To his brother, he whispered, "You brought her *here?* Are you an *idiot?*"

Jacob stared at his food but said nothing.

Sammy continued to talk softly. "You're just lucky he didn't catch you doing something."

Again, Jacob didn't answer.

Sammy stared at him. "Or did he?"

Abruptly, Jacob stood up, shoving his chair in the process. He picked up his plate and went into the kitchen. Sammy followed a moment later with his own dish. "He caught you, didn't he?"

Angrily, Jacob shoved his half-eaten dinner down the garbage disposal.

"What he'd do?" Sammy asked.

Jacob started to speak, then changed his mind. He shook his head.

"You're still alive. He obviously didn't maim you."

"I don't want to talk about it." Jacob began to wash his plate, scrubbing it well after it was clean.

"You want to wash mine while you're at it?" Sammy asked.

Jacob grabbed the dish from his brother and stuck it under the running tap, splashing water all over himself. Sammy went back into the dining room and began to clear the table, eating scraps of poultry as he brought the food into the kitchen. Dynamite turkey. Poor Eema. All her culinary talents going unappreciated. Still, he had to defend his brother against the onslaught. Jacob looked very upset and that was very out of character.

"C'mon," Sammy said. "Talk to me. What happened?"

Jacob shut off the tap. "Truthfully . . . he was actually pretty cool. Which worries me. It's like . . ." He shoveled leftover stuffing from the serving bowl into a smaller container. "It's like he's giving me this second chance." He exhaled loudly. "It's like if I mess up again, it's *all* over. That he'll send me away to military school or to the army or something —"

"C'mon!"

"Eema's right, you know." Jacob turned to his brother. "She is a bad influence. At least her friends are." He put the stuffing into the refrigerator and leaned against the kitchen counter. "I went to her girlfriend's party a month ago. Must have been around a hundred people there."

He licked his lips.

"I have never seen so many drugs outside a pharmacy. Sammy, they were doing *everything*. It was like this . . . this Babylonian orgy. I expected to see Nebuchadrezzar walk into the living room." He shook his head and looked away. "They kept passing stuff to me."

"Like what?"

"Like everything — pot, pills, LSD, coke —"

"You *didn't* touch the hard stuff, did you?"

"Only pot —"

"Thank goodness for small favors." Sammy put his hand on his brother's shoulder, but Jacob shook it off.

"I didn't do the hard stuff, but I didn't want to look like a wuss either. So I kept on taking hits of grass. I mean, I was really *hitting* on it . . . to look busy, you know."

The kitchen grew silent.

Jacob cracked his knuckles. "I got totally blasted. I didn't know what was happening. I totally freaked!" He winced at the memory. "I kept thinking like the police were gonna come in at any moment. And that I was gonna get busted . . . and that Peter was gonna lose his job . . . and it would hit the papers. And that Eema would cry and sit *shiva* for me. I kept wondering *why* I was doing it. Why I was even there."

"So why didn't you leave?"

"I don't *know!*" Jacob began to pace. "First off, I don't drive yet and I didn't have a ride and I was too zonked to walk or . . ." He stopped and turned to his brother. "You wanna know the *worst* part?"

"There's more?"

"I took off my *tzi-tzit* and *kipah* before I went," Jacob said. "I rationalized it by saying it would be a *chillul Hashem* — you know . . . to desecrate such holy things in such a rotten place. But the truth was that I was *embarrassed* to wear them. I was ashamed to look so . . . so Jewish." He closed his eyes and opened them. "Abba's probably rolling over in his grave."

Sammy waited a moment. Then he said, "You know, you're not as hard a case as you think you are —"

"Please!" Jacob pulled out a kitchen chair and sank into it. He lowered his head onto the table. "Spare me!"

Sammy sat next to him. He made several false starts, then got the words out. "You know what the trouble it, Yonkie? I'll tell you what the trouble is. You're way too smart for that school —"

"What are you talking about?" He lifted his head up. "I'm not a quarter the *gemara kopp* that you are."

"You don't do well in *gemara* because you hate it. You don't even try. But you whiz through the secular stuff like a speed demon. You know more math than I do even though you're two years behind me. Man, your friends are shaking their heads after taking the PSAT. I ask you how it went, you just shrug like it was nothing. No big deal. You didn't even call up to find out what you got."

"I don't care —"

"*I* called up," Sammy said.

Jacob stared at him. "*You* called up?"

"Yeah, I called up. I found your exam number on your desk and pretended I was you."

No one spoke for a minute. Then Sammy asked, "Are you interested in what you got?"

"No —"

"You got a fifteen sixty," Sammy interrupted. "You know how incredibly *good* that is? Jacob, I worked my ass off for the SAT and you still beat me by sixty points."

"PSAT isn't the SAT —"

"Yonkie, give me an effing break!"

"What difference does it make? The only thing

257

Yeshiva University requires is a male body with a *bris*."

"I think the academic standards are a *little* higher —"

"Not much."

Sammy shook his head. "How you *insult* your own people."

Jacob looked down. "I know. I'm terrible!"

Sammy leaned over and spoke softly. "Yonkie, *I'm* going to YU. I *want* to go to YU. It fits into what *I* want out of life. I'll probably be premed or predent and I want to be able to go to college and *learn* at the same time. YU is tailor-made for me. But it's not for everyone." He paused. "Have you ever thought about the Ivies? Lots of *frum* kids at Harvard —"

"Oh yeah, right!" Jacob sneered. "You got thirty thousand dollars, Shmueli?"

"First of all, there are scholarships —"

"Forget it —"

"Second of all, Peter sent his own daughter to Columbia. He wouldn't dare do less for you. He can't afford to show favoritism." Sammy grinned. "Eema would kill him."

"I'm not interested —"

"You should be!"

"Sammy, I don't have a chance. A, my grades aren't phenomenal, and B, I haven't done one . . . normal extracurricular thing in my entire life."

"So start now! Run for school office! Everyone loves you. You'd win easily."

"I don't want to run for school office. I *hate* school."

"So work on the school paper —"

"No."

"Join the basketball team. You're athletic."

"I'm not interested —"

"Do charity work. Do *something*, Yonkie! Deliver food to the elderly or work on a community teen suicide hot line."

As he entered the kitchen all Decker heard was the word *suicide*. His heart took off, and he suddenly forgot his pent-up anger. He asked, "What are you two boys talking about?"

The teens turned around. Neither had heard him come in. Jacob remained silent, but Sammy said, "Yonkie's interested in doing charity work. He wants to do the teen suicide hot line. I think it's a great idea."

"What?" Decker jerked his head back and furrowed his brow. "*Charity* work? When did this come up?"

"Just now," Sammy said. "I'd think he'd be great at it. What do you think?"

Decker pulled up a chair. "Taking on that kind of responsibility is a major commitment. You're working with real crises. And once they train you, you just don't show up whenever you want. You put in hours. It's time-consuming. It's grueling work. It's emotionally and physically exhausting." He turned to his younger stepson. "I can't *believe* you're interested in doing something like that."

"Gee, thanks for encouraging him," Sammy said.

"Will you just watch your mouth *for once?*" Decker shot out. "I'm really getting *sick and tired* of taking your sarcasm and sass."

Sammy shut down as if he malfunctioned.

No one spoke.

Then, Jacob licked his lips. "I think I could handle it."

But Decker was skeptical and suspicious, thinking that this latest stunt was nothing but appeasement, a shoddy attempt by Jacob to get on his good side. Decker was disappointed that Jacob would try so baldly to wash over his bad behavior. "And just when did you intend to do this?"

"Weekends."

"Jacob, if you do a hot line along with your studies, you'll have absolutely no free time left."

Jacob shrugged. "That's okay."

"You say that now, but when you're bogged down in work and all your buddies are out partying, I think you'll feel differently."

Jacob sat up and looked at his stepfather. "You're dismissing me. But I really think I have something to offer. I haven't had a charmed life, you know. I know what it's like to sleep with the covers over my head."

Decker softened his tone. "I'm not dismissing you —"

"Yes, you are, but that's not the point. The point is I know what it's like to feel intense sorrow. I mean I lost my father to a terrible death —"

"Yes, you did —"

"And just when Eema was pulling out of it, then came all that horrible stuff at the Yeshiva . . . you coming along to investigate, whispering all those questions to Eema that we weren't supposed to hear. Remember that day in the park when we first met? You basically told us to get lost."

"I don't remember it quite like that —"

"I know you didn't *say* get lost. Instead you tried to bribe us with a ride in the patrol car if we left you and Eema alone for about a half hour."

"I thought you enjoyed the ride."

"I did, but that's not the point."

Again, Decker missed the point.

Jacob said, "Dad, this big bruiser cop comes around and starts questioning your mother . . . I mean we knew something wasn't right." He looked at Sammy. "Right?"

"Absolutely."

Jacob got up and began to pace. "And then when that woman . . . that guard . . . was murdered. That was pretty damn traumatic."

Decker opened and closed his mouth. "I'm sure it was."

"You didn't think we knew about that, did you? Adults must think that kids are blind or deaf. Of course we knew about it. We just didn't say anything because Eema was so freaked out, and the whole place was going nuts. I mean, who had time to listen to a couple of pain-in-the-ass kids?"

"Jacob —"

"You know, Dad, it's pretty freaky to find out that the guy who'd been teaching you computers was arrested for being a rapist. I mean, I didn't exactly *know* what a rapist was, but I knew he was arrested for doing something bad. Stupid kid that I was, I thought he was arrested for showing us porn —"

As fast as Jacob was talking was as rapid as his mouth slammed shut. Quickly — as if he'd choked on the words.

The room fell deadly silent.

Decker's eyes darted between his stepsons. "That bastard showed you two *pornography?*"

The teens exchanged looks but neither spoke. They had been around seven and eight at the time of the mikvah rapes. Decker felt his heart drop, a sudden spurt of nausea counterbalanced by a geyser of raging anger. He whispered with fury, "Did that son of a bitch molest either one of you?"

Again, the boys traded glances but remained quiet. Finally, Sammy said, "Guess it depends on your definition of molestation."

Sweat drenched Decker's brow. He mopped up his forehead with a handkerchief, then clenched his hands to keep them from shaking. He stood up. "I don't want Eema to hear this. Let's take a walk."

19

The night was cool and dark, giving the illusion of privacy. They walked into the orchards, stopping under a navel orange tree scenting the air with its fragrant blossoms. But instead of smelling sweetness, Decker almost gagged on the cloying aroma.

Sammy immediately sat down. Jacob remained standing, leaning against the trunk, picking off bark. All of them shadowed, faces sketched in smudged charcoals. Obscure. That was good. It made it easier to talk.

Decker managed to speak quietly and calmly. "What he'd do?"

Sammy turned his face toward the waxing moon, the beams highlighting the boy's nose and lips. "We went to his computer club, you know."

Yes, Decker did know. He did know.

Sammy said, "There was this one time. I think it was a Thursday." He looked at his brother.

"It was Thursday," Jacob confirmed.

"Anyway," Sammy said. "He kept us after everyone else had left . . . both of us." He blew out air. "God, this was a long time ago . . ."

But Decker could tell that the kid remembered it as if it were an hour ago.

"Anyway, after all the big boys had left . . ." He chuckled. "Big boys . . . they must have been like ten. To me, they were big . . . anyway, Gilbert kept us late and said something like, 'Now I'll show you boys the *good* stuff.' "

He turned to his stepfather.

"He must have had a subscription to some on-line porn service — a subscription that the Yeshiva was paying for, ironies of ironies." A pause. "He showed us a bunch of pornographic pictures . . . really explicit stuff. It gave him a . . ." Sammy swallowed. "It gave him a hard-on."

With effort, Decker refrained from punching something. "Go on."

"It really wasn't all that bad." Sammy brushed it off. "He just like grabbed his crotch and said something stupid like, 'This is what it means to be a real man' — something stupid like that."

The boy stopped talking. Decker asked, "And that was the only thing he did? Just grab his crotch and say something stupid?"

Sammy said, "Actually, he made us touch it." He added quickly, "*Over* his pants."

"Touch it over his pants."

Sammy winced. "More like . . . you know . . . stroke it. But over his pants."

Decker felt like throwing up. "Did he ejaculate?"

"Uh . . . yeah." Sammy hugged his knees. "Although we didn't realize what it was at the time. All of a sudden his groin got wet. He turned real serious and said something like 'You *bad* boys —' "

Jacob interrupted. " 'Look *what* you bad boys —' "

"Yeah, that's right. 'Look what you *bad* boys made me do. You made me pee in my pants.' And we kept thinking how'd we make him pee in his pants? I remember one time we were talking about it — Yonkie and me. And Yonkie said, 'Why didn't he just go to the bathroom?' I kept wondering the same thing."

Sammy bit his thumbnail.

"Then he told us to go to the washroom and wash our hands. That we shouldn't go home smelling like pee —"

"I didn't smell like pee," Jacob said flatly.

"Oh yeah, get this!" Sammy began to rock. "He said something like, 'Even though you boys were bad, I'm not going to tell your Eema. So if you don't say anything, I won't either.' And we thought, 'Hey, great! Eema doesn't have to know that we were bad.' "

He chuckled, but it was anything but merry.

"Actually, it was more . . . disgusting than traumatic. And then later on, when you learn all these prohibitions against homosexuality, and you realize what happened, you start wondering if you sinned . . . or if you're gay because you touched a guy and made him come."

Decker said, "You know, none of that is true."

"Of course," Sammy said. "But it takes a little while to sort it out. It really doesn't bother me anymore. The guy was a pervert. I was a kid. And like I said, it was a long time ago."

No one spoke.

Decker asked, "And you're sure that's all he did to you?"

"That was it."

"You're not holding back, Sam?" Decker asked. "It was just that one time?"

"Yep! After that, we made sure we went home with the big boys. And then when all the stuff at the yeshiva started happening, Eema pulled us out of the computer club. Gilbert must have given her the willies."

The night became very still.

Decker asked, "And that was the *only* thing he did to you, Sammy?"

"Swear to God."

He turned to Jacob, trying to catch the boy's eye. "What about you, Yonkie? Was that the only thing he did to you?"

But Jacob wouldn't look him in the face. Decker felt his head go light. He turned to Sammy, hoping to extract some hidden information, but the older teen shrugged ignorance. Blind with fury, Decker was trying to keep control. But it was getting harder and harder. "What did that son of a bitch do to you, Jacob?"

The teen didn't answer.

Sammy said, "Maybe I should take a walk —"

"No, no . . ." Jacob rubbed his eyes. "It's . . . you can . . ." He sighed as only one can do when burdened by life at such a young age. "There was . . . this one time." He licked his lips and looked at his brother. "You were sick."

Sammy inhaled sharply. "What happened?"

"He caught me . . . I mean physically restrained me . . . held my arm . . . so I couldn't leave with the big boys." His lower lip trembled. "He goosed me . . . hard. He squeezed my balls for kicks. It hurt like hell."

Decker waited for more.

"That was it." Jacob slammed his lips shut.

Decker asked, "Over your pants?"

Jacob shook his head. "No . . . it was . . ." He tried to catch his breath. "I was a real skinny kid. My pants kept falling down when I would run or jump around." A breath. "Eema used to buy me jeans with elastic waistbands . . . only things that would stay on. . . . So he kinda slipped his hand . . ." He took a swipe at his eyes. "You ever notice that I always wear belts? And I keep them real tight?"

No one spoke.

Jacob said, "I kept struggling to break away. He just . . . laughed. He said to me . . . He said to me, 'What's wrong, Yonkelah? Afraid you'll *like* it?'"

"Asshole!" Sammy muttered.

Jacob said, "I finally did break away. I told him I was going to tell Eema. Know what he said? God, what a *shit* he was! Excuse my language . . ."

He looked up, he looked at his toes, anywhere but at faces.

"He said, 'If you tell your eema, she will *die* just like your abba did.'"

Jacob sniffed back tears, his complexion a ghastly white.

"Now I *knew* he was full of it. At seven, I *knew* people just didn't *die*."

Another sniff.

"But you gotta remember that all this strange stuff was happening . . . that Eema was already pretty freaked out. And then that guard was *killed*. And nobody *explained* anything to us. I mean, I was really *scared*." He turned to Sammy. "You were scared, weren't you?"

"Petrified."

"I knew I should have said something to Eema, but . . ." The teen wiped his eyes. "Anyway, I didn't wind up saying anything because he never did it again. And like Sammy said, Eema told us we didn't have to go anymore."

The boy leaned against the tree, hugging the trunk.

"It took me about a year to convince myself that Eema wasn't going to die. Then she told us we were moving to New York." He looked at his stepfather. "I really liked you. I didn't want to leave you. You took away a lot of the pain from Abba. But also, there was another side . . . I was relieved to get out of that place! It held so many conflicting memories — Abba when he was well and Abba when he was sick. You and Eema . . . of course, Rabbi Schulman . . . I love him. But then there was *him!* Mostly, I don't think about it. Then out of the blue, I get this image . . . it scares me. I feel like such a baby . . . you know, why can't I get *over* it?"

A sigh and a shrug. Then nothing.

Decker tried to speak, but the words lodged somewhere in the back of his throat. At the time of the murder and rapes, he had been in sex crimes and juvey, considered a top cop with years of experience. He had talked to numerous children who had been abused — emotionally, physically, sexually. One of the key signs of disturbance in young children was sleep disruption.

Jacob's night terrors.

Decker had seen them firsthand. Yet he chalked them off to anxiety from his father's death even though Yitzchak had died *two* years earlier.

Suddenly it all made sense. Jacob's friendly but detached manner, his quiet but secretive nature. Right before Decker's eyes, if he had bothered to take off the blinders. He had known that the boys had had contact with a *sexual* deviant. He had known that Steve Gilbert, a pervert and *rapist,* had taught both of them computers. He had known this! He had *fucking known this* and never once had he questioned the boys about Gilbert's behavior toward them.

Because at that time, he had been much, *much* more interested in Rina than in her two fatherless sons. All his attention had been focused on her. Even when he did spend time with her young sons, it was for the purpose of gaining brownie points with her. Always Rina, as he blatantly disregarded obvious signs of distress in a little seven-year-old boy. Even after witnessing Jacob's sexual behavior yesterday — especially precocious for a kid raised in a religious home — he still didn't put two and two together. Even the use of Jacob's *language:*

I can't talk if I know some kid out there is being raped.

Some kid. Not some *girl!* Some *kid!*

Any rookie cop could have done better.

If Decker had had just an iota of insight, had shown the *least* fraction of sensitivity that he had shown countless other *unrelated* children, he might have saved his *own* son — hell, *both* his sons — eight years of heartache and misery.

There wasn't a hole big enough to bury Decker's shame and guilt.

Jacob was talking to him.

Decker bit his lip. "Sorry, I didn't hear you, Yonkie."

"I asked if you were mad at me?"

Decker was speechless. Eventually, he mumbled out, "Am I *mad* at you?"

"Mad at me for not telling you?"

Decker blinked several times, holding back the tears. That was the *last* thing he wanted — sympathy from the boys. "No, son, I'm not mad at you. How could I be mad at . . ." He cleared his throat. "I'm mad at myself. I should have . . ."

He walked over to the boy and put a hand on his shoulder. Immediately, the boy leaned against his chest. Decker hugged him hard, as if the single embrace might right the wrongs. But that was impossible. Eight years of secrets and shame. They all had some distance to travel.

"I feel so damn lousy for you . . ." Decker regarded Sammy, sitting under the tree, his knees to his chest. Unnaturally silent. Where was the kid's mouth when he needed it? "For *both* of you," Decker said. "I just wish I would have . . . I . . ."

Sammy said, "You couldn't have known."

But he *could* have known. He *should* have known.

Jacob sighed in Decker's arms. "Could have been worse. At least Sammy and I had each other."

Sammy spoke softly. "You know, sometimes, I think about Gilbert . . . rotting away in prison. I remember him as being kind of a good-looking guy. So I think that maybe he's getting gang raped . . . often." He hugged his knees. "That makes me feel better."

Jacob broke off from Decker's embrace. "You *can't* tell Eema anything."

"I have no intention of telling Eema."

Jacob looked calmer. But he was still very pale. He said, "I still want to do the suicide hot line. Are you going to help me out or what?"

"Tell me when you want to start."

"This weekend."

"It's a deal."

A high-pitched voice yelled out, "Daddeeee!"

Rina saying, "Peter? Boys?"

"Yeah, we're here," Decker shouted back. "Just catching some air."

"I need to compose myself." Jacob walked away.

Wordlessly, Sammy got up and followed. A moment later, Sammy put his arm around his brother. Jacob kept his hands in his pocket, but didn't move away from his brother's touch. Decker watched as the figures grew faint in the distance.

The boys were so damn different. Yet Decker rarely heard them have words, let alone fight. He often wondered why they got along so well. Now he understood. Theirs was a bond formed from sorrow, loneliness and secret taboos.

"Daddeeeee!" Hannah shouted. *"C'mere!"*

Rina called out loud, "It's Marge, Peter. She says it's important."

Decker closed his eyes. "I'm coming."

"Daddeeeeeee!" Hannah started running to him . . . such unabashed joy in seeing her father. To her, he was still a hero.

How long before he blew that image?

20

Marge stood at the mouth of the nearly invisible driveway, a flashlight in her hand. It was a smart thing to do. Otherwise Decker would have missed the turnoff. He slowed, then stopped the unmarked. She opened the passenger door and slid inside. "You made good time."

Decker checked his watch. Five after ten. "One hour, five minutes."

"How fast were you going, Lieutenant?"

"None of your business. Who's minding the store?"

"Oliver's watching Pluto and his henchman." She caught her breath. "Henchman in the literal sense. His name is Benton. He whacks the heads off chickens. When I met up with him, he was covered in blood. Right now, he's cuffed to a post. With me down here, Oliver couldn't keep watch over him and Pluto . . . who, by the way, is screaming about civil liberties. But there's not much fire in his smoke."

Gingerly, Decker pushed down the gas pedal and the car crawled forward. Gravel churned underneath the tires. "Let me see if I understood you. You were about to check out the ranch house, but you saw a pool of blood in the middle of the living room."

"And bloody shoe tracks."

"Recent?"

"Still sticky."

"The thing is, you don't know if the blood's avian or human."

"Exactly."

"And Benton says it's chicken blood."

"Naturally." She stared out the windshield and into blackness. "And he has been killing chickens. Say I buy that he tracked some shit into the house. It's his explanation for the puddle that's lame."

"Which is?"

"He was bringing the pail of blood into the house, he stumbled and part of the bucket's contents spilled."

Decker said, "Well, golly, it happens to me all the time."

Marge chuckled. But her mood wasn't humorous.

"And did he tell you *why* he was bringing a pail of *blood* into his house?"

She wrinkled her nose. "He was bringing it into the kitchen to mix it with chicken stock, which he makes fresh from chicken bones. He says it makes a nutritious base for the Order's soups and stews."

"Yum," Decker said wryly. But that was his bias showing. Jewish dietary laws forbade the consumption of any type of blood. Even so, Decker ate liver, which was pretty damn sanguine.

"If he's telling the truth I'm going to look real stupid," Marge said. "Not to mention the fact that I ruined your evening."

"You did the right thing to call me."

"I sincerely *hope* I'm wrong. Who wants to be right? With that little girl missing . . ." She pointed into the dark. "Toward the left, Pete."

Decker nudged the steering wheel as the auto inched up the charcoal pathway. "Tell me about Benton."

"A big man with a blocky build. Concrete sort of guy. I think he's mentally slow. He didn't talk much."

"Pluto acted as the mouthpiece?"

"You got it."

"The guru was outraged?"

Marge considered the question. "To me, he looked surprised. I doubt that he spends any time indoors here, although he was aware that the house was a disaster zone."

"How would he know that if he hasn't been inside recently?"

"Maybe he knows Benton's forte isn't housekeeping. Because right before I went inside, he told me it was infested with rats and insects. I thought he was trying to scare me off. Remember, he was the one who protested our coming up. Still, he didn't seem nervous when I went inside." Marge's voice faded. "It was a good-sized puddle . . ."

"Dark as sin out here," Decker whispered. Quiet, too, but not restful. The stillness smothered gently like a down pillow. "How much farther?"

"About another half-mile. The houselights should come into view just around the bend."

"I take it you haven't called the locals?"

"Since you insisted on coming up even though I told you *not* to —"

"I came because I wanted to, Margie. No discredit to your professionalism."

He sounded tense. She asked, "Everything okay at home, Pete?"

"Been better. Anyway, I'll give the place a quick once-over. If the locals need to be called, I'll do it."

Rounding a curve, Decker saw lights, then a structure. The one-story ranch was *beyond* rundown. It was a shanty. As he neared it, he saw a hulking figure manacled to a slanted, square porch pillar. Next to it was a small shadow pacing back and forth. Decker parked.

Pluto was at the door before Decker was even out of the car. "If you think you can get away with this kind of blatant abrogation of civil rights —"

"Sir, do you want to wienie wag or do you want to get out of here?" Decker exited the car and loomed over the little man. "I can make this a very long evening for you, Brother Pluto. It's up to you."

Pluto's eye twitched. "Lieutenant, must you keep him handcuffed? You'd treat a dog better than that!"

Decker regarded Benton's wall-like shadow. "He's a big guy."

"I'll take responsibility for him," Pluto said.

"Nice but your responsibility won't do squat if he lashes out."

"Can't we reach some kind of compromise?" The guru seemed genuinely concerned for Benton's well-being.

Decker exhaled. "Wait here." He stepped aside and called Oliver over. "If I assign Pluto to Marge, can you handle that one by yourself?" He cocked a thumb in Benton's direction. The man was brick-solid.

"No problemo."

"He's muscle-packed, Detective. He could take you down in a snap. He could probably take me down and I got forty pounds and four inches on you."

"I hear you. I'll be careful."

Again, Decker eyed the farmhand. Leaning against the post, he showed no overt signs of aggressive behavior. But how quickly that could change. "Go uncuff him. I'll cover you just in case he turns rabid. If he behaves, bring him over."

Without hesitation, Oliver walked over to Benton and removed the handcuffs. The farmhand shook out his hands, then massaged his wrists.

Within moments, they began to approach. Scott was walking and Benton was loping. The farmhand had a square face with cheeks rough-ened by beard growth. His clothes were dirty and spangled with bits of feathers and viscera. His leathery hands were calloused and streaked with blood. He kept his arms at his sides. He smelled rank.

Decker asked, "How are you doing, sir?"

Benton's focus remained on the ground. "Better now that you got them things offa me."

"Are your wrists okay?"

The farmhand nodded, eyes on his feet.

To Oliver, Decker said, "Go help Detective Dunn with Brother Pluto. I want to be alone with Mr. Benton for a moment."

Oliver gave him an official, *yes, sir,* and was off. Decker took out a pocket tape recorder and turned it on, identifying himself and Benton into the small built-in mike. "You don't mind if I use this, do you? It's for your protection."

"Don't need no protecting."

"Do you know why I'm here, Benton?"

"Yes I do."

"I want to look inside your house —"

"It's not my house."

"Well, I want to look inside that house." Decker pointed to the hovel. "Is that okay with you?"

The farmhand shrugged. He reminded Decker of those Roger Hargreaves children's books — the ones with the simplistic names. Hannah had a few of them: *Mr. Busy, Mr. Tall* and *Mr. Funny.* Benton would have been Mr. Square.

"Do you have any idea what I'm going to find

inside?" Decker asked. The big man's eyes narrowed. "Yer gonna find the chicken blood. I've been slaughterin' chickens. I tole the lady that. I also tole her that my pail tipped over when I tripped. But she don't believe me."

"No one's saying you're lying. But I still have to investigate."

Silence.

Decker broke it. "So you don't care if I go inside and poke around?"

"Suit yourself."

"Be careful before you answer me," Decker told him. "Because if you say the wrong thing, it's down here on tape. It could come back to get you."

The farmhand was quiet.

Decker said, "Like if you think you might need a lawyer, Benton, I can get one for you."

"Don't need no lawyer." The ranch hand spoke defiantly. "Don't need no lawyer 'cause I didn't do nothin'."

A single ceiling bulb washed the room in a bilious pall. The smell was sharp and sour. As Decker crossed the threshold, the floorboards creaked beneath his weight and were sticky under his shoes. Once inside, it was as stuffy as a gym shoe — wet and warm and fetid. Yellowed walls were streaked by dirty rainwater from an obviously leaky roof. Decker could make out the sky through some of the bigger holes. Flies and gnats buzzed overhead, circling the dusty bulb and reveling in its illumination. One got too close and was fried on the spot. It dropped like a lead pellet, Decker's eyes following the fall. It joined its compatriots in a mass grave; dead insects had littered a floor encrusted with grime and spoiled foodstuffs. Whatever wasn't saturated with dirt was caked with grease. In the center of the trash heap sat a brown couch belching out stuffing. In front of the sofa lay an oval floor mat of blood that faded into shoe tracks of the mahogany whirls. The queasy knot inside Decker's gut erupted into full-blown nausea.

Marge said, "This was as far as I got. As soon as I saw that" — she pointed to the bloody pond — "I called Scott over."

Decker spotlighted the sanguine pool. He stared at the floor for about a minute. "It's not that big. Spill marks around the sides. See all the feathering around the perimeter? That happens when wood starts to soak liquid — in this case, the blood in the center puddle. If this had been the kill spot, we would have seen more blood, spray and vapor . . . some spewing onto the couch. What I'm looking at is consistent with something pouring down and splashing back up on the floor. As opposed to a live body with a pumping vessel or a dead body leaking blood onto the floor."

"So you think Benton tripped with the bucket?"

"Depends on if the blood's human. Then we

ask what he was doing with a bucket of human blood."

He arced the flashlight across the dung-colored walls. Repeated the sweep several times.

"Don't see any massive blotches of bloody spray."

Looking over his shoulder, he peered through the open door frame and into the darkness. He could make out Pluto's pacing shadow. Oliver was leaning against one of the porch's pillars. It was a wonder that it didn't collapse under his weight. He had his eyes fixed on Benton, who sat on a porch step, resembling a lump of granite.

Decker was soaked in the sweat of mental and physical exhaustion. "I'll take it from here. Go back and watch Pluto. That'll let Oliver concentrate on Benton."

"I won't argue with you." Marge raised her eyebrows. "Good luck."

Red swirls of shoe tracks led Decker to a stuffy, humid kitchen. Strewn across the countertop were a dozen chicken carcasses — all of them fully feathered and headless, their windpipes dripping rivulets of blood that ran down the cabinet doors and onto the floors. A kitchen table held baskets of fresh eggs. A small stove held a simmering cauldron. Decker gloved his hands, walked over to the pot and lifted the lid.

A murky soup swimming with bits of chicken and bone. Globules of blood were floating on the top. He grimaced and returned the lid.

Water from the tap was pouring into the sink. Decker turned off the spigot. The basin was filled halfway with bright red liquid — the same unnatural hue found in maraschino cherries and red dye fruit punch.

The stench became stronger, almost overwhelming. Decker took out some VapoRub and dabbed it under his nostrils.

Eyeing the top cupboards. No spray marks, no drips. Opening the doors . . . closing them. Cans of green beans, cans of tuna fish, cans of olives. A tin of sugar and a tin of coffee. A half dozen bottles of cheap beer. A bag of unopened pretzels. Lots of bugs — mostly dead, but some were still squiggling.

The refrigerator contained a quart of fresh milk, a couple of red apples and a half-used package of flour tortillas. An open jar of mayonnaise, a jar of salsa, an opened can of olives and a plastic tube of mustard. The freezer was frosted over and empty.

Turning his attention to the under-the-counter cabinets. Decker ran the strong intense beam from his halogen flashlight across the bottom wooden frame. Lots of recent drip marks from the bleeding chickens on the counters above, these emanating from the top and running down the full length of the cabinet door.

Again, a quick sweep of the light, across the baseboard and bottom molding.

One quick pass, then another until he stopped midway, breaking into a deep, nervous sweat.

His hand started to tremble. The flashlight's beam was focused on fainter, parallel lines which started at the bottom of the one lone cabinet and dribbled down to the baseboard.

Pale but noticeable. Older marks, but not *old*. Drier . . . browner. The fact that they had started at the *bottom* of the cabinet meant they had been made by something stuffed *inside* the niche.

His stomach bucking, Decker stared at the telltale discolored furrows. The cabinet was too small to hold an adult. But if a child was small enough . . .

He wiped perspiration from his forehead and neck.

Bending down onto his knees.

The drone of buzzing flies.

The terrifying smell of rotten meat.

He tugged open the door. Immediately, semiclotted blood poured out onto the floor as a black cloud of insects swarmed Decker's face. Batting them away while trying not to swallow. He jerked backward at the sight and stench. He arose in a flash, tried to stand erect, but instead swooned, holding his balance while gripping the counter, his fingers sinking into the squishy flesh of a raw chicken.

Closing his eyes, trying to find something breathable in this blanket of putrid air. It was the smell more than the body that had caused his light-headedness. The corpse was indeed grotesque. But thank God, it wasn't the kid.

He forced himself back down, again swatting

the buzzing insects. In the back of his mind, Decker knew he was looking at an adult male. But it was hard to discern exactly what was what. Someone had managed to cram the entire body inside the cabinet. But it had been done literally piecemeal.

The sloping shoulders of the headless torso held pulpy stumps that should have been arms. The thighs were pushed against stomach and chest. Just the thighs. Because the legs had been amputated at the kneecaps. The bottom portion of the legs and the disarticulated arms were piled in front of the torso — smoothish arms but there was hair on the legs. The hands had frozen into clawish clutches. The tips of the digits were gray and wrinkled.

And then there was the head — clay-colored, corrugated and desiccated, sitting atop the limbs like a flesh-covered skull and crossbones. A balding scalp topped a round, pudgy face. Vacant eye sockets. The orbs had probably fallen backward into the cranium. No beard or mustache. Decker didn't recognize him.

He went outside and called out to Marge. She took one look at Decker's complexion and paled. "Oh, my God —"

"It's not the kid or Andromeda —"

"Then who?"

"I don't know, but I suspect you do. Put some gloves on."

She started sweating. "Bad?"

Even if Decker had been calm enough to find

the words, he still wouldn't have been able to describe it. "This way." He led her through the living room and into the kitchen. Her gait began to teeter.

Decker asked, "Are you sick?"

"It's the stench." Marge breathed into her hands.

"It gets worse. Can you hold out?"

"If you're quick."

Decker helped Marge to a bent-knee position. "Keep your mouth closed and keep your hand over your nose." He opened the cabinet, releasing a dark funnel of flies.

Marge moaned into her palms. "Oh, my God!"

"Is it Nova?"

She averted her eyes. "Probably."

"Probably?"

"Definitely! Yes, it's him. Get me *out* of here!"

21

Sergeant Deputy Kirt Johannsen was a terse man. "What big picture am I missing?"

Decker started his story while Johannsen snapped gum. Talking outside in almost complete blackness, the only illumination being nickel-colored light coming from the shack's dusty side windows. The sergeant appeared to be in his early fifties — six-two with a stomach bordering on a beer gut. Round face, thick lips, a ruddy complexion, blue-white eyes that were almost transparent and a scalp glazed with white, thin hair. He wore sheriff khakis and held a wide-brim brown hat. After he had given the sectioned corpse a single glance, he had suggested they get some air.

Decker had gotten halfway through the saga when one of Johannsen's men approached. He was a freckle-faced kid with a gaping mouth, making him look stupid even if he wasn't.

"Sir?"

"What?" Johannsen had been listening intently, and was irritated by the interruption.

Freckles blushed. "The little guy over there . . . the one named Pluto, yellin' more than talkin' —"

"Get to the point, Stoner," Johannsen interrupted.

Stoner fidgeted. "Well, sir, he says we can't take Benton to jail till his lawyer gets here."

Johannsen sneered. "I don't need nobody's permission to arrest a man who has body parts in his kitchen cupboard. Take Benton in and lock him up in the *A* cell."

"What about . . . Pluto?"

Johannsen gave a near smile. "Since Abner ain't sleeping one off tonight, you can put Pluto in the *B* cell." He turned to Decker. "What's his part in all this?"

"He's a high-ranking member of the Order of the Rings of God. Just like Nova was."

"Nova's the guy in the cabinet?"

Decker nodded.

"What's Pluto's part in all this?"

"I don't know. I'm not saying he couldn't have done it, but he's been with my detective for the last nine hours." Decker pulled out a pack of cigarettes, lit one for Johannsen and then for himself. "I know you have to detain Pluto for questioning. And you probably have grounds to book him, too. But he's feisty. He won't go down without a fight. And the Order type of fighting is lawsuits."

Johannsen growled, "Damn weirdos. I told Horace and Mary Jane not to sell to them." He sucked in nicotine. "Not that I blame them. They got a real good price."

"The Order's complaints wouldn't stand up in court." Decker took a drag on his smoke. "But they could cause you interim grief."

Johannsen considered his options. "Stoner, this is what you do. Are you listening?"

"Yes, sir —"

"I mean really listening."

"Yes, sir."

"You, Hal and Doug take Benton in and leave that weirdo Pluto feller to Lieutenant Decker's people." He regarded Decker. "Is that okay with you?"

"That's fine with me."

Johannsen said, "I'll be at the jailhouse shortly. Keep Benton comfortable, but *don't* go asking him questions. You can't ask him anything until his lawyer's there. All you gotta do is make sure he don't escape. You think you can do that, Stoner?"

"Do we take the cuffs off of him, sir?"

Johannsen frowned. "No, Stoner, you *don't* take the cuffs off. You leave the cuffs on him at all times."

"Even when he's in jail?"

"Yes, even when he's in jail. Got it, Stoner?"

"I got it, sir."

"Then go do something." Johannsen waited until Stoner had left. He took a deep inhale of his cigarette, blowing out a thin wisp of smoke. "Don't go thinking badly about Stoner. Our jails are mainly for drunks . . . maybe an occasional husband who gets nasty with his wife. We don't get things like body parts in cabinets."

"Not my usual homicide either. What can you tell me about Benton?"

288

"A loner. But most of the people living on farms here mind their own beeswax. I see him when he comes into town to buy supplies. He don't cause any trouble." Johannsen took another puff on his cigarette. "He's got a woman."

Decker raised his eyebrows. "Really?"

"Really."

"Who?"

"Ruth Young. She's maybe fifty. Divorced. Lives about fifteen miles from here. She owns a pecan orchard."

"Do they do overnights?"

"I never paid much attention to their social life. But I guess I have seen his truck at her place at night." He shrugged. "Guess I should call her. First off, to make sure she's still alive. And second, maybe she'd want to know about Benton. You only found the one body, right?"

"So far. But I haven't done a thorough search. I wanted to call you first."

"Think there're others buried here?"

"No."

Johannsen looked surprised. "So you don't think that Benton's one of those serial killers?"

"No."

"Any psychology ideas why he did something like this?"

"I'm not even sure he did it."

"Glad to hear you say that. Benton isn't gonna win any genius awards, but even he wouldn't be that stupid to stuff a body in his own house."

Decker didn't argue, but he knew the fallacy of

that kind of reasoning. Over the years he'd had seen dozens of examples of egregious idiocy. "It's not the stupidity, Sergeant. It's the body. It was positioned. Someone was sending a message."

"What kind of a message?"

"Don't fuck with me."

"Well then, I'd say he got his point across pretty damn good. So you gonna grill Pluto?"

"Yep."

"The boy impresses me as a harmless fool."

"Perhaps." Decker ran his hand through limp hair. "So you never met Nova . . . the man in the cabinet. He's been up here before. He takes eggs and chickens down to the Order."

"Well, I've never seen him. Not that I recall."

Decker finished off his cigarette. "Did you ever meet Jupiter?"

"A couple of times."

"What was he like?"

"Friendly feller. Looked you straight in the eye when he talked. And damn could he talk — mostly about the stars and the planets. Some of it was over my head, but he seemed to know what he was saying. Benton told me he was a famous scientist once."

"Once."

"Benton also told me that Jupiter was in the process of inventing a time machine. 'Course I didn't give that much thought. You gotta take Benton with a grain of salt."

Decker took it all in. "Interesting."

"Is that possible? A time machine?"

"I don't know. Time machines had been one of Jupiter's pet projects back when he was Emil Ganz, the renowned scientist. His crazy ideas caused him lots of ridicule. Then he suddenly disappeared for ten years. When he returned, he was reincarnated as Father Jupiter, the spiritual leader of the Order of the Rings of God. When did Benton tell you about Jupiter's time machine?"

"Mebbe six months ago." Johannsen crushed out his cigarette. "I dropped by the place during one of my usual passes. The two of them had the telescope out. Matter of fact, Jupiter showed me the planet Jupiter. It was out back then."

"And this all took place about six months ago?"

The sergeant nodded. "Could be Jupiter was returning to his old passion."

"Seems like it." Decker thought a moment. "Not that I see any direct connection between time machines and Nova's corpse in the cupboard."

"Sir, this is beyond my ken." Johannsen donned his hat. "Look, Lieutenant. You come up here, you give me a call. You act real respectful. You share your cigarettes and talk to me like we're buddies. I appreciate it. But we both know I'm not equipped to handle a full-scale homicide investigation. Which this is."

Decker waited.

Johannsen popped a stick of gum into his

mouth. "I know I'm in charge. Which means I could do two things. I could call up Bakersfield, which I would do if there was no history. But since there is a history, I might as well give it to you. Do what you slickers do. Bring in your men and your techs and all your people. I won't get territorial."

"You're a gentleman, Sergeant."

"Just smart enough to know what I can and cain't do."

"Fortuitous that you should call."

After having removed Nova's head and the limbs from the cabinet, Deputy Coroner Judy Little worked on liberating the torso, moving slowly and meticulously. The heat had caused the stump to swell in its habitat, making its removal without tissue damage a tedious process. Dr. Little wore a mask. Decker could barely understand her muffled words even though he was kneeling beside her.

"Why's that?"

"Got a prelim report on Emil Euler Ganz aka Father Jupiter. He had arsenic in his system."

Decker felt his heartbeat quicken. "He was *poisoned* to death?"

"No, that's not what I said. When all the tests are concluded, I predict death by respiratory depression due to barb/alcohol combo. His BAL was .14, plus Nembutal and Seconal — both soluble in alcohol — were floating around in his system. The findings are consistent with what your detectives pulled up at the crime scene — the empty vodka bottle and the barbiturate vials. But, as a side story, there was arsenic in the hair and skin. Now, arsenic's a naturally occurring element in the body. It's always there in trace amounts. But he had more than normal."

"But not enough to kill him?"

"Can't answer that because I don't know what his LMD is."

LMD — lethal minimum dose. Decker asked, "Someone was poisoning him slowly?"

"Could be." She grunted as she sweated. "You know, if we could blast some air-conditioning in this hole, we could shrink this mother, making it easier to remove."

Decker said, "I have a couple more questions."

"Thought you might." When Little stood up, her knees cracked. She leaned against the counter. "Go ahead."

"You found arsenic in Jupiter's hair and skin."

"Exactly."

"But you don't think arsenic was the cause of death."

"That's right."

"If you had to go on record today, you'd say the cause of death was depression from barbiturates and alcohol."

"Three for three."

Decker thought a moment. "Could it be that somebody was trying to kill him with slow arsenic poisoning . . . so as not to arouse suspicion. But it wasn't working fast enough so he or she substituted barbiturates?"

"Conjecture is your bailiwick," Little said. "But sure, it's plausible. You know as well as I do that an OD on alcohol and Nembutal arouses far less suspicion than death by arsenic."

"According to Venus, Jupiter had been complaining of headaches and stomachaches for the last six months."

"Headaches and stomachaches — you know, nausea, cramps, diarrhea — are consistent with heavy metal poisoning in small doses. Substantial doses would have given him horrible abdominal pains, motor impairment, dizziness, nervous twitches. He would have been jumping out of his skin because heavy metals can cause exfoliation of the derma. You kick it up even further, he croaks. And it's not a pleasant death."

"Dr. Little?"

She turned around. "Hey, Anna. What's up?"

Anna was a young Asian tech, wearing blue scrubs, her features obscured by a face mask. She was holding a vial of red, viscous liquid. She said, "The blood isn't human."

"Chicken blood?" Decker asked.

"I haven't typed all the proteins yet so I cannot say what blood it is. Only that it is not human."

Little turned to Decker. "You don't look surprised."

"If the living room had been Nova's kill spot, the walls would have been spray-painted red."

"So you discovered this body based on a pool of chicken blood?"

"Dumb luck." Decker regarded the bloody glob of flesh still stuck in the niche. The nipples had been stained brown by dry riverbeds of blood. With the head and limbs gone, the torso was easier to stomach.

Head and limbs.

Abruptly, an image popped into his brain. Another skull and crossbones found in a box sitting on the shelf of a tool shed. He asked, "Arsenic's common in rat poison, isn't it?"

"Yep."

"It also has a bitter taste."

"You can hide it. Just mix small amounts in Coke or sweetened iced tea . . . like the Mensa killer did in Florida. George whatshisface? He did it with thallium."

"George Trepal."

"You can also inhale the powder. Maybe he snorted it in cocaine, or smoked it in crack."

"Possible." But Decker was thinking about the dozens of bottles of vitamins found in Jupiter's medicine cabinets. He said, "Or you could put the rat killer powder in a gel-cap and tell someone it was vitamins."

"That would work."

"Have you done any toxicological analysis on the bottles we pulled from Jupiter's medicine cabinet?"

"Nope. No reason to do it."

"Until now."

"How many bottles are we talking about?"

"Two dozen —"

"That's going to take a long time, Lieutenant. You're talking about opening up each capsule and sending it through gas chromatography. Plus, even if you find arsenic in the capsules, what *new* thing is it going to tell you? *I'm* already telling you he had arsenic in his system. The capsules aren't going to tell you who put it there."

"I still need it done."

"No problem. Just letting you know to settle in for the long haul."

"How long can you last with arsenic poisoning?"

"If it's done slow enough in small doses and at irregular intervals, you could last a while."

"Six months?"

"Sure."

"A year?"

"Possibly."

Little knelt back down and resumed working. She wedged her hands between the confines of the cabinet walls and the flesh and began tugging the torso.

"Like I said before, arsenic's a natural element. It doesn't disintegrate, doesn't flush out of the body, so there's buildup. In excess amounts, the first place it's usually laid down is in the hair and skin because of the rapid cellular turnover. To *really* see how long the poisoning had been going on, I'd have to section Jupiter's bones. Bone growth is like tree rings. If there's poison in the bones, you know it's been going on a long time."

"But he'd be sick during that time."

"Most definitely. Slow poisoning is a good way to keep someone incapacitated." One final pull and the bloodied clump was birthed from its partical board womb. "Yes!" Holding a red stump in her gloved hands, Little looked as pleased as if she were an obstetrician. "I need a double plastic morgue bag stat!"

Decker grimaced at the sight, but kept talking. "So you think someone wanted Jupiter alive, but out of commission?"

"I don't think anything. I'm just throwing out possibilities," Little said. "You know, Jupiter still could have killed himself, Lieutenant. The terrible effects of the poisoning could have driven him over the edge. He may have wanted to end his own misery."

"Sure, that's possible." Decker stood up. "Anything's possible. Even so, I'm liking Jupiter's death as a homicide a whole lot better than I did a few days ago."

22

Hearing the knock on the bedroom door, Rina put her book down. "It's open."

Jacob walked over to his mother, bent down and kissed her forehead. "Just thought I'd say good night."

Rina checked the time — twelve-thirty. "It's late."

"Just catching up. I've got a couple of tests to-morrow."

In his pajamas, Jacob looked about twelve. She said, "Sit down, Yaakov, I want to talk to you."

The boy sat. "I'm really sorry, Eema. It won't happen again."

"Yonkie, why didn't you tell me you got a fif-teen sixty on your PSAT?"

Jacob licked his lips. "Sammy told you?"

"Sammy?" Rina asked. "You told *Sammy,* but you didn't tell *me?*"

"No, of course not. *I* didn't even know. *Sammy* told me. He called up and pretended he was me. I was willing to wait until I got the card in the mail. But that's Sammy . . . he's gotta know ev-erything." Jacob shook his leg. "I just found out tonight. So who told you?"

"The school called." Rina sighed. "I had long talk with Rabbi Wasserstein and Mrs. Gottlieb yesterday."

She sounded so tired, and it was all his fault. His eyes darted from side to side. "What's going on?" *As if he didn't know.*

"Rabbi Wasserstein tells me you're getting C's in *gemara* and Halacha —"

"That's why I was up so late," Jacob interrupted. "I was studying. I know I'm doing bad, Eema. I'm trying to improve —"

"Yonkie, this isn't about your grades. It's about *you*." She spoke in a gentle voice. "Rabbi Wasserstein says your attitude toward school has changed in the last six months. You're not a problem kid — you're never disruptive — but you're not doing well because you don't seem to care. Half the time you sleep at your desk, the other half you appear apathetic. He thinks you're very bored."

"School's boring. I am bored." Jacob looked at the ceiling. *If only she knew. So trusting.* "But I can do better. It's no big deal. It's just a matter of doing all the busy work. I'll do better, Eema. I promise. Don't worry."

"Sweetheart, forget about me. I want to talk about *you*." Rina kissed his hand. "Mrs. Gottlieb says you're roughly two years ahead in math without even trying. You're only a sophomore. She says by the time you reach your senior year, there'll be no one left at school who'll be able to teach you."

"So I'll take some classes at CSUN. Or better yet UCLA." The kid smiled. It lit up his face. "I'll need a car for that."

Evading the issue. Rina said, "Jacob, I want you to listen and take what I have to say seriously. Okay?"

"This sounds bad."

"It's not bad. Just listen. Rabbi Wasserstein told me about a program that he thinks is tailormade for kids like you — those gifted in math and science —"

"Nerds."

"Jacob, let me finish, please."

"Sorry."

Rina said, "You'd be officially enrolled in high school at Ner Yisroel, but you'll take your science and math courses at Johns Hopkins."

"Ner Yisroel?" Jacob made a horrified face. "You've got to be kidding!"

"Yonkie, it's a golden opportunity —"

"They're fanatics!" Jacob cried out. "I'll die!"

"You won't die," Rina said. "You might even *learn* something."

Jacob bit his lip and was silent.

Rina said, "I know you're a social kid. And I know you like girls. This wouldn't be forever. It's for one year. I think you could make it through one year."

Jacob exhaled. His expression was still sour. "When would I go? Like for *next* year?"

"No, no, no," Rina said. "For your senior year. I'm not sending you and Sammy away at the same time. Selfishly, it would be too hard for me."

"So either way, I'm going to be here next year?"

"Yes. And that would be good, because your grades in Hebrew studies would have to come up in order to qualify. In addition, you'd have to do really well on your SAT, and you'd have to get eight hundred on the math portion of your SATIIs. Wasserstein doesn't think that would be a problem though — the eight hundred."

"Yeah, well, he's not taking the tests." Jacob cracked his knuckles. "I suppose I could do all right. I'm a good test-taker."

"Yonkie, everyone in the school thinks you're not being challenged academically, but no one knows how to fix the problem." Rina's eyes misted up. "I don't relish the idea of sending you away. Your life has been one big mass of disruption. But time is so precious. Why waste it if there's something better for you?"

"I know. You're trying to do what's best for me."

"It's a cliché, but it's true." Rina patted his face. "You don't have to make a decision. I'm just offering it to you as a possibility."

The teen was quiet for a moment. Then he said, "If I went to Baltimore in my senior year, Sammy would be in New York by then."

"Yes. The two cities are about a three-and-a-half-hour train ride or a forty-minute plane trip apart. You two could spend Shabbos with each other anytime you wanted."

Jacob shrugged. "I'll consider it. I know it's important to you."

"Jacob, it's not *me*. It's you —"

"No, Eema, it's *you*. If it was up to me, I'd drop out of school and like . . . sail around the world."

Rina was stunned, not by his words, but by his honesty. "Jacob, you're so unhappy. *What is it?*"

The teen shrugged.

"Do you feel burdened by being religious?"

He regarded his mother. *How did she know?* "Sometimes." He hesitated. "It's not just being religious. It's . . . just . . . I don't know. Everything seems so pointless. I mean, look at you, Eema. You're a good person. You believe in Hashem. You do all the right stuff, all the moral stuff. And then, bam!" He clapped his hands loudly. "Abba gets sick and dies. And suddenly you're a widow stuck with two small kids —"

"Yonkie —"

"And then you go on and remarry, thinking that life is going to be peachy. But then look what's going on. *He's* never home. And still you wait up all hours of the night. I betcha he doesn't even come home tonight."

"He's not coming home —"

"Told ya."

"Yonkie, this isn't your concern —"

"But it is, you know. Because I see you day after day with life dragging you down."

"Where is this *coming* from? I'm a very happy person!"

"Don't you ever get *lonely*, Eema?" Jacob was agitated. "I mean, night after night after night . . . how many books can you read?"

Rina regarded her son. "You are really angry at

Peter, aren't you?"

"It's not that, although I don't know why he's so against getting another dog."

"Look, if you really want another dog, we'll get another dog —"

"That's not the point."

"Jacob, your father was broken up by Ginger's death. He has a very hard time with loss. Not just his loss, anyone's loss! He feels personally responsible for the world's problems."

"What's his excuse? He never lost a father."

"Maybe it comes from being adopted, I don't know."

Jacob had forgotten about that. "Look, I love Peter. I know he does the best he can. And he may care about the world in the abstract. But I don't think he spends a lot of time considering other people's needs."

"Yonkie, he has a very demanding job."

"Eema, nobody forced him to take the promotion." Jacob rolled his eyes in self-disgust. "I'm whining. I guess if you don't mind being alone, why should I care?"

"Yonkie, Peter loves his work. And that's a very rare thing, to love what you do —"

"I thought he was supposed to love you."

"He does —"

"And that's why he leaves you alone all the time?"

Rina gave his words some thought. "You know, I must not mind being alone. Because I seem to marry men who aren't home a lot."

Jacob looked at her. "What do you mean?

Abba was home all the time."

"Sweetie, Abba was *never* home. Usually, he got up at around five for early minyan. Then he'd come back around a half hour later and take care of you kids until I got up . . . which was usually around seven. As soon as I was up, he left for the Beit Midrash to learn until dinner. He ate dinner every night with the family . . . that much he did. And he did spend time learning with you boys, too. But as soon as it was bathtime or bedtime, he was off. He went back to learn until midnight or whatever. I don't even *know* when he came home. I was always asleep."

Silence.

Jacob was looking at his lap. Rina realized she had just punctured a balloon. She said, "Honey, I didn't mind it. Honestly. Abba loved learning, Peter loves his job and I must love solitude. Especially after a day with your sister, who's a perpetual motion machine. You think that I'm staying up, pining over Peter. In fact, I'm lying down in a very comfortable bed, off my feet, with no one making demands on me, reading an interesting book —"

"Well, that sounds really exciting."

"Jacob, you want excitement. I've had enough excitement in my life. I want peace."

The teen laughed softly. "Guess I'm not giving you much of that." It was close to one in the morning. "I'm not only keeping you up, I'm keeping myself up. I should get some sleep."

"I love you."

"I love you, too." A beat. "Eema, I don't want you to think that I'm unhappy. Most of the time, I do great. I guess you know . . . sometimes things pile up."

"You're *bored*, Jacob. You need to find a passion other than girls."

He grinned. "If you're gonna have a passion, I think girls are a great one."

"I'm not saying girls aren't great. I'm just suggesting something *in addition* to girls."

Jacob thought about it. "You're right. I'm going to be sixteen in a couple of weeks. There're always cars."

"Are you doing this to aggravate me?"

"Maybe a little." Jacob laughed. "Good night." He turned serious. "I'll give the Hopkins program some real thought. Maybe it won't be so bad." A hint of a smile. "Actually, it may not be bad at all. There are girls at Hopkins." The smile turned into a broad grin. "*College* girls."

Decker was trying to have it both ways. It wasn't working.

Marge was talking. "Okay, say we arrest him. Then he's entitled to make the phone call to whoever he wants. At least to his lawyer —"

"That's exactly what we don't want. Pluto making calls before the search warrants for the compound are pulled! The last thing we need is him warning the others."

Decker tapped his foot.

"The idea is to stall him without ostensibly denying him due process." A pause. "Okay. Let's say we're detaining him, not booking him —"

"He's still entitled to a phone call even if he's detained."

"No, he isn't —"

"He's entitled to a lawyer —"

"It only becomes relevant if we question him. So we won't question him."

"So why are we detaining him?"

"Detaining him pending our current investigation. Until we can verify his story that he hasn't been up here for the last two days."

"Pete, that could take time — days. We can't detain him that long without a lawyer."

"He doesn't know that."

"Yes, he does. Even if he doesn't, *we* do! We screw up, they throw out everything we found on a tech."

Of course she was right. Decker frowned. "All right. Let's say we're detaining him and he's entitled to a phone call. And we're willing to give him one. But we can't let him use the line up here because it's blocked off, being part of the crime scene. And we can't bring him to an alternate locale to make a call, because . . . because . . . why?"

Marge shrugged. "We're too busy."

"Exactly," Decker said. "We're too busy. So we have no choice but to keep him locked tight in the car until our current investigation up here is completed to our satisfaction. Then of course when we leave the site, we'll try to find him a phone. But by then, it'll be three in the morning. And you know most everything will be shut down —"

"Pay phones?"

"They're always broken, Marge."

Marge was skeptical. "You're just lucky that his antiquated cellular phone has a signal that doesn't carry this far."

"Damn lucky."

"What if he wants to use our radio?"

"Can't let civilians use tactical lines. Against regulations."

"Not the tactical lines, Pete. Let's say he asks either Scott or me to place a call through the RTO."

"Then you don't get through."

Marge complained, "He's going to scream."

"Let him scream —"

"*You're* not dealing with him."

"I've been *dealing* with a dissected corpse, Margie."

She thought a moment. "I'll trade you jobs."

Decker grinned. "Easier to work with a dead asshole than a live one?"

"You got it."

"No dice," Decker said. "*I* choose the assignments. One of the perks of being a loo."

23

Modern-day holding cells were hermetically sealed, the only way to peek into the room being through a double layer of steel-meshed glass set into the steel-reinforced door. Sheriff Johannsen's jail consisted of two connected holding pens of ancient variety — steel-barred like the old-fashioned types used in Oater movies. As a matter of fact, Marge thought the entire office looked like a western film set. The window to the sheriff 's office held a decal of a big gold star. Inside were three scarred wooden desks sitting in a room that couldn't have been more than five hundred square feet worth of space. A linoleum floor had been browned by age, and walls held neon pink flyers of local events as well as official sheriff notices with everything thumbtacked to corkboards. A bare bulb hung from a lethargic ceiling fan. Scanning the area, Marge thought she noticed a gun vault. On second glance, it turned out to be a fifty-year-old icebox.

The cells were in the back and reached through a door cut into the back wall. The area was hot and stuffy even at night. A yellow bug light gave off dim illumination in sepia tones. Benton was sitting, bent forward, on a jail bench steel-bolted to the wall. His feet were planted on the ground, his knees apart, his cuffed wrists resting in front of his groin as if guarding it. He was sweating rivers — his face wet rather than damp — but he didn't seem to care. His clothes stank of perspiration, blood, dirt and shit. His hair was matted, his expression shadowed with dirt and darkened with uncertainty. When the cell door opened, he made eye contact with Johannsen, but refused to look at Marge or at Oliver. Marge leaned against one corner of the bars while Scott took up the other.

Johannsen chose to sit on the bench, keeping an eighteen-inch distance between Benton and him. "How you feeling, guy?"

The farmhand's voice was soft. "Been better, Sheriff, though I'm not complainin'."

"Stoner offer you some coffee?"

"Yeah, he did."

"Did you take it?"

"Yeah, I did."

"You want another cup?"

"No, I'm all right."

"A cigarette . . . you don't smoke."

"No, I don't."

A protracted silence.

Johannsen said, "I called Ruth up about twenty minutes ago to tell her what's going on."

A long pause. "Why'd you do that?"

"You know Ruth. She likes to help —"

"Don't need no help."

Johannsen said, "Benton, you're gonna need help and lots of it. You're in a tight position."

"I didn't kill no one, Sheriff. You know that."

"Benton, did you know that man in the cabinet?"

"Yes, sir, that was Guru Nova."

"Did you have anything against him?"

"No, sir. Not at all. Though I didn't knowed him so well. I knowed Pluto better."

"Pluto visit you recently?"

"Mebbe a week ago, I saw him."

"Anybody else been up at the ranch?"

Benton pondered the question. "No, just Old Guy Shoe trying to bum a free chicken."

Johannsen turned to Oliver. "They call him Old Guy Shoe because he walks around with old shoes around his neck. Strung together like a lei." He turned back to Benton. "What happened with Old Guy Shoe?"

"Nothin'."

"Nothin'?"

"I gave him some chicken heads and feet and he was happy." A pause. "When do I get outta here, Sheriff?"

Johannsen said, "First, these people here gotta ask you some questions."

"So ask already."

Marge said, "I think Pluto wants to have an attorney present during the questioning."

"Don't need some lawyer man. I didn't do nothin'."

"It's for your protection, sir," Oliver said.

For the first time, Benton's dull eyes focused on the detectives. "Then I'd like to call Father

Jupiter if you wouldn't mind it."

Oliver and Marge exchanged glances. Oliver jumped in. "That's going to be hard to arrange, Benton. I was hoping Brother Pluto would have told you by now."

"Told me what?"

Marge spoke softly. "Father Jupiter died two days ago."

For a brief moment, Benton didn't react. He sat frozen in his position with only his chest rising and falling. Then he said, "So that's why he wasn't coming up. I thought he was mad at me." He looked at Marge. "Wonder why Brother Pluto didn't tell me?"

"He didn't want to make you feel bad."

"How'd he die?"

Benton appeared to be absorbing the words.

"I can't say too much, Benton," Marge said. "But I'll tell you what it says in the papers. It's a suspicious death by overdose. Possibly a suicide —"

"Pigshit!" He blushed. "Pardon my language, ma'am."

"That's all right." Remaining in the corner of the cell, Marge squatted. That way she was eye level with him. She didn't want to ask anything about Nova. But what would it hurt to ask him about Jupiter's death? "Why do you say his suicide is pigstuff?"

" 'Cause he weren't the type to do that."

Marge waited. Nothing. She prompted, "Tell me why *you* think Father Jupiter wouldn't have committed suicide."

"Ma'am, I ain't like Brother Bob or Brother Pluto. I ain't smart. But I kin tell when a man's happy. When we used to take out the telerscope, I've never seen such a content being as Father Jupiter. The way he looked at the stars . . . like he was one with the heavens. He tole me that one day he was going up there . . . with the stars."

Oliver said, "That might have meant that he was going to kill himself —"

"No, sir," Benton corrected. "He was talkin' about his time machine. He was buildin' one." He looked at Johannsen. "I told you that, didn't I, Sheriff?"

"That you did."

"Father Jupiter tole me he was talkin' to a university 'bout it. About his ideas. He was real excited."

No one spoke for a few seconds. Oliver glanced at Marge. He said, "What university?"

"I don't recall. But he said 'twas a big one."

Marge said, "Southwest University of Technology —"

"That's it."

Again, the two detectives exchanged looks. Marge said, "His old haunt."

"Also where his daughter works," Oliver added.

Marge asked the farmhand, "Did Jupiter ever mention his daughter, Europa?"

"Don't recall," Benton answered. "Mebbe he did say something about a daughter. 'Course all the ladies at the Order of the Rings of God was his spiritual daughter."

"She's not from the Order," Marge said. "She's Jupiter's real daughter — his biological daughter. Jupiter was married before he became Jupiter. Did you know that?"

"No, ma'am, I did not. Still, it don't surprise me."

"How long have you known Jupiter?" Oliver asked.

"Ten years."

A decade is a long time. Marge asked, "How'd you meet him, Benton?"

The farmhand tensed in concentration. "Believe 'twas when I worked at Harrison . . . up in Saugus. Not too far from the Order. Mebbe twenty minutes by car."

"I know where Saugus is," Marge said.

"All right. So you know." Benton straightened his spine and scratched his nose with his cuffed hands. He was asked an important question and he had to answer it with the proper respect. "Father Jupiter jus' came up to me the one day. We talked some. Then he left."

"What did you and Father Jupiter talk about, Benton?"

He thought about that. " 'Bout me, I suppose. Did I like my job? Stuff like that."

They waited for more. But nothing came forth.

"Then what happened?" Marge urged.

Benton said, "He visited me another day.

Agin, we talked. I reckon this went on for a couple of weeks. Then one day, he asked if I'd like to run his chicken ranch up here in Central City. He said he'd pay me as much as I was making at Harrison, and I'd have a whole house to live in — not just a room. Sounded good so I said all right."

Oliver had taken out his notebook. "Do you remember the address of the Harrisons?"

"Not Harrisons. Just Harrison. No ess."

"Ah," Oliver said. "It's the name of a place, not the name of a couple."

"That's right."

The conversation was making Marge very curious about Benton's past relationship with Jupiter. "What kind of place is Harrison?"

"What kind of place?"

"What kind of people live there?"

"Oh." Again, Benton scratched his nose. This time, he also wiped his soaking face. "Lots of different people. Some were drying out on alcohol, some were drying out on drugs, some were just plain old folks. Me, I didn't do no drugs or alcohol. I was the handyman. They let me live there —"

"Who's they?" Marge asked.

Benton thought about that for a long time. "The woman who hired me was named Florine. That's all I knowed about her."

"How'd you find the job, Benton?" Oliver asked.

A stretch of silence. "I think one of the nurses

314

tole me about it."

"Nurses?" Marge asked. "Were you in a hospital, Benton?"

"Board and care," the farmhand replied flatly. "I came out of the army with a bad case of congestion that didn't go away. In the VA for two years, then they moved me to board and care in Newhall. Took a while for me to get better. A long while. The nurses used to ask me to fix things. They knowed I was good with my hands."

More silence.

"I recall that one of them mentioned Harrison to me. I worked there for five years. Never missed a day, though at times I was pooped. Got tired of people's bitches and messed-up lives. So Father Jupiter's offer sounded all right to me."

Saugus was in the Foothill division. Ten years ago Marge was working in Foothill as a detective in sex crimes. As far as she remembered, there weren't any murders resembling Nova's dissected body. If Benton had been a serial killer all those years ago, he had used a different MO. "How did Jupiter find you? Had he ever lived at Harrison?"

"Don't know."

"What was Jupiter's connection to Harrison?"

The farmhand shrugged. So much for Benton's power of conjecture.

"And this was around ten years ago?" Marge asked.

"Yes, ma'am."

"Did he talk about time machines back then?" Oliver asked.

"No, sirree. Back then, it was all about God and the heavens and the evils of modern science and scientists. That's why I was real surprised when he brought up the telerscope a year ago. 'Cause a telerscope sure is a science object. Still, it seemed to make him happy."

Oliver gave Marge a look. He said, "I need a word with my partner in private, Sheriff. Let's take five."

"No problem." Johannsen liberated himself and the two detectives from the cage. He locked the door behind him. "We'll be back, Benton. Would you like a cold drink?"

"No, I don't think so." He lay down on the bench. "Think I'll snooze a spell."

"You do that."

To Marge, Oliver said, "Let's take a walk."

They stepped outside under a star-studded blanket. The air was saturated with cricket calls, cicadas and the low croaks of lusting bullfrogs. The sheriff's office was in the middle of town — the only storefront still lit up. The rest of the shops were dark and shut tight, to be expected since it was almost one in the morning.

Oliver asked, "You believe Benton? About Jupiter being happy and not the type to kill himself?"

Marge said, "We should believe a man who has body parts in his kitchen?"

"Good point." Oliver smoothed back sweat-soaked hair. "So why do I feel we're missing something?"

"Let's start with what we know."

"A novel idea," Oliver said. "We've got Jupiter dead. And we know that he was being poisoned."

"Although not in lethal doses."

"And now we have his farmhand . . . who granted is a weirdo with a dead body in his kitchen . . . that's a big granted —"

Marge broke in. "Look, these are the facts. Either Jupiter ODed himself or he didn't OD himself. If he ODed himself, that contradicts what Benton says about Jupiter being a happy camper. If he didn't OD himself, then someone did it to him. And that goes hand in hand with the poisoning. The way it's laid out, it looks like the arsenic wasn't going fast enough so someone acted drastically."

Oliver said, "Agreed. So who wanted Jupiter dead?"

Marge said, "Dr. Little says that you can last awhile with arsenic in your system, but not forever. Because there is a build-up factor, each bit adding to each other. The poisoning couldn't have been going on forever — maybe a year or so."

"Which corresponds to about the time that Jupiter was rediscovering science . . ."

Marge said, "Europa told Decker that Jupiter was as sharp as a tack when it came to their scientific discussions."

Oliver said, "It seems to me that Jupiter was coming back to his old field after what . . . a twenty-plus-year hiatus?"

"Could be. But what does that have to do with someone pumping him with arsenic — not enough to kill him, but enough to make him sick as a dog —" Marge stopped herself. "It made him *sick*, Scotty. Maybe it also made him addled. Confused enough so he couldn't concentrate."

Neither one spoke.

Marge said, "The question I'm asking is: Was someone poisoning him to keep him from thinking about his former preoccupation with time machines?"

Suddenly Oliver's eyes widened. "Margie, suppose you were a scientist trying to establish a distinguished reputation for yourself as a hard-nosed cosmologist. And you have this father who was once brilliant but had been laughed out of the profession as a crackpot — a crazy, demented man who kept talking about building time machines. And finally, when you think he's out of the picture . . . well, suddenly he reemerges with the same crazy, embarrassing ideas —"

"*Europa?*"

"Didn't Benton say Jupiter was speaking to the people at Southwest U? Margie, she teaches there. She must cringe every time someone mentions his name."

"Europa hadn't seen her father in years —"

"*If* she's telling the truth."

Marge gave his idea serious thought. "She finally manages to get this albatross off her neck, and just when she's getting somewhere in her field, he reappears."

318

"Exactly," Oliver said. "So what would it hurt if she slipped a little arsenic in his vitamins to slow him down. You know, just slipped a little powder in Jupiter's drink or in his vitamin supplements —"

"Hold on," Marge said. "Who said there was arsenic in Jupiter's vitamins?"

"Deck mentioned it as a possibility —"

"So you don't know if there is or isn't arsenic in any of the vitamins."

"No, I don't know."

"This is all theoretical."

"Of course, it's theoretical. If we had facts, we wouldn't be debating anything." Oliver began to walk back to the sheriff's office. "Don't forget this, Margie. Europa is the beneficiary of a million-dollar cash life policy plus more if the death is ruled accidental."

"But that cash policy has been in effect for years. Why would she take him out now if it was only for the money?"

"Because he wasn't ruining her reputation until recently," Oliver countered. "And maybe Europa didn't want him to die. She only wanted him incapacitated so he wouldn't be an embarrassment. When the arsenic didn't work as well as she hoped, and he continued to go on with his time machines, *then* Europa was forced to do something permanent."

"So how did she OD him if she hadn't seen him for fifteen years? How would she even get into the compound?"

"She had help," Oliver said. "Bob."

"She hasn't seen Bob in years."

"So she's lying. Or maybe not. I don't know." Oliver shrugged. "No theory is without its glitches." They walked in silence for a moment. He said, "What's with this place where Benton worked? Harrison. Ever heard of it?"

"No."

"What do you think it is? Rehab?"

"Sounds like it," Marge said.

"And what do you think Benton was *really* doing there?" Oliver said drolly. "My guess is he was popping Demerol to keep the demons away. He looks like a mental case."

"We should be able to verify that," Marge answered. "What I'd like to know is *Jupiter's* connection to Harrison?"

"Good question." Oliver looked at his watch. "When's this lawyer gonna get here? Johannsen said he'd have someone here within the hour, and that was an hour ago."

"Let's just wait it out," Marge said.

"Stuck in shitsville. Bet they don't even have cable. Why do I get all the plum assignments?"

"Must be your charm."

Pluto exclaimed, "Your outrageous actions are in flagrant violation of citizen's rights. I am *not* going to let this pass. Someone will have your badge for this!"

Decker slowed his speed. The road was rutted and hard on the tires. "If someone wants my badge, he can have it. It would sure make my wife happy."

"Deliberately denying me access to Benton —"

"Just protecting you, Brother Pluto. You wouldn't want to be charged with collusion —"

"What?!"

"Anybody who has visited that farm in the last two days is under suspicion."

"Then that lets me out —"

"As soon as we verify your story."

"I'm not worried about myself! I'm *innocent!* I'm absolutely stunned by what you . . . discovered. It's horrid! It's obscene! It's repulsive. It's grotesque! I am deeply saddened about Brother Nova's untimely and violent death. He will be missed as the great man he was, and the perpetrator of this crime should be punished to the maximum. But right now I'm concerned about Benton!"

"So you don't think Benton was the perpetrator?"

"I can't comment on that."

So far, they hadn't found a kill spot on the ranch. But Decker had other ideas as to where the murder might have taken place.

Pluto was talking. "He needs representation. You and your lackeys are abrogating Benton's due process, knowing full well that the man does not understand the gravity of the situation."

"Benton will be protected. They're calling in an interim lawyer until you get someone up there."

"I know what *kind* of lawyer you chose. Some idiot out of Podunk U. named Jeb —"

"I have a cousin named Jeb. He's a pretty astute businessman —"

"What does *that* have to do with anything?"

"You just seem prejudiced against the name Jeb —"

"You think you can storm-troop your way over me. But you're sadly mistaken! And, on top of everything else, you won't even let me use the telephone."

"I've already explained this to you, Brother. The ranch's lines were being used to conduct emergency tactical information —"

"There are phone booths, Lieutenant."

"Sir, I can't have any kind of privileged information about a murder investigation transmitted through public airwaves."

"So I can't call on your private line. But I can't call on public lines either. You're clearly violating my rights —"

"I'm not violating your rights because I'm not charging you with anything . . . at least, not yet."

"So what exactly *are* you doing with me?" Pluto demanded to know. "You're not officially arresting me. But you are *detaining* me."

"In a manner of speaking, yes. Just until we can clear up a few things."

"But you won't let me make a simple phone call."

"As soon as we get to the station house, you can make your call." Decker checked his watch.

It was half-past one. "We've got another twenty minutes. Just hang on."

"Keeping me sequestered like some quarantined animal."

Decker gave up, turning a deaf ear to Pluto's rantings. The outrage, the indignity, the emotional stress, the forthcoming lawsuits, blah, blah, blah. The threats went through him like a bad case of the runs. White noise.

Decker heard his name over his radio. He picked up the mike and responded. His patience and his sneaky schemes were finally rewarded. The search warrants for the Order's compound and grounds had come through. He acknowledged the information and signed off. Pluto must have heard some key words. He started to ask questions.

"What's she talking about? What warrants?"

Decker said nothing.

Pluto became agitated. "What warrants was she referring to? She mentioned the Order. What do warrants have to do with the Order? You can't possibly believe that any of us had anything to do with Nova's murder! Do you honestly believe that any of us would be *so* stupid as to stuff poor Nova in our own ranch and then *allow* your people to go search it?"

The outraged Pluto was making some points. Decker said, "I don't know. Would you be that stupid?"

"I won't dignify that with a response."

"Fine with me. Let's enjoy the silence."

Pluto didn't take the hint. "You're only going to increase hostility and ill-will by allowing your men to trample again and again through our quarters. This horrible murder happened at the ranch. What does it have to do with searching the *Order* in the wee hours of the morning?"

Decker asked, "So you think Benton did it?"

"I told you, I won't comment . . . well, who else would have *done* it? Nova was a much-respected, much-needed member of the Order. Why would we foul our own nest?"

"Why do you think Benton did it?"

"He's obviously a bit off."

"Why do you say that?"

"Come *on,* Lieutenant. You met the man. Jupiter took on all sorts of charity cases. Benton was one of them."

"Where did Jupiter find Benton?"

"I don't remember," Pluto snapped. "I think Benton had been in rehab. In the early days, Father Jupiter often went to rehab centers to deliver messages of spiritual encouragement. Back then, he felt it was his duty to reach out to the weakest elements of our society. As the Order grew, more of his time was demanded at home. But often he'd assign me to pick up the slack. Which is how I found Moriah Farrander."

"You're a saint —"

"You asked me a question —"

"Which rehab centers did Jupiter enlighten?"

"Now you're being facetious."

"Do you have names?"

"No." Pluto sighed. "I suppose if you cooperated with me, I could cooperate and get them for you."

Decker was quiet.

Pluto said, "I'd like our dear brothers and sisters to feel a sense of security. While I realize I am not going to prevent you from invading, at least can you wait until morning?"

"Not a chance —"

"How is waking up our followers at an ungodly hour going to help you?"

"Brother, things have come up that necessitate the execution of the warrants now."

"Things? What things!"

"You'll find out soon enough," Decker said. "We're headed for the Order. You're finally going to get that phone call, Brother Pluto. And if I were you, I'd use it to call your lawyer."

24

Parked two blocks away from the Order were three cruisers, Detective Bert Martinez's Honda and Detective Tom Webster's Audi. Decker pulled behind one of the black-and-whites, shut the motor and got out of his car. He opened the passenger door.

"Out."

Pluto was surprised by Decker's authoritarian voice. Uniformed cops were approaching the car, their hands on their guns. The guru emerged from the backseat, his face registering apprehension. "What's going on? I don't like this."

Decker identified himself with his badge and gave the uniforms a hold sign. To Pluto, he said, "I need to confer with my two Homicide detectives. You want to get back to the Order, just stay put and cool your heels."

"Where are you going?" Pluto demanded to know.

The little man's eyes were glued to the uniforms. Decker figured that Pluto had probably been bullied in his young years. So what did he do with his personal power? Bullied others. Decker pointed to a spot about twenty feet away. "I'll be over there." He nodded to the police officers. "These fine gentlemen will take good care of you." To the uniforms, he said, "Watch him."

Martinez and Webster had already exited their cars. Decker met with them under the inkblot shadows of a scrub oak, dried leaves and twigs snapping under his feet. In the starlight, he could see all the gray poking through Bert Martinez's black hair. His mustache, however, was still dark — thick and the consistency of Brillo. His fleshy face drooped with wee-hour fatigue, but his brown eyes were alert and ready to do business.

Being younger and in better shape, Webster seemed to handle the late hours with aplomb. His hair was combed, his suit was pressed and even his socks matched. His face held few wrinkles and sags around his baby blues, making Decker feel like the wizened elder.

It was a role he didn't relish.

He could only imagine how Martinez felt. Still, the duo got along well although they had been working together for less than two years.

Webster handed Decker the warrants. "Everything's kosher."

Martinez added, "Checked and rechecked. But you can look them over if you want."

Decker did want to. As he read the legalese to make sure it was all there, he said, "Heard from Dunn or Oliver? I told them to call you two for updates being as I was stuck with Mr. Charm."

"Marge's last call was 'bout twenty minutes ago over the tach lines," Webster drawled. "The techs haven't found a kill spot in the house, so she and Scott are staying up north. They're planning on doing a grid search of the entire property at dawn . . . figured it would be easier to bunk out in Central City rather than to go back and forth."

"Makes sense." Decker checked his watch. Two A.M. "They sure as hell didn't pull an all-nighter with Benton. I take it they didn't get an early confession."

"If they did, they didn't tell us," Martinez said.

"Wonder why they quit so early?"

" 'Cause he's a stubborn shit," Webster said. "He's got his version and he's stickin' to it."

"What's his version?" Decker asked.

"He didn't do it."

Martinez said, "Dunn said he kept repeating the same mantra over and over and over. 'I didn't do nothin', I didn't do nothin'.' She felt they could have questioned him for a month and couldn't have broken him."

"I'm not asking for a month," Decker said. "But two hours is skimpy."

"The sheriff is keeping Benton locked up pending the grid search," Martinez said. "Dunn and Oliver were planning to question him again after they've combed the property. If they find any corroborating evidence, it'll shore up a case against him."

"Or, at the least, give them a line of questioning," Webster said. "Right now, they don't have dick because Forensics only found trace amounts of Nova's blood in the ranch house. She said that corresponded to drip marks in transporting the body from the front door to the kitchen."

"Who's she?"

Martinez said, "Dr. Little. We spoke to her around an hour ago. The body was drained of its blood way before it was stuffed into the cabinet."

"Benton slaughters chickens," Decker said.

Martinez and Webster exchanged looks, waited for Decker to explain the non sequitur.

"Don't you drain chickens by chopping off their heads and turning them upside down?" Decker asked.

Martinez shrugged.

"Beats me," Webster said.

"Nova's head was chopped off," Decker said.

"Are you saying that Benton mistook Nova for a chicken?"

"Funny, Tom —"

"I'm not responsible for anything I say at two in the morning."

"I'm just saying that Benton had experience in draining blood."

"You think he did it, Loo?" Webster asked.

"Right now, I have some doubts, but with proper evidence, I could be convinced."

Martinez said, "FYI, Loo, Benton had been with a woman for the past two nights — which, according to Little — was the time range for Nova's death. The woman's name was Ruth . . ." He started flipping through his notes. "Ruth . . ."

"Ruth Young," Decker said. "Johannsen told me about her. She alibied Benton?"

"Yep. But Marge was also quick to point out that Benton still had lots of hours alone in the house."

Decker ran his hands through dirty, sweaty hair. It was going to boil down to supporting evidence. To Tom, he said, "You just told me they found *traces* of human blood in the house."

"Consistent with the drippings of the drained torso as it was taken into the kitchen."

Decker recapped, "So after they've exhausted evidence collection at the ranch, Oliver and Dunn are going to requestion Benton?"

"That's what they told us," Martinez said. "They'll call you when it's light, and keep you posted." He took out a slip of paper. "Or if you want, Loo, you can call them. But the place they're staying has only public lines."

Decker considered phoning them, but nixed the idea. "Let 'em grab a couple of hours of sleep."

"A couple of hours sounds right fine to me," Webster said. "One thing before I forget. Marge wanted me to ask you if you ever heard of a place . . ." He took out his notepad and rummaged through the pages. "It's called Harrison. She thinks it's a rehab center located in Saugus."

"Harrison . . ." The name was familiar. Decker was trying to conjure up a mental picture. He had worked in Foothill division for over a decade — in Homicide, in Sex Crimes, in CAPS. Saugus was under Foothill's jurisdiction. "A green, two-story, wood-sided place converted to a halfway house. I think it had eight rooms plus a janitor's basement. It also had a wraparound porch. Drug and alcohol rehab, but it also took in some EMRs as well as nonviolent mental cases."

"EMR?" Martinez asked.

"Educable mentally retarded," Decker said. "A woman named Flora . . . no, not Flora . . . Florine . . . Florine Vesquelez. She was the coordinator. Not only of Harrison, but of several other halfway houses in Foothill. Far as I know, she's a straight arrow. What's with Harrison?"

"Benton worked there as a handyman for five years," Webster said.

"Worked there or lived there?"

"Both. It was where he met Jupiter. He claims that one day, Jupiter just showed up and started talking to him. Eventually, Jupiter hired him away to work at the ranch."

"How long ago did this happen?" Decker asked.

"Ten years ago."

Decker said, "So it was during my time at Foothill. I still know lots of people there. I'll check it out. Do you know if Jupiter was a resident at Harrison?"

"Not when Benton was there." Webster's eyes went to Pluto. "What's our mission with Mr. Shorty?"

"This is the situation," Decker said. "We've got two homicide investigations going at once — Nova and Jupiter. Most likely, they're related, but we don't know for certain. Jupiter's death

331

could have been a self-inflicted OD, but now it's looking closer to a homicide because he had more than trace amounts of arsenic in his system. Are we all together?"

"Like Siamese twins," Webster said.

"It appears that Nova's kill spot wasn't in the ranch house, though we don't know about the property yet. From what we *do* know, it's possible that the kill spot *may* be in the Order's compound, and someone dragged the pieces up north. Asnikov told us there was only four people other than Jupiter with access to the ranch — Venus, Bob, Pluto and Nova, but he's dead. If Asnikov's correct, the three remaining gurus must be regarded as suspects. Are you both with me?"

"Like army buddies in the trenches," Martinez said.

Decker went on. "I'll also have to interview the principals about Jupiter's death because this arsenic business sheds a whole new light on the investigation. The warrants give us permission to do a complete search and seizure. Anything we turn up, we can bag. Tom, you search the laundry area — the sinks and washers — for bloody clothes. Then check the toilets, the bathtubs and the pipes for hair and bone fragments. Martinez, start on Nova's room. You'll need to do an exhaustive search, see if you can't find something hidden. Lastly, we look for anything with arsenic in it. I'll start by checking out the toolshed in the back area. I remember seeing rat poison there."

Skull and crossbones.

"This is going to take time," Webster said.

"Probably until late this morning," Decker said. "Since you'll be tied up, and Dunn and Oliver are in Central City, I've got to assign someone to the MP cases of Lyra and Andromeda."

"What a mess!"

Decker thought, *Wasn't that the truth!*

As soon as the cars started pulling up to the compound, the three patrolling Dobermans responded with threatening barks. Decker got out of his unmarked and slammed the door shut. The others followed.

To the six uniformed officers, Decker said, "Take guarded positions in front of your vehicles, behind the doors with your guns drawn until I give you an all-clear sign. Then I want two of you on the north side, two on the south and two in the rear. Remember to wait until I give you the signal before you leave your positions. Any questions?"

There were none.

"Go."

Martinez pointed to the guard dogs. "What do we do about the alligators in the moat, Loo?"

No one could get anywhere near the open-barred gate, which, at the moment, was studded with sharp, Doberman teeth.

Webster asked, "You bring back any chickens, Loo? Maybe we can distract the critters."

Decker wasn't in the mood for wise-ass comments. His head throbbed and his annoyance was rapidly turning to anger.

Smirking, the guru said, "Looks like you have a problem, Lieutenant."

Decker held his temper. "Call off your monsters."

On home territory, Pluto was sure-footed. He responded in a huff. "They consider you the enemy. They're only doing what we've trained them to do."

"At this hour of the morning, this kind of barking is a legal nuisance —"

"So cite me."

"Look, buddy. It's two A.M. and I've got hours of work ahead of me. I've got all the necessary papers and you're hanging me up. I'm a hairsbreadth away from arresting you for obstruction of justice."

"Your fatigue is showing." The little man was enjoying his mini-voyage of a power trip. "And you didn't say please.

Decker gnashed his teeth and took out the handcuffs.

"All right, all right," Pluto said quickly. "No sense of humor."

He stood in front of the outside gate and quieted the dogs.

Unlocking the deadbolt.

As soon as Pluto entered the grounds, the biggest of the three animals jumped on top of him and licked the venal face. The beast almost knocked him down.

Pluto didn't feel amorous. "Get down, Dancer, right now!" He took hold of the animal's choke chain and, with a sharp yank, brought her back down to all fours. He turned to Decker. "It's all attitude, you know."

"You've got thirty seconds to get the dogs squared away before I take action," Decker said.

"I quake —"

"Twenty-five —"

"Come on, guys," Pluto said, milking his time. "The Gestapos need to get in."

Still holding Dancer by the collar, he ambled up to the front entrance with the other two beasts in tow.

Standing at the steel door, Pluto made a small, chunky shadow against a huge fortress backdrop. From Decker's perspective, the compound, backlit by gray starlight, looked like an impenetrable bunker. Pluto had left the outside gate open and Decker had thought about following him onto the premises. But two of the dogs were still untethered. Better to lag behind until the beasts were out of sight.

Pluto punched numbers into a panel. A moment later, a loud buzz rang out and he pushed the front door open. He took a step inside.

As the little man crossed the threshold, two booming blasts rang out, crashing through the stillness of the night. As former veterans, Decker and Martinez instantly hit the ground just as Pluto was blown backward as if caught in a gust of wind. Instinctively, the two men pulled a stunned Webster down with them.

Thick streams of liquid were squirting from the little man's chest and head. The guru fell, his skull cracking against the hard ground. Within a moment, a volley of return fire was unleashed as uniformed officers smoked up the air. It was answered by flashes of blinding hot light bursting forth from the compound's door.

They were armed with automatics!

"Fuck!" Decker shouted as he covered his head with his arms. "Fuck, fuck, *fuck!*" Belly pressed to the ground, he screamed, *"Hold your fire! Hold your fucking fire!"*

A couple of staccato beats from the uniforms, then dead silence.

Caught in the crossfire, one of the dogs lay dead.

A second beast stabbed the air with its piercing howls.

Decker raised his smarting eyes, trying to ascertain what was out there through a cloud of gunfire smoke. Dancer, the third and biggest Doberman, was whimpering pathetically, licking Pluto's head as it gushed blood.

From the hot fumes of fire emerged a loud voice. An evil Wizard of Oz orating through the stench of gunpowder. "I never did like that man."

The voice in the night.

Bob's voice. He shouted, "Tell them to knock it off! We have *kids* in here."

336

Decker's head was spinning. *"Hold your fire!"* he shouted again.

An elongated silence.

All Decker could hear was his frantic breath. He whispered, "Everybody in one piece?"

"I'm all right," Martinez whispered back.

"Tom —"

Webster was trembling so hard, he couldn't move. At last, he felt his crotch. "One piece."

More silence.

Then the voice again.

"You're very pushy, Lieutenant! You're like a fudge factor that can't be resolved. You're pissing me off!"

Decker managed to find his vocal cords. "It's unintentional, Bob."

"The road to hell is paved with good intentions. And that's what you've got here, Lieutenant. One long road paved to hottest Hades."

Another long period of silence. It was broken by the distant sounds of wailing sirens.

Bob screamed out, "You'd better call off *your* monsters, Decker! They start getting pushy, I'm not going to like it. Like I said, we have *kids* in here! And I know how much you and your buddies like kids!"

His gut churning, Decker screamed, "You hold your fire, Bob, we'll hold ours! We don't want anyone hurt." He looked at Pluto's lifeless body. The spewing had diminished to slow leaks and trickles. Blood-drained. "We don't want any *more* people hurt."

The sirens grew louder.

Decker shouted, "I'm going to crawl over to my cruisers, Bob. I've got to give my men some instructions . . . to prevent misunderstandings —"

"You're not an animal, Decker!" Bob shouted. "You want to move, walk upright like a *man!* I want to *see* you!"

Martinez whispered, "He's fucking nuts!"

Bob shouted, "Did you hear —"

"I heard you!" Decker shouted back. "I don't think that would be a good idea, Bob!"

"I've got kids here, Decker. Little kids with shiny faces. They'll make damn good cover photos for all the major magazines. You hear what I'm saying?"

Decker knew damn well what he was saying.

"It's like the elusive graviton," Bob went on. "It's out there but you can't see it. You're going to have to accept me at face value or we're going to have real problems."

Decker's face was mired in sweat. Webster said, "Don't do it —"

"Shut the *fuck* up and listen," Decker said. "As I get up, you two crawl over and take cover in the cruisers —"

"Sir, I —"

"That's a fucking order, Webster! As soon as you get to safety, find out whatever the fuck you can on who this Bob Ross is and what makes him tick! Call up Europa Ganz. She used to date the motherfucker —"

"Decker!" Bob screamed out. "I'm losing patience!"

"I make my move," Decker whispered to his men, "you make yours. Go!" Inch by inch, Decker forced himself to get to his knees.

As visible as the moon.

Slowly, he rose to his feet.

As visible as the sun.

He stood stock-still . . . waiting.

Nothing.

He started to inch backward to the cars.

Bob shouted, "Don't do anything funny! We got infrared scopes. You're as bright as daylight. And keep your hands over your head."

Decker held up his arms. "Free and clear." He stole a quick glance over his shoulder. Webster and Martinez had made it to safety.

"Don't move!" Bob shouted.

Decker stopped. "Bob, I've got to give orders to my men for everyone's protection."

"Then shout them out loud!" Bob screamed. "Why couldn't you leave well enough alone —"

The sirens were drowning him out. Cruisers flashing reds and blues, pulsating in strobic fashion. The cars pulling up one after another, each time more and more officers getting out, guns drawn, squatting behind open doors. Five, six, seven . . . Captain Strapp should be here soon.

More and more. A dozen in all.

Finally the sirens died down and all that remained were the silent gaudy car lights — as if someone muted the remote control and this TV cop scene was played out in silence. Decker's voice carried easily.

"Hold your fire!" he yelled. Then louder, just to make sure. *"Hold your fire!"*

Silence.

Flash, flash, flash went the overhead patrol car lights. Blue, red, blue, red, blue, red ... hypnotic.

Decker could feel his heart skipping beats, feel his head pounding against his skull. He couldn't stay out in the open forever, prey to some psycho's mental game.

"I'm going over to a cruiser now —"

"Stay where I can see you!" Bob demanded.

"No, Bob, I won't do that." A pause. "Remember the graviton. You don't improvise and we won't either. Trust is the name of the game."

No response.

"Bob, you hear me?"

Nothing.

With almost imperceptible movements, Decker walked backward to the nearest patrol car.

One second, two seconds, three, four, five ...

It took him almost a minute to touch a hood. His first instinct was to bolt for the door.

But that would have shown fear.

Don't ever let them see you sweat.

His face was sopping wet so it was too late for that.

Forcing himself not to immediately take cover.

Bob seemed to pride himself on some kind of perverse notion of trust. Decker decided to work on that. He shouted, "I'm still out in the open, Bob! Easy pickings. Completely open. That's how much I trust you, Bob. I know you see me —"

"Perfectly through the crosshairs!" the guru shouted back.

"And you can also hear me."

"Like a bell."

"I've got a cell phone in my pocket, Bob. Lemme give you the number."

Silence.

Decker gave him the number anyway.

Ten seconds.

Nothing.

Twenty seconds.

Nothing with nothing.

Flash, flash.

Thirty seconds.

The shrill ring broke the silence. Decker, startled, jumped, then managed to connect the line with his shaky hands. "Yo, Bob —"

"Why couldn't you just leave well enough alone, Lieutenant. Now look what you *got!*"

"I've got a mess."

"You've got more than just a mess, my friend!"

With one fluid motion, Decker slid into the safety of a nearby car, his hands trembling so hard he almost dropped the phone. He took in a deep breath and let it out with yoga precision. "I think we've got a stand-off, guy."

"You're one smart dude." A laugh. "That's exactly what we've got. And if you or anyone else tries to be a hero, you'll get one dead kid for every time you fail. In this Hollywood world of flash images and sound bites, that'll make for great Nielsen ratings. Your fuck-ups will be broadcast across the world."

25

From inside Martinez's Honda, Decker spoke fast and furiously. "We've got about five minutes before Strapp steps in and I'm off the case. I want you two out of here."

"What?" Webster started in. "Why?"

"If you two stay here, you'll be trapped into answering the captain's questions. Also, this is now a high-profile case. Most likely, the feds'll be called in. If you're here answering questions, you can't solve murders. If you're out, you can do some good. As long as Bob is talking to me, I'm forced to stick around. So you two go, and I'll make excuses for your absences."

"What kind of excuses?" Martinez asked.

Decker's mind was racing. In the distance, he heard the bleating of more sirens. "Did either of you skin yourself when we went down?"

Webster said, "I b'lieve I scraped my knee."

"Great!" Decker exclaimed. "I thought it might have been a graze wound from a bullet. I sent Martinez to take you to the hospital to have it looked at."

The wailing was getting louder, the brass was moving in. He said, "Tom, call up Dunn and Oliver. Tell them to come back to Los Angeles, but *don't* come to the Order until they hear from me.

In the meantime, fill them in."

"Got it."

"Next, find out everything you can about Guru Bob aka Bob Ross." Decker was talking rapidly. "To be thorough, you've got to check the databases. But in my gut, I still think Europa's our best bet. Grill her hard and once we have some background info on Bob maybe we can figure out *why* he's doing this. And if we can figure out the why, maybe that'll give us a strategy on how to play him."

The sirens were on top of them. Decker had to shout. "Eventually, we're going to plan a raid or infiltration. SWAT is going to need Marge, Scott and me because we've been inside the Order. I've been in parts of the compound, Marge and Scott have seen other areas. They'll want us to get together and create a floor plan. This is our ace in the hole — a way to keep everyone interested in us and buy some time until we know more. It would be nice if we found someone who's actually familiar with the interior of the place. Any suggestions?"

Webster spoke up. "What about Reuben Asnikov? Maybe he knows some ex-cult members who can help us out."

"Go for it," Decker answered.

"Cars are pulling up," Webster said.

Decker jumped out of the car just as the tires on Strapp's car spat gravel. He banged on the hood. "Go!"

Martinez gunned the motor and the Honda

sped off. As Strapp got out, Decker jogged away and tried to hide himself in the shadows. He dialed the Order. After twenty rings, he cut the connection and decided to face his boss. But within moments, *his* cellular rang.

Decker punched the button. "Bob, I'm about to be taken over." Waiting for a response. But none came. "What we have is upper echelon. Brass is going to take over. They'll probably call in the feds, although it isn't strictly a fed case. Someone'll probably confiscate my phone. I just thought I'd be a gentleman and let you know that it wasn't my idea."

"I don't like this. Feds are hotheads. Look at Waco."

"I'd be happy to stick around, Brother Bob, but like your own organization, we've got a pecking order. I'm way down on the food chain." Bob said, "Precisely what's wrong with our world. I'm trying to keep this small and personal — I mean we all know the players involved — and the government is screwing up. It's why we can't get anywhere in the space race. It's why we're behind in the arms' race. We have the science and the technology, but the bureaucrats hold us back. That and the fundamentalists. They're inherently afraid of progress."

"That may be, but there are still realities to deal with. Mine is my superiors."

"Well, I'm not dealing with your superiors or the feds, Lieutenant. You tell them that. And you also tell them if they try anything, I've got enough goodies in here to make Oklahoma City look benign."

Decker took in his words. Did he mean *bombs?*

Bob was saying, ". . . just tell them what I said, Decker!"

"Guru Bob, if you're going to blow up things, could you wait until I'm out of the picture —"

"Too late, Lieutenant. As far as I'm concerned, you're so much *in* the picture, you're hanging in a museum. But I'll tell you what. If I barbecue the place, I'll tell them you had nothing to do with it."

"It would be better if you held off —"

"Now you're getting pushy. You just want to stalemate me so you clowns can plan a raid."

"We can't storm the Order," Decker said. "It's a bunker."

"You got that right!" A stilted laugh. "Still, I'd like to see them try. It would be . . . amusing."

Someone tapped Decker on the shoulder — Strapp. Decker said, "Captain Strapp is here, Brother Bob. Would you like to talk to him?"

But the line had gone dead.

The Order of the Rings of God was getting its requisite fifteen minutes of fame with news personnel asking inane questions that had no answers. Misinformation was flying faster than sound, making it that much harder to sort fact from fiction. The good guys had set up camp behind a barrier of police vehicles — cars and vans. The media had been roped off at a distance, supposedly out of firing range, but zoom cameras were focused on strategic points. Within the hour, three different law enforcement agencies were called in, all of them pooling their ignorance.

As predicted, Decker immediately lost his command of the operation, replaced by Captain Strapp, who was then discarded in favor of the LAPD chief of police with the mayor in tow. Because Bob had mentioned bombs, the mayor had called in the ATF and the FBI to set up a task force with LAPD. The assistant director in charge (ADIC) of the Los Angeles branch of the FBI was out of town — in Sacramento — but was taking the first flight out in the morning. Explosives had turned everyone fearful. Both the police and the FBI had their own SWAT teams and hostage negotiators specializing in these kinds of delicate situations. Quantico had been apprised, the attorney general's office had been notified and there was phone contact between the on-site agents and the White House.

Ordinarily, Decker would have been ousted hours ago. But because he held sway with Bob, as predicted, the higher powers kept him on. Everyone ready, set and waiting to go except for one minor fact. *Nothing* was happening.

The techno-wizards had set up several James Bond superspy vans equipped not only with the standard SWAT MP5 rifles but also with alien, high-powered sniper gear. The weapons were sleek, heavy and lethal, outfitted with the latest in infrared scopes and sights. The van also held state-of-the-art cameras and surveillance equipment.

All of it would have been invaluable *if* the Order housed its people in tents. But as most of the place was shielded by thick, reinforced concrete block — and none of the policing agencies had X-ray vision — no one really knew what was happening on the *inside*. Warehoused in one of the FBI steel-plated monsters-on-wheels, Decker remained phoneless and jobless, cramped and hunched over, staring at static monitors. His cellular phone had been taken from him. Wired to FBI tape recording machines.

Everyone waiting for it to ring.

With him were a trio of feds. There was Supervisory Special Agent Jan Barak, a technical equipment specialist. She appeared to be in her mid-thirties with a round face and a nervous expression. She wore a black pants suit, black shirt and sneakers without socks. There was also Special Agent Darrel Lombardo, who seemed a bit older — an African-American with a receding hairline. Decker couldn't discern his assignment. He suspected Lombardo's job was watching Decker.

The final member was Bennett McCarry, special agent in charge. This rank was known as an SAC but pronounced Ess Ai Cee, never as the acronym SAC. Decker found this out when he had referred to McCarry as a SAC and was duly corrected. McCarry was Caucasian — a dapper man in his forties, dressed in a gray suit, white shirt and black-and-white geometric tie, which hung loosely around his neck. His face was long and lean, his pink cheeks sprouting light stubble. He had a prominent chin, high cheekbones and deep-set eyes. His expression was as taut as steel wire. He manned the tach phone lines — giving orders to his people, taking orders from faraway superiors, coordinating the whole mess with the mayor's command post a few vans down. During the interludes, he asked Decker pointed questions.

"How you'd get into this fiasco?"

Decker countered, "Same way you got into Waco and Ruby Ridge."

McCarry glared at him, waiting for a proper response.

Decker said, "If you ask me a specific question, I can give you a specific answer."

McCarry ground his teeth together. "What do you know about Guru Bob?"

"You want a physical description?"

"You can start with that."

"A thin guy around six-even. Lean with a goatee. Get me a police artist, I'll get you a picture. His hobbies appear to be gardening and women. He told me he had been a student at Southwest University of Technology. He was a disciple of Emil Ganz's work."

"Aka Father Jupiter," Agent Barak said out loud. "The head of the Order —"

McCarry interrupted. "Jupiter died several

days ago. Suspicious death. An OD. A Heaven's Gate copycatter — empty bottle of vodka and pills."

Decker nodded. "Earlier this evening, the coroner informed me that there had been arsenic in Jupiter's system."

McCarry perked up. "So now it's homicide."

"Not necessarily. Dr. Little still thinks booze and pills killed him. Could have been accidental, could have been suicide. But with the autopsy findings, I was able to pull warrants for a full-scale search and seizure of the Order. Which I couldn't do before because I didn't have probable cause. We got here around two in the morning —"

"Who's we?" Agent Lombardo piped in.

Decker said, "Pluto and I. Pluto's the dead guy Bob blew away. He had called off the guard dogs — the Dobies — and was entering the premises when Bob opened fire."

McCarry asked why Decker was with Pluto at two in the morning.

"A good question," Decker said. "Wait until you hear the answer. We had been up at Central City, at the Order's chicken ranch, trying to pry out a swollen, disarticulated, decapitated torso stuffed into the kitchen cabinet."

The trio went slack-jawed . . . without comment.

Decker went on. "The body turned out to be another high-ranking member of the Order — a podiatrist who called himself Guru Nova. The corpse was less than two days old because we had interviewed him around forty-eight hours ago. He signed Jupiter's death certificate, ruling it as an OD. We wanted to know *why*. He was squirrelly around us. Obviously, he felt fear from somebody. And from his outcome, his fears were well grounded."

Barak's mouth opened and closed. "Did Bob cut up Nova, also?"

"Bob's high on our hit list. A distant second suspect is the ranch's hired help — a man named Benton, who's holed up in the Central City jail. I left a couple of my guys up there to interview Benton so that I could come back down here and execute search warrants for the Order. When Bob opened fire on Pluto, I was about thirty . . . forty feet behind him. My guys and I dropped. We managed to reach safety. I called in the incident." A pause. "Now you're up to date."

McCarry played with his tie. "Why'd Bob kill Nova?"

"I don't know that he did."

"Well, why did he shoot Pluto?"

"Beats me."

"You must have a theory."

"I have several and they're all incomplete. Before I shoot off my mouth, I'm waiting for more facts."

Barak asked, "So Bob's taking over the Order?"

"Looks like it."

"Anyone else in his way?"

Decker told them about Venus.

McCarry asked, "Any idea if she's alive?"

"Nope. If he calls, I could ask him to put her on the line. But Bob's an irritable guy. He's not going to like demands."

Barak said, "You said Bob was a disciple of Ganz."

"Yes I did."

"So he was a scientist . . . once?"

"I don't know if Bob actually worked as a scientist. He was majoring in astrophysics at Southwest U. when Ganz resurfaced as Father Jupiter. Bob followed him into the Order of the Rings of God, and the rest is history."

"What do you mean resurfaced as Jupiter?" McCarry asked.

"What do you know about Ganz?"

"Cult leader of the Order of the Rings of God. Been around . . . what, ten years?"

"Fifteen."

"He used to be a well-known scientist."

"Twenty-five years ago, Dr. Emil Euler Ganz left his job and all his prestige at Southwest University of Technology and walked off the face of the earth. For ten years, his whereabouts were unknown. Fifteen years ago, he came back as Father Jupiter and started the Order."

"Where'd he go in his ten-year absence?" Lombardo asked.

"No one knows. From all accounts, Jupiter had just vanished. His family thought he was dead. Ganz's wife hired people to look for him, but they got nowhere, and she gave up. Then, suddenly, Ganz resurfaced as Jupiter."

"How convenient."

"Not for the wife."

"Where is the wife?"

"She died four years ago."

"Who told you this?"

"Ganz's daughter."

"Ganz had a daughter?"

"Ganz has three children. The daughter is the only one with something to gain from Ganz's death." He explained the insurance policy.

McCarry frowned. "You keep coming up with these zingers. What else haven't you told me?"

Decker shifted positions and met McCarry eye to eye. "I'm not holding back, Special-Agent-in-Charge McCarry. But I do have a two-day jump on you."

McCarry asked, "Can you tell us why there's no Bob Ross matching Guru Bob's description in our computers?"

"Your computers are either incomplete or Bob Ross isn't his real name. Which wouldn't surprise me. Most of the cult members have changed their names. Right now, the majority are astral names — Venus, Pluto, Andromeda —"

Barak asked, "So why is Bob just . . . Bob?"

"Asserting his independence, maybe." Decker shrugged. "Venus's real name is Jilliam Laham. Originally, she was a friend of Ganz's daughter, Europa. Andromeda's name is Lauren Bolt. She's missing, by the way. She, and a twelve/thirteen-year-old kid named Lyra, disappeared from the Order around eighteen hours ago."

"Are you putting me on?" McCarry asked.

"Wish I were. Yesterday Pluto called up the station house in a rage. He all but accused us of kidnapping them. Which is one of the reasons we were up at the ranch . . . sure you don't want to write this down?"

McCarry's disbelief was cut short by the ring of the cellular. The tapes clicked on and he connected the call. "This is Special Agent Bennett McCarry of the FBI. Talk to me."

Guru Bob was pissed. "Get me Decker!"

McCarry had experience with these types of situations. He had worked with the Freemen in Idaho and Montana. The trick was to keep cool yet remain firm. He said, "He's not available. What can I do for you, Bob?"

"It's guru to you, shithead. Besides, I don't talk to idiots I can't see —"

"I'll step outside —"

"Don't interrupt!" Bob was shouting. Decker could hear him through the receiver, see his voice waves spike on the monitor. "You have a minute to *make* Decker available, Special Agent *McCarry* or I'll pulverize seventy-six children to dust. I've got plastics as well as conventional explosives strategically set throughout the entire compound. So don't even think about a sudden raid. We've made over three hundred pounds of the shit — sulfuric acid, nitric acid, toluene along with gel explosives. I've got TNT stored not only in cell batteries with long-range detonators, but we've also got stuff in shootable projectiles and pellets. If you think I'm bluffing, I'll send a sample from our chem labs. I aim at your face, Special Agent *McCarry*, and you're cosmic vapor."

"I understand, Bob. I don't think you're bluffing. I'll give you Deck—"

"*Stop* interrupting me! As long as you're on the line, just shut up and listen! Don't even think about turning off the *electricity*. We have backup power. If you start in any way, shape or form to flex muscle, I'll flex *mine*. And I'm looking at a detonator switch and my finger's getting itchy!"

McCarry said, "Bob, I believe you. I'll try my best —"

"Like Yoda said, there is no try — just do or not do." A raspy breath. "And you know what I'm going to *do* for you, Special Agent McCarry? I'm going to call the media circus and tell them your name. So when they report the seventy-six dead kids flying in the air, they can announce to the world that Special Agent Bennett McCarry *tried* his best!"

"Wait a minute, wait a minu—"

But Bob had hung up. McCarry cursed. He had a loud voice and his swearing reverberated in the van. He was sweating as if trapped in a hotbox.

Decker raised his eyebrows and held out his hand.

Wordlessly, McCarry gave him the phone.

26

The apartment was a mile from the university, easily within biking distance. Europa obviously took advantage of that fact as evidenced by the European two-wheeled racer in her living room. An athletic woman, she had hung her walls with pictures of herself skiing down a steep, snow-packed slope; battling choppy, white waters in a raft; standing in a vegetation-packed forest decked out in hiking gear and showing off a glorious view while precariously balancing on a mountain bike. Other photographs included ice-cold landscapes of stellar-laden skies. Her concession to the ordinary was a prefab entertainment unit containing a stereo receiver, a CD player and holder, and a small TV. There was also one particle-board bookshelf filled with paperback novels. The furniture consisted of two tan, overstuffed leather love seats topped with patchwork throw pillows, a free-form wooden coffee table piled with magazines, a pair of low-slung, bag-type chairs and a telescope.

After waking Europa up, Martinez and Webster gave her a two-minute rundown on the turmoil at the Order. She immediately switched on the TV. At three-thirty in the morning, the unfolding events had full network coverage and were on most of the local and cable news stations as well. The men gave Europa a chance to dress. But when she returned to the living room, she was still in her green terry-cloth bathrobe. She was holding a beat-up photo album, the cover torn and tattered.

Brushing her soft bangs off her face, she said, "I found a few old pictures of him." She rubbed her eyes. "I don't know if they'll help."

She showed the detectives the page where the photographs had been mounted askew. The man in the snapshot was as thin as spaghetti. He had hair past his shoulders and sported a long, full beard. He wore bell-bottomed jeans, and his shirt print was of a melee of gawdy, tropical fruit. He had his arm around a woman who was also skinny as wire. She had stringy, dishwater hair and her ears were adorned with large hoops. Accoutrements included wire-rimmed glasses and platform shoes.

Europa noticed that Webster was staring at her. "Hippie dress. You're probably too young."

Webster smiled. "You flatter me."

Martinez stared at the photographs. "More like . . . hippie-cross-disco."

"Astute," Europa commented.

"Hippies would have been wearing earth shoes."

"College protester or former vet?" Europa asked him.

"Vet."

"Poor you."

"I know," Martinez said. "I saw Hell and missed all the fun."

She studied herself in the snapshot. "You're absolutely right. This was post-hippie time, although Southwest was never a bastion of antiwar sentiments. They couldn't afford it, since the war machine built half of the current campus . . . *state-of-the-art* labs. We have one hell of a particle smasher — two and half miles long. They don't come cheap." She removed the snapshots from the album.

"You can have these if you want. God only knows why I kept them. Bob wasn't the love of my life."

She glanced at the TV. Nothing but sweeping exterior shots of a lifeless compound. A sudden cut to the police and FBI commotion yards away.

Martinez took in the pictures. "Bob's last name is Ross? He never did tell us."

Europa said, "When I knew him, it was as Robert Ross — playing the WASP. He claimed he was an Easterner." She spoke with her nose up in the air. "Yeah, Easterner all right. New Joisey. Have a seat. Can I get either of you anything?"

"No thanks." Webster parked himself in one of the slouch chairs. "So Ross is his *real* last name?"

"Maybe," Europa said. "With Bob you can't tell. He was always hiding things. This is not supposition, this is fact. He was expelled from Southwest early on. Why didn't I tell your lieutenant this juicy bit before? Because Bob wasn't the focus of his investigation — my father was — and it didn't seem important. Now it does. Sit down, Detective Martinez."

Martinez sat on one of the leather couches. She took a seat on the opposite arm.

"Bob showed up at my dorm one day, asking questions about my dad," Europa said. "That wasn't unusual. After all, Southwest had been the great Ganz's school and I was the great Ganz's daughter. I found it annoying — everyone asking about my father — but I was polite about it."

"What kind of questions did he ask?" Webster inquired.

"It was about a year before Dad's miraculous reappearance. Back then, the school's favorite parlor game had been *Where in the world is Dr. Emil Ganz?* Basically, Bob asked me if I had any inside dope as to the whereabouts of my dad. As if I'd be holding back."

She clutched the photo album and sighed.

"Anyway, Bob was barely maintaining a C average. And this was *after* grade inflation. Schools were still sympathetic to the students even though the draft had been abolished. Ten years earlier, Bob would have flunked out. His average in real grade time was closer to an F."

"Why was he doing so poorly?" Webster asked.

"Hard to keep all the math straight when your brain's saturated with hallucinogens. Still, there were other druggies at the school who did fine. Bob was a weird case. First of all, I think he only got into Southwest because of connections."

Martinez was scribbling notes. "Who sponsored him?"

"I don't know if someone sponsored him or his dad gave money or if he was a legacy . . . you know, an uncle who's an alumnus. It's impolite to ask."

Suddenly, she stopped talking. Her face registered anguish.

"I can't believe Bob gunned down that poor guy just like that. Was there some kind of internal politicking . . . you know . . . was this guy a threat to him?"

"I don't know," Webster answered. "Do you reckon that Bob might react violently if threatened?"

"Bob always had a suspicious nature." A laugh. "Small wonder. He was doing illegal things. Guess that would make you look over your shoulder. Anyway, backtracking for a moment — to Bob and school. How should I put this?"

She mulled over her ideas.

"Bob had some real interesting flashes. Mental flashes —"

"You mean visions?" Martinez asked.

"No, no, no," Europa answerd. "Although I'm sure he had plenty of drug-induced trips. I'm talking about mental mathematical flashes. Partial solutions to age-old problems — which divides the kids from the adults in abstract math and physics."

"I'm lost," Webster said.

"It's hard to explain," Europa said. "The true geniuses often have these epiphanous, *mental* pictures of a mathematical solution — a drawing or chart or a diagram or an object — way before they even begin to work with the math. Einstein actually visualized his theory of relativity. He saw space bending in the presence of dark matter, he saw time distorting and objects foreshortened. All of them — Euler, Fermat, Gauss, Bohr, Heisenberg, Hawking, the famous Feynman diagrams, the Riemann sums, which are the basis of calculus. The greats seem to possess this uncanny ability to formulate images that answer mathematical problems. Of course, they need the numbers to prove them correct. But the numbers are rarely the starting point. When Einstein tried to fit his theory *around* the math, he made one of the biggest blunders of his life."

Webster asked, "So Bob had these genius mental pictures?"

Europa smiled. "I believe the word I used was flashes. He got some momentary flashes, but they never resolved into anything meaningful because (a) resolution takes perseverance and patience and work ethic, and Bob had none of those qualities, and (b) math was not Bob's forte. Sure, he could teach calculus to a bunch of engineers. But you need more than the basics to be a brilliant astrophysicist. I don't know if Bob was lazy or if he just didn't have it up here."

She touched her temple.

"They kicked him out?" Martinez asked.

"Yes, he was kicked out, but not for failing. He was expelled for embezzling. He should have gone to jail. But because he said he'd leave quietly, they let him go."

"Tell us about it," Webster said.

"He worked the register at the cafeteria. When things got hectic at lunch, people would put down a buck for a ninety-cent item and leave without their change. Bob didn't ring up the sale. Instead, he pocketed the dollar.

"The other way he pilfered cash was by adding lunch items in his head. He was a mental calculator. He'd always give the customer the correct total — tax and all. He wouldn't ring up those sales either. He'd keep the money, and make change from his pocket. And he was clever about it. He rang up just enough sales to make it look like there was activity. Still, he'd pull fifty, sixty bucks a day. Five days a week. You figure it out."

"He must have carried around a lot of pocket change."

"Nah. Whenever he needed change, he'd feed the register a twenty, and take the change from the drawer. Everything always balanced. Finally, a disgruntled girlfriend finked on him." She shook her head. "He always had this way of getting people to do his dirty work."

"Yourself included?" Webster asked.

"Not stealing, but he talked me into drugs. We tripped together. I was lonely and we both missed my father." She paused in thought.

"Actually, Bob possessed lots of my dad's lesser qualities — egotistical, grandiose, paranoid, sharp-tongued, glib —"

"A pathological liar?"

"Well, there was a psychopathic quality to him — the substance abuse, the stealing, the lying, the feeling that people were out to get him. Which was only reinforced when they *did* catch him stealing. Putting others down to bolster his own ego. Yeah, you did well in linear algebra, but grinds are usually good at the easy stuff. Wait till you hit number theory or group and ring theory."

She shook her head.

"You know, sexually, he wasn't good. But he always managed to make me feel like *I* should feel grateful. He was so full of himself. Still, I'll say this much for him. He was one of the few guys who never made fun of me or my father's wacky ideas."

"The time machine," Martinez said.

"Yeah, the time machine." She rolled her eyes. "How'd you know? Your lieutenant must have told you."

Martinez nodded. "I was just talking to some of my colleagues who had been spending the night in Central City. Did you know that your father had purchased a chicken ranch up there for the Order —"

"A *chicken* ranch?" She laughed. "Okay."

"The hired hand up there — his name is Benton — told us your father had a telescope up

363

there. He often took it out to look at the night-time skies."

"And your point is . . . ?"

"He said that your father had revived his interest in time machines."

Europa looked blank. "Really?"

"What do you think about that?"

"About time machines or my father's interest in them?"

"How about time machines in general?"

"My specialty is subatomical particle spin. I leave the time machines to H. G. Wells."

"What do you think about your father's recent interest in them?"

"I don't know what to think. The tragic part is my dad's ideas about superluminal links had scientific data to back him up."

"What kind of data?" Webster asked.

She smiled. "Do you really want to know the answer?"

"It's complicated?"

"Technical. It has to do with photons given off as electrons descend from an excited delta position to one at rest. There are theories that if the same photons shared the same space and were given off at the same time, they'd forever have instantaneous communication. Hence, *super*luminal — faster than light — travel. That was Dad's starting point. The trouble was, his entire project . . . it took on a paranoid quality. I remember only in bits because Mom shielded us from most of his erratic behavior. But I do remember him saying that he *had* to build this machine to escape the aliens who had already planted evil thoughts in his friends' brains. We'd be next if we didn't escape soon. As a kid and coming from Dad, I was very frightened. Not only by aliens but by my father's belief in them. Back then, Emil Euler Ganz had a lot of cosmic credibility."

"I can see that," Martinez said. "How old were you?"

"Twelve, maybe. I was fifteen when Dad disappeared. At first, Mom was concerned, but not overly so. As the days passed, she became frantic. I was *petrified*. Because deep down, even at fifteen, I had thought that the aliens succeeded. Given what he had been talking about, I thought it was eminently logical that he had been kidnapped by space creatures."

She didn't speak for a moment.

"Somewhere . . . in my child's mind . . . I still believe it. Because how else do you explain a ten-year absence?"

"There are mountaintops in Nepal," Webster said.

"True. For all I know, he took off somewhere. But being kidnapped by space creatures sounds so much less mundane."

Martinez asked, "Was Bob interested in your father's time machines?"

"If he was, he never told *me*." She drummed the photo album she was still hugging. "The Order suited Bob. Lots of easy marks to boss around and plenty of young, vulnerable girls to have sex with. Plus, he really did admire my father's work. I'm sure he kissed Jupiter's butt. Dad was a hopeless sucker for flattery. It sure worked in Jilliam's case — excuse me, Venus. You know that I knew Venus. She was my childhood friend."

"Do you think it's possible that Bob and Venus are an item?"

Europa thought about it. "Maybe. But I don't think so. Sex wasn't Jilliam's thing. When I knew her, she was searching for the spiritual. Although if she did hook up with Bob, sex has to be a factor."

"Although he wasn't good," Webster answered.

"Not with me."

Martinez asked, "Without getting graphic, can you fill us in on why he wasn't good?"

"I can get graphic. Doesn't bother me." A shrug. "He was never fully tumescent. Which I thought was strange because he always climaxed even with the flag at half-mast. It wasn't very satisfying."

"I wouldn't think so," Webster said. "Did he need things to make him interested?"

"No kinks that I could ascertain. He liked the usual adult hetero porno. I don't remember seeing homosexual stuff or child stuff. He did have a couple of B and D magazines. But we never did that kind of thing. He just never got fully hard. I suppose I didn't thrill him."

"Why do you think he embezzled money?" Webster asked. "Was he poor?"

"Nah. Besides, money isn't the calling card at Southwest. Brains is the ticket. My opinion? He stole for kicks."

She sat back in her chair.

"I saw him in the cafeteria a couple of times pulling his shtick. Taking the money and changing it from his own stash. He winked at me when he did it." She waited a moment. "I looked down at his pants for some reason. He had a hard-on. Unbelievable what comes back from the memory banks. It's when you *don't* think about things . . . that's when they come to you."

She threw up her hands, glancing at the TV.

"I hope this ordeal resolves. The Order has a lot of children. I have a couple of half-sibs inside — a sister and a brother. The boy's from Venus, the girl's from another one of my dad's lovers."

Martinez asked, "And you've never met them?"

"I suppose I could have set it up. But I didn't want to." She shook her head. "Just too damn sad!"

Webster's pager went off. He glanced at the number. To Martinez, he said, "The boss."

Europa said, "Phone's over there."

He thanked her and called the number. Decker answered midway through the first ring. "Where are you?"

Uptight and all business. Webster answered, "At Dr. Ganz's —"

367

"Learn anything?"

"Quite a bit. Bob was kicked out of Southwest for starters."

"Doesn't surprise me. Did Europa confirm that his last name was Ross?"

"That's what Bob told her."

"It doesn't kick out on any of the FBI's computers."

"She felt he was working-class New Jersey."

"Ethnic?"

"Maybe."

"Ross could be a Jewish name."

Webster turned to Europa. "Could Bob be Jewish?"

"More like an anti-Semite. He sure was jealous of a lot of Jewish kids. Made comments to that effect. Coming from New York or Jersey, I figured he was probably Italian or Puerto Rican."

"Did you hear that?" Webster asked Decker.

"Yes, I did." Decker thought of Italian variants on Ross — Russo or Rizzo . . . that name struck a familiar chord. Then he remembered that Rizzo was a character in *Grease*. Then there was Ratso Rizzo in the seventies movie *Midnight Cowboy*. Man, he was showing his age. He lowered his voice. "Is she being cooperative?"

"Very."

"Put her on." Decker squirmed, trying to get more elbow room. The van was small and McCarry was on top of him. Over the line, he heard, "This is Dr. Ganz."

"Thanks for helping us out."

"God, I'm sorry about the situation."

"Maybe you can help. Detective Webster tells me you know quite a bit about Bob Ross, or whatever his name is."

"It was fifteen, sixteen years ago."

"Let me ask you this. Do you think Bob has the technical knowledge to build bombs. I don't mean things like small pipe bombs. I'm referring to major charges."

"An intriguing question," Europa said. "Let me put it to you this way. The Order was originally made up of disenfranchised engineers and scientists. If two lay-nothings could blow up half the federal building in Oklahoma City, it wouldn't surprise me if these nutcases had nuclear capacity."

27

Standing outside, behind the shield of vehicular metal, Special-Agent-in-Charge McCarry unfurled the first of many scrolled architectural plans that the Order had filed with the city planner's office. But he couldn't concentrate on an engineer's map of lines and circles. Instead, he found himself staring at the stagnant bunkers. What kind of activity was going on inside? More than that, why hadn't the son of a bitch called back and asked for Decker? Stringing them all along, but that was to be expected.

The architect leaned over the map, smoothing out the page with the palms of her hand. She placed rocks on the corners of the paper to keep it from curling up. Then she adjusted her bifocals. In her sixties, Adele Sawyer had been only tangentially involved with the original project. She had never even seen the finalized plans. But she was the first one the feds had located, and the only one to come down on such short notice. Her gray hair was tied back into a thick ponytail. She wore a cable-knit sweater and jeans.

Adele started to explain the plans. "As I recall, Jupiter wanted a large enough entry hall so it could double as a meeting place — a room where the members could get together to discuss common problems —"

"Where'd he get the money for something this big?" McCarry groused. "How much did this thing cost? Four million? Five, maybe?"

The older woman was unfazed by McCarry's brusqueness. "Actually, the external structure isn't much more than boxes strung together. Slabs of steel-reinforced concrete. Hard as hell to penetrate, but not all that expensive to build because there's no detail."

Staring at the blue-inked dimensions, McCarry tried to get a fix on the actual size. He glanced at the command post a couple of cars away. The mayor was briefing a troop of his lackeys, getting ready to present them to the media. Los Angeles was nothing but a three-ring circus. He glanced at Decker. "You've been inside. What can you tell us about it?"

Decker tightened his coat and waited for the first glimpse of dawn. How many hours before people turned on their television sets for the morning news? How many hours before the few gawkers became a major crowd control problem? How much time before a terrible stalemate with lives at stake became bedlam? Eyes focused back on the blueprint. He pointed to an area. "This is the entry?"

Adele nodded.

"It's got high ceilings as I recall."

"Fifteen feet according to the plans."

"There's a big stained-glass window in the ceiling."

"So we can penetrate from the top?"

"Not without a battering ram," Decker said. "It's steel mesh over steel bars. At the time, I wondered why it was constructed with so much metal. But it was a big mother window so I thought the steel was necessary for support. There are some small dormer windows at the junction between wall and ceiling. They're also barred — well, you can see for yourself. Do you have the exact dimensions?"

"The exact outside dimensions are a foot by eighteen inches," McCarry answered. "Even without the bars, they're too small for any of my current men to penetrate. Unless they're like arrow slits. Small on the outside and bigger on the inside. What do the plans say?"

Adele said, "Twelve by eighteen on the outside and inside."

"Around the size of a small doggie door," Decker said.

McCarry said, "I'm wondering if we can take the bars off — spray them with liquid nitrogen from a long distance and crack them apart — if we have anyone who's small enough to fit inside. A woman maybe."

"Lieutenant?"

Decker turned around. It was Webster and Martinez with Europa Ganz in tow. She was also dressed in a sweater and jeans. She and Adele — with their grayish hair and fresh faces — could have passed for mother and daughter.

McCarry asked, "Who are you?"

"They're from my department," Decker answered. "The woman is Dr. Europa Ganz — Jupiter's daughter. The one I called about Bob's capacity to fabricate explosives."

"Of course." McCarry shook hands with her, showing a glint of animation. "So you must know the inside of the place."

"Actually, the last time I was inside the Order was something like fifteen years ago."

"Then why are you here?"

"I was wondering that myself."

Decker said, "Sir, she knows Bob Ross —"

"*Knew* Bob Ross," Europa interrupted.

"A Bob Risso, Russo, Rizzo. Something about that name is sticking in my head." Decker was exasperated. "I can't pull it up . . ."

McCarry asked, "Since you know Ross, what can you tell us about him?"

"*Knew* him!" Europa corrected again. "As in *past* tense."

Martinez said, "I got hold of Asnikov —"

"Go for it," Decker said.

"Who's Asnikov?" McCarry snapped. "The deprogrammer? What's going on here? If you're running an independent investigation and keeping us in the dark —"

"Special Agent McCarry, I'll be happy to enlighten you, just as soon as I know what's going on —"

"So what does Asnikov have to do with anything?" McCarry stiffened. "I'm in charge of this task force —"

"Excuse me," Adele interrupted. "If this spat is going to take a while, I'll get a cup of coffee."

"I'll come with you," Europa said.

"No, you stay here," Decker said. "We need to talk to you —"

"But I told those two everything I know about Bob." Europa pointed to Webster and Martinez.

"Told them what?" McCarry asked. "What's going on?"

"Excuse me," Adele said. "I'll just be over —"

McCarry said, "Someone please *fucking fill* me in!"

Decker nodded to his men. They told him what they had learned from Europa in less than a minute. Europa verified their accounts with the occasional nod.

After they had finished, Decker said, "She knows both Venus and Bob. Plus, being Jupiter's daughter, I thought she could give us a psychological profile —"

"Me?" Europa asked. "I barely knew Dad when he lived with the family. He jumped ship when I was fifteen."

"You've been in contact with him," Decker said.

"Strictly pleasantries," Europa answered. " 'Thanks for calling, Dad. Talk to you later.' Plus, I haven't spoken to Jilliam or Bob in fifteen years —"

"Still, you know more than we do," McCarry broke in. "Why do you think Bob is doing this?"

"If you mean killing people, I have no idea."

Martinez said, "You told us he had a paranoid quality to him."

"But back then, he'd been stealing. Plus, he was heavily involved with drugs. The combination would make anyone paranoid."

Decker seized a thought. "Dr. Ganz, what if Bob had been *caught* stealing again? How do you think he might react? Maybe paranoid?"

"Who'd he be stealing from?" Webster asked.

"Jupiter's the only one with money," Decker answered. "It would have to be the boss."

"But Jupiter's dead," McCarry said. "Are you saying that Bob killed him?"

"Not necessarily," Decker said. "What I'm suggesting is *maybe* Bob's been slowly poisoning him — keeping him doped up and essentially brain dead — so he could rip him off —"

"Poisoning?" Europa interrupted. "My father was *poisoned* to death?"

"He had arsenic in his system —"

"When did you find this out?" Europa demanded to know.

"About twelve hours ago," Decker answered.

"Good Lord!" Europa sighed. "How long had the poisoning been going on?"

"The coroner couldn't tell. She mentioned something about looking at his bones to get a more exact time frame."

"Did your father start the Order of the Rings of God with independent wealth?" McCarry asked.

"I . . . I don't know," Europa answered.

Decker asked, "Did your father have money

when he did his disappearing act?"

"I was fifteen. How would I know?"

"Maybe your mother said something to you?"

"We never talked about Dad. The subject made her very bitter." She tried hard to bring memories into focus. "I never remember my mother *worrying* about finances. But we certainly weren't wealthy. I know she spent a great deal of money trying to locate Dad. It had to have come from somewhere."

"But you don't know anything about your father's cash reserves when he took off."

"No. But he must have been living on something. He was gone for ten years . . ." Europa paused. "My memories are a bit cloudy. But if I recall correctly, I remember Mom having it harder financially *after* he came back. But by then I was an adult. I was more attuned to things like money problems."

"Or maybe your father decided to reclaim some of the money you'd had been living on," Martinez said.

Europa said, "That's very possible."

"Can we get back to Bob?" McCarry asked. "You said he was paranoid?"

"I said he had a paranoid quality to him." A hesitation. "Not unlike my father actually."

"Bob admired your father," Decker remarked.

"Hero-worshiped him."

"What about his own family?" McCarry asked.

"He never said much about them. He grew up back East. I had the feeling that he didn't get along with his father —"

"That's it!" Decker shouted. "That's *mother-friggin'* it!"

"What?" Martinez asked.

Decker clapped his hands once. "In the editorial section of yesterday's paper, some guy named Rizzo or Russo wrote a scathing letter about Emil Ganz. Basically saying that Ganz had plagiarized every important piece of research he had ever done —"

"That's nonsense," Europa said.

"I gave you the paper, Bert —"

"It's in the car. I'll get it."

Europa became agitated. "My father had lots of negative characteristics, but I never heard *anyone* say anything remotely concerning plagiarism."

"Was Bob's father a scientist?" Decker asked her.

"I have no idea what his father did."

"The Russo/Rizzo in the paper owned some kind of holistic imports business —"

"Oh, my goodness!" Europa shrieked. "Bob did tell me something about a family business."

"So there you go," Decker said. "If I remember correctly, the letter Russo/Rizzo wrote dealt with Ganz's integrity in science."

"I'd like to interject a point," Webster drawled. "Dr. Ganz, you told us that you thought that Bob had a sponsor for gettin' him into Southwest Uni—"

"I thought maybe —"

"Maybe it was his own father," Webster suggested.

"If Bob's father had been an important person to Southwest, Bob wouldn't have been expelled," Europa answered. "Sad, but true. It's who you know."

"What if the plagiarism accusations were true?" Webster asked.

"It's nonsense —"

"But if they were, maybe Southwest took Bob in just to shut up his father," Webster said. "After all, Ganz had been their pride and joy."

"Not at that time," Europa countered. "He was a subject of ridicule."

Decker said, "But think how bad it would have looked for the university if one of their acclaimed top professors had been a research thief. Supporting a dishonest scientist is a lot more damaging to a name than supporting a crazy one."

McCarry said, "I don't know why we're wasting time with this. Bastard Bob hasn't even called back —"

"That's not surprising," Europa said. "Bob loves games."

McCarry asked, "So he's viewing this whole thing as a game?"

"No doubt."

McCarry spit on the ground. "Lots of hostage situations. But I always get the psychos."

"Lots of criminals are psychos," Decker pointed out.

"Yeah, but most psychos are dumbshits — low

378

IQ's with learning problems. Bob doesn't fit that category. Even among psycho leaders who tend to be a brighter bunch, Bob would probably stand out as one of the smartest. Plus, he can build bombs." He turned to Europa. "Am I right about this?"

"Bob is very bright."

"Ted Kaczynski with an army of zombies behind him," McCarry said. "A hostage situation with lots of kids and a paranoid but bright leader. We're in big trouble."

"He's waiting for you to make a move," Europa said. "Wait him out. Because every time *you* move, you show pieces of your hand. Point of fact. *If* you want to keep Bob engaged, you give him games, not warfare. He's not interested in brute force, he's interested in finesse."

"I thought you didn't know this guy," McCarry said.

"I don't know him per se," Europa said. "But I know game players. Southwest is filled with them. See, Special Agent in Charge McCarry, like most army men — or paramilitary if you will — you're thinking in terms of a two-person, zero-outcome game. Meaning someone *has* to lose. And losing, in this case, is losing very big. Instead of win/lose, you should be thinking in terms of a win/win — the Nash equilibrium point — where all parties are at their optimal position —"

"What the *hell* are you talking about?" McCarry asked.

Europa gave a long sigh, as if it was a burden to deal with the lowly non-math sector of the population. "Don't make a move until the odds are stacked in your favor."

McCarry's cellular phone rang. He picked it up, turned his back to the group and spoke in hushed tones into the receiver. Martinez returned, newspaper in hand. He gave it to Decker. "The letter was written by Dr. Robert Russo, Sr."

"Dr. Russo" — Decker scanned the letter and read out loud — "Mediocre physicist . . . plagiarizer, thief, kidnapper, *adulterer*." He looked at Europa. "What do you know about that?"

"Nothing." Her voice was stiff. "Can I see the letter?"

Still reading, Decker said, " '. . . probably running from some irate husband who just got tired of Ganz messing with his wife . . .' " He gave the newspaper to Europa. "Upon rereading this, it looks like Ganz was having an affair with Russo's wife."

"Bob's mother," Webster said. "You know, maybe it was *Ganz* who got Bob into Southwest University of Technology. Maybe he did it out of guilt. Or out of pressure —"

"My father wasn't around when Bob got into Southwest," Europa said.

"Maybe he was, and *you* just didn't know about it."

Europa frowned, then read the letter carefully.

"This is patently *ridiculous!*"

"What part is ridiculous?" Decker asked. "The plagiarism or the affairs?"

"I didn't know anything about Dad's personal life. But I do know he's no plagiarist. Academics is filled with petty people. This guy is psycho!"

"Then he probably is Bob's father," Martinez said.

Webster checked his watch and talked to Decker in a low voice. "It's time for Asnikov. Maybe we should leave before Mr. Fed has other ideas."

"Go ahead." Decker waited a moment. "If you can, bring Asnikov down here when you're done. He might know something about the physical layout of the Order. Plus, it'll make McCarry feel better."

Europa was still holding the letter. "Actually, the letter is similar in tone to Bob's rantings during a bad trip."

"What letter?" McCarry asked.

Europa showed him the newspaper clipping.

"Jesus!" McCarry answered. "So Ganz was screwing this guy's wife — who's probably Bob's mother?"

"I'd bet money on it," Decker said.

"Bob Junior must have had one hell of a rotten relationship with Bob Senior if he turned his own father's archenemy into his personal hero."

"So Bob *poisoned* my father to death?" Europa asked.

"Drugs and alcohol murdered your father,"

381

Decker said. "Suicide still hasn't been ruled out."

"What about the arsenic?"

"According to the coroner, it wasn't what killed him."

Decker paused. "You know, *if* Bob was ripping off your dad, it made sense to have kept your father alive. Because now that he's dead, I'm betting that all of Jupiter's money goes to you — or at least to the living heirs."

"Why? What do you know about my father's finances?"

"He had a million-dollar life insurance policy with you as the beneficiary," Decker said.

Her eyes widened. "I don't believe . . . are you *sure?*"

"I think so —"

"You *think?*"

"I've heard something to that effect, yes."

"Then why haven't *I* heard about it?"

"Because your father's death has been ruled suspicious," Decker said. "First, the cause of death has to be determined before an insurance company will pay. If it is ruled a homicide, you have to be cleared as a suspect. But I'm not talking about the insurance policy — which is clearly yours. I'm thinking that Jupiter must have had bank accounts. We know he took money from his parishioners."

"He did?" Europa asked.

"Condition of joining the cult," Webster said. "You give up your worldly assets to Father Jupiter, who spends the money for the good of the group."

"It's the communal money — in Jupiter's bank accounts — that Bob could have been embezzling. Now that he's gone, unless otherwise stated, Jupiter's money goes to the closest living heirs."

"My brothers and me."

"Unless Jupiter has a will stating otherwise. And even if he did, you could contest it."

"So now that my father is dead, the money Bob was embezzling is mine."

"And Bob's life on easy street is down the toilet." Decker hesitated for a moment. "Although I'm still not sure how Nova plays into all of this."

"Who's Nova?" Europa asked.

"Another guru from the Order," Decker said. "We found his dissected parts in a ranch owned by your father."

"My God!" Europa exclaimed. "That's horrible. And *that* was Bob's doing also?"

"Probably," Decker answered. He looked at McCarry, who was staring at the blueprints. Staring, but not absorbing anything. "You're awfully quiet."

McCarry jerked his head up, then rubbed his forehead. "My boss is taking the six A.M. down from Sacramento. I'd like to have a plan formulated by then."

"You're about to be displaced," Decker said. "Forget it. No way I'm working with your boss,

McCarry. We started this mess together, we'll end it together."

McCarry was shocked. That kind of loyalty was unheard of. Made him suspicious. What did Decker have up his sleeve? He asked, "Is it my good looks?"

"McCarry, I refuse to break in another fed," Decker said. "If I have to recap my story one more time, I'll puke."

28

"Ner Yisroel?" Sammy asked. "You've got to be kidding!"

Rina refrained from rolling her eyes. "How about a 'Good morning, Eema'?"

Sammy plunked himself down at the kitchen table. He was dressed in the school's uniform of blue pants and white shirt, but he hadn't put on his shoes. "He'll die."

"He won't die." Rina took out Hannah's cereal bowl. "If you really cared about your brother, you'd be encouraging him —"

"Are you saying I don't care about Yonkie's welfare?"

"Shmuel, it's too early to fight. If you're going to spar, do it alone." Rina walked out of the kitchen.

"How can you spar alone?" Sammy called out.

She ignored him and went into Hannah's room. The preschooler was swallowed up in her covers, her only sign of life being tight, orange ringlets. Rina pulled the comforter back. "Good morning, sweetheart."

Hannah opened her eyes, blinked and closed them again. She held out her pipestem arms for an embrace.

"Ah." Rina hugged her. "This is my daily dose of sugar."

She kissed her mother. "Is Daddy gone?"

"Yes, Daddy is gone."

A pout in her voice. "But he didn't say good-bye."

"He didn't come home last night."

Hannah opened her eyes. She was confused. "Where was he?"

Good question. Rina said, "He slept at his work."

"At his work?"

Rina nodded.

"Why?"

"Because he was very busy and didn't have time to come home."

Hannah remained puzzled. "They have beds at Daddy's work?"

"Yes, they do."

"But not all works have beds."

"No."

"Only Daddy's work?"

Rina nodded.

"Can I see Daddy's bed?"

"One day."

"Today?"

"No, another day."

"Do they have pillows?"

Rina smiled. "Yes, they do." She got up from Hannah's bed. "Can you get dressed by yourself or do you need help?"

"I'll get my dress on. And my socks. And my

shoes. But you help me with the buckle."

"Fine." Rina stood. "Come into the kitchen when you're dressed."

"Are you making me oatmeal?"

"Yes. Is that okay?"

"It's okay." Hannah sat up and rubbed her eyes. "Can I watch cartoons?"

"For a few minutes."

"Then I'll get dressed very fast."

"Good for you."

With a sigh, Rina braved the kitchen again. Sammy was playing with a bowl of Rice Krispies. His bare feet were now covered with socks. The shoes were still a mystery. He looked up when his mother came in. "I'm still here."

"I see that."

"You don't like me anymore."

Rina laughed. "I love you —"

"Yeah, but you don't like me."

"Shmuel —"

"I'm serious."

"You argue with everything I say."

"I think I know Yonkie very well . . . better than you."

"I'm sure you do. Still, the program's a good one. He needs a challenge."

"I agree. But not Ner Yisroel."

"Nothing's carved in stone. Besides, it's not between you and him, it's between him and me."

"In other words, you're ignoring me. See, you don't like me anymore."

Rina didn't answer. It seemed the smartest maneuver.

Jacob came shuffling into the kitchen. "Morning."

Rina kissed the top of his yarmulke. "Morning."

Jacob washed his hands and said the accompanying prayer of *Al N'tilat Yadayim*. Pouring some orange juice, he drank it in a single gulp.

Rina asked, "Did you finally get to sleep?"

He slumped into a chair. "I got a few hours."

"You need more sleep," Rina said.

"I need a lot of things," Jacob countered.

Sammy slid him a clean cereal bowl. Jacob asked, "Anything besides Rice Krispies?"

"Apple Jacks."

Jacob frowned and pushed the bowl aside. "I'll pass."

"You have to eat something."

"I'll grab a bagel at school —"

"Yonkie —"

"Cartoons! Cartoons! Cartoons! Cartoons!" Hannah sang as she danced into the kitchen.

Sammy moaned. "Are *Looney Tunes* at six-thirty really necessary for her psychological well-being?"

"They're very violent," Jacob added.

Rina ignored them and turned on the kitchen TV. Immediately, images of a bunkerlike complex filled the tiny screen. Police lights were flashing in the background. Rina felt her heart jump as she stared at the pictures.

Did he call last night?

"I want cartoons!" Hannah insisted.

"Shhh!" Rina scolded.

"One man dead . . ." the TV stated. "It's a grave situation with no end in sight out here in the West Valley . . ."

"Oh, God, it's local!" Rina exclaimed.

Sammy was suddenly awake. He sat up. "What is it, Eema?"

"Go check the message machine and see if Dad called."

"He didn't come home —"

"Just do it!"

Sammy got up.

Jacob had his eyes glued to the TV. His heart dropped into his stomach. "Is everything okay?"

"I don't know!"

"I want cartoons!" Hannah whined.

Jacob stood, reluctantly taking his eyes off the TV. "C'mon, Hannalah. Let's watch in my room."

"In your room?" She jumped up and down. "Goody."

Sammy came back. "Nothing on the machine."

"Damn him!" Rina swore.

The boys stared at her. They had never heard their mother curse before. Sammy said, "Want me to call the station house —"

"No!" Rina paced. "I'll do it. It's nothing. If it was something, I would have gotten a phone call by now. I just wish he'd . . . turn the sound up, will you?"

"Come on!" Hannah said, tugging at Jacob's shirt.

"Just a sec—"

Rina yelled, "Take her out of here now!" She dialed Peter's cellular.

The line had been cut.

Fabulous!

Jacob scooped up his sister and left the kitchen. Rina hung up the phone with a slam, picked up the receiver and punched in the station house's number. "He knows how I worry and he never . . . yes, this is Rina Decker. Is my husband, Lieutenant . . . Don't put me on hold! I just want to know —"

But she had been sent into an electronic void.

"You'd think after seven years he'd have the decency . . . yes, this is Rina Decker. I was wondering if . . . well, do you know *where* he is . . . do you know if he's all right?" A pause. " *'I'm sure'* isn't good enough . . . connect me to someone who knows something or I'm going to storm the place!"

She stamped her foot.

"God, these people are infuriating."

"He's fine, Eema," Sammy said. "Like you said, if something happened, you would have heard about it."

"What's going on over there?" Rina asked him.

"Some sort of hostage situation —"

"Fabulous!" Rina felt her head go light. She leaned against the counter. Sammy saw her face go white and gave her a chair. "Sit down."

"I'm all right —"

"Sit down!"

Call-waiting beeped in. Rina depressed the flash button.

"It's me. I'm fine!"

Rina broke into tears of relief as well as anger. "Do you think you might have called and left a message?"

"They confiscated my phone. All the other phones are tied up. This is literally the first chance I've had to get an outside civilian line. You were worried. I'm very sorry."

She gave out a couple of choked sobs. "It's fine." A sniff. "Sorry I jumped down your throat."

"I understand. Honestly, it couldn't be helped."

"As long as you're all right."

"I'm fine."

"It's good to hear your voice."

"Same here. I love you. You heard about the situation from the TV?""I'm looking at it as we speak."

"Can you tell me what images they're flashing?"

Rina regarded the monitor. "Exterior shots of a group of buildings. The Order, right?"

"Yes. Same on all the stations?"

Rina picked up the remote control and searched through the networks. "Basically."

"No faces?"

"Not so far."

"Good. I've got to go."

In a small voice she said, "I love you."

Decker felt his throat clog. "Baby, I love you, too. So very much. Kiss the kids for me. Tell them I love them. I mean that."

"I know you do."

"I don't know when I'll see you."

He had such a longing in his voice. Rina said, "Whenever you can, it'll be right. Promise me you'll be careful."

"Always."

"No heroics, please?"

"Honey, they're waving to me. I've got to go."

He disconnected the line. Rina hung up the phone, realizing her hands were clammy. She rubbed them together and looked at Sammy. "Go tell the other two they can come in from exile."

"He's okay?"

"He's fine." She stared at the TV. "But he's going to be camped out there for a while. Don't expect him home until Shabbos. And maybe not even then."

"He told you that?"

"Not in those words, but the intent was there. Unless this ends quickly." She stared at the TV. "From what he told me, the cult is pretty self-sufficient. It's going to be a while." She wiped her tears away. "Oh, my, my. You never appreciate something until it's gone."

The kitchen grew quiet.

"Go tell the others to come in, Shmuel. Yaakov

must be scared out of his wits." Rina kissed her son's cheek, then splashed water on her face. "And put on your shoes, Sammy. It's late. Yaakov has exams. Life goes on."

But the teen dawdled.

She looked up from the sink. "What is it?"

"Life goes on," Sammy repeated. "Boy, I've heard *that* one before."

"I heard the details in transit — on the car radio." Asnikov opened the door to his outer office. "The cops aren't saying much. The reporters assume you're playing it close to the bone. What's more likely is you don't know much. The Order has run a tight ship all these years. Not many leaks, ergo not much detail."

Martinez said, "Maybe you can help us on that account."

"Don't see how." He turned on the lights to the reception area, walked through the space, then unlocked the door to his office. He flipped those switches, then removed his jacket, draping it across the back of his desk chair. "Now that you've got a mess on your hands, maybe you gentlemen have an understanding of what I do. I liberate human beings from these kinds of dungeons before their monstrous leaders crack up and take everybody down with them."

With a click of the remote, Asnikov turned on a ceiling-mounted TV. The cameras were still panning across the buildings. Everything static and status quo. Sunlight was breaking through the overcast, turning the bunkers' concrete from steel to gold. The wall clock read six-thirty.

Asnikov's mandible was grinding against his upper jaw. The sound was audible. He pointed to his Stickley-styled couch with the primary-colored pillows. "And as long as you're here, have a seat."

Webster said, "Sir, it would help us if you came along with us."

Asnikov's green eyes bore into Webster's. "Along where? You aren't taking me to your station house, are you?"

"No, sir. We'd like you to come to the Order."

"You have a warrant to take me there?"

Martinez noticed that the deprogrammer had flinched, though not more than a fraction of a second. "No, sir, we don't have a warrant. We're asking for a favor."

Again, Asnikov eyes drifted back to the TV — to the metal gauntlet of law enforcement cars and vans. He spoke while watching the monitor. "What do you think I can do for you?"

"Help us with the Order's physical layout."

"I don't know the physical layout." Asnikov returned his attention to Martinez. "Those bastards have had spies out for me. I haven't been able to get within a mile of the place without someone shooting at me."

"An exaggeration, Mr. Asnikov?" Martinez asked.

The programmer smiled cryptically. It held malice and bitterness. "What I'm telling you is

I've never been inside. Believe me, I'd *love* to be part of the raid that breaks those sons of bitches. But I don't know anything — just like you."

"So you're telling us that you've never helped anyone escape the premises?"

"Exactly."

No doubt about it. Martinez knew that something was making him nervous. "Maybe one of your people has helped someone break out?"

"Nope." Asnikov remained adamant. "I wish I could help . . ."

He let the words hang in the air.

End of conversation. Webster kept it alive with another tactic. "What do you know about Guru Bob?"

"Why?"

"Just gathering information," Martinez said. "For starters, is his last name Russo?"

"Someone's done some homework. Most people think his last name is Ross. That's what he used when he was at Southwest U. of Tech. He left without graduating."

"Actually, he was kicked out," Webster said. "Either leave or be expelled."

Asnikov raised an eyebrow. "Then you know more about him than I do. In the past, I hadn't given Bob much thought. As long as I've known the Order, Pluto has been the gatekeeper. Being as infiltration is my stock-in-trade, I've always concentrated on how to get around *him.* Ignoring Bob was probably a mistake. Could be why I've had problems."

"What do you know about Pluto?" Martinez asked.

"What do you know about him?"

"Nothing," Martinez said. "Right now, we're still trying to get a fix on Bob."

Asnikov nodded. "Pluto's given name is Keith Muldoony. He came from dirt-poor beginnings in the backwoods of West Virginia — from a big family. At one time he was their shining star. Not only the family hero but a role model for the entire town. Keith was a *college* graduate."

"From where?"

"Community college. Nothing fancy, but considering his surroundings that was some deal. His major was psychology. He actually worked in a hospital for a year. Impressed the relatives with his job because he wore a white coat. When I talked to them, that's the first thing they told me. 'Ole Keith worked in a hospital and wore a white coat.' Guess a white coat is heady stuff for a kid whose relatives are either on welfare or in jail."

"What did he do in the hospital?"

"Not much more than an orderly from what I could ascertain. Probably in the mental ward, being as he majored in psychology."

Webster said, "It's a long way from West Virginia to the Order."

"Yep."

"What brought him out here?"

"Jupiter. Pluto came out to join up with him. Together, they started the Order."

"Where'd he hear about Jupiter?"

"I don't know. But for a while it was just Jupiter and Pluto and a few oddball followers. Venus, Nova and Bob came later on." Asnikov took an empty coffee urn and went into the bathroom. A moment later, he started fixing up six cups' worth of full-strength brew. "He should have been next in line. Best-laid plans of mice and men . . ."

Martinez wasn't about to give up. "Mr. Asnikov, surely you must know some ex-Order member. Someone who can help us out with the physical layout of the place."

"Sorry."

"Sorry what?" Webster asked. "Sorry, you don't know an ex-Order member, or sorry, you won't help us out."

Asnikov's eyes went to the TV. "We're going around in circles. Is this your idea of getting something done, or are you just putting in the hours to satisfy your boss?"

"And you don't know anything about Lauren Bolt?" Webster pressed.

"We're back to her, are we?" Asnikov smiled. "Bunch of maniacal, murderous ghouls tell you that I kidnapped Lauren Bolt, and you *believe* them?" He shook his head. "You certainly haven't learned much these past few days."

"Why are her parents still out of town?" Martinez asked.

"Beats me." Asnikov pointed to his inner office. "I got a polygraph in there. I use it on prospective clients to weed out the psychos. Hook me up. Ask me questions about Lauren Bolt and/or her parents. Gentlemen, I guarantee you, you'll hit more blanks than a washed-out stud."

Martinez tried one last time. "Mr. Asnikov, we all know your files are confidential. But we've got an exceptional situation. They're holding scores of children as hostages. Do you have children, sir?"

"Detective, I'm on *your* side. I happen to be familiar with some of the young adults in there."

"Who?"

"They are ongoing cases. I can't tell you because of confidentiality. And even if I did tell you, it wouldn't help. Because they're still on the *inside,* and that fact is a testament to *my* failure!"

No one spoke. The coffeemaker gurgled.

Asnikov's jaw bulged as he poured himself a cup of full-strength espresso. "What do you *want* from me? I know bits and pieces. But if I tell you some misinformation and that causes a major screw-up, not only will my reputation be justifiably ruined but *I'll* feel personally responsible for every life that's lost. *Wait* them out. That's what I *do.* I wait until I *know* what I'm doing."

"Waiting is good — *if* you have time!" Martinez said.

There was strain on Asnikov's face — the humiliation of failure. Webster felt he was at the breaking point. He said. "Sir, why don't you just come down and give us your insights into the Order. You've been studying the group a lot longer than we have."

"I don't want to be part of your raid. Because I know you're going to screw up. I have absolutely *no* confidence in law enforcement."

Webster started to speak, but Martinez held him back. Bert pulled out a card. "Fair enough. If you change your mind, give me a call. Or better still, feel free to drop by the Order. As long as we have this situation, you've got a standing invitation."

Asnikov put the card in his breast pocket. "I suppose it's to my credit that you think I know so much." His face became grave. Again, his eyes went to the TV. "My sister died at Jonestown . . . along with my niece — a three-year-old with a cherub face and beautiful curls. My parents have never recovered from their deaths."

He finished his coffee and opened the office door.

"I'm not without empathy."

29

Decker squinted into the sun, then tented his eyes under a roof of fingers. "So you're telling me that Asnikov's hiding something?"

Martinez said, "No, I said *I* think he is —"

"Then sic a judge on him!" Decker said. "I'm not playing footsies when there are lives at stake! We got the law behind us, i.e., eminent danger to an individual or individuals outweighs patient/doctor confidentiality. Let's use it."

"Loo, we don't know anything definite," Webster said.

Decker turned to Tom. For once, the permapressed Southern boy looked wilted. "So Asnikov *isn't* hiding anything?"

"Maybe he was acting a little cagey —"

"What does *that* mean?" Decker was trying to keep the edge out of his voice, but it wasn't working.

Webster told Decker Asnikov's parting line — a sister and three-year-old niece who died in Jonestown, Guyana.

"Something like that in your history — like a personal connection to every kid holed up in a cult. I think he'd help, but confidentiality is holding him back."

"So we'll take the decision out of his hands.

Let's get a subpoena to search his files."

Martinez said, "Even when we get one, Loo, it's going to take time to go through all his files."

Decker stared at the bunkers. "If Bob decides to hunker down for the long run, we'll have *lots* of time."

Martinez chewed the ends of his thick mustache. "*If* Bob decides to hunker down . . ."

"If," Decker repeated. He checked his watch. Seven-thirty. He'd been up for over twenty-four hours. His heavy eyes lifted from his wrist and landed on an FBI van. McCarry was inside, updating his boss. The agent wasn't a bad sort. But he was an inconvenience: another body with another set of orders. Someone who could screw things up. Decker supposed McCarry felt the same way about him.

Martinez asked, "What now?"

Decker said, "Go out and file a petition for the subpoena. At least you'll be doing something. Me?" Decker pointed to his chest. "I sit around, scratch my balls and wait."

"Kinda like baseball players," Webster remarked.

"Wish I made their money."

"Bob hasn't made phone contact?" Martinez asked.

"Not in the last four hours."

More silence . . . mind-numbing silence.

Webster asked, "Where's Europa?"

"We sent her home."

"Why?"

Decker shrugged. "No new insights. She pretty much told me what she had told you. We've got her pager number if something comes up. But there was no reason to keep her here. Especially since Bob didn't want to talk to her."

He stuck his hands in his pockets, brushed loose bits of packed dirt with the tip of his shoe.

"I thought she might have been able to flush him out. From the looks of things, Bob doesn't want to talk to anyone. The inactivity is making the Brass nervous. Both LAPD and fed SWAT teams are talking raid."

Martinez looked at the buildings. From his perspective, they resembled fortified castles. "How are they planning to break in?"

"Maybe freeze the bars, break them off and shoot some canisters of tear gas through the windows, then find someone small enough to crawl inside. First, they're trying to figure out if the windows are electrically hot-wired and/or attached to detonators."

"How do you do that from a distance?"

"Beats me. I'm no weapons expert. They've got scanning machines, they've got every conceivable weapon and the latest in high-tech gismos. What they don't have is an *insider's* knowledge. You get us an insider from Asnikov's files, you give us one hell of a magic bullet."

Silence.

Ten seconds . . .

Twenty seconds . . .

A minute . . .

Decker's eyes shifted from the lifeless compound to the buzzing press area. The hordes were being contained by a band of yellow tape, a half-dozen police officers and a lot of psychology.

"Which judge do you want us to wake up, sir?" Webster asked.

Decker gave him a name, then an alternate if the first wasn't available."Do you have a phone number?" Martinez asked.

"In my office." Decker fished into his pocket for a ring of keys. "Marge and Scott are there now . . . at the station house. I should say they *were* there. I told them to come here around ten minutes ago. They arrived back in town while you two were interviewing Asnikov."

Webster said, "Why're you bringing them out here? I thought you wanted them out of the way so they could work independently."

"Captain's orders. He wants their input because Scott and Marge have both been inside the compound."

Again, no one spoke. The trio stared at the buildings, their skin tone pallid from lack of sleep and a wash of dirty sunlight. Again, Decker checked his watch — seven thirty-eight. Talk about time slowing to a crawl. Maybe in a former life Einstein had been part of a multi-disciplinary law enforcement task force in a no-win hostage situation. Then again, Albert had probably had lots of empty hours as an employee of the postal system in Switzerland. Back then, disgruntled clerks didn't have guns, so things must have been pretty damn slow in the mailroom.

McCarry was still conferring with his colleagues.

Decker was still waiting for Bob to call.

Very, very quiet.

"The key, Loo?" Webster asked.

Decker let out an absent chuckle as he sorted through the ring. "Be nice if I could keep a train of thought."

"Probably has something to do with sleep deprivation."

"No doubt." Decker unlatched the key from the ring and handed it to Martinez. "Either of you know how to work my electronic Filofax?"

"Haven't a clue," Martinez answered.

"I can figure it out," Webster said. "That's why Bert and I make a good team. I can do the Filofax, and he pulls me down to the ground when someone's shooting at me and I'm standing like some frozen squirrel."

But Decker wasn't listening. He was distracted by familiar faces in the distance. Dunn and Oliver were trying to get past an army unit's worth of security personnel. Martinez saw them, too.

"Bert, go rescue them," Decker said. "We'll all compare notes, then I'll explain how to use my Filofax."

Five minutes later they took positions beneath the feathery boughs of one of the many elms. Decker sat huddled in his wrinkled brown suit,

sucking on a cigarette. His four nonsmoking homicide detectives waved away his smoke.

"How can you puff on that thing at . . ." Marge
looked at her wrist. "At eight forty-five in the
morning —"

"*Seven forty-five,*" Decker said.

"Oh, that makes it even better." Marge was irritable from lack of sleep. They were all drained
and tense. With careful deliberation, Oliver gave
them a step-by-step recap of their night up at
Central City. Before they had returned to Los
Angeles, they had once again grilled Benton the
farmhand in the Central City jail. This had been
done at five-thirty in the morning.

"It wasn't one of my best interviews," Marge
said.

"Doesn't matter," Oliver said. "Benton slept
through it."

"Not true," Marge said, "he talked. He said he
didn't do it — over and over and over and over
and over —"

"He was talking in his sleep, Margie. Just like
I'm doing now." Oliver stifled a yawn. "Since we
rushed back here, someone should go back to
the Order's ranch and do an evidence search in
the house and premises now that it's light outside. See if we can find a kill spot for Nova."

Decker said, "I'll send someone else up. Right
now, Strapp wants both of you here."

"I'm touched," Marge said.

"If SWAT decides to raid, they'll need your
input, since you've both been inside."

"You mean it's not my charm?"

" 'Fraid not."

Marge clutched her hands into fists. "When are they going to raid?"

"I don't know even *if* it'll happen let alone *when*," Decker said. "In the meantime, as soon as McCarry's done with his boss and the architect, Brass'll want to talk to you."

"What's he like?" Oliver asked. "McCarry?"

"Uptight and nervous — like all of us. He seems fairly competent . . . as if he'd *like* to do a good job. For himself, for the bureau. The feds got Wacko Waco to live down."

"Where's Strapp?" Marge asked.

"With the police chief and McCarry."

"They've excluded you?" Marge asked.

"When they called the meeting, I excused myself, claiming I had to be ready in case Bob called," Decker said. "Too many friggin' people on this task force." Another drag on his smoke. "Too many people, too many opinions and too many meetings."

Oliver couldn't help it. This time, he let go with a full-mouthed yawn. "Do you know if they've scheduled any meals or naptime into our watch period?"

Webster muttered, "Good luck with that."

Marge turned to Martinez and Webster. "What have you two been up to?"

Bert filled them in. When Martinez was done, Oliver said, "So Asnikov was a bust."

"The Loo doesn't think so," Webster said.

"We're getting a subpoena for Asnikov's files just as soon as he explains how to use his electronic Filofax."

Martinez said, "Did we tell you that we found out Pluto's real name? It's Keith Muldoony."

"Muldoony?" Decker squinted with bleary eyes. "Irish?"

"Could be," Webster said. "But Pluto was a dirt-poor Appalachian white . . . originally from West Virginia. I thought most of them were English stock."

"*West Virginia?*" Dunn said. "Now that's a surprise. I spent some years in Fayetteville, North Carolina, on the base. I can usually spot regionalist speech."

"Ditto," Webster said. "He fooled me, too."

Oliver said, "You know, *that* makes perfect sense to me — Pluto being a country boy. I saw him slaughter a chicken. He just whacked its head off without a *moment's* hesitation. Then he offered to help Benton clean up the bird shit in the coop. I should have guessed that he'd once lived on a farm." He thought a moment. "A guy like Bob . . . he would never have done that."

"Oliver, I could see Bob killing a chicken," Marge said. "He shot Pluto in a heartbeat."

"Shooting is urban," Oliver said. "Whacking the head off a squawking chicken with a single ax blow is pure country. And talk about spray. Can't picture a guy like Bob getting dirty."

Marge said, "If he killed Nova, he sure as hell got spray."

"Not if he shot him first and carved him later." Oliver paused. "Maybe he wore galoshes and a slicker."

"How did *Pluto's* name even come up?" Decker asked.

Martinez said, "We'd reached a dead end with Asnikov so I brought him up to keep the conversation going."

Webster said, "Old Reuben claims that Pluto's from a large, uneducated family. However, he managed to graduate from community college."

"Psychology major," Martinez added. "He became the family's local hero because he got a job in a hospital."

"Wore a white coat," Webster said. "That impressed them all."

"Pluto worked in a hospital?" Decker's eyes darted from face to face. "What did he do?"

"Asnikov thought that he worked as an orderly."

"An *orderly?*"

"They wear white coats, Loo," Webster said.

"You mean Pluto was the guy who emptied the bedpans?" Oliver grinned, deepening the bags under his eyes. "How fitting."

"I've been thinking," Martinez said. "Maybe Bob resented Pluto because the little guy had pulled himself up by the bootstraps."

"So that's why Bob gunned him down?" Webster made a face.

"I've heard of stranger reasons," Marge said.

"Also, Pluto graduated college while Bob was kicked out."

Decker said, "You can't compare Southwest U. with a local community college. In the smugness and prestige department, Bob had it way over Pluto."

Martinez said, "According to Asnikov, the Order was founded with just Jupiter, Pluto and a few followers. Bob came in later."

Oliver said, "I could see a guy like Bob, who thinks he's hot stuff, resenting being pushed around by dirt-poor, white trash like Pluto."

Marge said, "But Bert just said that Pluto wasn't white trash. That he went to college."

"But he started life as white trash," Oliver said. "Origins are everything."

"I don't buy it," Webster said. "*Why* would Bob — even hating Pluto and being jealous of him — just open fire and cause himself all this mess? On the surface, Bob seems like a sensible man. There's gotta be another reason for him lashing out."

"I never met Bob," Martinez said. "But I assume the man has charisma."

Decker nodded. "Fair assessment."

"Loo, if there had been a legitimate struggle for power in leadership, who do you think would have won the vote? Pluto, Bob or Venus?"

"Hard to say," Decker answered. "Pluto was acting as the leader. But Venus and Bob weren't interfering in Pluto's quest for power."

"If Bob had chosen to challenge Pluto, would

it have been a head-to-head competition?"

Decker thought a moment. "Don't know. But they certainly were peers as far as rank went."

Martinez said, "But you don't know if Bob would have won a popular election."

"What are you driving at, Bert?" Decker asked. "Shooting the enemy was the only way for Bob to take control?"

Martinez said, "Maybe he could have won an election, but maybe he didn't want to wait to find out. So he took control the fastest way he saw fit."

"What he has isn't real control, Bert. The minute he steps outside, he's a dead man."

"But maybe that's good enough for him. Because now — at this moment — he's king of the mountain. Sounds to me like typical psycho thinking. Impulsive — act now, pay later."

Oliver said, "The man is attention-starved. He not only has control over the Order, but now he has the press. You got the press in your palms, you've got control of the entire *country*."

"Jupiter's dead, Pluto's dead, Nova's dead . . ." Martinez ticked them off with his fingers. Then he stroked his mustache. "I think Bob not only likes control, he likes *killing* people."

Webster asked, "So you're saying that all of a sudden, Bob discovers homicidal urges?"

"Who said he *just* discovered them, Tom?" Martinez said. "Could be he's always *had* 'em. We know from Europa that Bob got a thrill out of cheating —"

"It's not the same thing as murder."

Decker wasn't sure about that. Criminals loved the thrill of the notorious. He was warming up to Martinez's ideas — a psycho killer in a cult. Because sects like the Order were magnets for disenfranchised people who longed for a guru to lead them into a new life. Breaking ties with family and former friends. No outside communication. No one keeping track of their whereabouts. Perfect prey for a predatory person . . .

"Look at Jonestown . . . look at Heaven's Gate . . . look at Waco. Their leaders talked their members — supposedly rational human beings — into mass suicide, killing themselves and, in the case of Waco and Jonestown, their kids as well. If leaders could get their members to do that, surely they could justify a couple of murders that were 'necessary for the good of the community.' "

"What a field day for a psycho," Martinez said. "Imagine a closed-door cult with lots of potential victims, and lots of privacy to do your dirty work. Tailor-made for a serial killer. Who knows? Maybe Bob disguised his murders as sanctioned killing — you know, like human sacrifices disguised as rituals or rites."

Marge said. "You know, we've worked Homicide in this area for what . . . four years —"

"I've worked this area for twelve years," Oliver said.

"About three years after the Order started," Marge said. "I take it you've never heard of

411

human sacrifices?"

"No, but how would I know?"

"It's a valid point," Decker said. "As long as the privileged attendants kept their members under lock and key, we wouldn't have *any* idea who's even inside those buildings let alone what was going on." He stared at the compound. "Bob could have been murdering people for years, burying the bodies on the grounds, and we wouldn't know the difference."

No one spoke.

Softly, Decker asked, "Who knows what's under those rows of vegetables?"

Marge said, "Now you're just being gross."

"But it makes some sense, Margie," Oliver said. "Because who's going to stop Bob?"

"Jupiter for one," Webster said. "Unless you think he was a homicidal maniac, too."

Oliver arched his eyebrows. "A cult of serial killers —"

"C'mon!" Webster said.

"Suppose there were killings and Jupiter didn't know," Decker said. "Maybe every time someone disappeared, Bob blamed it on Asnikov."

"Just like yesterday," Marge pointed out. "Andromeda and Lyra disappeared and who did they blame? Asnikov!"

"Even if I accept that premise," Webster said, "which isn't exactly straightforward . . ."

Decker smiled. "A few logical leaps —"

"Why would Bob ruin his perfectly quiet, psycho, serial killer setup and start murdering in the open like he did with Pluto? That certainly blew his cover."

"Things were closing in on him," Martinez said.

"Also, psychos have a self-destructive need for attention," Decker said. "Oliver said it perfectly. Guru Bob is one attention-starved boy. Maybe he got a hint of the attention with Jupiter being gone, and he got hooked."

"Loo, the idea is to get attention without getting *caught*."

"Then you're anonymous," Martinez said. "That's no fun."

Decker paused for a moment. "Let's back this up from the beginning. What precipitated this whole ordeal?"

"Jupiter's death," Martinez said.

"Right," Decker said, "Jupiter dies — maybe even poisoned to death. My take? Someone wanted him incapacitated, but alive. Because while Jupiter was alive, he could get away with things that he couldn't do if Jupiter was dead."

"Like killing people?" Webster was incredulous. "Y'all think that Bob was murdering people and Jupiter turned a blind eye?"

Decker said, "Seeing Bob in action, I think it's possible that Russo was using Jupiter as a shield for his dirty work. Could be Bob had convinced Jupiter that his victims were enemies of the Order and had to be destroyed."

"Why would Jupiter believe Bob?" Webster asked.

"Because why would Bob lie? If the old man had been kept isolated, getting his information from only his gurus —"

"To believe Bob, the old man would have to be crazy —"

"Maybe he was. Remember the videotape? Jupiter talking about breaking them in *his* land. We thought he was referring to outside people like us. Maybe he was talking about his enemies within the Order."

"Even if Bob could convince Jupiter that the killings were necessary, don't you think that Venus or Nova or Pluto would have stopped him?"

"Two out of the three people you just mentioned are dead," Decker pointed out. "Maybe they tried to stop him and Bob took umbrage."

Marge looked wan. "This is making me sick. I'm beginning to think that maybe Andromeda and Lyra were Bob's latest victims."

Decker shrugged in a noncommittal manner. But it wasn't convincing.

Webster was still skeptical. "Y'all are jumping around a bit . . . all this speculation."

Oliver asked, "You got anything better to do with your time?"

"Actually, he does," Decker answered. "He can go get a subpoena."

"As soon as you get us the judge's phone number," Webster retorted.

Decker frowned. Another thought came to mind. He said, "Look at Nova. That wasn't an ordinary murder. That was a showpiece! Whoever killed him really enjoyed himself. Arranging the body in skull and crossbones. Bragging about what he had done. Typical of an organized serial killer."

Webster said, "Shooting Pluto in the open certainly wasn't organized."

"But it was effective," Oliver countered. "Bob realized his days were numbered, so he didn't care anymore."

Martinez said, "You know, if Bob is this sadistic, pleasure-seeking murderer, I think he'd enjoy taking the whole cult down with him — going out in a perverted blaze of glory."

"Y'all just creating fantasy —"

"No, we're creating a *scenario*, Tom," Oliver said.

"Okay," Webster said. "Suppose I bought Bob Russo as a serial killer. Suppose I even bought that Bob killed Nova and Pluto because they were a threat to his power base. Why in Mother Mary's name would Bob decide to kill Pluto in the open like that?"

"He cracked under the strain," Martinez said.

Webster waved him off. He looked at Decker. "Are you going to explain the Filofax or not?"

Decker said, "You push the *enter* button, then type in the name —"

Marge's cellular burst into a shrill ring. Startled, she pushed the button and connected the line. "Detective Dunn."

Through the receiver came a fierce, whispery female voice. "You've *got* to get us out of here!

415

He's gone completely *insane!*"

Marge snapped her fingers to get Decker's attention. Her heart was beating like a boom box. "Venus, is that you —"

"Listen carefully! Because I only have seconds to talk before he shows up." She dropped her voice. It was barely audible. "If you *don't* do this right, we'll all *die!* You hear me! Because he's booby-trapped the doors and windows. The back door from the garden to the kitchen is probably the easiest to defuse. Because he's been going in and out of it. So he has to set up something that's easier to arm and disarm. Got it?"

"Got it —"

"Right now he's working on electrically wiring the outside fences. So you don't have much time. Now there's a hole underneath the fence midway between . . ."

Static!

Frantically, Marge punched a roam button, hoping to find a suitable frequency to let her airwaves in. But it didn't do any good. The phone was dead.

Marge swore.

"Venus?" Decker asked.

"I assume so since she's the only one I gave my card . . . wait! I gave Terra my card, too. It could have been Terra."

"Your card had your cell phone number on it?"

Marge nodded. "Venus's voice is throaty. Terra's more meek. But I couldn't tell. All I heard was a scared whisper."

"Did she say something about the back door?" Martinez asked.

"She said all the doors and windows were booby-trapped, but the back door was probably the easiest to defuse because Bob has been going in and out of it. She said we'd better work quickly because Bob was working on electronically wiring the outside fences."

Decker said, "Think the call might have been a trap to rope us into action? Europa said that Bob likes playing games. She said that if we waited him out, he'd make a move. This could be it."

Silence. Then Marge said, "*Maybe*. Except the voice certainly *sounded* terrified."

"Could be legit," Decker said. "But it could be acting. Cults attract the fringes, and so does Hollywood. Lots of past thespians have wound up with some mighty strange gurus."

30

After apprising the LAPD brass and FBI of the latest communications, Decker and his crew waited for instructions. Marge was interviewed first, her phone immediately confiscated. Lots of questions; for every ten people, there were eleven opinions. The diversity led the top brass to convene yet another task force operative in the form of — guess what? — another meeting. Even had Decker been invited — which he wasn't — he would have excused himself. With so many people calling the shots, chances of a screw-up were great.

The consensus was that the phone call had been a trap. Marge took the role of the lone voice of dissent. She stood against the elm tree, staring at the lifeless building, sipping coffee from a paper cup. With her were Decker, Oliver and Special-Agent-in-Charge Bennett McCarry, who had joined the group by default. Their own small task force — one devoid of power and importance, but at least her voice could be heard. She rubbed her eyes, blinking back glare from the overcast, mid-morning sky. Mr. Sun was trying valiantly to break through the pewter clouds.

"If Bob really wanted to hook us, why didn't

he use a kid on the phone? He knows we'd be more likely to take risks for children."

"Kids are unreliable," answered McCarry.

"Not the Order's kids," Marge responded. "They've been programmed to be little robots."

Recalling her interview with fourteen-year-old Vega, thinking about the glimmer of light behind the young teen's eyes as she spoke about the Little Prince's adventures into magical worlds. Such a bright child, yet she had lived out her short life behind concrete walls, her mind crammed with hard-nose sciences, and the false faith of a guru, dropout astrophysicist. A pain shot through Marge's heart.

McCarry was talking. ". . . like she was talking under someone else's orders?"

"The woman on the phone?" Marge asked.

McCarry almost repressed his annoyance. "Yes, Detective. The woman on the phone. Did she sound like she was repeating someone else's orders?"

Marge pondered the question. "To me, she sounded genuinely scared."

Oliver said, "Even if it's a ploy to draw us out, we still can't ignore it."

Decker said, "I'm sure the current task force is working on it."

"Why aren't you with them?" Oliver asked.

"Guess I've been kicked out of the loop." Decker yawned, then faced McCarry. "So what's your excuse for hanging around us losers when you could be part of the bigwigs?"

McCarry shrugged. "I like losers. Feel at home with them."

Decker smiled. He knew a couple of reasons why McCarry elected to stay. First, Decker had clout — albeit minimal — with Bob. Maybe the FBI agent wanted to ride his wave. But more than that, Decker sensed that McCarry had grown tired of useless meetings. He was beginning to warm up to the agent, sensing a reciprocal thaw. There were small signs of mutual trust. Things like McCarry getting Decker's people fresh coffee when he had exited the task force's trailer.

The agent asked, "Where are the other two? Blondie and Mustache?"

"Martinez and Webster?" Decker rephrased. "They're petitioning to subpoena Reuben Asnikov's files."

"Which judge are they asking for the warrant?" Marge asked.

"Ryan."

"Good choice."

"Asnikov's a first-class bastard," McCarry shot out. "Sitting on information while there are kids inside."

"Asnikov claims he's never rescued anyone from the Order," Oliver said.

McCarry asked, "You ever mention him to anyone in the Order? See their reaction?"

Marge said, "Couple of times."

"To them, he's the devil, right?"

"In the flesh."

McCarry sipped coffee. "You don't elicit naked hatred unless you've messed them up. Over the years the L.A. Bureau alone has received close to fifty kidnapping complaints against him."

"Kidnapping complaints from the *Order?*" Marge asked.

McCarry shook his head. "The Order would never contact the FBI about Asnikov. First of all, they're kidnappers themselves. Second, the gurus all have clouded pasts, I'm convinced of it. No, most of the complaints against Reuben have come from divorced parents. Kidnapping kids for one parent or the other. You know the scenario. Dad decides to stick it to Mom by kidnapping sonny."

Decker asked, "Does Asnikov kidnap for the custodial or noncustodial parent?"

"He swings both ways. We have at least fifteen cases where he's taken the kid away from the court-assigned parent. Although in a few cases, looks like the court made a mistake. I'd say the bulk of his work consists of returning kids to the custodial parent."

"Nothing wrong with that," Marge said. "That's restoration."

"In theory, no." McCarry's eyes turned steely. "It's his methods."

"It's your kid, you have the legal rights, the system is failing you . . ." Marge shrugged. "I don't see a problem."

"It's vigilante justice," McCarry said.

"To me, it's plain justice."

The agent didn't press it. Decker looked around the area teeming with steel and flesh — cars, trucks, SWAT vans and other assorted vehicles along with newspaper and TV people with cameras, spotlights, makeup personnel (mascara and foundation run in the fog) and sound booms and mikes. In the last two hours, the bodies seemed to have multiplied by mitosis. An ant farm in macrocosm. Everyone just waiting for *something* to happen.

Decker said, "We could cut the manpower in half without losing anything."

"At least by half," McCarry agreed. "What a waste of money." To Marge, he said, "My techs are wiring your line to our tape machine in one of our equipment vans. They should be done in fifteen minutes. You'll need to stick around in case someone calls you."

Oliver said, "In the meantime, Loo, I think we should look for the alleged hole in the fence. See if it even exists. I've got a pair of binocs in the trunk of the car."

"Sure, go look, Scott. Who knows what you might find?" To McCarry, Decker said, "Does anyone in your agency have any idea if the compound's doors and windows are *really* hot-wired?"

"Nobody," McCarry answered.

Oliver spoke. "The phone call said that Bob was in the process of wiring the fence. I'm just wondering if maybe Bob already has. Like he has a switch to turn it on and off. So we plan our move thinking that everything's copacetic. Then the moment Bob sees us futzing with the fence, he flips on the juice, turning us into crispies."

But Decker was staring off into the distance.

Marge asked, "What're you looking at?"

"At ten o'clock . . . just before the ropes." Decker pointed several hundred feet to the left of the cordoned-off press area. "Looks like some kind of security break."

Several uniformed men were interrogating a woman wearing jeans, a black turtleneck sweater and red Keds sneakers.

They were more than interrogating her; she was handcuffed. She was rocking on her feet. On closer inspection, she was stamping them on the ground.

Her body language seemed young . . . the energy with which she moved. She was thin with long, stringy brown hair. She appeared to be shouting although Decker couldn't hear from where he stood. Within seconds, the officers had closed rank around her, and she was buried beneath a blanket of blue security uniform shirts. Then the seas parted, and two of the men started dragging her off, the toes of her red sneakers digging tracks into the ground.

Marge said, "C'mon, Scott. Let's check it out."

Oliver took the last sips of his coffee and tossed the cup in a brown shopping bag that had been designated as garbage. "I'm with you, babe."

Decker rubbed his forehead as he watched them jog toward the scene. He saw them flash ID, then talk to the group of officers as the woman was being shoved unceremoniously into a black-and-white. At first, Marge seemed to be nodding with a distracted air. But within moments, her entire expression underwent a radical change. Even at this distance, Decker saw her eyes widen several diameters.

As the police car began to pull out, Oliver bolted to the front of the cruiser as Marge rushed over and banged on the passenger window. Decker heard her screaming, but again he couldn't discern any intelligible speech. Abruptly, the police car braked, and jerked backward. Marge didn't even wait until the car was motionless. She yanked open the back door and stuck her head inside.

Without a word, Decker began to run toward the car. He could hear McCarry sprinting behind him. Obviously, he had the same idea.

As Marge attempted to help her out of the car, the girl kicked up dust, legs flailing in every direction as she tried to break from Marge's grip.

"Get your fucking paws off of me!"

"Just calm —"

". . . come here, risking *my* life, and you morons try to *arrest* me!"

"The officers didn't know —"

"So they should shut up and listen! I *knew* I shouldn't have come back!" The girl continued to struggle against Marge's grasp. "Let go of me, you idiot!"

Marge released her hold, and the girl flew backward, landing on her butt. Wordlessly, Marge gripped her arm and pulled her back to her feet.

The girl said nothing for a moment, wiggling her hands. "Think you can take your B and D fun bands off my wrists?"

Marge said, "I'm on your side —"

"Listen, girlfriend, you want to build rapport, take the handcuffs off!"

Breathlessly, Decker stopped in front of the girl, looking deep into her eyes, recalling the lone fuzzy picture of Andromeda that he had seen. It could have gone both ways. "Are you Lauren Bolt?"

"Depends who's asking," the girl answered defiantly. "Who're you?"

"Lieutenant Peter Decker — LAPD. Where's Lyra?"

"None of your damn business!"

"Just tell me . . ." Decker was still breathing hard. "Tell me that she's okay. Please." A breath. "All I want you to say is that she's okay!"

For the first time, the girl seemed to sense concern. "She's okay."

"Safe?"

She nodded.

"That's good." Decker put his hand to his chest. "One less thing to gnaw at my gut."

"You've been looking for her?"

"Looking for the *both* of you. The Order claims that you were kidnapped by Reuben Asnikov."

A disdainful snort. "Sounds like something the Order would say." Another snort — more forceful. "Sounds like something *Pluto* would say. Pompous ass. Is he really dead?"

"Yes."

"Wish it would have been *Nova* —"

"Nova?" Marge asked.

Lauren regarded Marge. "You know him?"

"We've interviewed him," Oliver said.

A light of recognition behind the eyes. "That's right. I was still there when you did. Guess he forgot to tell you he's a perv! They're *all* perverts. But he's the worst because he likes kids."

"Nova's dead, ma'am," Oliver said.

A smile spread across Lauren's lips. "Now if you could just get the rest of them, my life would take on meaning."

"Do you work for Asnikov?" Marge asked.

"No. But he's the reason I've come . . . well, *one* of the reasons. Even if he hadn't called, I would have probably come down." She looked at her feet. "Because of the kids. You get . . . attached . . ."

She looked up and squinted in the harsh light.

"He got me just in time. We were about to jump ship for Australia."

"But you *don't* work for Asnikov," McCarry stated.

Lauren's face flared up in hostility. "I just said

426

that, didn't I? Are you deaf?"

McCarry tapped his foot. "I thought you came here to offer us help."

"That's up to you, bub."

Decker regarded her. She had to have been in her early twenties: so skinny you could break her with a bear hug. Yet here she was, mouthing off to a swarm of security officers, lashing out and swearing like a sailor, not the least bit deterred by authority. She was brash and rude and physical. No wonder they had slapped cuffs on her. Yet Decker understood her blatant gall. She had needed it to infiltrate the Order.

One of the arresting officers stood on the outside of the group, his hand on his hip. "Do you want me to take her in, Lieutenant?"

"No," Decker answered. "Leave her be."

"Yeah, leave me be, bub," she said.

Marge took McCarry aside. "I'll fill you in."

Decker gave her an A-okay sigh as he studied the young girl's face, her familiar patrician features blurred by rage and impudence. He computer-aged her visage about sixty years. "The Farranders said that Maureen was their youngest so you couldn't be Lyra's aunt. I'd say you're Maureen's niece . . . the daughter of one of her older sisters."

Lauren glared, but said nothing.

"Maureen?" Oliver asked.

"Known as Moriah in the Order." Decker faced Lauren. "When I was hunting for Lyra, I interviewed your grandparents. You look like

427

your grandmother."

The girl tensed. "The selfless Ceese — a bastion of altruism!"

Decker said, "We're all prisoners of our past —"

"Not all of us, bub!"

"No, not you. You're the righteous cousin on a mission to save Lyra. *Good* for you, Lauren! You did it! You got her out and probably saved her life. That's no exaggeration. Now help us get the other kids out and you'll be a true hero."

At once, Lauren's eyes welled up with tears. "First, take the damn hardware off me."

Decker glanced at the officer with the ring of keys. "Remove the handcuffs."

The man was dubious, but listened to orders from a superior. Within moments, the girl was rubbing her wrists. Freed of the shackles, she seemed less sure of her position. Quiet but guarded.

She said, "I suppose I owe you something. The police investigation disrupted the Order's robotic schedule." A long look into space. "You gave me the break I needed."

Decker asked, "How long had you been underground?"

"A little over two years." Lauren wiped her eyes. "It was hell, but I'd do it all over again. Especially after what I know. No way I'd let her rot there."

"You couldn't have known Lyra before you went inside," Decker said. "Chances are you never even met her. She was raised inside the Order. What made you go after her?"

She hugged herself. "That's me! Always a sucker for the underdog. The kind of kid who brings home stray cats and baby birds." The girl looked away, her face still holding sadness. "I can't stop thinking about the other kids."

"Join the club," Marge said. "Did you know the dangers going in?"

Lauren shrugged. "Reuben pretty much gave me the details. He told me *not* to do it. He told me how dangerous the Order could be. He told me that Pluto'd be watching my every step. He told me if I stepped out of line, I'd be physically punished. He told me that Bob would come on to me because I was young and cute. He told me that I'd have to sleep with him and if I didn't, I'd pay dearly. He told me there was a very good chance I'd *never* get out. He told me he couldn't help me — no one could — because the Order was impenetrable. He told me to think it over . . . not for days, but for months. And I did."

"But you went anyway," Decker said.

"I don't think I believed Reuben. The arrogance was a good thing. Because if I had really known . . ." She looked away. "I had worked with poor kids — kids in the inner city — much to my mother's horror." She looked at Decker. "Did you meet *Mom?*"

Decker shook his head no.

"A mini Ceese. See, I grew up in a family who thought that people should only be vanilla-flavored. When I realized that chocolate had lots to offer, I got to thinking about Maureen's kid. No one else in the family was interested in saving her . . . charity begins at home."

A tear rolled down her cheek as she stared at the bunkers.

"It eats me up. There're *good* people inside, sir. Decent people who're looking for God in all the wrong places. It's not *them*. It wasn't even *Jupiter*. Yeah, he was psycho, but more into his visions than into power. It's the mad four below him — Pluto, Nova, Venus and Bob. You don't know the half of it."

Oliver took out his notepad. "Apparently not if you're telling us that Nova was a pedophile."

She focused in on Oliver's face. "Chester the Molester."

"He seemed like a wimp."

"Most pedophiles are," Lauren snapped back. "How'd he die?"

"Exsanguination, most likely," Decker said. "Someone carved him up and stuffed him in one of the kitchen cabinets at the Order's ranch. The local law is holding the ranch hand named Benton for the murder. Does his name ring a bell?"

Lauren shook her head no. "I wasn't even aware that the Order owned a ranch."

"Jupiter owned it. Now it probably belongs to his daughter, Europa. Benton runs the place, although *I* don't think he popped Nova. I think Bob did it."

"Sounds logical," Lauren said. "After Our Father Jup— After Emil Ganz died, Bob moved in like a cockroach."

"I always picture Pluto as the roach," Oliver said.

"Pluto's more like a T-rex. He destroys what gets in his way."

Bob as the roach and Pluto as T-rex. Like Oliver, Decker would have thought it was the other way around.

Marge asked, "Why would Bob kill a wimp like Nova? Was he a threat to Bob's power base?"

Lauren gave the question some thought. "Not really. Nova was the weakest of the four."

"So why would Bob kill him?" McCarry asked.

"Because Bob enjoys killing people," Lauren said.

No one spoke.

"Even so, there *has* to be more." Decker stopped for a moment, his mind flipping through the file of the original case. Back to the very beginning. A spark in his brain ignited. "Jupiter was found dead at around five in the morning. Nova was writing out the death certificate a half-hour later. And Europa called the police shortly after that." A pause. "Some woman from the Order called Europa to tell her that her dad had died. It *wasn't* Venus."

Decker looked at her pointedly. Lauren bit her lip.

"C'mon, Lauren. You couldn't have called

without help because only gurus had phones. Someone instructed you to *make* that call. Process of elimination tells me it *had* to be Nova. *Why* would he want you to call up a violator?"

"He was frightened by Jupiter's death. Bob and Pluto had wanted to bury Ganz on the grounds like the others —"

"The *others?*" McCarry said. "What *others?*"

"The others that had 'expired' along the way," Lauren answered. "No doubt they were murdered —"

"You know that as a *fact?*" McCarry asked.

"I know that rebellious members had a way of disappearing —"

"Jesus!" Marge muttered.

Decker asked, "What else did Nova confide in you, Lauren?"

"He said Ganz's death was too big to hide. That Ganz was too famous and he had children. He was worried about Europa, the daughter. Ganz had kept up contact with her. This time, Nova wanted to go through proper channels. He said if we didn't call the police in now, it would be big trouble later on when Europa found out about her father's death. Everything and everyone would be investigated. That would have been the death knell for us . . . for them . . . the Order."

"Thinking he could waylay us before we dug too deep," Oliver said.

Lauren nodded. "He told me to phone Europa even if it meant breaking the vows and overstepping the chain —"

Decker blurted out, "Overstepping the *chain* . . . breaking the vows." He tapped his foot. "I've heard that expression before."

"It's one of the Order's most basic laws," Lauren said. " 'Never break your vows and never overstep the chain of command.' The gurus used to lecture it to us over and over and over and over."

Decker hit his forehead. "Oh, my Lord!"

"What?" Oliver asked.

"When I first met Pluto, I asked him about the phone call to Europa. He said whoever did it would have to be *addressed* because he had overstepped the chain, and had broken his vows."

He made a face. *T-Rex here we come.*

"It was *Pluto* who killed Nova. He was *addressing* Nova's insubordination. That little motherfucker knew all along that he'd carved up Nova. He knew it when you two went up there. And he knew you'd find the body. But he didn't care because he knew we'd arrest Benton!"

"Loo," Oliver said. "Ms. Bolt just said that it was *Bob* who enjoyed killing people."

"Bob kills for sport — for pleasure. Pluto killed to keep his power base absolute. He couldn't have men like Nova — who overstepped the chain and broke vows — get away with colluding with violators. Especially since Nova was a privileged attendant — a *guru.* That position demanded complete loyalty to the Order. And since Nova couldn't be trusted anymore, Pluto killed him."

"Then why did Bob kill Pluto?" McCarry asked.

"Because Bob knew his power base was finished. While Jupiter was alive, but zonked out from arsenic, Bob pretty much had free rein. Even though Pluto was second in command, Jupiter still ran things. But once Ganz died and the free ride had ended, Bob knew he had no constituency. Better to die a leader than live under a little totalitarian putz like Pluto. And after Nova's death, maybe Bob figured he was next on the chopping block anyway."

"So who killed Jupiter?" McCarry asked.

Marge said, "The place housed two homicidal lunatics and a child molester. Take your pick."

Lauren took a swipe at her eyes. "I keep seeing the *children* — obeying whatever they're told." The young girl bit her lip. "We've got to do something. They do terrible things. They made us watch."

"You witnessed murder?" Decker asked.

"Punishments," Lauren said softly. "They claimed they served as purification as well as warnings for the rest of the Order."

"What kind of punishments?" Decker asked.

"Burning iron pokers on the stomach and soles of the feet, branding the back with the six-six-six of the devil. If it was a second offense, Pluto would amputate digits — fingers, toes."

There was silence. Oliver thought of the little man hacking off a chicken head. He asked, "And if it was a third offense?"

This time when Lauren bit her lip, she drew blood. "There wasn't a third time. The offenders would . . . disappear."

"Was Jupiter present during the punishments?"

"You know, I never remember seeing him at the rites of purification." A sob escaped her throat. "The sadism always came from his underlings."

"What about Nova? Did he participate?"

"He'd take the atoner's . . . the victim's vital signs. To make sure the punishment didn't go *too* far."

"Like the Spanish Inquisition," Decker said. "The torturers always had a doctor present during the process to make sure the victim didn't actually die . . . so the person could be tortured again."

To Lauren, Marge said, "The victims were given only two chances?"

"Yes."

"And no one protested?"

Lauren said, "You know, I found out real quick that protest is an invention of a free society. Everyone was *terrified!* No one said a word!"

More silence.

Lauren went on. "Pluto had convinced the congregation that the process was necessary for atonement. If the victim didn't undergo the torture, he'd die a violator and never reach the next level. Venus led them in chant while Bob or Pluto performed the horror. *Everything* was ritualized."

"How'd you get around them?" Marge asked.

The young woman's face was full of pain. "I played up to Bob." She threw up her hands. "Hey, placating the enemy with sex is a time-honored tradition."

Immediately, Decker thought of Chanukah. Most people knew about the brave Maccabees fighting off the Greek Syrians. Few knew about the heroics of the woman, Yael. After the Syrian defeat, the enemy general, Sisera, escaped to Yael's house for shelter. She wore him out to complete fatigue by bedding him. Afterward, when he had fallen into a deep sleep, she drove a tent peg through his brain. "How *did* you escape, Lauren?"

Lauren blinked. "Used a time-old tradition of convicts. I tunneled my way out. I started digging on day one." A shrug. "I always had my fingernails. On good nights, I had a spoon."

Along with the others, Decker was stunned. All that for a little girl she had never met. Someone should study her superior morals and ethics.

Lauren brushed strands of hair from her face. "I did what I had to do."

"Anyone else from the Order know about your tunnel —"

"Maybe that's the hole in the fence," Oliver interrupted.

"What hole?" Lauren asked.

Marge explained the phone call.

"I didn't dig out midway between any fence. I came out way *beyond* the fence, in the middle of the wooded area behind the compound. I would never have dug in the open. Way too vulnerable. Reuben and I talked about it before I went in. He said to dig out in the mountain brush where there was plenty of cover. I don't know what hole your caller's talking about."

"You think the call is a trap?" McCarry inquired.

"Depends who called. If it was Terra, no, it's not a trap. She's *terrified* of Bob."

Decker nodded. "If you met up with her again, you'd think she'd be on your side?"

"Well, she's terrified of Bob. But she's also terrified of defying him."

"If Venus had made the call, would it be a trap?"

"I don't know. I will say that she has a lot invested in the Order, so I don't see her trying to bring it down. Venus also commands respect. You don't mess with her. People have tried and things have happened to them."

"What things?" McCarry asked. "Don't tell me *she's* a serial killer."

Lauren was pensive. "Like I said, I never *saw* anything. But her enemies, like the enemies of Bob and Pluto, had this way of disappearing."

"Talk about declining populations," Marge said. "It's a wonder the Order didn't murder itself out of existence. It's unbelievable!"

"Not at all," Lauren said. "When there are no absolutes and *people* make up the rules, anything is fair game." A pause. "I'm not a big one for organized religion. But God has its good points. If the Ten Commandments were given by the Ultimate Creator, then those rules have to be *immutable.* And that's not bad. Because when human beings *change* the norms, they always fuck things up."

McCarry snapped her out of her musings. "Tell me more about this tunnel."

She told them all she knew. How she chose her spot — in the teens' classroom. Because the gurus weren't the least bit concerned with the kids. And the classrooms were always empty at night. She'd sneak off and dig. She'd time her digging with the cries from the infant nursery next door. Every night, she'd scratch away. She was lucky. Out here, in the valley, the soil was loose. Not like the clay soil that held up most of the city of L.A.

"We should contact SWAT," McCarry said. "I'd play it like this. We lead the Order into thinking that we're looking for an imaginary hole —"

"It may be real," Lauren said. "Maybe someone else was trying to dig out. I'm just saying it isn't part of *my* tunnel. Its location doesn't even sound like one of my red herrings."

"Red herrings?" Decker asked.

"I dug some fake holes outside. Also Reuben's idea. In case I'd make an escape and get discovered midway, my pursuers wouldn't know which hole was real and which one was a dead-end. I dug two fake tunnels while I was at the Order.

They don't lead anywhere. One goes about twenty feet and dies, the other's about forty."

Decker was flabbergasted. "Can I harness your ingenuity and market it?"

"I was trying to save my life . . . Lyra's, too. Incredible how creative you become."

McCarry said, "If we look for this imaginary hole in the fence midway between somewhere, we can draw Bob into thinking we've fallen for his trap. In the meantime, SWAT will tunnel —"

"Uh, there's a problem with a raid," Lauren said. "My tunnel was barely big enough for me. It's all belly-crawling. Can't lift your head more than six inches off the ground. At some points, I really had to contort to make it through. You'll *never* get your *regular* men through there. A small man would even be doubtful."

"What about my size?" Marge asked.

"Maybe —"

"We'll do the raid with women," Marge said. "I'll lead."

"You're not familiar with the pathway," Lauren said. "The turns are tricky. If any part of the tunnel has collapsed, you'll be lost."

"I'll risk it!" Marge said.

Decker looked at her. "Margie, that's insane."

She ignored him. "It'll have to be done at night."

"Night, day, it doesn't matter," Lauren answered. "Tunnel is as dark as jet fuel. Slimy, too."

"I was thinking of dark as coverage in the mountains —"

"Ah," Lauren said. "Good point!"

"We'll need miner's caps for starts," Marge said. "Protective gear, equipment, gloves, masks. Don't want to pick up any lethal virus nesting in the soil."

"A lightweight oxygen tank may be helpful," Lauren said. "Just in case."

"You're not worried about gases igniting."

"It's not that far down."

"How far?"

"Six feet maybe."

"It's too dangerous," Decker said. "Forget it!"

"What do you mean, *forget* it!" Marge was outraged. "It's okay for men to raid and risk their lives, but when it comes to meek women —"

"I'd forbid *anyone* under my command," Decker said. "Marge, for chrissakes, you're a *homicide* cop, not Indiana Jones!"

"*She* made it out!"

"She had two years for test runs. Besides, the Order wasn't looking for a raid when she broke out!"

"Pete, they're not going to be looking for a raid coming up from a *tunnel* —"

"They'll be looking for a raid in any way, shape or form. Through the doors, through the ceilings, under the floors. They're going to be scrutinizing everything!" He threw up his hands. "If this is going to be done, at least let SWAT handle it —"

"*I've* got a major advantage over SWAT."

Marge poked her chest. "*I've* been inside the Order."

Oliver said, "Marge, to use the advantage, first you've got to *get* inside."

"I can do it —"

"She just said you're too big!" Decker insisted.

"Maybe not," Lauren backtracked.

Marge turned to her. "Are *you* willing to go back in?"

"Yes." She nodded fiercely. "I couldn't live with myself if I didn't give it my best shot." She looked at Decker. "Loo or Pete or Decker or whatever your name is, if she's willing to go in, so am I. You need me. I'm your only hope."

McCarry said, "You'll need professionals with you."

"Then no more than three people," Lauren said. "I've loosely calculated the oxygen level for the given area. The tunnel can support around three sets of lungs without trouble."

"We'll take supplemental oxygen canisters," Marge said. "So I'm one, and Lauren's two. We'll take one more." She turned to Decker, "Who's our best on SWAT?"

"Probably Sharon Jacobs."

"Is she here?"

"I don't *know!*" Decker was agitated. "This is sheer suicide!"

Marge said, "Pete, I keep hearing the voice of that kid I interviewed —"

"Who?" Lauren asked.

"Vega —"

"Oh, she's wonderful! Brilliant, too."

"I'm going and that's it!" Marge turned to Decker with a determined look on her face. He had seen it too many times in the past. It said, "I hear you, I'm disregarding you."

McCarry said, "Special Agent Elise Stone has been with SWAT for ten years. I know she's here. Been here since the beginning."

"We'll take her," Marge said. "Lauren'll lead, then I'll go, Elise Stone'll bring up the rear." She looked upward. The sun was stronger now. The harsh light made her eyes burn. "We've got about twelve hours to concoct some kind of workable plan. We'd better light a fire." She threw her arm around Lauren. "C'mon. Let's go save some kids."

31

Reuben Asnikov was brought down to identify Lauren Bolt: to verify that she wasn't a plant from the Order. He did the identification with glee, not only feeling vindicated by her appearance but relieved and grateful, stating that perhaps *maybe* the kids had a glimmer of a chance.

The children. The foremost consideration — the drooling infants with bald heads and lopsided smiles; the toddlers with wet thumbs, teetering gaits and curious eyes; the preschoolers learning how to count while pushing rubber blocks through shape-sorters; school-age children with missing front teeth, bright eyes and gangly limbs; the giggling preteens on the verge of puberty; teenagers carving their way into adulthood.

Decker wondered if *any* of them would ever reach their majority.

After Bolt and the deprogrammer gave their respective affidavits, Lauren was led to a trailer to rest while indemnity papers were drawn up. The legal phraseology alone would take hours, the lawyerspeak needing to be exact. She'd have to acknowledge the dangers — disclosed and undisclosed — in the operation. She'd be required to sign a stack of papers, waiving her rights to sue the city or any individuals associated with the raid should she undergo any sort of harm — either physical or mental, be it loss of limb or life. Decker kept hoping Bolt would get cold feet. But as time passed she became more resolute, determined to rescue her kids.

Asnikov was free to go, but he had elected to stay on. He wore a white button-down shirt, most of it covered by a gray cable-knit sweater, and black pants. On his feet were black socks and rubber-soled shoes. Staring at the compound, he chewed gun, snapping it loudly. Even so, his jaw muscles were working much harder than necessary.

The deprogrammer said, "Lauren's a great girl, but she's foolhardy."

"The impetuous nature of youth," Decker said. "We old farts take meetings, she just goes in and does it."

"I never thought she'd make it." Asnikov's eyes were directed forward. "It ate at me . . . her being there and my inability to help her. In the beginning, we talked about implanting communication devices on her body. In the end, she decided against it. She was completely on her own."

"She never tried to get hold of you?"

"The parishioners don't have access to phones. And even if she could have pilfered one, it would have been too dangerous to call. They monitor everything." He looked at Decker. "I told her not to do it. But I'm glad she did. She succeeded where I had failed."

"She was lucky," Decker said. "But *this* time is different. They're going to be *looking* for infiltrators. It's one thing to escape the compound, another to raid and liberate it."

"Agreed," Asnikov said. "Why don't you stop her?"

Decker clenched his jaw. "If I had known she was going to pull a stunt like this, I would have had her arrested in the beginning. Now, it's out of my hands."

Asnikov's expression remained flat. "You're against the raid?"

In its present form, Decker was very much against the raid. But he didn't comment.

Asnikov said, "Lauren once told me she was part cat. That's why she moves so quietly. Hope she's right because she could use nine lives." He shook his head. "Three of us versus one hundred plus of them. Some odds. All we have is the element of surprise." He smiled. "Lauren saved you the bother of subpoenaing my files."

"Saved you the bother of us sorting through your cases," Decker said.

"It wouldn't have mattered to me. Sure I have office files. But most of the important info is filed up here." He pointed to his temple. "When are they planning to go in?"

Decker said, "I don't know."

"You're being sly."

"No, I'm not. I don't have an ounce of guile in me at the moment. Too damn tired."

Asnikov nodded with understanding. He said,

"In a way, I'm jealous of Lauren. Wish it were me going in."

"Hero's complex, Asnikov?"

"Bet your ass. Every time I free up a human soul, I feel real good about it. Sure beats that sick and helpless feeling you get when the camera pans across your dead sister. This should be sweet revenge if you can pull it off." He tightened his jaw and the muscle swelled. "I'd give anything to liberate that concentration camp!"

The comparison wasn't exactly parallel. But it wasn't far off the mark. A maniacal leader with three murdering henchmen, and a pedophile as the resident doctor. Just multiply the numbers and it could have been the SS.

Sweet revenge if you can pull this off, Decker thought. *A big if.*

He looked at Asnikov, whose eyes were far-off stars in a distant galaxy. His posture was rigid, his face had gone hard. His jaw was chomping hard and loud, but there was no sound of snapping gum. Instead, it had been replaced with the rasping noise of enamel gnashing against enamel.

Awakened by the harsh ring of the phone, Decker startled, then bolted up. Like a fireman called into action, he jump-started into immediate action. He looked at McCarry, then at the communications expert, Special Agent Jan Barak. She gave the a silent countdown on her fingers. Then with precise timing, Decker picked up the receiver.

446

Bob asked, "What're you doing out there, Lieutenant?"

Without missing a beat, Decker answered, "Not much, Bob. What are you doing in there?"

"I just took a terrific nap. Feel better than ever. How about yourself?"

"I'm fine."

"You don't sound fine. You sound tired. They don't give you much in the way of a break, do they?"

"I like doing my job, Bob. Protect and serve. That's our motto."

"Well said, Lieutenant Decker. Because we all have jobs to do. It's cosmically ordained by the universe. Take a look at the planetary motion of our own solar system. Everything's in perfect gravitational balance. Perfect orbits until some giant meteor or comet comes along and knocks everything off-kilter. Then there's that old entropy again rearing its ugly head. Total chaos. You understand what I'm saying."

"Keep the status quo. I'm with you, Brother."

"No, I don't think you are, Lieutenant." A pause. "Well, maybe *you* are, but some of your workmen have other ideas. Because we're noticing some movement out there . . . we can see you mapping out the perimeter of our home. From the front to the back . . . from our public entrances to our back doors in the brush of the mountains."

"Sure it's us? There are lots of creatures out there."

"I'm not worried about the pumas. I'm talking about the two-legged creatures. For the dark, we've got infrared scopes on our rifles. You want to be sitting ducks, it's up to you."

"I hear you."

"I'm still not sure that you do," Bob insisted. "Tell them we've got weapons with fantastic ranges. I mean I just don't *get* it, Decker. Why would any man volunteer to be target practice?"

Decker said, "I'll find out what's going on."

"Lieutenant, I *know* what's going on. Are they keeping you in the dark?"

"What do you want me to tell them?"

"Just what I'm telling you. I'm giving you fair warning, Decker. The most holy Order of the Rings of God considers anything that invades our personal space up for grabs. It doesn't matter if you come in the front or back door, get my drift."

"You hold the top cards, Bob. We've known that from the beginning."

"So why are they *fucking* with me? Don't they believe me? Do they need a demonstration?"

"No, Bob, that's not necessary —"

"I'll give them one if you hold on. Honey, come over here for a sec."

"Bob, don't —"

A deafening blast over the line. Decker dropped the phone and jumped back, holding his ears as cannons shot through in his brain and fireworks exploded through his optic nerve. Staggering on his feet while his heart drummed

448

against his sternum. Someone touching him.

He whirled around, teetered, then tried to focus.

Jan Barak looking at him with worried eyes. She was talking to him, but he couldn't hear a damn thing. McCarry, too. The agent was mouthing silent fucks.

A deep breath . . . trying to turn the head volume from multiforte to just plain forte. Eyes darting about, he spied the fallen phone and picked it up, gingerly placing it against his right ear as his head screamed in protest.

Into the receiver, he said, "Bob, are you there?" Silence. His own words had been miked with reverb, everything echoing inside his skull. "Bob?"

McCarry slapped his forehead. Barak appeared to be talking to him. Decker ignored them and tried again. "Bob, are you with me, guy?"

No response. Then McCarry's voice, though hushed, became suddenly audible. ". . . line's dead."

"Oh." Decker hung up. "Man, that smarted."

McCarry was still talking, ". . . to a doctor —"

"I'm fine —"

"Decker —"

"I can hear you, can't I?" He knew he was shouting by the feeling in his throat. Certainly not by the sound of his voice. To his own ears, he sounded muffled. For the most part he *could* hear, although McCarry sounded as if he were speaking inside a belfrey. "Give me a few minutes, I'll be fine —"

"Decker, don't be an ass, you've got . . ."

But his words were fading out. The agent ended his speech by mouthing the word *bastard*.

Decker felt an upsurge in his gut, the world spun about him. He sat back in his chair, threw his head between his knees. Barak came over, touched his shoulder. He let her hand remain there for a moment, then he sat back up, his eyes landing on one of the van's perimeter monitors.

"Look!" He pointed upward.

All eyes followed.

The Order's front door had opened just wide enough to eject the body. It arced upward, then landed ten feet from the entrance, lying like a broken marionette with tangled strings. A frail frame in a long dress. Probably a woman even though its entire head was wrapped up in several towels. Very wet towels soaking up copious amounts of blood. Decker could discern that the cloth was saturated even though the monitor was black-and-white.

Definitely a woman. But who?

Because Lord only knew what her face looked like.

32

Crouching in the brush, Marge felt her thighs
bunch as she froze stock-still. Looking and listening. Throughout the night, there had been
random shots coming from the small windows
that lined the Order's main gathering halls.
Nothing organized, but enough to get the adrenaline going. The task force had talked about
hurling canisters of tear gas through glass, but
over the past twenty-four hours, the cult members had covered most of the panes with wooden
planks.

Again, she glanced around, checking over her
shoulder. The only sounds were the nocturnal
voices of nature, everything *appearing* calm. But
how quickly that could change. Forced to play
the interminable waiting game. A second, then
two . . . three . . . four . . . counting slowly . . .
slowly.

Garbed in nylon camouflage fatigues and thick
boots, she knew most of the perspiration pouring off her forehead was coming from tension
and fear. Because the night was cool and the
clothes were lightweight. Still, she sweated —
on her face, under her arms, between her legs,
rivulets running down her thighs and calves. She
dabbed her forehead with her sleeve at the rim

of her miner's hat.

More waiting . . . twenty-six, twenty-seven, twenty-ei—

An owl hooted, then swept down from the trees, rustling branches as it nosedived to the ground. Moments later, it soared upward with a wiggling field mouse in its talons. Highlighted against a three-quarter moon, it flew across the sky, its wings cutting through the air. While still in flight, it plucked the mouse from its claws with its beak, held it there, then landed on a ghoulish oak tree twenty yards down. Moments later, the mouse was carrion.

Marge's heart hammered against her chest. The bird's sudden movements could bring unwanted attention to their operation. Quickly, she pulled back sharply twice on the rope tied around her waist — the stop signal to the others.

Tugs answered her back.

Then nothing.

Start all over, Dunn. One, two, three, four . . .

They had decided to use the rope for messages because it was far less noisy than two-way radios. Of course, they had the boxes for backup.

As a matter of fact, they had everything — dried food, water in pouches, locating devices, communication devices, protective gear, flashlights, ammunition with regular scopes and infrared scopes, grenades and mace. The gear loaded Marge down, made trampling silently through the brush even more difficult. But she did what was necessary.

Several more minutes passed. Then she felt a Morse code pull against her waist — two long and one short. Lauren was requesting to go forward. Marge passed the message down to Special SWAT Agent Elise Stone. From the rear, she received the sign to proceed. Marge forwarded it to Lauren.

A big game of telephone. Hoping that, unlike the childhood diversion, the signals stayed true.

Another step forward. Another stop.

And so it went. For what seemed like hours.

In fact, it took Marge a full two hours to traverse a mile.

To the others, Lauren whispered, "We're going to have to drop the electronic junk. They have lots of honing devices, being paranoid and all. We can't afford to risk it. We're also going to have to leave behind the heavy stuff. You two are pretty large. You'll never make it through the tunnel all bulked up like that."

Elise Stone was a couple inches shorter than Marge, but also thick-boned. Her short blond hair peaked from her miner's hat. "We'll remove *our* bullet vests. But you keep yours on."

"I can't *move* in it. I feel like a mummy."

"Lauren," Marge whispered. "You're the front person, the first one in. You *have* to be protected. You're a small girl. Just do it."

"I'll sweat to death."

"You'll sweat, but you won't die," Elise said. "Where's the entrance?"

"The boulder you're standing next to."

Elise looked down and to her left. Her face registered surprise. "How'd you *lift* that thing?"

"I didn't lift it, I rolled it millimeters at a time. Back then, the one thing I had was time."

Elise tried to heft it. "Thing must weigh five hundred pounds. Where's the crowbar?"

Marge pulled the tool out of her knapsack. She wedged it between the granite and the ground. "This is where we use that leverage thing."

"What time is it?" Elise asked.

"Two-fifteen."

"When is sunup?"

"Six-thirty."

"Jesus, that's not good," Elise said. "We'd better haul ass. Lauren, out of the way."

The young girl moved aside.

Elise grabbed the middle part of the crowbar, Marge held on to the tip. On the count of three, they exerting maximum force, heaving down on the metal pole, pushing so hard they grunted. The solid orb of stone rolled inches. The two cops exchanged glances.

"Do the rocks in these mountains have a high metal content?" Elise asked.

"Just keep going," Marge said.

"Keep going," Elise echoed.

A half hour later, two thirds of the opening to the tunnel was exposed. Drenched in sweat, Elise said to Marge, "I think I can make it through. What about you? You're the biggest of us. Can you fit down there?"

Marge dropped to the ground and inched in head-first. Immediately, her shoulders caught.

She surveyed the situation, then raised her body. "I think if I wiggle my shoulders from side to side, I could probably clear it eventually." She raised her body back to a standing position, feeling strong and fit. All those years of push-ups and sit-ups had finally served a practical purpose.

Elise began retightening the rope around her waist. "Then let's do it."

Marge said, "First, we should wedge the boulder so it doesn't roll back and cover the opening."

Elise made a face. "Be nice if I had a brain."

The two cops worked together. After the boulder was safely rooted, they did a checklist for the final time as they secured the rope around their bodies. They left their backpacks at the opening, taking out only what was necessary — miner's cap, a flashlight, bottled water, a small canister of supplemental oxygen and a semi-automatic with magazines. Adjusting the surgical mask over her nose, Marge regarded Lauren's covered face. "Sure you're up for this?"

"Definitely."

"Are you ready?"

"Ready as I'll ever be."

"Then go for it, girlfriend."

Lauren hugged Marge with force. Then, without hesitation, she dropped to her belly, turned on her miner's hat and crawled down into darkness. Seconds passed, then a full minute. The opening became darker and darker until Lauren's hat light became nothing more than a raindrop of illumination. Finally, Marge felt the tug around her waist.

"Time to go."

Elise said, "Good luck, Dunn."

"Best wishes to you, too, Stone."

Marge made final adjustments to her mask, then crept into the ground. Immediately, her upper body was wedged between the dirt opening and the boulder still blocking part of the tunnel's entrance. Marge shifted her shoulders to the right, then to the left, cramming her body down the shoot. She kept repeating the motions until the soil about her torso loosened, giving her that extra needed millimeter of free space. She felt herself slide through the adit, and moments later, she was encased in a dark, moldy channel.

Completely sealed off from life-giving air! As if she were buried alive. Hell, she *was* buried alive! Only a small entrance hole furnishing all three of them with natural oxygen. Their backup supply wouldn't last more than a half hour. If the ground should give way, Marge knew she'd be finished. She fought off waves of panic, hearing her own anxiety-riddled panting through the mask.

Slow down, you're fine, she chided her brain. *Breathe deeply . . . breathe regularly. In and out . . . in and out.*

Instant biofeedback. As she heard her breaths slow, she was able to retard her choppy gasping.

Ahead was a unidirectional tube. Nowhere to go except forward. Struggling, she managed to stretch her gloved hands in front of her body and claw at the ground with her nails. Pulling herself along. Slithering on her belly like a snake.

More like a lowly worm, she thought. *Don't think about yourself. Think about the kids! Or that poor innocent woman shot by a maniac murderer simply to prove a point. Discarded like a broken toy. Or poor Pete and his ringing ears.*

Although truthfully, compared to being buried alive, ringing ears didn't sound so bad.

Grit scratched her flesh; she could feel it through her clothing, rubbing against her quadriceps, her shins, her abdomen and chest. She tried to lift her face upward only to hit her hat on the ceiling. Clumps of dirt rained down as dust clogged her eyes.

More panic.

Breathe slowly . . . breathe deeply. In and out . . . in and out.

The light on her hat was functional, thank God, but she couldn't see much. She waited for several moments, then felt a pull about her waist. A signal from Lauren — although there was no visual *sign* of Lauren.

As Marge continued, the only thing visible to her eyes was the ground beneath her belly. The air was sodden and dirty, the smell metallic like an approaching electrical storm.

At first, the tunnel was dead quiet . . . not even a hint of any ambient noise. But as Marge listened more closely, she could make out dripping sounds . . . a plop here . . . a plunk there. Groundwater. It had rained recently. How much was down here? Was she going to get caught in a pool and drown? No, if anyone would get caught it would be Lauren — *No, no, no, don't even think about that. Keep going!*

Marge heard scratching, like mice skittering in an attic. But mice didn't live six feet below. Moles did. Maybe it was a mole. Do moles bite?

Don't think about it.

More likely it was Lauren moving forward, her light body skimming across the soil.

Another tug.

Marge moved toward the direction of the pull. As she went on, she felt the channel constricting, the circular walls closing around her body.

It wasn't her imagination. There was definitely less room to move.

God, suppose she got stuck in the middle? Could they pull her free without the tunnel collapsing?

Don't think about it!

Counting slowly . . . one . . . two . . . three . . .

Breathe normally, she commanded herself. *One . . . two . . . three . . .*

Trudging deeper into the gully — tighter and darker. The soil had become saturated with groundwater, turning the pinched alley into round walls of slime and ooze and an occasional germ-infested puddle. Marge could feel the goop streak her clothing.

No one in front, no one in back. Completely alone for all that *she* could see.

If the terror and the claustrophobia ever became unbearable, they had a predetermined message of a half-dozen hard pulls on the rope, repeated twice. But Marge would be damned if she would be the first to cry out.

Just keep going.

Her heartbeat reverberated inside her miner's hard hat. She knew she was gasping as her lungs took in sharp intakes of air.

Keep going, her brain screamed. *Stop thinking about your own terror. Instead, think about the abject fear of those kids!*

But as the cylinder narrowed, compressing her body even farther, she felt pins of panic stick her bones. She lifted her eyes upward, hoping to spy a glimmer of light from Lauren's hat. Ahead was only a dark hole of black sludge.

Don't panic! Don't —

All at once, she felt the rope tighten about her waist. The action was being passed to her from the front. Lauren was asking permission to once again move forward.

Marge stopped . . . tried to catch her breath.

Concentrate, Dunn! Hundreds of people are depending on you! Think of that poor girl shot through the head! That's what caused all the urgency!

Bob on a killing spree.

Another breath.

Slower . . . slower.

Remembering what had been discussed,

Marge managed to squeeze her hand against her body and tug on the rope twice, passing on the communication to Elise.

Waiting.

Seconds later, the tug was answered.

Elise giving the signal that she was about to enter the cold, clay pipeline.

More seconds passed.

Elise giving Marge the signal to continue. Marge passed it to Lauren. A count to ten, then she crept forward on her stomach.

It was now more like *sliding* because the tunnel was very wet. It reminded Marge of the old Slip-n-Slide . . . the hours she had spent in the hot summers of Fayetteville, sliding on a thin sheet of water-coated plastic. There had been an in-ground pool at the base, and she had used it occasionally. (The colonel had demanded that all the Dunns be proficient swimmers.) But no one in her solidly rooted working-class neighborhood had a pool in the backyard. Not like here in money-rich L.A. Even the shoddiest apartment house had a pool.

So think of the tunnel as a Slip-n-Slide.

Another quick breath.

And you're not surrounded by darkness, you're just closing your eyes . . .

Never realizing how claustrophobic she was. How in the world had Lauren pulled this off? Not only had she crawled through it and saved Lyra's life, Lauren had actually *built* the damn thing.

And the newspeople keep ragging that there
are no more heroes in this world.

Think of Lauren's heroism, she demanded.
*Think of the Slip-n-Slide. Think of anything except
how you're buried six feet beneath earthquake
country with no way except a goddamn rope to communicate. And the rope wouldn't do you a fuckin' bit
of good if the whole tunnel was to collapse because the
others would be fucking buried along with you.*

Again, she felt the dread of unbridled fear.

A draw around her waist.

Lauren was moving closer toward the destina-
tion.

That was good, Dunn. Very good.

*Just remain cool, remain super cool. Think of the
kids. The kids, the kids, the kids!*

A pull back toward Elise.

Again the message was passed along tele-
phone-style.

Keep going, keep going!

Her head felt light.

*No, Dunn, no! You're not going to faint. Slow your
breathing down.*

A drag on the rope . . . Lauren telling her to
stop.

Marge passed the signal down.

Then she stopped.

Counting softly, but this time, she counted au-
dibly. She wanted to hear something besides the
dribbling of groundwater. She wanted to hear
something besides Lauren's scratching. Most of
all, she couldn't stand the horrible silence that

engulfed her when Lauren wasn't scratching or the water wasn't dripping.

One . . . two . . . three . . . four . . . five . . . six . . .

Don't panic, don't panic!

Thirteen . . . fourteen . . . fifteen . . .

The message to keep going.

Pass it on back, Dunn, pass it on back.

Shimmying on her belly, she proceeded. Nothing in front, nothing in back.

Nowhere to run.

Nowhere to run.

Wasn't that a song title?

That's good, Dunn. Think of song titles.

Just keep on truckin', girl, keep on truckin'.

The seconds slowly converting to minutes — first to one minute . . . then two . . . then five . . . then ten . . . fifteen . . .

Inching forward, her face and mask painted with ground muck as she wondered just *how* many gnats, mosquitoes and pathogens was she inhaling or smearing into her pores.

Keep on truckin'.

Gettin' good at it now, girlie. You can do it.

Another signal to stop.

Pass it on down, Dunn. Pass it down.

Counting slowly. One . . . two . . . three . . . four . . . five . . .

Thirty seconds passed. Then a minute. Then two.

Don't panic, don't panic!

Three minutes crawled by, then four.

Again, the panic. Too much time was passing.

She signaled to Lauren — *tell me what's going down, girl?*

Her question remained unanswered.

Marge's heart took off in flight. *Oh, God Almighty, please tell me what the hell was happening? Please just let her be okay!*

Again, Marge attempted to relay another message to Lauren via the rope.

Again, her signal wasn't returned.

Good God, was Lauren intercepted? Should she and Elise turn back?

Wait it out, Dunn! A few more minutes. Wait it out!

After ten minutes, Marge felt a pull from behind. Stone was now asking her what was going down. Damned if she knew.

Another minute, then she'd give the turnaround signal.

Ten seconds . . . twenty . . .

What to do! What to do!

Thirty . . . forty . . .

At last, there was a draw about her waist, the sign coming from Lauren.

A sweet, *sweet* sign!

Lauren had given her a message via rope pulls, and what a message! She had made it to the entrance to the Order.

Stop until further notice.

Marge passed it to Elise.

Again, minutes passed. But this time Marge felt better waiting. Because if one of them had made it, surely she and Elise would make it as well.

Lauren was safe.

Five minutes passed. Then Marge felt a drag on her rope. Lauren was telling her to press on.

Pass it down to Elise.

With renewed vigor, Marge inched forward. Her breathing had calmed, and clarity of thought filled her brain. She didn't realize it, but there were tears in her eyes.

33

A slender hand reached down, grabbing the mud-caked glove. Peering upward through the narrow hole, Marge could see Lauren's dirt-encrusted face, her finger over her lips in warning. Digging her feet into the slimy wall of the tunnel, Marge tried to root herself. Though Marge must have outweighed Lauren by fifty pounds, the young girl pulled with reserved force, lifting Marge's head and shoulders above the murky canal. Unfortunately, Marge's lower body remained compressed inside the tunnel. Her gloves weren't much help. Slick with muck, they held little traction. Still, she pressed the greasy palms against the floor's flat surface and attempted to liberate her torso. But the gloves slid out from under. Lauren clutched around her shoulders before she sank down.

"Good catch," Marge mouthed. "One more time."

She repositioned herself, then slowly hefted her body. Feeling her biceps and triceps distend as she levitated from the cylindric tomb. When she was far out enough to bend her knees, she twisted her waist and swung her long legs outward. Expelled from the primordial ooze, Marge collapsed onto the floor. Her lungs now breathing real oxygen, she felt literally reborn.

Lauren reached over and turned off her miner's cap light, whispering directly into her ear. "Are you all right?"

"Perfect," Marge whispered back.

The space was raven black. But Marge knew that they were in one of the Order's two classrooms — specifically the supply closet. As Elise Stone approached, her hat gave off a crescent of light. Marge's eyes adjusted, and she could discern several robes, hanging from the closet's pole, swaying like poltergeists. Slowly, she rose to her feet.

Lauren spoke in hushed tones. "The nursery is next door. We shouldn't talk unless necessary. Never know where they planted bugs."

Marge agreed. In silence, they waited for Elise, scraping gunk from the friction treads of their shoes. The last thing they needed was to slip. Pulling out Elise was easier because there were two of them. As they waiting for Agent Stone to catch her breath, Marge took out a penlight and honed in on the robes. They were white. She took one down and wrapped it over her dirty clothing. "Better camouflage than what I have on."

Elise and Lauren followed her lead. Going through a final checklist, Marge reread her instruction sheet.

"Change of plans, Lauren," she said. "They want us to go out first with older kids."

"What? Why not the babies?"

"Babies go last," Elise stated. "They're more

likely to cry and expose us. If we take them last, and they do attract attention and screw us up, at least the older kids will have made it out."

Lauren whispered, "But the nursery is the closest to us. The kids' bedrooms are several doors down. We'll have to walk down a hallway to get to them. I'm sure someone will be guarding the corridor. Talk about exposing ourselves before we've rescued a soul."

"I'll take care of the guard," Marge answered. "You just convince the kids to follow you. From what I saw of them and how well they were trained, that's not going to be easy."

Lauren sighed. "I hope you know what you're doing."

Marge *didn't* know what she was doing. But neither did anyone else.

"What about this thing?" Lauren pointed to her bulletproof vest under the white robe.

"Keep it on."

Elise said, "I'll keep watch. You'd better hop to it."

"Somebody gets in your face, you know the drill."

"I know. Shoot to kill," Elise said.

Marge checked her Beretta, making sure the magazine was shoved in all the way. When Lauren started to move, she held her back. "I go first —"

"But —"

"I got the gun —"

"But I got the vest," Lauren protested. "Besides, I know where I'm going."

"Good point," Elise chimed in.

Marge said, "We'll go out together. But first let me check out the room. Besides the security camera focused on the teacher's desk, anything else that I should be aware of?"

"Not that I know of."

Marge said a quick silent prayer, then turned the handle of the closet door. Carefully, she opened the door just enough to peek out. All she could see were blotches and shadows. She extended the door another hairsbreadth. Nothing. Abruptly, she pushed the door out all the way.

No shots fired.

Carefully, Marge tiptoed out of the closet, into the open. First, she located the security camera. It was mounted over the white board, aimed at the teacher's desk. Figuring for a certain amount of camera view spread, she knew which surrounding areas to avoid.

Another step forward.

The lack of standard windows in the room was a good thing. True, she couldn't see out, but no one could see in either. A hint of moonlight streaked in from the upper windows, silver-plating the empty desks and chairs. She turned on the penlight and shone it around the room. Nothing unusual. She held out the palm of her hand, giving Lauren a wait sign, casing the room to ensure that they were alone. After a few moments, she turned off the penlight and beckoned Lauren forward. Together, they pressed on to the hallway, avoiding the security camera's tattletale eye. Marge nudged the door a crack, then peered out into a dark corridor.

Nothing but stillness.

Motioning Lauren forward, they crept into the umbra, taking baby paces toward the bedrooms.

One step . . . two steps . . . three and four . . .

Marge pushed her arm against Lauren's chest to stop her.

"Footsteps!" she whispered.

Pressing Lauren against the wall, Marge screened the young woman's body with her own. She could feel Lauren's rapid heartbeat, smell her sweat. Or maybe it was her own. Within seconds, a white-robed sentry appeared, staring into the grayness with vacant eyes — a malevolent ghost devoid of any comic-book charm. As the head turned in their direction, Marge didn't give its eyes an opportunity to focus. She leaped out and slammed the butt of her gun into his solar plexis, then against his thick skull. Immediately, the guard went out. Marge caught him (the weight felt like a man) before he hit the ground. To Lauren, she ordered, "Check his pockets for a radio or walkie-talkie."

Lauren rummaged through his clothes, then pulled out up a small box.

"Bring it into my line of vision." Marge looked the apparatus over while holding the limp body. "Okay. You can leave it on. Just *don't* press the red button. That will pick up our voices. Get his feet and we'll carry him back to the closet."

Lauren lifted the man by his ankles, but stared at the face. "This is Brother Ansel. He's one of those who does purification duty — a first-class asshole."

Marge nodded, feeling better that she had cold-cocked a first-class asshole. Carefully, they carried him into the empty classroom, again taking measures to avoid the security monitor.

Elise stared at the lifeless bulk of flesh. "Is he dead?"

"Don't think so." Marge laid the body on the closet floor, and checked for a pulse. Strong. And he was also breathing. She examined the depression in his skull. It was thick with blood, but not spurting. "He'll recover, but he's going to have one hell of a headache."

Elise said, "After I tape and tie him, I'll bandage the wound."

Marge handed her the squawk box. "His name is Brother Ansel. He's in charge of torture. He's an asshole."

Elise said, "So if someone calls in, I'm a torture freak named Brother Ansel."

"You've got it," Marge said. "C'mon, Lauren. Now that he's out, we've got to step on it."

Again they made their way into the foyer, moving rapidly and quietly. Lauren stopped in front of a door. "This is where the teens sleep."

"Boys and girls?"

Lauren nodded.

Marge raised her eyebrows. She opened the door, peeked inside. Eight beds, seven of which were filled with sleeping adolescents. No adult supervision. An ideal situation *if* no one went ballistic. To Lauren, she said, "Make them listen to you like you did when you were their teacher."

Lauren was breathing rapidly, sweat streaming down her brow. She took a deep breath, then started with Vega, gently shaking her shoulders. The teen startled, then brightened.

"Sister Andromeda!" the girl shouted.

Lauren clamped her hand over Vega's mouth. "Shhhhh!" She removed her hand and spoke. "Vega, this is an emergency. We've got to go now!"

The frail teen pushed black hair from surprised blue eyes. "Go where?" she whispered.

"No questions. You must trust me and follow me. And you *must* be very, very quiet."

"But where are you going —"

"I said no questions!"

"Yes, Sister Andromeda." Having displeased her elder, Vega looked crestfallen. Lauren softened her expression. "Vega, I'm counting on you to help me with the others."

"I will help you, Sister Androm—" She stopped talking and stared at Marge. "Surely we are not going with the *violators!* Guru Bob said they might be coming to —"

"Vega, listen to me!" Lauren spoke quietly and with intensity. "If you don't do as I say, terrible, terrible things will happen. People will die!"

"But Guru Bob says that death is a good thing. It means we will join Jupiter."

Lauren bent down and gently held the girl by her face, looking deeply into her eyes. "This is going to be very hard for you to accept, my sweet Vega. But Guru Bob is *wrong!* Now it is up to you . . . who you choose to believe. *Bob?* Or *me?*"

Vega licked her lips. "I will follow you, Sister Andromeda."

Lauren kissed her forehead. "Thank you, thank you. Now you must help me convince the others." Methodically, she began to arouse the others — first four girls, then two boys. They were equally excited about Andromeda's return, but also confused about what their teacher was asking them to do.

The oldest was a girl named Asa — brown eyes and curly red hair — a teen version of Little Orphan Annie. She said, "I trust you, Sister Andromeda, but we should not go without asking Guru Bob. This is not procedure. This is breaking vows and overstepping our bounds. It is also joining up with a violator."

The others nodded in agreement.

Vega said, "I agree it is odd, what Sister Andromeda is telling us to do."

An Asian boy of around thirteen piped in, his teeth wide and strong. His name was Orion. "Perhaps our Sister Andromeda has been corrupted by the violators. This is what Guru Bob has warned us against."

Pointing the accusatory finger.

"I think this is a trap."

They were running out of time. Talking at first

in whispers, but the conversation, though still soft, was growing louder. Marge regarded Lauren with pleading eyes.

Do something!

But it was Vega who stepped forward, her voice growing in command. "Yes, she is a violator . . . one from the corrupt outside. But I assure you that *she* is not corrupt. She is a dreamer like our most holy Father Jupiter. A traveler of the stars of imagination."

"How do you know?" asked Asa.

"I have talked to her." A tear streamed down Vega's cheek. "She understands our most beloved book — *The Little Prince*. She has read it in French."

Looks of admiration. Vega straightened her spine. "I shall *go* follow our teacher, Sister Andromeda. I will trust her. I will go with the violator because I have read her heart. I suggest that all of you do the same. But if anyone should choose to stay, please . . . I beg of you . . . do not divulge Sister Andromeda's secret."

A long pause. Then Orion said, "Our Father Jupiter was an explorer of different worlds. So shall I be an explorer. I shall preach his word in the sphere of the violator." He stood up. "I will join up, too."

Asa was the next to agree to come with them.

With three down, the others followed with scant protest. Marge told them to put their robes over their pajamas, then peered down the hallway.

Empty.

"Quietly and quickly," she said.

She lined them up and took them back to the empty classroom. Once inside the closet, away from the camera's lens, she began tying ropes around their waists. Their blind obedience to authority turned out to be their best asset. To Lauren, she said, "You go first, they'll follow with Elise bringing up the rear —"

"But with all those people in the tunnel, the oxygen will be used up quickly."

"Lauren, time's our worst enemy. We've got to take a chance. The kids have meditated. Tell them to breathe slowly and deeply." Without hesitation, Marge held out her canister of oxygen. "In emergencies, use this."

Lauren was reticent. "What about you?"

"I've got a good set of lungs," Marge said. "Least that's what all the boys used to say. Now go!"

Vega asked, "Are you going to take the other children with you?"

"As soon as you all have made it to safety."

"Then I shall stay behind and help you."

Marge looked at Vega, holding her fragile shoulders, which were attached to a *determined* young lady. "If you do that, you may not make it."

"Correct," Vega answered. "But it is a chance I shall take. I am not afraid of death. But I am afraid of neglecting my duty. As our Father Jupiter stated many times, duty is paramount. Now my duty is to you. And you will need help to convince the children."

"Let's move it," Elise said. "The rescue team should be coming within the hour. If we miss the reconnaissance group, we're screwed."

"All right, Vega," Marge said. "You can stay with me."

"Correct."

To Lauren, Marge said, "As soon as you can, come back and help me with the younger ones."

A muffled groan came from under a blanket. Brother Ansel was joining the present world. Marge kicked the bundle, and all was quiet. One of the kids asked about the noise.

Lauren said, "It is our Father Jupiter giving us words of encouragment. Let's go."

Vega tried to reassure her friends. "This is our first adventure into space. We shall make it positive and scientific and full of spirituality. Always remember our Father. Let us meditate and pray."

"To our Father Jupiter and his eternal spirit," Orion joined in.

The teens bowed their heads in solemnity. Elise was antsy, but held herself in check. Too much prodding could backfire. Lauren kissed the children's cheeks — one by one. "Well spoken, my dear children. To our Father Jupiter. Now let us begin."

Without another word, Lauren crept back into the murky channel of black ink. Working quickly, Marge and Elise threaded the children through the darkened needle. "Keep your heads down,"

Elise told them as they entered the tube. As she was about to go in, she regarded Marge. "Good luck."

"Same."

Agent Stone disappeared underground.

Moments later, the closet was stark still and quiet, the only sounds were the whispers of breathing.

Time dragged.

In the silence and fear, it dragged even slower.

Vega said nothing, sitting on the closet floor, waiting for the next step. Completely prepossessed without any overt signs of fright and dread. That made some sense. How could she have any concept of danger . . . any concept of *reality?* Her young life had been lived in altered reality.

Again, the tarp emitted groans.

"Who is under the blanket?" asked Vega without emotion.

Marge knew the girl was too sharp to accept a lie. "Brother Ansel."

"You have captured him."

"Yes."

"Tied him up."

"Yes."

"You consider him an impediment to your operation."

"Correct." Marge bent down and peeked under the blanket. Ansel was moving his head from side to side. Slowly, he opened his eyes. When he saw Marge, he tried to get up, but

Marge shoved him back down to the floor. She put a gun between his eyes. "One sound and you're a dead man. I'm not screwing around."

Frightened eyes. The head nodded in comprehension. Marge looked over the bloody gauze taped to his wound. Elise had not only done a fine job of restraining and muzzling him but of bandaging him as well.

Abruptly, static beeped through his intercom. Marge threw the cover back over Ansel's head and stepped out of the closet. She didn't want Ansel's moans to be picked up over the squawk box. Vega followed her and shut the closet door.

She asked, "Do you know the codes?"

"Codes?" Marge's chest started drumming. "No, of course not."

"The planets are in orbit," Vega answered flatly. "Brother Ansel's voice is medium in range for a man. A little bit nasal."

Marge nodded, depressed the button. A wave of static hit her ear, accompanied by a cryptic question. Marge looked at Vega. Vega nodded.

She said, "The planets are in orbit."

Through the electronic interference, Marge made out another cryptic question. Internally, she started to panic, but managed to maintain her composure for Vega. Even though the teen seemed much calmer than she.

Vega whispered in her ear. "Say, 'I repeat. The planets are in orbit. Do you copy?' "

Marge took a deep breath, spoke low and with

a twang. "I repeat. The planets are in orbit. Do you copy?"

More static.

No response.

"Do you copy?" Marge asked slowly.

One second . . . two seconds . . . finally, a crackly "Roger" and then a sign-off.

Letting go of the button, Marge exhaled quietly. Words of appreciation could not begin to tell the little girl what was in Marge's heart. She thought about it, then decided the best compliment would be to appeal to her intellect and sense of adventure. She asked, "Did you know, Vega, that in my world . . . the violators' world . . . that they send people into space?"

"Correct," Vega answered. "Astronauts. Our Father Jupiter was instrumental in sending them into space. But he has developed more spiritual ways of space travel — ways that do not require rocket ships."

Marge whispered, "Of course. Spiritual journey is always superior to anything physical. Still, with someone as brilliant and as spiritual as yourself, if you don't mind my saying so, I think you would make a fine astronaut."

Vega regarded Marge with curiosity. "But I am a girl."

Marge said, "There are many women astronauts." A pause. "You know *that,* don't you?"

Vega said nothing. Her face was impassive.

"But I daresay," Marge continued, "that you are as brilliant and as spiritual and as heroic as the best of them."

Vega's eyes held back tears. "I am a child."

Marge smiled, holding back her own tears. "So was the Little Prince."

Vega's lower lip trembled, as her eyes erupted and salt water flowed down her cheeks. She didn't answer and Marge left it at that.

Finally, Vega said, "It is not good to fill the mind with fantasy when there is work to do."

She was right, and Marge told her so. The teen had so much to offer the "violators' " world. So much innate goodness along with a fervent desire to *do* good. Here, living in the confines of repression with murderers as leaders, was a morally superior being.

Vega said, "I must pray that I made the correct decision for duty."

At this particular time, prayer sounded like a fine idea. So Marge prayed for the lives of the babies and children still housed in the building, prayed for the innocent adults subjugated by monsters and prayed for Lauren and Elise. She also prayed for her *own* survival. But first and foremost, she prayed for Vega's welfare. Marge felt that after all the girl had done, she deserved top billing.

34

It was taking too long.

In theory, Marge had prepared for the unexpected, but she hesitated from implementing a major shift in plans. Time was indeed crawling, but reality dictated that a minute was still a minute. She didn't want her distorted perception to translate into rash actions, especially since Vega was under her charge. The teen, though steeped in prayer, sensed Marge's apprehension. Abruptly, she stopped meditating and regarded her newfound ally.

"You think something has happened to them?"

Marge tried to keep her voice level. "No, not at all."

"Time has passed."

"Yes."

"Maybe the tunnel has collapsed?"

"I sure hope not."

"But you do not know."

"No." Marge refrained from sighing. "That's true."

"You think that they were captured?"

Marge said, "Vega, I doubt that. We have many trained professionals watching for them. They should be safe."

"But we are watching, too," Vega said. "We are watching you."

Marge reminded herself to keep her breathing steady. She bent down and looked into Vega's eyes. "What is the Order watching us do?"

"Encroach upon the perimeters." She waited a moment. "There are things that will happen if the violators get too close. The adults think we children do not know. But we do know. We do not talk, but we listen."

"What do you know, Vega?"

"I know the plans that Mother Venus and Guru Bob have made. I know what will happen if the violators break through. We have been instructed to follow our Mother Venus and Guru Bob into the temple. Together, they will take us to the other side."

"The other side." Marge paused. "Guru Bob wasn't referring to a *physical* other side, am I correct?"

"You are correct. Our Mother and Guru Bob refer to a spiritual journey."

Marge felt imaginary brass fingers tighten around her neck. "Mass suicide."

"Guru Bob and our Mother have told the adults that it is preferable to end their lives in this sphere rather than be corrupted by the violators. There are many in the Order of the Rings of God who agree. Contingencies are being set up."

Marge wet her lips. "What kind of contingencies?"

"There are wires being strung around the

temple to end our earthly visit. Guru Bob plans to do it just as our planet was created — in a Big Bang. This appeals to him and to the circular nature of Father Jupiter's mission. Creation and destruction — the endless cycle."

Marge could do without the destruction part. "So Guru Bob *does* have explosives?"

"Correct. He has many types. But I think that Guru Bob and our Mother Venus will not detonate anything unless they feel that the spiritual journey is the Order's last hope."

Vega kept talking about Mother Venus being in on the plans. The more Marge thought about that phone call, the more she was convinced of its validity. If it wasn't Venus, then it had to be Terra.

Where was Terra now? What was she feeling?

Vega broke into Marge's thoughts. "It is in the violators' interest to tell Guru Bob that you are not planning anything."

"We're not planning anything."

"You have planned this."

"This is different," Marge bristled. "This is for the children."

"It is different to you. But it would not be different to Guru Bob."

Marge stopped talking. Her ears began to hear things — scratching from below. *Someone* was crawling through. She took out her Beretta just in case that it wasn't Elise or Lauren. A minute later, she heard Lauren's frantic whisperings.

"Help me up!"

Marge grasped her dirty hand, and pulled her out of the hole. "Is everything —"

"I don't know, I don't know!" Lauren was breathing hard. "I left before . . ." She was panting. "It took us a long time to get everyone through. Elise says we're way behind schedule. When I left, she still hadn't communicated with the reconnaissance team. But we both figured I'd better get back before you started to panic."

"I wasn't panicking —"

"Whatever." Lauren was still gasping. "It's bad out there, Detective. Lots of shots being traded. It could be why we can't get hold of the rescue team. They don't want to bring attention to this area. I don't know why the police are closing in so fast, especially because we don't have all the children yet."

"Maybe Bob has killed more peop—" She stopped talking. Vega was listening . . . always listening. Marge regarded her watch. They were *way* behind schedule.

Lauren said, "I really think we should do the nursery first. They're the most vulnerable."

Marge said, "All right. Let's go."

Lauren pointed to the lump under the tarp made by Brother Ansel. "What about him?"

"He's a real liability. While you were gone, I gave him a mother dose of baby sedatives to keep him quiet."

"Weren't we saving it for the infants to make them sleepy?"

Marge shrugged. "You do what you have to

483

do." She made sure she had her gun and Brother Ansel's radio. "Wait here while I verify that the classroom is empty."

She ventured forward. This time she heard some scurrying noises. It was four-thirty in the morning. The Order was waking up. She signaled to Vega and Lauren to follow. The three of them tiptoed to the door connecting the classroom with the nursery. Quietly, Lauren tried to turn the handle.

"It's locked," she said.

Marge said, "Then we'll have to go through the hallway."

"Let me go first," Lauren said. "If someone sees me, I'll arouse less suspicion."

"I shall go with you," Vega said. "I will not arouse any suspicion."

"No, Vega, you stay with me." Slowly, Marge turned the knob to the classroom door, cracking it open to peek through the slit.

Silence.

She stepped into the passageway. It was empty, but she could hear nearby footsteps.

"The Order's filled with early risers," Lauren said. She took the lead, tiptoeing to the nursery door.

Opening it a smidge.

Peering inside.

Everyone was sleeping, and all was quiet.

Very quiet considering it was a nursery.

Lauren went inside with Marge and Vega at her heels. She closed the door.

All of them waited for their eyes to adjust to the dark.

After they did, Marge made out a shadowed figure in the corner. A woman was sitting in a rocking chair, lids closed, her head tilted back. She held a sleeping infant in her arms. At one point, she must have been feeding it because a nearly full bottle was resting on the infant's chin, dripping down its sleep suit.

Lauren approached the figure. She whispered, "Terra?"

No answer.

She tried again. "Terra, love, it's Andromeda."

Nothing. Terra sitting as still as a mannequin.

Vega said, "Perhaps she is deeply asleep."

"Something's way off," Marge said. "It's eerie. There's no . . . movement . . . no . . ."

She stopped herself, realizing she was sweating. Glancing first at Lauren, then at Vega. "Nobody move."

Marge walked over to the closest crib.

Looking down into the cot, at the sleeping form. A pillow-sized bundle wrapped in a dark-colored pajama blanket. The baby seemed to be a little girl of around a year. She was resting on her side. She had smooth, porcelain cheeks, and curls fell over her eyes. Marge reached down to touch her, hands shaking with fear. She felt the baby's forehead. As soon as her fingers brushed against the infant's brow, a bolt of electricity shot down her spine.

The skin was dry and cold.

Carefully, she turned the child onto her back.

No resistance. Not a stir. Her arms flopped outward as if stuffed with cotton. Marge's fingertips touched the soft folds of the baby's neck at the jugular. No detectable pulse.

Marge fought back nausea as she took in Lauren's questioning eyes. She moved on to the second crib, then to the third. Within moments, Lauren understood the significance of Marge's actions. "Oh, God!" She reeled backward. "Oh, dear God, no!"

Marge said, "Go examine the toddlers on the mattresses —"

"Oh, God, Oh, God —"

"Shhhh!" Marge chided. "Quiet, Lauren! Someone will hear —"

She stopped whispering, discerning voices from the outside hall. *Male* voices. Abruptly, the nursery door flew open and two ghostly white-robed men stomped in.

One was saying, "We'll take the bodies and bring —" He saw Marge's white-robed figure. "Who the hell are —"

Marge didn't let him finish. She hauled off and punched both of them in their groins with quick one-two jabbing stabs. As they doubled over, she whacked her gun over their heads. They crumpled to the floor, moaning and holding themselves between the legs. A final swift kick to the heads with her boot, and they both went out.

The Order was closing in!

Marge barked instructions as she felt the gelid

babies for any signs of life. "Inspect the toddlers just to make sure we didn't overlook a living one."

Immediately, Vega went to work, but Lauren was shell-shocked. "Dear God, it's just like Jonestown. Someone must have fed them poison in their formula —"

"Lauren, get to work!"

"I can't believe Terra would do that," Lauren sobbed. "If she did, someone must have *forced* her because she wouldn't have murdered —"

Vega interrupted. "I think they are all dead —"

"Oh, God!" Lauren wailed. "How could she kill them! Why would she —"

"*Shut up!*" Marge snapped with intensity. "We're being invaded. Get to work, dammit!" She felt for Terra's pulse. Nothing. "Go help Vega with the toddlers! We've got about ten minutes before people are going to wonder where these two knocked-out assholes are."

Terra's skin was as smooth and frigid as a floe. Marge pushed her shoulder and the body slumped over. She felt the cheek of the infant resting in Terra's arms. Immediately, she broke out in cold rivers of sweat.

"Omigod! This one's *warm!*" Her heart started to soar. "She has a pulse! And she's *breathing!*"

Marge glanced at the bottle: It was full. The baby probably fell asleep before she could ingest enough poison to kill her. Feeling her head go light, Marge realized she'd been hyperventilating. She willed herself to breathe slower.

To Vega, she said, "Lauren and I have to get the school-aged kids *if* they're still alive. We've only got minutes left. Vega, do you think you can crawl through the tunnel by yourself, holding on to her?"

"Yes, I can do it."

"Vega, it's dark and slimy and scary and very, very long and —"

"I can do it, Detective Marge." A brief smile. "You said I would make a very good astronaut. If I cannot crawl through a tunnel, how should I succeed in space? Give me the living baby."

Marge's eyes clouded with tears. She kissed the teen's forehead. "No matter what happens, *don't* come back for us! Go get rescued, Vega! Go out and become the great woman you're destined to be!"

Vega kissed Marge back, then took off with the groggy infant in her arms.

"The younger children are always chaperoned," Lauren said. "The adults will scream when they see you."

"So I'll shoot them if necessary. Let's go!"

Out from the hallway and into the first of the children's bedrooms. Marge threw open the door, immediatcly hit by a strong beam of fluorescent light. A white-robed woman spun around, her empty eyes attempting to focus in on Lauren's face. She was holding a plastic jug, three quarters filled with maraschino-colored liquid. "Sister Andromeda?! You've returned to us —"

"C'mon, Ceres, we've got to get out —"

"But we are getting out!" Ceres pronounced. A vacant smile spread across her lips. "That is what we're doing now, Sister. I'm helping the children leave before the violators take over."

About thirty children were standing in a single-file line, their eyes still half-closed from being awakened so early. They seemed to range in age from four to ten. On a trestle table sat forty paper cups, containing the unnaturally deep pink liquid. Marge swept her arm across the tabletop and knocked over the cups, the tainted punch spilling over the surface and onto the floor. Ceres stared at her, a look of bewilderment stamped across her face. "What are you do —"

"Sorry, Sister," Marge interrupted. Pulling her fist back, she decked Ceres in the face. The woman buckled, then collapsed onto the floor amid the gasps of the children.

"Quiet, children!" Lauren said. "You *must* be quiet!"

Sensing their teacher's anger and urgency, the children froze, their expressions ranging from sheer fright to horror. Yet not one of them dared to move a footstep.

Marge was on overdrive. "Lauren, take them into the tunnel."

"But there are others —"

"I'll get the others!"

"No, *I'll* get the others!" Lauren insisted. "The children will follow me easier than you."

She was right. Marge said, "Tell these kids that

489

they *must* listen to me, no questions asked."

Lauren repeated Marge's words, using the authority of Sister Andromeda.

Marge looked down the corridor. Finding it empty, she said, "Come on, kids, this way! And hurry!"

With frantic hand gestures, she moved them toward freedom. She had succeeded in getting half into the classroom when another guard rounded the corner. He saw her a few seconds before she saw him. With shaking hands, he pulled out his gun. He would have had her if he'd been a pro. But he wasn't because he hesitated.

Marge didn't. She shot him twice in the head.

Another white-robe ghost down, Marge thought. This one out for good. It was as if she had been cybertransported into some Pac Man–type video game, her mission to kill the evil white-robed apparitions before they got her.

"Hurry!" she yelled at the kids. "This way! Quick, quick, quick!"

Now shoving them into the classroom, toward the trapdoor in the closet. "Down the hole! It's a tunnel, kids. A long, dark tunnel. You can get through it! You can do it! Once you're through it, you're safe."

She shone a flashlight into the pit.

"Now all of you! Get down on your hands and knees and crawl!"

No one moved. Some of the younger ones began to cry. Marge honed in on the older children — specifically a tall girl with black eyes and short, black curly hair. "Get them inside before it's too late! Move it or we're all going to *die!*"

Terrified, the girl remained paralyzed. Marge shook her with all her might. "Do it or I'll tell Andromeda that you disobeyed!"

The girl nodded, tears streaming down her cheek. Quivering and crying, she began ushering the little ones into the black hole, pushing them inside the bowels of the earth when they refused to go in of their own accord. As they wailed, the older children took the little ones' shaking hands and dragged them along.

"Go, go, go!" Marge rushed the youngsters inside, holding back the oldest girl. "What's your name?"

"Centura."

"I'm Marge, Centura. And you're not only going to help me, you're going to be a real hero just like Father Jupiter." Shoving another tiny child into the black hole. "Go, go!"

When the last of them were underground, Marge handed Centura a flashlight and said, "It's up to you to get the kids through. Help the little ones make it if they're too scared to move on their own. There'll be people waiting to help you out the other end. Now move it!"

The child's eyes were pouring water. But dutifully, she ducked into the pit. As soon as the children were inside the pipeline, Marge rushed back to help Lauren. She was leading another group of school-aged kids toward the classroom.

"The last of them?" Marge asked.

"Yes —"

More voices. Adult males. Marge saw them, took aim, shot all of them in the stomach.

Running to freedom with the remaining children. When they were all inside, Marge slammed the classroom door, wedging a chair up against the handle to keep it locked.

Andromeda turned on her miner's cap and the flashlight. "Let's go! Down the hole! Move it!"

More cries and wails. Some refused. Marge resorted to brute force, literally hurling them down the squalid void before they could protest, and shoving them back underground when they tried to turn around and pop back through the closet's trapdoor.

"Go, go, go!"

The moaning was heartrending. Marge felt like an ogre, but horrid visions of murdered infants made her work fast and furiously. Screaming, yelling, physically rough with them until the kids realized they had no choice. The direction was only one way!

Waiting for the last of them to be securely underground! When that final child had been plunged into the pit, Marge tore off her robe, turned on her miner's cap and thrust herself down the dank, narrow tube.

Once again, panic welled up in her chest as mud and grit surrounded her every pore. But her heart was beating so rapidly, she scarcely noticed her fear. Completely engulfed by muddy earth, she felt as if the tunnel had narrowed within the last two hours. Her body dragged against the slime, the dozens of feet in front of her kicking pools of sullied water into her mouth and face.

Without warning, the ground opened its mews and roared. It shook them fiercely like salt in a shaker, raining down mud and soil, further pinching off the already constricted tubing. High-pitched screams filled the conduit.

Marge coughed up muddy phlegm and spit it from her mouth. "Keep going!" she screamed, pushing bodies forward. "Keep going, keep going! We're going to make —"

Another blast!

Hard and furious!

From above the underground belly convulsed! Dirt dropping in chunks and clods, collapsing onto them, tumbling onto the children amid frenetic coughs, sneezes, choking noises, screams, cries and wails. Marge's lower body was buried beneath an avalanche of loose soil. She couldn't shake it off — no room. With determination, she dug her nails into the treacherous terrain and clawed her way out of the wreckage.

"Go, go, go!" she shrieked as she coughed up muck. *"Faster, faster!"*

Abruptly, the temperature inside the ground began to soar, turning the tube into a steamy mudbath.

"Quick, before the next one!" Marge gasped out. *"Hurry!"* All that precious oxygen being used up.

"Hold your breath if you can . . ." But her head

became woozy. Stars danced in front of her face.

No, you're not going to pass out! The children need . . .

Deep breaths.

They need you . . .

Blacker and blacker.

Stop a moment . . .

Just a moment . . .

The stars began to recede. Her head was now pounding. But a pounding head was preferable to a light one.

The temperature continued to climb.

The ground surrounding them hot to the touch.

Baked *alive*.

The child in front of her stopped moving — a boy of around eight. Marge didn't know if he had frozen or passed out. She didn't care. With great effort, she began heaving him forward, using the reservoir strength of her palms. His body was heavy, his bones felt leaden, but there was *no* choice. If she didn't get him through, *she'd* never make it through.

Heave!

Rest!

Heave!

Rest!

Hot, hot, hot, hot!

Heave!

Heave, heave, heave!

Youch! Hot, hot, hot!

But miracles happen in the most unusual

places. The boy suddenly regained consciousness. Though groggy, he was able to move baby
steps forward.

"Go for Father Jupiter!" Marge urged him between gasps. "Go. Go . . ."

"Hot!" he moaned.

"We're almost . . ." *Don't talk, Dunn!* Big gasp!
Save your energy.

The tunnel getting narrower and narrower.

Marge working harder and harder.

No more strength!

Hotter and hotter.

Baked alive.

Baked Alaska.

Delirium, here we come!

No, you can do it!

Go, go . . . gasp, gasp . . . go, go . . . gasp . . .

The stars coming back . . .

Her strength ebbing . . .

A deafening roar followed by violent tremors
of the earth. Mud tumbling over her head, inter-
ring her weakened body in hot, dungish coals,
charring her nostrils, stinging her mouth and
cheeks, searing her eyes . . .

Keep go —

But she had nothing left.

Sinking.

Fading, fading, fading . . .

The ground trembled, and her limp body gave
way to the "other side."

Feeling a jerk on her leg . . .

Something on her . . . pulling on her.

The boy maybe? Grappling for help?

Poor kid.

Still caring even at her last breath! But what could she do?

With her body buried under pounds of dirt and her lungs suffocating, she gave up. As the last bits of light were snuffed from her consciousness, Marge retained this vague notion that she was somehow breathing real air.

35

Another fireball exploded in the charcoal sky, rocking the earth, spewing flames into the cosmos as the sizzling air scorched Decker's nostrils. Momentarily thrown off balance, he fell backward into the gulley, landing on his hipbone. His clothes had been thickened by layers of ashes and soot, his hands made sore and raw from rooting in the muck. Within moments, the blast was followed by a volley of machine-gun fire in his direction.

"Drop!" he screamed.

He threw himself across the pile of children, the last of the crew that had made it out before the tunnel had collapsed, and the entranceway had caved in. He had about five minutes to rescue Marge before she drowned in sludge.

"Fucking assholes!" Head down, he groped around with his fingers until he felt the handle of the automatic. Getting off the children and onto his knees, he peeked over the top of the trench, then let go with a barrage of bullets. *Take that, you goddamn motherfuckers!*

The exchange of gunfire, though seemingly protracted, lasted no longer than thirty seconds. As soon as it subsided, he slithered out of the trench, leaving the children in the hands of the rescue operation. Quickly, while dodging bullets, the joint LAPD/fed SWAT team loaded the youngsters into a shielded truck.

Dawn was coming in fast! Good, because they had light to work by. Bad, because they were all more visible. Creeping on his belly to the crater of mud, Decker plunged his hands into the gook and began digging like a possessed beagle. McCarry, Stone, Oliver, Martinez and Webster were excavating alongside him, all of them prone, their heads covered by hard hats. Oliver, Webster and Martinez were using their bare hands as shovels. Stone and McCarry had the advantage of small tools.

How many minutes had passed?

Two . . . maybe two and a half?

Maybe three, four minutes left to save her.

"C'mon, Margie, do something to let me know you're there!" Decker's arms were elbow-deep in slime, his fingers grabbing to feel something. "Why don't the jerks leave us alone and just blow themselves to smithereens?"

McCarry swore as he spaded gunk. "The kid said Bob wanted to go out in a big bang. Looks like he's getting his wish."

"I got a wish for him," Decker said. "I wish I could flay him slow —" His fingertips rippled over the smooth surface of skin. He tried to grip it, but the flesh slipped out of his grasp. *"There's someone down here!"* he yelled. *"I felt something, I felt something."*

Frantically, the crew began unearthing mud.

But hostile gunfire erupted, forcing Decker to pull his arm out and cover his head.

"*Goddamn* them!" Decker said, his face hitting the ground. This time, McCarry and Oliver shot back, allowing Decker to dive back into the bog, trying to salvage whoever was left, *including* his closest friend and partner for the last fucking ten years!

Maybe three minutes left to go.

Work, Decker, work! Work!

"How many kids were there before Marge?" Decker yelled.

Stone answered, "Lauren doesn't remember —"

"How the hell does she know —"

"She didn't have time to count —"

"It's here! I got something, I got . . ." Decker's arm had once again disappeared into the mire, his face dancing cheek-to-cheek with the blackened pool. For a second time, he felt flesh, dug his nails in hard and deep. "I've got someone! Pull me up, pull me up!"

Webster, Martinez and Oliver wrapped their arms around Decker's body and began to tow him backward as the others unearthed the soil around his arm.

Decker talked to God. "Just let me hold *on!* Just let them hold *off* —"

Again, the air broke with gunfire blast. But this time, being *so* close, no one stopped working. The men kept dragging, the others kept spading, all of them praying that the bullets' trajectories would fly off-course.

Grunting as they pulled Decker, who held on with untold strength, trying to draw the body up from the bowels. Soon the buried limb became visible. The men grabbed onto the thin arm, hooking their fingers into the slippery skin, gaffing it like a fish. They tugged on it while the others dug around the flesh. Moments later, a mud-drenched youngster was ejected from the boggish hell. A quick wipe of his face showed him to be a preteen boy.

Marge had about two more minutes left! As the others continued their frantic rooting for Marge, Decker shoved open the boy's mouth, stuck his fingers down the kid's throat and tried to clear an airway without making him gag. Aspirating muck was a surefire way of giving the kid a very dangerous pneumonia. When he sensed some air space in the throat, he covered the boy's nose and mouth with his own mouth and gave three quick breaths. He looked down at the child's body to see if his air had produced a rise in his chest.

Nothing.

Decker jammed his fingers down the boy's throat a second time, then administered three quick puffs. This time the kid's thorax swelled.

"I got a fuckin' airway!" he screamed as sweat streaked down his sullied face. "Fuckin' hallelujah! I need a medic! Where are the fuckin' medics? I need some help with CPR!"

"They're behind the trench!" Elise cried out as

she scooped up goop.

"How far?"

Stone didn't answer. Distraught, she had finally shattered, allowing herself deep sobs as she spaded muck with her trowel. Oliver glanced at her, trying to keep a lid on his own emotions. But he was losing the battle. Conjuring up images of his partner under pounds of pressure and mud . . .

"Come on, baby! C'mon!" He spoke to himself. His strength was draining, but pure, raw adrenaline kept him going. "C'mon, honey, you've *got* to be there!"

Something crashed and blew up a hundred yards away. The ground responded by vomiting out rocks and chunks of granite.

"Motherfuckers!" Martinez screamed, his arms deep within the ground. "Motherfuck— Oh, Blessed Mary, I think I feel something!" He plunged his arm as deep as he could go. "I've got something! I think it's a piece of clothing! Dig here! Dig around me!"

As dirt flew out in all directions, Decker continued to breathe life into the boy's lungs. He had called someone for cardiac depressions, so now Webster was at the child's chest.

"Pulse?" Decker asked.

"Not yet —"

"C'mon, kid, you can —" He looked over at Martinez. "You got her yet?"

"Not yet —"

Webster said, "And one, and two, and three, and four and five."

Decker breathed into the boy's mouth, hoping to revive this young and fragile life. He never pictured death as revenge on evil individuals. But as he struggled, as the others sweated and labored, all he could think about was torturing Bob Russo. It scared him that he found pleasure in the images.

Webster was still counting, "And one, and two, and three, and four and five."

A breath.

A one, a two, a three, a four, a five . . .

A breath.

"Faster!" Martinez screamed at those around him. "I'm losing . . . she's slipping down . . ." He was practically facedown in the mire. *"Faster, faster!"*

Like quicksand, the wet hole was covering itself up almost as quickly as they dug. But slowly, slowly, the pit became a bit wider, a bit deeper. At first, it was inches, then a foot. Finally, enough gunk was unearthed to reveal Martinez's hand gripping onto a small patch of cloth. McCarry and Stone locked onto the fabric and pulled, hoping that the strong protective SWAT garb would hold fast.

Like pulling a dinosaur out of the tar pits.

Tugging harder and harder.

Dig, tug, dig, tug, dig, tug —

Webster saying, "And one, and two, and three, and four and five . . ."

A breath into the lungs. Decker shouting, "You get her?"

"She's coming."

"Is her face out?"

"Not yet. It's coming —"

"And four and five."

A breath. "Got her?"

Another spew of gunfire.

"Shit!" Decker yelled as he protected his head. "Shit, shit, shit!!"

The police answering the fire.

"Got her —"

"It's coming!" Martinez said, grunting.

Slowly, the piece of fabric was turning into part of a pant leg, then a leg with a boot. McCarry hammer-locked his arms around the femur, and towed it upward as others continued to spade around it. Within moments, both legs were exposed. Five men grabbed and pulled.

Webster still shouting, "And one, and two and three —"

Suddenly, the boy hacked up mud, then broke into spasms of coughing. Decker turned him onto his side as the child threw up gunk. Webster broke into unexpected tears, then slithered back to the crater to help shovel away crud from the exposed body.

The boy's breathing was erratic, the pulse unsteady. But Decker could no longer hold off. He needed to help. He needed to be part of the operation to save his partner and friend!

"Get him to a paramedic!" he ordered Webster.

He gripped her legs along with the others and pulled.

The two legs . . . then the hips . . .

Long legs, wide hips . . . an adult in camouflage. It *had* to be her.

Please, God, let it be her!

About one more minute before oxygen damage kicked into the brain.

Decker tugged with such intensity that he felt the vessels in his face bursting. Screaming, "Pull, pull, pull —"

"We're pulling, goddammit!" McCarry shouted back.

Two legs and a hip.

The hips and then the stomach, then the chest.

One more goddamn minute.

A second passed, then two, then three . . .

Suddenly, she was out, sliding with so little friction, that they all fell backward.

She was completely lifeless — without breath, without pulse, without the rudiments of involuntary nervous synapses. So thickly caked in gook, her face had become a smooth, ceramic convex surface of mud. Frantically, Decker wiped away the goo from her face, sticking his fingers down her throat and in her nostrils.

Maybe fifty seconds — maybe less.

With Marge being the last of the lot, McCarry could only think about getting his people out alive. While attempting to tow Marge into the shielded trench, the special-agent-in-charge snapped commands regarding vehicle clearance of the area. But Decker didn't hear a thing. He was too busy trying to clear Marge's nose to get an airway, creeping on his belly as they dragged her amid punctuated bursts of machine-gun fire.

Finally, they returned her to relative safety behind the protective ditch. Twenty feet away stood the pickup vehicles. Seeing the body, a trio of hard-hatted paramedics dropped down from the van's cargo door, and, while crouching, sprinted a gurney over to the body. As they loaded her into a four-wheel-drive Suburban that had been converted into a bullet-proof ambulance, McCarry ordered his rescue team into the fed's armored vehicles.

Without hesitation, Decker slipped into the back of the ambulance before the cargo door was slammed shut. His presence made the small working space even more cramped and crowded, but no one protested his being there. The key turned in the ignition, and the motor kicked in. A depression on the gas pedal, and the four-wheel drive lurched forward, reeling over the unsteady, bumpy terrain. Surrounding him were McCarry's armored trucks, all of them desperately trying to negotiate the unstable earth beneath them.

Dry-eyed, Decker held Marge's frigid hand in his own cold grip, and stared out the rear window while EMTs toiled frantically on Marge's unresponsive bulk. They cleared, they cleaned, they intubated, feeding her fresh oxygen with a mask strapped over nose and face. They swabbed, and injected meds while monitoring her flat vitals signs. Immediately, a tech started chest compressions, which were read out on the screen as little spikes resembling Etch-a-Sketch mountains. The doctor over the radio was asking questions. He could barely be heard over the outside noise and internal static.

A paramedic was talking to Decker.

Focus, Pete. "Pardon?"

"You have to let go of her and move back."

The EMT was holding resuscitating paddles. Comprehension in Decker's brain. He couldn't hold onto her body because he'd get electrically zapped in the process. Reluctantly, he dropped her hand, letting go of the physical connection.

"Paddles in place?"

"In place."

Abruptly, the jeep was jerked side to side by an explosive outburst. The ground roared, blackening the soft morning light with sand, dirt and grit. Rocks and pebbles stabbed the plastic windows while stones pounded the steel doors. The inside temperature zoomed upward.

The driver cursed as he swerved to the left, then to the right, then to the left again. But he never stopped moving forward. He turned his head and peeked over his shoulder.

"Everyone okay?"

Decker couldn't answer, couldn't find sound in his throat. He looked out the side windows. McCarry's crew still appeared upright; at least the trucks were still on four wheels.

With great courage, he allowed himself to look at her, at her gray, dirt-streaked face now masked and tubed. Yes, air was entering her lungs, but were they still too soggy to absorb life-giving oxygen?

Gunfire pellets hailing onto the vehicle, reverberating inside like an echo chamber.

"Those goddamn fuckheads!" The driver swore while trying to steer the wheels. The car skidded, almost overturning before it landed on all fours with a clunk and fishtailed.

The driver kept going.

Twenty feet . . . thirty feet . . . forty feet . . . the Order's bunker inching away, slowly receding into the distance.

Drenched with sweat from the soaring, internal temperature, the techs set up the paddles again. Though it must have been close to ninety degrees, Decker was still shaking with cold.

"One more time," the paramedic gasped.

"Can you go faster?" one man asked the driver.

"Not if you want to get there alive."

"Eric, paddles in place?"

"Paddles in place, Terry. Fire when ready!"

Zap.

The body jumped, and all eyes went to the monitor.

A large spike peaking to the top of the screen, corresponding to the transmitted electrical impulse.

Then a flat line.

Moments later, several erratic spikes appeared with corresponding audible beeps.

Then another flat line.

But then another beep . . .

Then another beep . . .

Then another . . .

And another . . .

"First try out!" The paramedic, though breathing hard, was grinning. "Man, you never get *that* lucky!"

Decker stared at the monitor, tears streaming down his cheeks. Without taking his eyes of those beautiful spikes, he asked, "Is she breathing?"

"Not on her own."

Decker continued to study the monitor. The pulse was getting stronger, more regular. "Her *heart's* beating. It's beating on its own!"

"Yes, sir, this is true," Eric, the tech, answered.

"Her lungs *have* to kick in."

"Well, she's getting oxygen."

Decker regarded Marge's face, stroked it tenderly, erasing his dripping tears off her plastic oxygen mask with his fingertips. "You're halfway there, Dunn. C'mon, baby, I *know* you can hear me! We've got this connection so don't crap out on me now!"

Another eruption bombarded the mountainside. Again, visibility was wiped out. The ambulance shook and jerked, then skidded over the rocky ground as equipment was hurled across the interior of the car. Stone and rock pummeled the vehicle.

But within an instant, the darkness transformed into total, sun-blinding daylight as chemical explosions of fire and hard material spewed into the early morning ethers.

The blast was deafening. Decker held his ears and winced in pain. But the earth refused to be hushed. After the initial burst, it suddenly opened up its jaws, and bellowed out deep, shattering belches. The ambulance was seized by the ground's fury, tossed and blown as if storm-swept. As Decker rocked in the van, his eyes adjusting and peering through the petroleum winds outside, he could make out the bunkers exploding in fiery, domino fashion.

One violent meteor blast after another.

Boom! Boom! Boom! Boom! Boom!

An inferno had erupted like a hot volcano. Within seconds, the buildings that had once comprised the Order of the Rings of God were a memory. Completely eradicated. All that was left was hot fire, shooting flames, belching smoke and glowing, white ashes.

36

After four hours of sleep, a nurse woke Decker up to check his vitals. The interruption irritated him, and he blurted out that hospitals were the worst place in the world for recuperation and why didn't she just leave him the hell alone. Rina said something to him — and to the nurse — but he didn't process any of it. Instead, he endured the poking and prodding in a state of semiconsciousness, then dropped back to sleep as soon as the white-garbed devil made her exit.

The next time he woke up, he thought about Marge, how he should *be* with her. All he had to do was throw on a robe and take the elevator down one floor because he really did want to hear her talk.

Really talk.

Not just hear her moan and groan and say things like, "I hear you" and "yes." He wanted to hold a conversation even if it were conducted in monosyllables. But the idea of physically *moving* seemed insurmountable or, at the very least, a supreme effort. Besides, his bedside clock told him it was 4:06, and that looked to be 4:06 in the morning rather than 4:06 in the afternoon, although in hospitals — like casinos — it's impossible to tell time.

The kicker was Rina sleeping on the cot. Some orderly had brought it in for her yesterday and placed it right next to the hospital bed. Decker figured Rina wouldn't be sleeping at 4:06 — oops, now 4:07 — in the afternoon. She'd either be awake, maybe reading a book or talking to a nurse or perhaps she'd be home, taking care of Hannah . . .

Who *was* taking care of Hannah?

Probably his in-laws. Or maybe Cindy.

He was very proud of his logic. It indicated he had the capacity for rational deduction. Again, his blurred and darkened vision fell on Rina lying on the hard surface, wrapped up in a sheet. He flashed to the montage of carnage at the Order, to the body pieces being transferred to the morgue by the coroner's office. Lots of sheeted gurneys covering hundreds of incomplete corpses. He wanted to wake Rina up just to make sure she was still alive, even though he *knew* she had to be very much alive. Hospitals didn't put patients and corpses in the same room.

So he didn't wake her up, thinking that yes, she was alive and maybe he should let her sleep. And maybe he should sleep himself.

The next time his brain tuned in, he found Rina's cot empty. For one panic-stricken second, he thought that maybe he had been right, that she had been part of the bloodbath. But more likely, it meant Rina was up and about, and it was a permissible waking hour. Murky sunrays shot through the hospital room's postage-stamp window. (Didn't they dust in here?) Slowly, he swung his long legs over the edge of the mattress, then attempted to sit upright.

The world started to spin, his cerebral cortex knocking around his cranium like a BB in a tin can. He dropped his chin to his chest and held his temples, trying to stave off the increasingly loud ringing between his ears. Then he thought that perhaps if he stood up, it would get better. Shoving his weight upward, he stood on bended knees while reeling on the soles of his feet.

Rina saying, "Just what do you think you're doing!"

Decker sank back onto the mattress, too tired to defend himself. Reality was starting to intrude — where he was and what had transpired. After being checked in for observation, after hitting the pillow, he had been too exhausted to dream, too spent to have nightmares. But he knew they would come. The ordeal had been too much to fathom in his waking world. It had to come out somewhere, and the subconscious was as good a place as any.

Hopefully, it would come out after he had finished with all the questions and had done all the paperwork. That's what awaited him — hell and red tape. But the self-pity didn't last more than an eye blink. He was alive, Marge was alive, his kids were alive and most of the Order's children had been saved.

C'mon, Deck. Give yourself a break!

He asked Rina what time it was. His words sounded foreign to his ears.

"It's seven-ten."

Seven-ten. Checked in at two-thirty P.M. yesterday, he'd been sleeping for something like fifteen hours. Interrupted hours because of the damn nurses . . . who were only doing their job, he knew. But it was still irksome. He finger-raked wet, carrot tresses. He must have been sweating in his sleep.

"I need to see Marge," he announced.

"She's sleeping."

A few seconds delay to process what she had said. *She is sleeping.* "How do you know she's sleeping?"

"Because I was just down there."

"How's she doing?"

"Her vital signs are very strong."

"Is she breathing on her own?"

"Very much so. She has supplemental oxygen, but they took her off the ventilator hours ago."

Decker nodded. He could feel the fog lift from his head. "Maybe I'll just go down there and watch her sleep."

"You need to take care of yourself, Peter. You need to rest."

Rina's voice seemed soft . . . or more like muted. His head was still buzzing, but at least he could hear. Then she stopped talking, and the only sound that presented itself was this annoying hum in his brain.

"I said *gomel,*" he stated proudly. *Gomel* was the

Jewish prayer said upon deliverance from danger. "Or at least my version of it."

Rina nodded. "It's truly a miracle you're on two feet."

"I'm not exactly on two feet." Decker sank into the pillow. "How long do I have to be here?"

"It's a twenty-four-hour observation."

"You mean incarceration."

Rina looked at him. Moisture had filled her eyes. Her lower lip began to quiver. She bit it hard, but it didn't stop the tears.

"Ah, honey!" Decker reached out to her. "I'm perfectly fine! Just a little . . . sleep-deprived!"

She sat on the edge of his bed and locked her arms around his neck. He managed to drag himself into a semiupright position and drew her close, draping his arms around her warm, sweet-smelling body, trying to absorb her light to illuminate his foul darkness.

Their tears mixed, both of them crying silently. Like two enjoined puzzle pieces, they remained separate units, but one entity. They stayed that way until the nurse came in, chirping that it was time to take his blood pressure.

It was hard to reconcile this Marge — sleeping between crisp, white sheets — with the muddy corpse they had pulled out a day ago. Though inhaling through an oxygen mask, Margie was breathing on her own. Tube-fed, but her body was getting nutrition. Her heartbeats were strong and regular. So engrossed by the high-tech life preservation machines, he hadn't noticed the pajama-clad package sitting by Marge's hospital window. The young teen was staring out the yellowed pane, her elbows leaning against the ledge, her forehead touching the glass.

Decker cleared his throat and the girl swung around. Immediately, she sat up ruler-straight.

"You can relax, Vega." Decker tightened his robe belt around his waist. "As a matter of fact, you *should* relax. You should probably be in your room with the others."

"I am fine." She looked away. "I had to see her. Just to make sure."

"Yes, I know how you feel," Decker agreed. "I had to see her, too."

Vega glanced at him, but didn't respond.

Decker asked, "How are you feeling?"

"I am well."

"Does anyone know you're here?"

Vega lowered her head, shook it from side to side.

"Then maybe you should get back to your room. You wouldn't want to worry the staff with your absence."

She made no effort to move.

"Vega?" Decker asked. "Did you hear me?"

"Yes, Lieutenant." But she was affixed to her chair. "It is wrong that I disobey, and do not tell the nice nurse where I am. I am very bad."

Decker sidestepped Marge's bed and came over to her. He sat on the floor, again tightening his robe. If a nurse walked in, he didn't want her to think that he was a pervert. "Vega," he said softly. "There isn't a bad bone in your body."

Vega studied him with confusion on her face. "Bones cannot be good or bad. They are just bones."

Decker took a moment to organize his thoughts. "Vega, you are a *very good* young lady. You know that, don't you?"

She said, "I saved the baby. That was very good."

Decker exhaled outloud. "No, that was an incredibly *heroic* act! Extraordinary! That went beyond being good! But you, just by being *you*, are good. Do you understand what I am saying."

But she didn't understand.

She said, "I am good when I do good things, I am bad when I do bad things."

"No!" Decker shook his head vehemently. "It doesn't work that way. Good people — like you — they are *always* good even when they make mistakes."

"I did not say a mistake, I said I am bad when I do *bad* things."

"That still isn't correct. You can be disobedient, do a naughty thing. But that doesn't make you bad. That makes you a good person who was disobedient or naughty. *You* are still good. Am I making any sense to you?"

She said nothing.

"Let's take an example." Decker tried appealing to her logic. "You listened to Marge.

516

Now, the Order said you did a *bad* thing, that you disobeyed the rules. But I know you did a *good* thing. Most important, *you* know you did a good thing — to listen to her. If you hadn't listened to her, she would be dead."

A tear fell down her cheek. "All the people in the Order of the Rings of God are dead. Maybe by listening to Marge, I caused them to die."

"Oh, no, no, no, no, no!" Decker said. "They had made plans to die long before Marge or Lauren — Andromeda — or Agent Stone had appeared through that tunnel. Furthermore, they were going to kill other people before they died. You *know* that because you saw those . . ." He swallowed hard. "You saw the babies. If you had stayed, you would have been murdered just like the babies were murdered."

She had been staring into Decker's eyes. This time, she looked away. "The babies are now in a better world. That is not so bad."

But her tears had thickened. Decker wanted to hug her, but held back. Everything in this world — the violators' world — was foreign to her. Who knew what constituted comfort to Vega? Was comfort even a word in her vocabulary?

Vega said, "Many adult people have come and talked to us. Most wear white coats like those in the Order. Perhaps they want us to think that we are talking to friends, not violators, by dressing like us."

"Actually, doctors in the violators' world wear white coats."

"So they do not have ulterior purposes?"

"No."

"These doctors," Vega said. "They talk to us in groups, they talk to us individually. They ask us questions, they give us tests. The woman who gave me a test said I was very, very smart."

"You are very, very smart."

"I overheard some of them talking. They said that we were all very smart, that we had an outstanding knowledge of math and science that went beyond our years. They said also that our reading comprehension was very high."

"I'm sure that's all true."

She faced him, wiping away tears. "If Father Jupiter and his followers produced such smart progeny who study and try to understand the physics and metaphysics of the universe, why is everyone saying that Father Jupiter and the Order are so *bad!*"

She sniffled.

"The violators should *not* say the Order was bad! It was not bad. It was *not* bad!"

Decker nodded.

She wiped her nose on her hospital gown. "The violators do not understand! They say we are smart, yet they say the Order is bad. That is a contradiction! They should not say that! It is very *wrong* for them to say that!"

It was painful for her to hear such criticism, and she was defending her people. Was it done out of habit, out of loyalty or out of guilt? Because when given her first brush with free will,

Vega had opted for Marge over the Order. Because she knew instinctively what was *really* right.

He didn't dare explain it to her. That kind of stuff was better left to the pros.

The kids were being extensively evaluated. Before he dropped off to sleep, Decker had spoken to the head honcho — some shrink doctor who had worked for years as a police consultant in the Westside substation. He was also reputed to be a top-notch child psychologist. The Brass had put him, among others, in charge of setting up the adjustment program. Still, the doctor had taken time out to talk to Decker. Though Decker knew psychopatter when he heard it, he still found himself talking to the man. The guy clearly understood cops.

Decker said, "I'm sure there are lots that we violators don't understand about Father Jupiter and the Order of the Rings of God. But I'll tell you what *I* understand."

"What is that?"

He ran his finger down the bridge of her nose. "I know that you are a very good lady. And I know that you will do *great* things in this world. You will not only be a great scientist — if you choose to be a scientist — but you will be a very moral scientist because you are a very upright individual."

She said nothing.

A *moral* scientist. Decker flashed to the accusations leveled at Emil Euler Ganz aka Father Jupiter. Perjury. Adultery. Plagiarism. A sadistic man who took pleasure in ruining careers according to his own daughter's recollections. Yet others saw him as a god and a savior. Where was the truth? If it existed, it certainly wasn't absolute.

"A very *moral* scientist and a *moral* person," Decker went on. "Because you are a moral girl. You were born that way."

Vega said, "I think that everyone is born a *certain* way, Lieutenant. But that is not *all* of it. It was our Father Jupiter, our teachers *and* our gurus at the Order who shaped my being. You are trying to separate the *Order from me*. But that is an impossibility."

Decker regarded her young, wet face. Of course, she was right. The irony of it all — this morally superior creature coming from a cult steeped in immorality, and run by venal, murderous leaders. She had now been emancipated from the manacles of these maniacs. Would freedom and choice corrupt her pure spirit?

Vega said, "People should stop saying untrue things about the Order of the Rings of God, and our Father Jupiter. He was a *holy* man. The violators are wrong to say mean things about him."

"What things specifically bother you?"

"They say that Father Jupiter was wicked and crazy. They do not know. He was a *prophet!* God's hand-chosen whose mission was to spread His word. *They do not understand!*"

Decker agreed. "That's true. They don't understand."

She looked out the window. "They do not know of the Order's wonderful teachers. They did not see the care, the charity that was given to the less fortunate. We never lacked for food. We were always clean and warm. We were *constantly* immersed in wonderful knowledge." She shook her head. "They do not understand!"

They don't understand, because all that's left for the public is a human boneyard. Such a tragic, *avoidable* event! An utter *waste* of human life. A minute more and Marge would have been gone. Decker said, "Maybe someday you will write a book and explain it all to us. Try to make us understand."

"I would like that very much."

Decker gave her a brief smile, his eyes drifting over to the hospital bed. Vega noticed the subtle shift in his attention.

"Detective Marge will be all right?"

"I hope so." A pause. "I think so."

"She is your friend?"

"Yes, Vega, she is my friend."

"Maybe when she gets better, she can be my friend, too."

"Vega, she already is your friend."

The teen's face brightened. "How do you know?"

"She spoke highly of you the first time she met you. Why do you think she went into that tunnel and risked her life? It was because she cared about you."

Vega appeared to think about his words. Then

she cleared her throat. "She said I should be an astronaut. I think I will listen to her."

"A fine idea."

"I would like to explore space," Vega said. "Ideally, it would be wonderful to fly without a ship — like the Little Prince. But that is fantasy. So I shall be an astronaut and fly in a spacecraft. It is second-best, but we are bound by the rules of physics."

"You will make a fine astronaut, Vega."

"Thank you," Vega said. "And maybe one day, if I am fortunate, I will see the Little Prince."

Decker smiled. "In space?"

"No, Lieutenant Decker, he does not exist in space," Vega said gravely. "Perhaps one day, I will meet him in my dreams."

"You're looking better."

Decker pivoted around to the door. It was Dr. Little — the esteemed coroner in the flesh. He winced at his own mental pun. "Hey, Judy."

"They've determined you're fit for human consumption?"

"Something like that." He stopped packing up. "I'm feeling pretty damn consumed."

"I'm sure." She sat on Rina's cot. "They put you through the usual battery of tests, Lieutenant?"

"Yes, they did, and all of them were a pain in the ass." He threw his shaver into a small photographer's bag and perched on the side of his bed. "They gave me lots of those hand-eye tests. You know, stand on one foot and touch your nose while closing both eyes. Something designed by a sadistic neurologist who takes great glee in making you feel uncoordinated."

Judy smiled. "I take it the results were okay?"

"If there's brain damage, it was there long before the Order ever existed."

"When are you leaving, Pete?"

Decker checked his watch. "My wife and kids should be here in a half hour. The welcoming committee. I'm surprised they didn't hire a band. You've met my big girl, Judy?"

"Don't believe so."

"She's a cop."

"You jest."

"It's the truth. I wasn't happy about her decision, but she's happy. That's all that counts." He smiled to himself. "She's a great kid. All my kids are great."

"Not too proud, huh?"

"Everyone's entitled to some obnoxious crowing."

Little asked, "They have hospital clearance passes, right?"

"I believe so. Why?"

"Security's very tight. Much stricter here than at the crash site."

"The Order's children are here."

"That's right. Everyone wants a peek at the kids. What are they expecting to see? Little robots?"

"Probably."

"The guards have been fending off news-people left and right." Little gave him a small smile. "When they're not posing for pictures."

Decker laughed. "Uh, snap my good side."

"Just about. Took me over a half hour to get in."

"Hope it's a lot shorter to get out." He zipped his bag up. "I hate hospitals. I'll be thrilled to say good-bye to this place." He thought about Marge. "At least as a patient."

Little had a pained expression on her face. "How's your head?"

"It booms, it hoots, it rings, it whistles. Got a friggin' percussion section inside my brain. They keep saying it'll take time to heal, so what choice do I have? Captain Strapp's told me to take a week off . . . more if I need it. As you know, the department has excellent disability."

"I'm sure you'll be fine."

"Let's hope that goes double for Margie."

"How's she doing?"

"Marge . . ." He sighed out the name. "Well, according to the pros, she's well-oriented . . . knows her name and the current president. Her cognition . . . like that word?"

"Pretty damn fancy for a cop."

"I know much more than I let on." A pause. "I think Marge *knows* a lot more than she can communicate."

"Is she talking?"

"Yep, and that's a very good sign, although she speaks in very short sentences. She recognizes everyone, knew me and Scott and the guys instantly."

"That's good."

"She even remembers working on the Ganz case — recalls bits and pieces of the chicken farm she visited right before she came down to the mess at the Order. She realizes she belongs in the hospital — she can't breathe too well and she's aware of the oxygen mask — but she doesn't know *how* she got that way. She's confused about the details, doesn't know what happened to her. Everyone thinks that's normal."

"Her body underwent a massive shock. Sometimes the mind shuts down along with the body."

"I know. I saw it all the time in 'Nam."

"You were in Vietnam?"

Decker smiled. "Tell me I don't look old enough."

"You don't look old enough."

The smile turned into a grin. "You lie beautifully."

"I believe the correct PC terminology is that I'm 'honesty impaired.' "

Decker chuckled, though his heart held no levity. Abruptly, he turned sober. "Yeah, I saw just about everything in 'Nam. What happened at the Order . . ." A shrug. "It wasn't all that different. War is war." He rubbed his brow. "Hell of a lot shorter tour of duty, I'll say that much."

"At least it's over," Little said.

"Still got a mound of paperwork to deal with.

Plus, until Marge is back on her feet, it's not over for me."

A moment of stretched silence.

"She's going to be fine," Decker stated with bravado.

"I'm sure she'll make a quick recovery," Little agreed.

He asked, "How's the graveyard going?"

"Gruesome," Judy admitted. "Excavating thousands of body parts mixed with all the blood-stained rubble. It's going to take months to fit all the pieces together."

"So I guess you haven't the faintest idea if Bob and/or Venus are among the dead?"

"Right now we're picking out teeth for ID purposes. We've sent out for dental X rays. Now we have to play mix and match with not a whole lot of intact material. Meanwhile, we've got scores of grieving family members hanging on by a string. Some haven't heard from their missing loved ones in years. They're hoping that their relatives had left the Order before this all happened." She threw up her hands. "If I were them, I'd be clinging to whatever I could hold."

"Me, too. Did you call up Annie Hennon?"

"The tooth fairy?"

"I think her official title is forensic odontologist."

"We phoned her, sure." A sigh. "She's down in the ruins with the best of us . . . sorting through the ashes. Nice of her to do it, too. She has a full-time private practice."

Little stared up at the ceiling.

"I've seen hundreds of corpses, Lieutenant. I've done autopsies on thousands of bodies. Nothing prepares you for this kind of horror." She stared at him. "Listen to me . . . moaning about my lot when you just went through the battle lines."

"We all have our own private millstones around our necks." Decker shrugged. "At least I'm going home."

"That's good." Little plunked out some notes from her jacket. "This is after the fact, but I found out the likely source of arsenic for King Jupiter."

"Go on."

"His vitamins," Little continued.

Decker thought back to all those bottles he had initially tagged and bagged. He had taken a peek inside a few of the plastic containers. Most of the complexes had been in the hard, tablet form. He asked Judy about that.

"Lots were solid pills, but some were in capsules. Specifically, the herbal preparations like the gingkoba and ginseng. It appears that someone had mixed the preps with a couple of micrograms of arsenic powder, then stuffed it back into the capsules."

"Not hard to do."

"Not at all."

"All the signs of a typical poisoner — nonconfrontational, cowardly, sneaky. Plus, you can stick around and watch while the recipient suffers." Decker scratched his head. "Sounds exactly like Bob."

"Bob was confrontational when he needed to be."

"That was after Jupiter had died."

"Ah." But Judy still seemed disturbed. "Bob's *real* last name was Russo, correct?"

"Yes, of course." Decker looked at her. "Why do you ask?"

"Because someone said something about Bob changing his name from time to time."

"Oh . . . that." Decker nodded. "Europa, Jupiter's daughter, mentioned that when she first met Bob, he told her that his name was Ross. Later, we found out it was Russo."

"But Russo is his real last name."

Decker regarded her face. "What are you driving at, Judy?"

"The poisoned bottles had Bob's name on the labels."

Decker was confused. "You mean the bottles were prescription?"

"No, not at all. The supplements were OTC. I'm talking about the *maker's* label. It said Russo Holistic Supplements. I looked up the company. It's a legitimate enterprise. The company's president is —"

"Robert Russo!" Decker completed the sentence. Then buried his face in his hand. "Good grief!"

"Not a coincidence?"

"The company's president is Robert Russo, Sr."

"Bob's father."

"Well, I've never done the DNA test on them, but I'd swear to it in court." Decker stood and began to pace. "Bob Senior *detested* Emil Ganz. In a letter to the editor written a couple days after Ganz's death, Big Bob accused him of perjury and adultery — probably adultery with *his* wife."

"Little Bob's mother?"

"Yep."

"So Little Bob poisoned Jupiter to avenge his father's honor by using Daddy's supplies? *Très* Oedipal. Where's the Greek chorus?"

Decker said, "From what I've seen and heard, Little Bob hated his real father. Little Bob told me that Emil Ganz was his hero and his spiritual father. I got the feeling that Little Bob even hooked up with Jupiter to *spite* his dad, certainly not to please him."

"Then something must have changed Little Bob's mind about Jupiter. Because there was definitely arsenic in those capsules."

Decker was quiet.

"What's wrong?" Little asked.

"The bottles that had the arsenic capsules. Did the lab people take test samples from un-opened or opened containers?"

Little thought a moment. "I don't know."

"Does the lab have any *unopened* bottles of Russo Holistic Supplements?"

"I don't know. You'd have to ask —" Little stopped talking. She chuckled with surprise.

529

"Are you thinking that the arsenic came from *Big Bob*?"

"Big Bob really detested Ganz."

"Pete, how would Big Bob know Ganz was taking his pills?"

"Judy, he owns the company. He knows who he ships to. He must have known that his company was shipping boxes to the Order —"

"Why would he know that? I'm sure his company ships out hundred of boxes a day."

"You detest a guy with that much passion, so much that you carry a grudge for years, you pick up on things like that."

Judy raised a skeptical brow.

Decker said, "It would be a snap for the manufacturer to slip a little arsenic in the capsules."

"That's not the point —"

"On the contrary, Judy, that is the point."

She pocketed her notes. "Pete, even if Big Bob had been aware that there were pills being shipped to the Order, he still wouldn't know that the preparations were meant for Jupiter specifically."

"Maybe the boxes had Jupiter's name on it."

"Do you know if they did?"

"No. I'd have to check Big Bob's inventory labels." He paused. "Try getting a warrant to check that out."

"Even if they were shipped to Jupiter, Big Bob takes the chance of poisoning people along with Jupiter."

"So maybe that's why there wasn't a lethal

dose in any one capsule. Or maybe Big Bob simply didn't care." Decker stopped ambling. "This is a question with a *simple* solution. If the lab has unopened bottles, we'll test the samples for arsenic contents. If they do have arsenic, then we'll know that the poison came from the manufacturing side."

"That doesn't pin it on Big Bob."

"With poison in the unopened bottles, I could pull a warrant to comb Big Bob's outfit. Then I could check the inventory number labels and see if they match the tainted bottles. With enough evidence, I could possibly arrest Big Bob for attempted murder."

"But the arsenic didn't kill Jupiter."

"Big Bob doesn't know that," Decker said.

"But a jury will."

"We'll worry about that later."

"And if the lab doesn't have any unopened bottles?"

"Then maybe we'll be extremely lucky and find some unopened, untampered bottles lying in the rubble. Most likely, the bottles are now dust and ashes. In that case, we'll never know which Bob did it."

"So one of the Bobs got away with poisoning Jupiter."

"Neither Bob got away with anything. Presumably, Little Bob's dead. That means Senior Bob lost his only son." Decker thought a moment. "Actually Senior lost Junior to Jupiter a long time ago. And even if the father had exacted his judgment on Jupiter, in the end, the cult destroyed his boy. *Midah keneged midah*. That's a Hebrew term. The English law equivalent is measure for measure, but what it *really* means is what goes around, comes around. And that, my friend, is the whole damn story of life!"

37

He felt her eyes burning a hole in his back. He could hear her voice even before she spoke. She said, "You must have played high school football."

His eyes still on the photographs, Decker answered, "Yep."

Silence.

She said, "God, that was terrible of me."

Decker's eyes shifted focus, from the stark moonscape to Europa sitting behind her desk. She seemed smaller than he had remembered. It was probably her posture. Her shoulders were stooped, and her head jutted forward and downward.

"What was terrible?" he asked.

"My elite-snobbism bias. Summing you up based on physical appearances."

He analyzed *her* physical appearance — pale skin bordering on wan. She wore a charcoal skirt suit with a white blouse. In just a few weeks, her short-cropped hair seemed to have sprouted tufts of gray.

She appeared depressed, and who could blame her? According to the news, her lunatic father — the fallen angel of astrophysics — had spawned a society of maniacs and devil worshipers. The rumors weren't all that far from the truth. Europa had to feel angered by her father's legacy, burdened by it as well. All the crap she had taken from colleagues when Ganz had become Jupiter. Once again, she was taking crap now that Ganz's group had been annihilated. The newspapers tarring and feathering her father even though he had died days before the Order's holocaust.

Decker said, "You made an educated guess based on my build, Doctor. I look like an ex-football player."

"That's not it. I said *high school* football instead of college football. Because you're a cop, I assumed you didn't go to college. Sorry."

Decker smiled. "Now we're playing true confessions?"

"I amaze myself," she answered. "We say that the space taken up by a human body is finite, but I seem to have an infinite capacity for guilt."

And didn't that tell it all. Decker said, "I didn't go to college actually . . . well, not until much later on. By then, I was too old to play football."

"What did you study?"

"Poli sci. Then I trudged through three years of law school — night school. Actually all of my higher education was night school. Anyway, I graduated with honors and passed the bar. First try. Not bad for a cop, eh?"

She smiled weakly. "It's good for anyone."

"I worked with my ex-father-in-law," Decker went on. "Estate law — wills and trusts. I lasted six months, deciding to go with my strengths."

"Law's loss is law enforcement's gain."

"Thank you. I think I'm good at what I do." Decker took a seat opposite Europa. "Still, I keep wondering if I handled the Order properly. Specifically Bob."

"What do you mean?"

"Maybe if I had been more skilled, I could have talked Bob down."

"For what it's worth, Lieutenant, I don't think there was anything anyone could do. Bob was determined to make his own notorious place in history."

Decker asked, "Why'd you ask me about football, Doctor?"

"I don't really know why." A pause. "Maybe because my father liked football."

"Did he play?"

"I don't know. Shows you how close we were."

"But you know he liked the game."

"He'd watch the big games — the Rose Bowl and the Super Bowl. When I was real little, I'd sit with him, although I never understood all the rules."

Decker smiled. "No one does. We're all faking it."

Another weak, fleeting smile. Her eyes were tired and sad.

"So when you were little," Decker said, "you watched the games with your dad?"

"The Rose Bowl mostly. It was a New Year's Day tradition. Once, when my brothers were just babies, he took me down to his office at the university. Just me. I remember watching the parade from his vantage point on the sixth floor. That building is long gone since they put up the Space Sciences Center. But back then, we saw everything. The visibility was amazing. After the parade, we watched the game on TV."

"Nice memories."

"One of the few."

"It stayed with you all these years."

"Yes, it did."

"Guided you through some pretty dark times."

She regarded his face. "You're not the type to play shrink. Exactly why *are* you here, Lieutenant?"

"Tying up some loose ends," Decker said.

"What kind of 'loose ends' are you talking about?"

"After the destruction of the Order, I was given some time off. Not that much time, but enough to poke my nose into other people's business —"

"What does *that* mean?"

She had turned testy. He felt she knew what was coming.

"Does the name *Harrison* ring a bell?" Decker asked.

She continued starc at him, then averted her eyes.

Decker said, "Remember we told you about the Order's chicken ranch . . . which I guess is yours now. Anyway, Benton, the farmhand who we initially had questioned for Nova's murder, used to work at Harrison. Matter of fact, that's how your father met him. According to Benton, he just showed up one day."

She didn't answer.

"It's now a halfway house," Decker continued. "But during the Reagan/Bush years, it was used as a community mental health facility after most of the major psychiatric hospitals had been shut down because inpatient funding had dried up. Harrison was cheap to run. Back then, it had some live-in mental patients. And since it was given federal grants for rehab work, it generated all kinds of paperwork."

Her shoulders stooped farther. "Can you cut to the chase, Lieutenant?"

"The current administrator is a woman named Florine Vesquelez. She's worked there for over twenty years, and is very organized with the files. She allowed me to peek at some of the past cases. Guess whose name showed up as an inpatient resident?"

She sighed. "Keith Muldoony."

"Any idea who the *real* Keith Muldoony was?"

"Haven't a clue."

"It's Pluto."

"Oh." She scratched her nose. "That makes sense."

"Was it Pluto's idea to register your father in Harrison's care under the name Muldoony?"

"Beats me. At the time, I was kept totally in the dark."

Decker nodded.

Europa sighed with resignation. "You don't believe me. That I had nothing to do with it." A shrug. "Well, sir, that's *your* problem."

Decker thought a moment. "Doctor, can you ride this one out with me?"

"Do I have a choice?"

"You can tell me to leave," he answered. "I have no legal right to be here."

She regarded his face. "You did all this poking around on your own?"

"Yep."

"And you want nothing from me?"

"Pardon?"

She was quiet.

Decker smiled, but he was disturbed. "You think I'm trying to blackmail you, Doctor?"

"Are you?"

"Is that what Pluto did?"

She was quiet.

Decker said, "I'm just a curious fellow with time on my hands. What we say goes no farther than this room."

"I'm supposed to believe you?"

"Well, Doctor, if you don't, that's your problem."

She smiled weakly. "Go on. Get it over with."

"First off, I'm wondering how Pluto convinced you to bring your dad back to Los Angeles from West Virginia."

"He didn't convince me of anything. I told you I had no idea what was going on. Bringing Daddy back to L.A. was all my mother's doing."

"Your *mother* brought your dad back?"

"Yes, although I didn't know it at the time."

"Why would your mother suddenly bring your father back to Los Angeles? I'm assuming she was the one who committed him to that tiny mental hospital in West Virginia in the first place."

"I assume."

"To get him out of the way."

"More like to keep him out of public view. Prevent him from making himself a total object of ridicule. When in fact he was an object of pity."

"So why would she risk exposing what she'd been trying desperately to hide."

"I don't *know* why, Lieutenant. And Mom's dead. So I guess we'll never really know why?"

Decker was silent.

Europa said, "Again, this isn't firsthand knowledge. But I think Pluto threatened to expose Dad's mental problems if she didn't cooperate."

"Ah!" Decker nodded. "So I wasn't far off. Blackmail was Pluto's kind of thing."

"I'm sure you're right."

"You must have been angry at your mother when you found out the truth. That your father hadn't disappeared, but was wasting away as a mental patient."

"A bit miffed." But her expression spoke of fury, not of irritation. She got up from her desk chair and went over to the coffeepot. "You like yours black, right?"

"Good memory."

She took out the coffee urn and began busying herself in mundanity. "Actually, I didn't talk to her for a long time. So in a sense, there were years when both my parents were lost to me. Then afterward . . . a long time afterward . . . when I saw firsthand who or *what* my father really was . . . I began to calm down."

She poured water into the machine.

"I started putting myself in Mom's place. During Dad's disappearance . . ."

She made quote signs with her fingers at the word *disappearance*.

"During his disappearance, Mom was still being honored as the wife of Dr. Emil Euler Ganz. Southwest was still paying her a stipend, which helped care for her three children. After all, no one had really known what had happened to Dad. And he had received threatening letters over the years. So foul play didn't seem out of the question."

"Like those letters in the newspaper after he died?"

"I suppose. Although as a child, I never read the contents. But I knew that they existed."

"So that thing you told me about your mother hiring detectives was a lie?"

"No, she did hire detectives to keep up the pretense." She smiled. "None of them found Dad because Mom had done a remarkable job of hiding him. West Virginia is a long way from Los Angeles. Since he was an inpatient, he didn't generate any paper trails. And I imagine, he was either too crazy or too zonked out to reveal his true identity to anyone. He was truly lost to the world for years . . . until Pluto came along."

"Your mom should have hired me. I could have found him."

Europa managed a moribund chuckle. "I believe you."

Decker thought a moment. "I guess your mom didn't want to lose the few benefits left in her marriage."

"Exactly." She nodded. "She had already lost Dad to insanity. Why lose everything?"

"Then Pluto discovered your dad's true identity while working there as an orderly."

She turned on the machine and the coffee began gurgling. "They say that mental patients are always pretending to be people in famous professions. Even if Dad had said he'd been a famous scientist, I doubt most of the workers would have believed him. But somehow Pluto had seen the truth. He must have been perceptive on some level."

"Extremely perceptive and extremely crafty. So when he told your mother to bring Dad back to L.A. she cooperated."

"She must have."

"Whose idea was it to bring your father specifically to Harrison? Hers or Pluto's?"

"Don't know."

"And your mother had your father committed there at Pluto's behest?"

541

"You saw the records, you must know the details better than I do."

"Under the name Keith Muldoony."

She shrugged.

Decker said, "That's the name you found him under."

"This is true."

"And all of this was kept secret from you."

"Kept secret from me, kept secret from the world." She poured him a cup of coffee. Decker formulated ideas as he sipped the black goo.

She took a swallow and asked, "What's wrong?"

"I don't know a thing about West Virginia law. I know in California, it's hard to have a person committed without his permission."

"Maybe Dad had himself committed voluntarily?"

"Doesn't sound like your father?"

"No, it doesn't. But perhaps Mom had been medicating him to keep him quiet."

Her reasoning made sense. Decker asked, "And after your mother committed your dad to Harrison, Pluto never contacted your mom again?"

"Not that I know of."

"No contact until he called you up anonymously and told you about this man named Keith Muldooney over at Harrison, claiming to be the great scientist Dr. Emil Euler Ganz."

"It came in a letter actually."

"On your twenty-first birthday."

This time, Europa's mouth dropped open. She shut it quickly. "You certainly did your homework."

"No, I just figured that Pluto had contacted you the moment you reached your majority."

"Ah!" She nodded. "Yes, of course. That would be the whole point. My being old enough to take responsibility for my father."

Decker said, "Because your mom had refused to have your father released to her care."

She was silent.

He asked, "Did you show the letter to your mother?"

"Yes." A long pause. "She became physically ill . . . almost passed out. When she recovered, she tore the sheet into tiny, tiny pieces and told me to ignore it. At that moment, I knew the whole thing had to be true."

Decker waited.

"I went down to Harrison . . . saw him . . ." Tears in her eyes, she turned suddenly irate. "They had him working as a *janitor,* for Chrissakes! He was totally blitzed out on Thorazine! He drooled when he talked. His hands shook. He was a goddamn zombie! He was swallowed up by fear! This was my *father!* I owed him something for my genetics alone. I *couldn't* allow such a great man to continue to live under such demeaning conditions."

"Your mother had no problem with it."

She bolted up from her seat. "My mother had three kids to raise and Dad had been scaring her with his crazy thoughts and theories."

"But you weren't aware of it?"

"As a child, you have the tremendous capacity to deny reality. Sure, he had crazy ideas. But he was always a man with crazy ideas. And he got lots of scientific recognition for some of his *crazy* ideas! How was *I*, at twelve or thirteen or fourteen, supposed to know which of his ideas were brilliance and which were insanity?"

A good point. Decker told her so.

She sat back down, trying to calm herself, holding her coffee cup to mask shaking hands. "Toward the end, Mom claimed that he got threatening! What else could she do!?" She pounded her desktop for emphasis, then threw her head back. "She must have felt it saved our lives to get him away from us."

"Maybe it did."

"I don't know . . ." She looked up. "Things certainly didn't work out well in my family. My brothers, though brilliant, never reached their full potential. Both of them dropped out. Emulating Dad, I guess. Because they really never knew him as Dad the scientist, just . . . Dad the nutcase. One's now a hermit in India. I haven't heard from Jason in five years. The other — Kyle — he spends most of his time whaling with the Eskimos in Alaska. He did say he'd come down for Dad's funeral if that *ever* gets under way."

Decker asked, "Why didn't your mom initially commit him closer to home?"

"I don't know why!" she blurted out. "Maybe

544

fear of discovery. Or maybe she wanted him far away." Eyes watering, she cried out, "Who the *hell* are we to judge her actions!"

"You're right, Europa. I'm sorry if I offended you."

"It's all right." She closed her eyes. "Nothing I haven't wondered myself." A hesitation. Then she opened her eyes and said, "I understand why she lied to us as youngsters. What I *can't* understand was why she continued the lies after we were grown. Finding out in some anonymous letter was dreadful! She should have *told* me!" Under her breath. "She should have *told* me."

"So at twenty-one, you took on the burden of caring for your father. You hired a lawyer and became his conservator."

She said nothing. Then, "Twenty-two actually. Took me a year to organize my thoughts."

"Noble of you," Decker remarked.

"Noble, but shortsighted. As soon as Dad was released, Pluto grabbed him. At first I was relieved. I was a struggling college student with meager means of support, and here was this guy, who had known my father for years back in West Virginia, still willing to care for him . . . to attend to his needs. It wasn't until they formed the Order that Pluto's true intentions finally dawned on me. Dad, for all his craziness, was still a magnetic, powerful and completely mesmerizing leader. Pluto was completely the opposite. He could offer a shipload of drunken sailors a dozen whores, and they'd walk away from him. He was simply *repulsive* in the true sense of the word. There wasn't any way he could attract followers. But what he could do was manage my dad, who could attract followers."

She rolled her eyes.

"Talk about teamwork — what's it called? *Folie à deux?* Two crazy people getting together, each one feeding the other's grandiose delusions and wreaking havoc?"

Another big sigh.

"It was a losing battle from the start. Pluto kept stoking Dad's crazy thoughts . . . completely manipulating him."

"But once the Order was established, it was your dad who was in charge."

"I think Venus helped in that regard — decreasing Pluto's hold over him. For that reason, I should have been grateful to her. Although, at the time, I was pretty damn angry at her."

"Pluto manipulating him, Venus manipulating him. But you were the one with the true power. Yet you never considered recommitting your father."

"I know this sounds strange, but I couldn't stomach the thought of my father locked up again. Like he was nothing but some psychofreak . . . which he was."

"You acted out of kindness."

"It was a toss-up. Medicated and controlled, or crazy but free. I felt, rightly or wrongly, that he deserved to live his warped life in some kind of dignity."

"Even though your father's insanity had turned him — and you by extension — into laughingstocks among the scientific community."

"Yes, he made quite an idiot out of himself. But that wasn't the worst part. He had these crazy theories about aliens and time travel. Some of it — the time travel part — was grounded in sound science. *Most* of it was highly implausible. If he had kept his time machines at the theoretical level, it wouldn't have been so bad. But he started trying to build one using money from his old bank accounts. Dad may have been delusional, but he knew his bank numbers."

"Funny how that works," Decker said.

"Tragic is more the word. He took out almost all of Mom's hard-earned, penny-pinching joint savings before we caught on. Mom blamed *me* for everything. She kept saying if I had left well enough alone, none of this would have happened. So here I was, at twenty-one, responsible for both my parents' problems."

"No wonder you let Pluto take over."

"I did, but it was a mistake. At least Pluto didn't take the money and run, I'll say that much for him."

"Maybe your father never *gave* it to him."

She hit her forehead. "Of course, he didn't. Dad must have used the money to form the Order."

"He had savings when he died, you know."

She shrugged.

Decker said, "It all belongs to you."

"No it doesn't," she said. "Dad's *insurance* policy money belongs to me. But his savings — which are in the high five figures — belong to all those poor children who are now without parents. The savings might have belonged to my half-siblings. But they died in the explosion."

A heavy sigh.

"You want to know something?" she exclaimed. "I think the Order made Dad better. Better meaning more sane or more . . . conventional. The sect gave him a title, gave him a forum for his lunatic ideas, gave him respect, gave him a home and a woman. The times he had called me around my birthday, he had sounded much less paranoid than when he had first been released from Harrison."

She rubbed her mouth.

"Back then, he had been in so much . . . *pain*. Terrorized by his own shadow, looking at me with waifish eyes. Like I was going to *hurt* him. The paranoia and psychotropic drugs had just . . . stripped his soul. He wasn't like that when I talked to him. Sure, he was off, but . . . not like he had been at Harrison. Maybe the insanity was still present. But at least the dread and fear were gone."

Decker nodded.

She said, "I've heard that sometimes the paranoid hallucinations lessen with the aging process. That the voices may be there, but the patient is rational enough not to listen to them."

Decker asked, "He heard voices?"

"Auditory hallucinations are the most common kind. Even as a kid, right before he left, I remember him saying that aliens were going to come get us if he didn't build his time machine and fly away."

Decker remembered her telling him that. "He still heard those voices, Doctor."

She sat up. "How do you know?"

"Right before he died, he was planning to build a time machine."

She thought about Decker's words. "So maybe he wasn't get-ting better at all. Maybe he was still afraid of aliens. That's too bad."

"Maybe he'd get better, and then maybe he'd sink." Decker spoke softly. "Maybe the roller-coaster ride between sanity and insanity finally drove your father to do the extreme. It could be the voices told him to take flight with vodka and pills. Maybe that's why he killed himself."

"Didn't you say he was poisoned?"

"He was poisoned, but not with enough arsenic to kill him."

"So you think he took his own life?"

"Yes, I now think your father committed suicide."

"I don't know if that makes me feel better or worse."

"At least he died peacefully," Decker said. "Which is a lot more than I can say for the others."

The room became silent. Then she said, "If I

hadn't freed him, the Order might never have existed."

"So you think this whole thing is your fault?"

She made a face. "No, of course not!"

Decker said, "Your father, though mentally ill, must have been a very powerful man. He was the undisputed leader of the Order of the Rings of God, and, as such, he controlled not only his regular cult members — who were no doubt not the most stable tops in the toy box — but also his gurus, who were out-and-out flaming psychopaths. For years, the Order, under Jupiter's leadership, lived in peace with its neighbors. If Bob hadn't self-destructed, the Order would be standing today with Pluto at the helm. It was your father's *death* that started this whole ugly chain of events."

"But his release from Harrison played some part in it."

"You go back far enough, Dr. Ganz, and everything was related. Don't the scientists say that eons ago, the four major physical forces that rule the universe were once one big megaforce right before the Big Bang?"

"Yes, that's the theory." She set her elbows on her desk and propped her chin up with her hands. "You know, it's strange how things are connected. You really never know the long-term consequences of anything, do you?"

"No, you don't, Doctor," Decker said. "And that's why I believe in God and not science."

38

Two weeks of respite, and Decker was going stir-crazy from boredom. Dying to get back to work. Until he *did* go back. Then he wished he hadn't been so anxious to return to the grind.

Actually, the first day wasn't all *that* bad. But he was glad when it was over. It was good to get home. Work had provided a wonderful refuge, had kept Decker's mind occupied on details so he didn't actively think about dead babies, adults in an inferno and scores of body parts. Yet every time he had passed Marge's empty desk, he had felt his stomach turn over. She was doing great, due back within a month's time. But her very absence had reminded him of things he hadn't wanted to think about. And he knew he wasn't alone in that regard. The entire Homicide detail would have benefited from a healthy dose of Prozac. Instead, they had opted for ye olde cop bar, inviting Decker to the festivities. He declined, saying that at least his family deserved a father figure if not an actual father.

Opening the front door, he was surprised to see Marge sitting on his couch. He grinned and hugged her fiercely. "Staying for dinner?"

She hugged him back. "No, Loo, not tonight."

"No?" Decker let her go. "What are you running off to? Who's the hot date?"

"Four lost adolescent girls still assigned to DPSS."

"Ah!" *Kids from the Order.* Decker sat down, patted the empty cushion next to him. "It's wonderful of you to give of yourself . . . remain in such close contact with them."

"I have no choice. As long as those children are without homes, I have to go to them."

"Does Lauren Bolt go with you?"

"She did for a while. But . . . she couldn't take it . . . the press and everything. Hey, even heroes need a break."

A well-deserved break to say the least. Decker pictured Lauren's face as she'd emerged — a shell of a human being. But weren't they all.

"Anyway," Marge continued, "she's off with Lyra to Australia. Now that Lyra's mother is dead . . . blown up with the rest . . . anyway, they're going try it down under for a while."

"Sounds good."

"Doesn't it though."

"You should think about it — for a vacation, I mean."

"Australia?"

"Australia, Fiji, Hawaii." He smiled. "Darlin', you've got the time. Take advantage."

"Not right now." She smiled back. "At the moment, I'd like to stay close to home. And then there're the kids."

Decker looked at her — his partner for over ten years, his friend for over fifteen. "Margie, the kids are in the hands of professionals who are very able people —"

"I don't want to hear this —"

"You should *relax* while you have the chance."

She took his hand. "Peter, I know you mean well. Everyone means well. But I *need* to do this." She shook her head. "You just *can't* understand where I've been."

He was quiet.

"None of the pros think it's bad that I'm there with the girls. Matter of fact, one said it's probably good therapy for me. I think he's right."

"Margie, it's wonderful that you're there to be a solid rock for them. But I'm just wondering what happens after the kids are placed? Where does that leave you?"

She managed a kind smile with wet eyes. "I'll be fine."

This time, Decker took her hand. "You get attached to the buggers. Like leeches, they get under your skin."

"It's true." She pulled her hand away and stared over his shoulder. "In fact, I have Vega staying with me —"

"*What!*" Decker said. "What do you mean, 'staying with' you?"

Her eyes bore into his. "I don't know how I can say it any more clearly. Vega is staying with me."

"For how long?"

"Maybe five, six years —"

"Are you *nuts!*"

"Well, thanks for the support!" Marge stiffened. "I'm glad I spoke to your wife before I talked to you."

Decker started to speak, but backed off. "Okay . . ." He tapped his foot. "That's really great . . . I mean, you're great to do this." Under his breath, he muttered, "I hope you know what you're doing —"

"No, I *don't* know what I'm doing!" she cried out. "I just know I have to do this! Pete, *you* don't see Vega's little face every day. You don't see that pathetic look in her eyes, that 'God, help me please, I'm drowning' look! She's so damn lost! They're all so *damn* lost!"

She wiped her eyes.

"Pete, I was given something, a very, very special gift." She swallowed hard. "The gift of a *second* chance at life. I was literally brought back from the dead, no small thanks to you —"

"I didn't do anything —"

"From what I heard, you did *everything.*"

He didn't answer.

"Peter, what kind of human being would I be if I didn't reach out to them . . . to her? How could I not . . ." She turned her head away and held back tears. "I know I can't save the world. I'm a cop, for God's sake, and I know the injustices that exist. I'm powerless to change the world. But maybe . . . just *maybe,* I can make a little difference to a very vulnerable lost girl."

"I . . ." Decker bit his lip. "I think that's very wonderful of you. I'm just . . . concerned about where it leaves *you.* Your life changes with kids.

Margie, it's irrevocable . . . irreversible. You can't go back when it starts to get rough. And it's going to get rough."

"I'm *not* going to change my mind."

Decker looked into her eyes, though it was her heart that was talking. "Okay."

She asked, "Would you give yours up for anything?"

"Of course not. But I have a little help." He took in a deep breath, let it out slowly. "Honest to God truth? I couldn't do it without Rina. I'd muck everything up. Lord knows, I muck up enough even *with* her."

"If you had to, you'd rise to the occasion of single parenthood."

"Please, God, don't ever test me!" He prayed with sincerity. "What about *you*, Margie? What about your love life? How do you think your dates are going to take to your new responsibility?"

"If they don't take to her, I don't want them in my life," Marge answered. "Christ, Decker, I'm thirty-six with no candidate on the horizon. My clock is ticking like a time bomb. I *like* children. I was a juvey cop for ten years. I may not look the part of an earth mother, but I'm not devoid of maternal feelings."

"There's always the Girl Scouts."

"Now you're being glib."

"I am," Decker admitted. "I'm sorry."

She felt tears well up in her throat. "Peter, I didn't *ask* for this. It was . . . given to me — this challenge. I have to live with myself. I can't turn my back on her. Not now . . . not ever." She stood up. "I've got to go."

He got up from the couch, held her by the shoulders. "If I didn't know better, I'd say you actually look happy."

She rolled her eyes.

He said, "You could have brought her with you. Here, I mean."

"She's with the others — her spiritual brothers and sisters. Everyone agrees. It would be tragic to immediately split them all up."

"They're all orphans?"

"Orphans yes, but not without family. Some have aunts and uncles. Some have grandparents. But the legalities take time. Not to mention the adjustments. And then there's the paperwork for guardianship or adoption."

A pause.

"And then there are others, like Vega, who are totally without family." She shook her head. "Completely alone."

"Don't mention them to Rina. She'd adopt the world if you'd let her." Decker was only half-kidding.

"She's calm, isn't she? Especially considering all she's gone through."

"Very calm." Decker was in awe. "Child rearing. Some people just have more tolerance for life's ambiguities."

Margie kissed his cheek. "If you call to-morrow, and I'm not home, don't worry. If all goes well, I'm taking the four stunned girls to their first outing at the mall."

"Good luck to you."

"Originally, I wanted Disneyland. The head shrink thought that might be a bit too much sensory overload."

"A man with a brain."

Marge smiled — a sweet, sweet smile. "See you later." She craned her neck and shouted out, "Bye, Rina!"

"Wait!" Rina came running out of the kitchen, holding a Lucite salad bowl. "So we're on for tomorrow?"

"I'll meet you at ten sharp."

"You're *part* of this?" Decker asked.

"Cindy, too. Like it or not, we're partners in crime." She stood on her tiptoes and kissed Decker's cheek. "How was your first day back?"

"Yeah, how was that?" Marge asked.

"Good, actually."

"Hope to be with you in a month."

"Nothing would make me happier."

Marge paused. "Anything new?"

"Yeah, as a matter of fact, Judy Little found —" He glanced at Rina. "I think I smell something burning."

She smiled knowingly at Marge. "He thinks he's protecting me." She patted his cheek. "I'll let him labor under that delusion. See you tomorrow."

She left the room. Decker waited a moment longer, then whispered, "A partial jawbone — a mandible with two back molars. It was burned but the amalgams held. Annie Hennon has matched them to one of Venus's X rays."

"Ah . . ." Marge nodded. "So she was there?"

"Appears that way."

"And Bob Russo?"

"Still nothing definitive," Decker said. "But that doesn't mean anything. The place is one big boneyard. Ironically, the only bones *not* there are *Ganz's* bones. *His* are still in cold storage, waiting to be tested for arsenic poisoning — if we can ever locate his vitamin bottles —"

"What do you mean?"

"It seems the bottles have been temporarily mislaid —"

"What?" Marge was shocked. "The lab *lost* the bottles?!"

"*Supposedly*, they checked the suckers back into the evidence room. But Evidence doesn't have them. So now *I've* got to play Sherlock fucking Holmes, trying to figure out where the lost evidence bags are. This all came down today, by the way. Hit my desk as soon as I walked into the squad room. I spent half my first day back trying to track down the lab's fucking paperwork —"

He stopped talking, waved his hand in the air.

"You can tell I'm getting better psychologically. Petty things are getting to me." He smiled. "Next time you come, bring Vega for dinner. Maybe her manners will rub off on my kids."

"More likely, theirs will rub off on her."

"Ain't that the truth." Decker heard Sammy's car engine chunking along. "Hold on." He opened the front door and shouted, "Don't block her car, Sammy! She's about to leave."

Ignoring his stepfather, Sammy turned off the motor. He stuck his head out the window. "Just tell me when and I'll move the car." Then he, Jacob and Hannah got out of the Volvo. The boys walked under the load of overstuffed backpacks, but Hannah was as free as the wind.

"Daddeeee," she shouted.

"Hannah Roseeee," Decker answered, picking her up and swinging her over his head.

Marge stepped out, into the misty dusk air. "I'm leaving now, Sam."

Sammy tossed his stepfather the keys. "Nice catch, Dad. One-handed. Can you move the car for me? I've got lots of homework."

Marge stared at the teen, who was completely oblivious to what he had just done. She started laughing.

Decker laughed with her. He jingled the keys while carrying Hannah on his shoulders. "And you're doing this voluntarily?"

"I'm crazy," Marge said.

Aren't we all, Decker thought. But he took Hannah, strapped her into the backseat, and moved Sammy's car anyway. He actually took it as a compliment that Sammy had stopped treating him with kid gloves. Things were starting to get back to normal.

He went back into his house, put Hannah

down, her little feet refusing to plant onto the floor. Finally, he got her to stand up. "Why don't you go watch cartoons, sweetie."

"Will you watch with me?"

"Can I rest for a minute?"

"Daddy, you can have *two* minutes."

"So magnanimous!" He kissed her soft, silken cheek. "I think it's *Scooby-Doo.* I'll see you soon."

She scooted off. He plopped onto the living room sofa, threw his head back and stared at the ceiling. Moments later, Jacob took up the cushion next to him, laying his head on Decker's shoulder.

"Tired?" Jacob asked.

"A little." Decker kissed his son's forehead. "How about yourself?"

"A little."

"It's after six," Decker said. "Where did you guys go?"

"Sammy and Hannah picked me up from the Teen Hot Line Crisis Center."

"Oh!" Decker sat up and so did Jacob. "How'd that go?"

"Well . . ." Jacob cracked his knuckles. "Grandpa never raped me, so I guess I'm one hell of a lucky guy."

Decker winced.

"And I discovered that divorce . . . it's a very lousy thing. Maybe . . . maybe even worse than losing a parent."

"Depends on the divorce."

"Well, the ones the hot line got were *pretty*

nasty. Then again, no one calls when everyone's getting along. Or at least faking it." Jacob thought a moment. "We got a couple of abuse cases — physical abuse. Parents whacking their kids close-fisted. That's one of the center's main criteria for reportable abuse. Slugging with a fist."

"Did you actually talk to any of the callers?"

"No. I just listened in on the tape recorder. Wow! I *marvel* at the counselors. They're *my* age, and they handle the callers like seasoned pros. I wouldn't know *what* to say. I'd just like . . . freeze. Or worse, I'd say the wrong thing and send someone into the Pacific Ocean without a life jacket. It's really amazing . . . what they do."

"They learned, Jacob. And you'll learn, too."

"I hope so."

"They were nice to you?"

"Real nice. It was . . . okay. It felt good actually." He threw his head back onto the couch pillow. "Some people have it very rough." He turned to his stepfather. "I wasn't being facetious, you know. I think I am lucky."

"I'm glad."

"I have a mother who loves me very much. I had a father who loved me very much. And I have a stepfather who's cool."

Decker grinned. "I'm cool?"

"Very cool." He kissed Decker's cheek. "Play you some chess after Hannah goes to bed?"

"It's a deal."

He stood. "Well, I've put it off long enough.

Gotta go tackle *gemara*. Is Eema almost done with dinner?"

"I think so."

"Tell her I may just eat in my room. My grades in *gemara* really suck. I've got to study."

"Are you thinking about that Johns Hopkins program?"

He shrugged. "Maybe. See ya." He turned and went into his bedroom, slamming the door behind him, which caused Decker's head to ring.

It rang for ten seconds, then twenty seconds, then thirty seconds.

Then suddenly the switch turned off.

And there was nothing.

Nothing except for the ambient noise of Hannah's cartoons on the TV, Sammy's CDs being played a little too loud and something frying in the kitchen.

Home noises that were comforting.

Blessed solitude. Breathing deeply . . .

A minute passed, then two.

Sitting in his house, settling into his sofa with nobody calling his name, nobody beckoning him to the phone, no demands *and* his head wasn't ringing.

Nothing but peace.

Doesn't get much better than this!

He rested another moment. Then he got up from the couch, heading for the bedroom.

Scooby-Doo awaited.

We hope you have enjoyed this Large Print book. Other G.K. Hall & Co. or Chivers Press Large Print books are available at your library or directly from the publishers.

For more information about current and upcoming titles, please call or write, without obligation, to:

G.K. Hall & Co.
P.O. Box 159
Thorndike, Maine 04986 USA
Tel. (800) 257-5157

OR

Chivers Press Limited
Windsor Bridge Road
Bath BA2 3AX
England
Tel. (0225) 335336

All our Large Print titles are designed for easy reading, and all our books are made to last.